TWISTED

Book 1 in the TWISTED Series

By Brittany Hawes

Deep Sea Publishing

COPYRIGHT PAGE

Deep Sea Publishing ISBN: 1939535476
Deep Sea Publishing ISBN-13: 978-1-939535-47-4
Deep Sea Publishing E-Book ISBN: 1939535468
Deep Sea Publishing E-Book ISBN-13: 978-1-939535-46-7

www.deepseapublishing.com
Printed in the United States of America
eBook created in the United States of America

Table of Contents

Acknowledgements

The first and most important acknowledgment must be given to God. I cannot even begin to express the happiness and joy that He has given me in allowing me to pour out this story and allowing it to be put into these pages and into the hands of others. Without Him, none of this would have been possible. He put all of the following people in my life, all of whom were beneficial in the making of this book.

To my beautiful mom, Connie, who has given my siblings and I all of her love and support since the day we were born. Thank you for your unconditional love and for always supporting me in whatever I do. You have helped me grow from a shy, little girl to the happy, young woman that I am today. Thank you for being the example that I hope to be to my kids one day. I love you with all of my heart, Mama!

To my funny, talented, and beautiful family, who have loved and supported me all of my life. My dad, Herbert, who helped grow the creativity in my being. Thank you for always listening to me, praying for me, and sending me all of those funny stories. I still have them! My brother, Armand, who is always able to make me laugh. Thank you for reminding me to live life how you want to and for introducing me to art. Best brother ever! My sister, Madisen, who I can share any and everything with. Thank you for always putting up with my silliness and reminding me to chase my dreams. Best sister ever! My aunts, uncles, and grandparents, who were beneficial in my upbringing. I can't even begin to put how much I love all of these people into words. Thank you for always being there for me and I love you all!

To my best friend, Tiffany, and second family, thank you for always opening your arms to me and getting to know me before judging me. You were one of the first people to accept me when I first moved down to Florida. Thanks, Tip, for always having my back and for helping me to have the courage to show my stories to others!

.

To the team at Deep Sea, thank you all for giving me the chance to get my voice out there in the exciting world of writers. It's a bit scary, so I'm glad to have such a dedicated team to guide me. Thank you!

To anyone I may have not put on here, you are most definitely not forgotten! There are so many people who have helped me achieve this lifelong dream, I couldn't begin to list them all. Thanks to all of you!

Brittany

Prologue

When I was a kid, I would always let my dad carry me around on his broad shoulders, even though I was (and still am) terrified of heights. But I only let him *after* he did something to win my favor. Yeah, I was a brat.

I remember one time in particular, around nine years ago. I was only eight then and as big of a tomboy as I am now. My parents and I were taking a walk down the crowded sidewalks of our hometown, the beautiful city of Los Angeles, California. We had come across a small ice cream parlor that had just opened and was selling ice cream cones for half-price. I had begged and begged Dad to buy me an ice cream cone with three scoops of strawberry ice cream, my favorite flavor. My mom had lightly punched my dad on his arm and playfully demanded one for herself, too.

Oh, my mom. She was the best role model a girl could ask for, and not just because of her amazing academic history. She graduated from her high school at the top of her class and with many full-scholarship offers from colleges all over the country. She chose Harvard and then went on to medical school. After a lot of hard work, she was able to start her first year of residency at a L.A hospital, which is where she first met my dad.

My parents' favorite story in the world to tell me was of how they first met. My dad had been a doctor at the hospital when he first laid eyes on my mom.

"She was a real beauty, I tell ya, Little Lola," he would say to me, his eyes crinkling up with the wide grin that would spread across his face. "She carried herself as if she ran that entire hospital. I knew right then and there that I was in love and, as handsome as I was, she was gonna fall for me just as quick."

My mom's side of the story was a bit different. "Your father tried hard, extremely hard, to get my attention. He left me flowers, chocolates, stuffed animals…" she would pause to laugh, "…but I just threw them away. I was at that hospital to learn, not to fall head over heels for some cocky doctor." She would always pause here and look at me with a smile, but I knew she wasn't really looking at me. I could tell by the dreamy, far-off look in her eyes. She was looking at her memories, back to her days as a young intern at the hospital.

"But then, I let him take me out to the park. I figured he would buy me something to eat, which was the only reason I let him take me." We both always got a good giggle at this.

"But then, we started talking and smiling and laughing...we had so much fun, just sitting there on a park bench." She would smile and shake her head. "We stayed out there for hours, just talking. That became our new tradition—going out to the park bench to talk and laugh. We became best friends out there."

The next part was my favorite part, mostly because it involved myself. It was only natural. I was a kid and could care less about old people falling in love.

"One day, during my second year of residency, your father was late for our date out in the park. It was cold and I wasn't going to wait out there all night. I was just about to leave when I felt someone put something around my neck." She would reach out and reenact the gesture on me, which made me smile.

"I can't afford the ring yet, but I hope you'll accept this as a marriage proposal," Dad would tell me with a laugh. "That's what I told her after I put that gold necklace around her neck. She reached up and said..."

"This is supposed to be a wedding proposal?" My mom's incredulous face was hilarious at this point as she told me the story. "I told him I'd keep the necklace but the answer was no until he put a real ring on my finger. You can bet your little butt that he went out and bought me this ring the very next day." She always flashed her huge, shiny diamond ring at this point, smiling from ear to ear. "We were married the next summer. But, I had a little secret." Mom would reach up and pull out a gold necklace from beneath the collar of her shirt with a golden heart-shaped locket dangling from it.

"I kept his first marriage proposal and after you were born..." She let me flick open the locket and I smiled every time I saw the pretty photo of me as a baby, being held by my mother as my father hugged the both of us. Beside it, inscribed in gold, were the words "Forever & Always". I can still clearly remember that picture of us, as well as that story, as clearly as that fateful day we went out for ice cream.

I remember sitting around one of those outdoor tables at the ice cream parlor, watching my parents lick their dripping ice cream cones. Dad would always get mint-chocolate and Mom would always get cookie dough. We laughed around the table for hours, passing each other our cones of pink, green, and white until everything, even the cones themselves, were devoured.

Afterwards, Dad had hoisted me up on his shoulders, grabbed Mom's hand, and we went strolling through the crowded streets of L.A. I clearly remember them tucking me into bed that night and telling me they loved me. I can still remember the brush of my dad's stubbly chin as he kissed me good night and the softness of my mom's thick, curly hair as she tickled me on my stomach. They said they would see me when the sun came up again, except they never did.

Because that was the day my parents disappeared.

Chapter One

The Dream came again that night.

I was eight years old, barefoot and giggly. My hair was short and done up in black, bouncy curls. I was dressed in a white cotton sundress with bright, golden roses swirling around the hem. That was weird. As a child, I always preferred to wear shorts or overalls so I could have the freedom to run around and play. The only time you would catch me in a dress would be on Sunday morning at church.

What was even weirder was the fact that I was in the air and walking on clouds. With each step I took, it felt as if my bare feet were sinking into cool, soft batches of cotton candy.

Suddenly, I felt someone pick me up from under my arms, and the next thing I knew, I was on Dad's shoulders, just like old times. I held back a squeal of surprise and instead forced myself to look down. We were far above those fluffy clouds now, and I could see the blues, greens, and whites of Earth below.

We were in outer space. Comets and meteors passed us by in a blur as we trekked across the universe. I started to panic once we began to pass familiar planets such as Saturn and Jupiter.

"Dad," I tried to say, but my voice came out as barely more than a squeak as my throat constricted. I couldn't breathe. It felt as if someone had wrapped their hands around my throat and was squeezing the life out of me.

Dad continued to run. That's when I noticed his expression. A grim, serious frown plagued his normally cheerful face and he kept his dark eyes staring straight ahead.

I began to beat at his head, wrench at his shirt, pull on his ears, but my blows might as well have been ant bites. He ignored them. I gave up and turned my attention to where we were going. A bright light was in the distance. I couldn't quite make out what was the source of the light, but it sent a chill down my spine.

We moved towards it in slow motion, when suddenly, whatever invisible platform we were on, disappeared.

We fell.

* * *

"Daddy!" I awoke with a start, sitting straight up. My head hit the ceiling of my current address, a damp cardboard box turned roof, and I fell back down on my back onto the sidewalk. My chest heaved and my forehead was sticky with sweat. I swiped at my face and tugged my thin, ragged blanket tightly around myself.

"Just a dream, Lola, just a dream..." I repeated softly, hating myself for letting "The Dream" scare me. I had been having it almost every night since my parents' disappearance nine years ago.

It was the same each night. I would ride my Dad's shoulders into outer space and then we would plummet back toward Earth. I could never figure out what exactly we were searching for up there but I knew it had something to do with the light. I couldn't make out the mysterious object that floated just inches away from us every time, yet we could never reach it.

"You okay, Lola?" I rolled over to find the woman I only knew as Carolina staring over at me in concern. She was peering at me from beneath her own dirty blanket, a perturbed expression on her smudged, round face.

I took a shaky breath to calm myself before I was able to answer her. "Yeah. Go back to sleep, Carolina." The middle-aged woman gave me another look before she rolled back around to face whoever was sleeping on the other side of her.

That was one of the downsides of being homeless—you had absolutely zero privacy.

I had been living without a real home for the past nine years and had been living in the infamous Skid Row for about one. My parents disappeared when I was only eight. I had to find a way to survive on my own. After the food in the refrigerator had ran out and the electricity had been cut off, I broke into my parents' safety box and took off on a bus to my aunt's house in a small town in northern California. I had lived there and went to school until I was sixteen. My aunt and I had had our differences, so I had stolen some of her money and ran away, back to L.A., where my parents and I had lived. I had been living here for the past year and life hadn't been as easy as I had hoped.

Twisted

After finding my parents' original home newly occupied by a couple with a pack of brats of their own, I had been forced to take up residence in the only place possible—the streets. Luckily, I had found a nice church that offered it's courtyard as a rest area. It was for women and children to sleep at night without worrying about being robbed from or worse.

I still had to struggle to eat, sleep beside drug users, and pray that I never got caught up in the wrong things. It was a tough life.

Sometimes, I wondered if I should just go back to live with my aunt, but I just couldn't bring myself to do it. Call it pride, call it whatever you want. So, here I was, sleeping on the ground, cold, hungry, and surrounded by people that, although I hate to admit it, were a lot like me.

I brought a hand to my chest, feeling the out of control beating of my heart. *It was just a dream…just a dream….*Still, I knew I wouldn't be able to go back to sleep. I shimmied out from beneath my cardboard roof before reaching my arms skyward to stretch. I shooed away the rats nibbling at the food wrappers near my feet, then stood up.

I carefully stepped over the endless rows of people lining the ground in their blankets and dodged the ragged tents that sometimes housed five or more people when they were allowed to be pitched. Usually, I would avoid walking around during the night, but the sun was just peeking over the horizon, so I decided to take chance.

No sooner had I slipped out of the gates of the church when someone grabbed my arm.

"Yo, little Lola! Let Mr. Frederick get a few dollars for some food!" a scraggly voice begged. I sighed, already knowing who the owner of the voice was.

"Why don't you just wait for one of the churches to serve breakfast and eat there?" I asked as I spun around to face the gnarled old man known as "Frederick D" due to his striking resemblance to the abolitionist of the same name.

Frederick D gave me a sheepish grin, revealing the one tooth he still had, which clung like a stubborn child to his pasty gums. "Girl, it's only 6 'o clock! Frederick D needs food right now!" he explained indignantly. I sighed and shook my head at him. I knew this money would most likely end up going toward something besides food because, let's be real—where in Los Angeles could you buy a decent meal for a few dollars? But I still reached in my pocket, dodged the pocket knife I kept for protection, and grabbed the only bill I had left in my pocket—five dollars. I handed him the crumpled bill. Frederick D's eyes lit up at the money in his hand before he quickly tucked it away in his pocket. He sent me another happy grin.

"Thanks, little Lola! You're a good girl, sweetie, when you're not yelling at people," he half-complimented me as he gave his pocket a happy pat. Suddenly, his expression turned serious. He looked over his shoulders, like he suspected someone was watching before he beckoned me to come closer with a crook of his veined finger. I looked around as well, before I leaned in, just a bit.

"Since you're a nice girl, ol' Frederick is gonna let you in on a secret," he began. He paused for a brief second to look around once more. "Keep your hands away from guns. They're one of the only things that can undo you, Lola." With that weird, foreboding statement off of his chest, Frederick D ambled off, still rambling to himself. I stared after him, not knowing what to think.

Let's face it: a lot of homeless people are crazy. Frederick D would most likely be put in that category. But, in light of the strange Dream I had just awakened from, it was easy to see why I felt a bit freaked out.

I decided to cast it off as Frederick D having a bout with senility and continued on with my morning stroll. It wasn't the most cheerful walk.

People pushing around empty shopping carts, boys no older than me shoving needles in their arms, and poor families huddled together to keep warm in the cool October morning air—it was a sad sight. All of us who had ended up here at Skid Row had one thing in common--we had nowhere else to go. Fortunately, the city council had recently begun working on housing projects for our street, so the number of people stranded without a home or a way to get one was steadily decreasing. Unfortunately, at least for me, these housing projects were mostly geared toward helping the disabled, drug-heads, and criminals. Where did that leave me?

Not that I hadn't had my share of criminal activity in my day, but that's another story.

I sighed as I patted my now empty pockets. I really needed to stop being so generous with my money. Now I didn't even have a dime to my name. That was a problem, mainly because of someone called Blackeye.

I knew I had to do what I always did in situations like these, and that meant travelling north to the more populated area of Los Angeles. Travelling there was never an easy task, especially since the shoes I had on were so worn out, the soles were beginning to rub away. But public transit wasn't an option, seeing as I was penniless, so walking was my only other alternative. I hiked up my cargo pants and began on my way.

***

Around thirty minutes later, the rundown houses began to shift into towering skyscrapers, and hobos were replaced with people dressed in Armani suits with Dooney & Burke accessories. The traffic was much louder and a lot less considerate here, so I stuck to the sidewalks, inadvertently putting myself by people who wanted nothing more but to keep away from the "dirty hobo." I ignored them for the most part and pressed on.

I wandered around the noisy streets of Los Angeles, throwing any and everyone who dared to give me a disdainful glance one right back. Most tried to do all they could to avoid me, like I was a diseased animal. I knew I wasn't the friendliest person in the world, but I didn't exactly bite. I was hoping someone would show me some sympathy and hand me a dollar or two, but so far, no luck. I wasn't going to get a cup and beg for money, although I had nothing against people who did. Sometimes you just had to do what you had to do. I still held tight to what little pride I had left and liked to work for my money, doing little odd jobs I could find.

I passed by a store's glass windows and paused to inspect myself. My short, spiked red-dyed hair was messy and unkempt, my brown skin looked dry and ashen, and my ensemble of a burgundy hoodie and black cargo pants looked wrinkled. My light brown eyes looked wider and more sunken than usual and I knew it was from lack of sleep. I looked like some sort of crazy drug-head seventeen year old girl who had gotten in a fight with a pair of scissors and a pitcher of red Kool-Aid (the last part of that actually wasn't too far from the truth).

Everyone who passed me by seemed to be clones, like they were all pumped out from some factory. Their hair was bottled blonde, their bodies were tall, lean, and athletic, and their faces were all touched up in one way or another. I glared enviously as a pack of girls who were my age walked past me, giggling and talking loudly. They were all dressed in the trendiest clothes and each wore a pair of designer shades. They didn't spare me a glance as they passed by.

Sometimes, I wished that I would wake up and be one of them: normal, happy, and carefree. Sometimes, I wished that my biggest worry was the upcoming test in Biology. But life had handed me a different set of cards and I was going to have to play my hand either way.

"Hey. Hey! Do you want this?" A tiny voice yelled from behind me, making me nearly jump out of my skin. I turned around and was surprised to see a little blonde girl staring up at me.

She was holding out an M&M cookie in her tiny hand and wore an angelic smile on her face. It was so sweet and innocent that I almost gagged. I really didn't like kids. But I couldn't turn down free food, especially not from a kid who looked like a modern-day Shirley Temple with her honey-blonde curls tied up in two adorable pigtails.

"…Thanks." I stooped down to her level and took the cookie, then gave her a small smile. The little girl grinned back, revealing two missing front teeth, as she watched me devoured the warm cookie in two bites. In an instant, she had another one out. I laughed and shook my head.

"Don't you want to save some for yourself? Or maybe your mom?" I asked. I suddenly realized that the small girl was all alone. I shivered at the possibility of someone so young having to live the way I did, yet I saw it all the time in Skid Row, thanks to strung-out parents.

"My mommy says she doesn't eat cookies 'cause they have carbs or something," the girl said with a shrug. I let out a sigh of relief. At least the kid had a mom. Where was this mother of the year and why was her daughter out here alone?

The girl gave me a defiant pout before she shoved the cookie toward me again, then gave it a firm shake as well. "C'mon, just eat it!" she said, still pouting. I laughed and took it gratefully, although I couldn't help but wonder where she was producing these cookies from. Beggars couldn't be choosers, I guess. At least they weren't stale. I munched the soft cookie silently as the girl looked on.

Finally, she spoke. "Why are you all by yourself, huh?" I swallowed down the rest of my cookie and wiped my hands on my cargo pants. I wasn't in the mood for story time but she had just given me breakfast.

"I don't have anywhere to go," I replied with a shrug. The girl scrunched up her face, her big, blue eyes crinkling with confusion.

"Your mommy and daddy can't just bring ya home?" she asked, innocently, while twirling a blonde curl. A dull pain throbbed in my chest and I looked away.

I wished every day that my parents would show up and take me anywhere but where I was. I refused to believe that something terrible had happened to them and that they were dead. If they were, someone would have contacted my aunt and let her know. I still held strong to the belief that they were still alive, but just missing. Every day, I had to reassure myself because with every day that passed, it grew harder to believe.

"My mommy and daddy went missing. So now I live by myself," I explained in a tight voice. The girl nodded, as if she understood, but her face was still etched with concern and bewilderment.

"Mary-Anne! Get over here! Right now!"

The little girl and I looked up as a shrill voice tore through the morning air. A blonde woman adorned in expensive furs and glitzy jewelry was standing outside of Macy's, her arms loaded with bags bearing the store's logo. She stared at me, a look of mild disgust and horror on her pointy face. She beckoned the little girl over with a quick wave of her hand.

"Yes, Mommy," the little girl replied in a sour voice before skipping over to where her pointy mother stood. She tugged at mother's pencil skirt and pointed at me. "That girl doesn't have a home or a mommy or a daddy. Can she live with us?" she asked. I tried to fight back the small flicker of hope that lit up inside of me as the mother looked at me with new found interest. The interest in her eyes quickly faded as she gave me the once-over.

"Don't talk to strangers, Mary-Anne, especially not to dirty ones. She doesn't look very becoming." With that last blow, the mother grabbed her child's hand and led her away. Mary-Anne gave me a sympathetic look and a small wave. I waved back, and forced a smile. I wished all people could be like Mary-Anne. I'd be in cookie paradise and living in a mansion by now.

With a grunt, I straightened myself back up and ran a hand through my short red hair. For some reason, my encounter with Mary-Anne, the cookie girl, had helped lift my spirits. The little girl reminded me of myself, in some ways. She had a lot of spunk. I silently prayed that she led a good life and that one day I would be able to repay her for her kindness.

It was time to get on with my schedule for the day. It was the same every day: Getting money and trying to find my parents.

***

I started on the next block, outside of the Ritz-Carlton. It was one of the most ritziest and expensive hotels in Los Angeles, so I made sure to keep well out of the way of the guests. I lingered around the entrance area, out of sight of the snobbish celebrities, snobbier millionaires, and honeymooning couples that bustled in and out. A huge, panting woman carrying five expensive-looking suitcases caught my attention. She was wearing a huge sunhat on top of curly brown hair and a pair of sunglasses that screamed designer.

Just what I was looking for.

I approached her, mock concern on my face. "Excuse me," I asked her, using my best "Harvard student" dialect, "Do you need help with those?" The woman looked at me, her eyes lingering on my dirty cargo pants, and then she smiled at my face, which I prayed was clean.

"Why, yes, miss, that would be very kind," she clucked in a southern accent. I gathered her bags up from her broad shoulders and heaped them onto mine. I almost broke in half under the weight. *What was she packing—her refrigerator and two children?!*

"My room's just on the tenth floor. We can take the stairs for exercise," the southern belle declared. I held back a curse word and simply smiled a big, plastic smile.

"Great."

***

After a grueling fight with a couple flights of stairs and some nosy employees, Southern Belle and I stood outside of her room, panting like dogs and sweating like pigs. I thought that she would pass out by the third floor so we decided to take a five minute break after every other flight of stairs. It had taken us almost thirty minutes but we had made it.

I wiped my brow and forced a grin at her.

"There you go, ma'am!" I sang cheerfully, while I mentally strangled her for making us take the stairs when there was a perfectly working elevator nearby.

The woman smiled at me, her face red from exertion. She stuck her doughy hand in her jeans' pocket and pulled out a crisp fifty dollar bill. I had to stop myself from salivating.

"Why, thank you so much, young lady! Take this, please." She handed me the bill and it took all of my self-control to not jump around with joy. The Ritz-Carlton guests never failed to tip big.

"Thanks! Have a wonderful day!" This time my cheerfulness was definitely not forced. I hurried back out to the front of the hotel, ready to help anyone else that seemed like they were loaded and unsuspecting.

Well, it wasn't the easiest job but this was a good summation of how I earned money. I did odd jobs like this by being in the right place at the right time. When I had first run away, I'm ashamed to admit that I had resorted to running with the wrong crowd and stealing to get what I wanted. A close call with the law and a firsthand look at how my actions had caused someone else to suffer had set me on the right path.

"Excuse me." A deep voice followed by a heavy hand on my shoulder snapped me out of my thoughts. I instinctively yanked away and turned around to face whoever had grabbed me, thinking it was one of the employees.

But no, it was not an employee. At least, he didn't look like one. A handsome silver-haired man stared back at me, a broad grin spread across his handsome features.

He was wearing an expensive, white designer suit and holding onto one of those fancy straight canes, which served no purpose other than decoration. The first thing that entered my mind when I saw him was that he looked too young to have a silver hair. The second thing was that he looked like he was loaded, judging by his attire. I straightened my pose, realizing that I was acting like an escaped prisoner.

"Can I help you?" I asked a little coldly. If there was one thing I hated besides heights, it was being snuck up on.

"Actually, I was hoping you could. Your name's Lola Phillips, is it not?" he asked, innocently twirling his black cane. I narrowed my eyes at him, confused.

How did he know who I was? I took a step back and crossed my arms in front of my chest.

"What do you want?" I asked.

"The question is, what do *you* want, Lola?"

Okay, I was getting creeped out now. Deciding this man was crazy or someone trying to sell me some lousy product, like a limited time offer for Pillow Feet, I gritted my teeth and decided to play along.

"I want you to get away from me," I replied sweetly before turning away from him. I frowned at the sight of a small old lady just entering the hotel. She looked as if she bathed in money, judging from the tiara adorning her white hair. I imagined the tiara on my short, spiky hair, paired with my stained cargo pants, and it was a match made in heaven.

Suddenly, the man stepped in front of my view of the elderly woman, his face now serious. The man pointed his cane at my face, making me angrier than I already was. I resisted the urge to take his cane and break it over my knee. Besides, I doubt I could pull off such a feat without breaking my own knee.

"Are you sure that's what you want, Lola?" he asked, his voice sounding calm and playful, though his face read told a different story. "What if I told you I could help you find what you're looking for?" My heart nearly stopped as my mind instantly went to my parents.

How could he know what I was looking for? The thought of this man toying with my mind and making my heart beat out of control unsettled me.

I pushed his cane out of my face, and then shoved him back with both of my hands, sending him and his fancy cane to the ground. The man's mouth hung open and he stared up at me, wide-eyed. He looked so shocked that I would've laughed if I wasn't so nervous.

"You don't know anything about me," I warned, before spitting by his polished shoe and storming away from the hotel. I glanced back over my shoulder and was surprised to see that the mysterious man was nowhere to be seen. I felt a familiar shiver run down my spine as a slight breeze rustled my hair. I tore my eyes away from the hotel. I fingered the fifty dollar bill in my pocket but, for some reason, I couldn't find too much joy in it.

I broke out into a sprint, wanting to put as much distance between me and the Ritz-Carlton as possible.

Chapter Two

It's not hard to lose someone in downtown L.A.. I made it all the way back to Skid Row before I even let myself think about stopping to catch my breath. I looked over my shoulder every time I heard something behind me and felt relieved when I saw that it wasn't the stranger.

As much as I hated to admit it, the man had certainly got under my skin. I wondered how he knew who I was and how he knew I was looking for something. It was enough to make any person somewhat jittery, which is why I nearly jumped out of my skin when I heard someone's voice behind me.

"Girl, you look as if you've been runnin' de Olympics."

I breathed a sigh of relief after my mind had calmed down enough to think reasonably. I'd recognize that strong Jamaican accent anywhere. My old friend Tara stood before me, shaking her head and laughing.

Tara was a pretty, enthusiastic girl with a beautiful smile that made you smile back no matter how down you were feeling. She had gorgeous black and brown dreadlocks which hung below her waist. Today she had them tied back with a colorful ribbon in a low ponytail.

"I feel like I just ran a marathon, too," I said with a laugh as she pulled me into a hug.

Tara and I had met when I had first run away from my Aunt's. We had hit it off instantly. She was a few years older than me and had showed me the ropes on how to make it living alone. She had been living out here for the past three years and I honestly admired her.

Tara suddenly backed away from me and scrunched up her face, her jade eyes squinting in disgust. "Ooh, you smell like you did, too. What have you been up too, Lo?" she asked, while waving her hand in front of her nose for extra benefit.

"The usual. Trying to get money down at some hotels," I explained as I joined Tara in leaning on the building we were standing beside. I decided not to mention my run-in with the crazy man and his cane.

"It must have been a hotel for dogs, 'cause that's what you smell like."

"I get it, I stink!" I cried out in exasperation as Tara gave another hearty laugh, her dreadlocks bouncing with her heaving shoulders. After she was through getting herself a good knee-slapping laugh, she wiped her eyes and looked at me. Her face took on more serious look.

"You alright? You seem a li'l shaken up," she asked with concern as she continued to study my face. I gave her a smile and pushed her playfully, successfully knocking away her serious expression and replacing it with a lighter one.

"I am fine, Tara, smelly, but fine," I assured her. I patted my red hair and frowned. "Although the dye job you gave me last week isn't." I was still a bit sore at my bright red hair. I had wanted a change in my natural dark brown hair color, so I had turned to Tara, Skid Row's dependable hair stylist. She had got me my desired red dye but somehow, my precious hair had turned out to be the color of a red chili pepper.

Tara shrugged and flipped her dreads over one shoulder. "Ya said de red, and ya got de red."

"I didn't mean Clifford-the-Big-Red-Dog red!" I complained, while pointing an accusing finger at my pitiful head of hair. And of course, the dye was permanent. The only way to change the color would be to dye it again, and though I could be pretty brave, I wasn't ready to take another risk.

"Hush, hush, child." Tara shushed me with a wave of her hand, which was loaded with rings that her "supplier" bought her. "It's cute! Don't let nobody tell you differently." Suddenly, the serious look was back on Tara's face, and her voice became quieter. "But anyway, I be needing to tell ya some-ting."

I nodded, letting her know she had my full attention. Tara glanced around, making sure that no one was watching us. She leaned in close to me, so that only she and I could hear her next words.

"Blackeye wants to know if you have his payment." My chest tightened a bit at the name "Blackeye" and I felt my breathing quicken.

"Yeah," was all I could manage to say.

Tara nodded and backed away from me. "He be waiting for you 'round de corner." After another hug and a quick goodbye, I left Tara and followed her directions into one of the nearby alleys. I wasn't surprised to see the tall, tattooed man awaiting me.

"Okay, here's your money," I told the tall man as I tossed my wadded up fifty dollar bill at him. The man was what many would call my supplier, but there were definitely no drugs involved. He easily caught my hard-earned money with one hand, unfolded it and studied it carefully, as if I had somehow managed to scrounge up a counterfeit bill. That would've taken much more work than just getting real money.

"Would you like for me to go steal you a microscope so you can study it more closely?" I asked in a voice dripping with sarcasm. My supplier gave me a sharp look, making me instantly shut my mouth. Even I knew not to push this guy's buttons too hard.

He was known around the streets as Blackeye, because of all the fights he was involved in and because of the fact that he was never seen without the color black on. I personally thought that was the stupidest nickname I had ever heard, but I wasn't about to tell him that. He was over six feet or pure, tattooed muscle and didn't joke around.

Blackeye, finally deciding that my bill was the real deal, stuck it in his dirty jeans pocket and gave me a tiny nod. He reached into his other pocket and handed me a phone with a charger.

I studied the scratched up cell phone in my hand. It was an antique, ancient artifact with an antenna and no touch screen, and buttons that sounded squeaky when pressed.

"Who'd you steal this from—Fred Flintstone?" I asked incredulously. Blackeye shot me another one of those looks, so I shut my mouth and just barely held back a sigh. I needed a phone if I was going to be able to get in touch with anyone that could help me find my parents, not to mention be able to track down the guy who sold me everything I needed.

"You should be happy I got you anything. You've been slacking on your payments lately," Blackeye rumbled, his voice sounding a bit more threatening than usual. I shrugged and stuck the phone in my pocket. It was time to go.

"Yeah, well, it's hard trying to get you money every day and do the stuff I need to do, too," I huffed, while turning around to leave.

I was stopped short when Blackeye grabbed the top of my hair and yanked me back to him. I cried out in pain and surprise.

"Who are you talkin' to?" Blackeye hissed in my ear. His hot, rancid breath made me wrinkle my nose, but I said nothing. I tried to squirm away but his grip on the roots of my short hair only tightened. I stopped struggling and could only stand still and listen as he continued.

"Don't forget that as long as you owe me all of that money for getting you the stuff you need, you belong to me."

I didn't reply, mostly because there was nothing I could say to that. My chest heaved up and down with anger. I regretted the day I had met this oversized gangbanger with every breath I took.

I had been desperate and hungry. He had found me lying in the street, half-starved, and he had helped me. He was also the reason I had begun stealing. I had thought the world of him back then, but now, not so much. It turned out he was one of the biggest drug dealers and pimps in L.A. and I had just managed to get tangled up with him. I didn't know he would start to charge me for the food he got me and the clothes he stole for me.

Luckily, I had been sneaky enough myself to steal most of the stuff he wanted me to pay back, so I hadn't been sucked into his brothel of prostitutes, unlike my friend Tara. In fact, Tara had been one of the people who had helped steer me clear of that path. I could see from the worry lines and tired expression on Tara's face that that road wasn't easy.

"Ok, I get it. Let me go!" I howled as I winced from the pain he was causing me. He held his grip a moment longer before pushing my head forward and releasing his grip. I quickly pulled away from him and turned around so that I could see what his next move would be. You could never tell with Blackeye. He just laughed and fixed me with a steady glare.

"Just remember…I own you," he warned, his dark eyes telling me he meant every word. I continued to stare him down. He spat by my shoe and then walked away, leaving me alone on the sidewalk. I waited until he had turned the corner before I sent him a well-deserved bird and then lowered it just as quickly. The last time he had caught me shooting him a bird, he had slapped me so hard, I had seen stars for the next week. I prayed for the day that I would be able to pay him off and then finally be able to leave this life.

I walked out of the alleyway, rubbing my sore head. I took out my new/old cell phone and played around with it. I was happy to see that at least the service had already been started and the phone was fully charged. I was surprised to already find the inbox full of text messages. Curiosity got the best of me and before I knew it, I had begun to go through them.

Most of them were from Blackeye's numerous girlfriends, asking him where he was and if he would ever come and see them, and a few were from some of his fellow gang members. I read one from his mom saying:

HENRY I NEED YOU TO GO GET ME SOME FEMININE PRODUCTS! JUST SAY THEY ARE FOR YOUR MOMMY! MWAH I LOVE MY BIG BOY!"

I got a good laugh out of that one. Just as I was getting to the more recent ones, the phone vibrated and I almost dropped it. I shook the phone a couple of times angrily and then checked the number. I didn't recognize the area code. I opened the text and nearly dropped the phone again as I read what was typed:

LOLA, IF YOU CHANGE YOUR MIND, COME TO BOULEVARD3 ON SUNSET BLVD 2NITE. I WILL B THERE. AND U WONT REGRET YOUR DECISION 2 COME.

I stared at the screen for a couple of seconds before I angrily pressed the End key and shoved it in my pocket.

I already knew who the text was from. The man from the Ritz-Carlton. His piercing silvery eyes and knowing smirk floated across my mind, and I just as quickly banished it. How he got my number the second I had got the cell phone was beyond me.

Suddenly paranoid, I made my way into the nearest public area, which was a community park. I sat down on the nearest bench and stared at my cell phone; a thousand questions soaring around my mind.

Boulevard3 was one of the biggest and well-known nightclubs in LA. I heard Leonardo DiCaprio had visited there a few times.

How was I supposed to get in there? *Hello, I'm seventeen, Mr. Mystery!* What was I going to wear? And was I really considering going to meet that guy? I leaned my head back and growled incoherently at the sky, catching the attention of two chubby kids on the nearby slide.

I was going to go. I was going to go to Boulevard3. I had to figure out what this man was offering and why he wanted to help me. I was willing to take any risk if it helped me find my parents. But the biggest question still remained—how was a homeless seventeen year old going to get into one of the hottest nightclubs in Los Angeles?

***

By that night, I was desperate. After bumming a few dollars to catch a bus to Sunset Boulevard, I had spent the entire day looking through stores that might have inexpensive outfits one might wear to a club. Of course, they didn't have anything I could afford.

Fortunately, I still had a fake ID that Tara had hooked me up with a long time ago. She told me that it was insurance, in case I ever needed to go anywhere or got into any trouble. I guess the situation I was in called for it.

The license was under the name of Talia J. Michaels. The 19 year old on the ID slightly resembled me; that is, if I gained fifty pounds, had blonde hair, and was Caucasian. So now all I needed was the money to get into the club, maybe some makeup to make me look older, and a new, hot outfit. And that basically meant I was going nowhere.

When I was around five or six, my mom used to call me Sticky Fingers. I could steal anything from anyone without getting caught. I was a little evil genius. Eventually I ended up stealing Mom's wedding ring and got my butt spanked so hard I cried anytime my dad was within a ten foot radius of me for the next two days. I grew out of the phase and vowed never to steal again. Desperate times called for desperate measures and I had crossed the desperate line a long time ago.

I loitered around the outside of the Hot Stylez clothing store, trying to decide whether or not to go in. I had told my parents I wouldn't steal ever again (pinky promised, in fact), but as said before, desperate times called for desperate measures. And I had broken the promise many times before.

I walked into the store. It was as glam on the inside as it looked on the outside. Neon colors lit up each wall and announced the latest trends and hip sayings in bold, capital letters.

PATTERNS

GO GREEN

LET OUT YOUR INNER ANIMAL

The smell of cheap perfume and mints filled the air. A few customers were browsing through the clothes, not bothering to look up as the chime announcing my entrance rang out.

I looked over nervously at the clerk, who was filing her nails and blabbing on her cell phone while dealing with a customer, all at the same time. I figured she was occupied at the moment. I went over to a metal rack of clothes containing dresses and sifted through them, trying to look casual. There were dresses of all shapes and sizes; red ones with deep V-necks and green ones with high slits all lined the rack.

I wiped my sweaty palms on my pants and looked over my shoulder. No one was looking. I slipped a black mini dress off the rack and tucked it under my arm in one swift motion, then glanced around again.

I was being so obvious. But luckily, no one was paying attention. I spotted an emergency exit on the far side of the store and headed toward it. *Only a couple of feet away.... Move, feet, move!* I basically sprinted out of the door and kept running until I was a couple of blocks away from the store.

Stopping to catch my breath, I realized that I was grinning like a maniac. I threw my head back and laughed triumphantly. Sticky Fingers had struck again!

I held up my new dress and admired it with pride. It was a short black mini-dress with silver sequins adorning the top in a slanting pattern. It would look perfect on me I stepped back into the alley and quickly changed into my hard-earned dress. It fit like a glove. Now that the semi-hard part was done, it was time to move on to phase two of my "Meet up with Mr. Mystery" plan: Sneak into the Boulevard3.

***

I stood in line with the rest of the "party people", set on getting inside of Boulevard3. I was surprised that there weren't that many people in line. In fact, I hadn't recognized that the building they called Boulevard3 was even a nightclub. It looked more like a country club.

I had successfully flared my pixie cut up into a decent style and had scrounged up some black studded stilettos from Tara that were currently making me five inches taller and five steps away from falling flat on my face. I noticed a few guys checking me out, so I guessed that I didn't look too bad-looking. I knew that I wasn't exactly ugly in the first place (even when I was wearing my dirty cargo pants) but I couldn't fight the urge to laugh behind my hand. Little did the guys know that they were checking out a hobo whose latest address had been part of a cardboard box.

The line was moving. I stepped forward, my hands starting to feel sweaty as I came closer and closer to the awaiting bouncer, who looked like two George Foreman's combined. How was I going to get past him? There was no way he would believe I was 18. I was too chicken to try and hand him the fake ID which now, I'll admit, looked nothing like me.

A couple of guys at the very front of the line were starting to shout and I couldn't help but overhear their conversation with the bouncer.

"What do you mean we're not on the list?! We went online and put in for reservations!" the shorter one was saying, his voice getting louder by the minute. The bouncer, I now noticed, was holding onto a list. He scanned through the papers and then gave his head a firm shake.

"Nope, no Josh Davidson or Trey Jones. You'll have to step out of line, boys. If you're not on the list, you're not getting in." he explained. After some not-so-kind grumbling, the unfortunate guys lumbered away, casting everyone in line looks that dared us to say a word.

By this time, I was literally pouring sweat. I hadn't known there would be a list. No one said there was going to be a list.

There wasn't too much time to worry because, before I knew it, five other girls and I were in front of the bouncer. The girls were obviously together, because they all looked exactly the same, down to their platinum blonde hair and acrylic Hello Kitty nails.

Suddenly, a plan came to my mind. I scrunched myself up to the girls and smiled.

"I'm so excited! Aren't you excited, uh, Brittany?" I asked the blonde closest to me, hoping Brittany was actually her name. She looked at me as if I were crazy.

"How do you know my name?" she asked in a nasally voice. I just giggled and smiled at the bouncer.

"Brittany's excited, too! Isn't it ladies' night?" I asked, praying that it was. The bouncer gave me a nod and a smile. I let out a breath I didn't know I was holding in. That meant the money was no problem. But the list was another thing...

"IDs?" George Foreman's look-a-like asked, holding out a big, meaty hand. I watched enviously as the other girls showed him their IDs. The bouncer looked at their IDs, then at the list. After a while, he nodded and motioned for them to go in. He even gave them a big, sunshiny smile! The girls grinned back, their teeth white and perfect, before they strutted inside, their blonde extensions swinging in unison behind them. Brittany was just about to show her ID when I decided to set my plan in motion.

"Brittany, you little witch! Was that Dustin's picture I saw in your purse?!" I yelled loudly, putting my hand on my hip for extra effect. Those years in Drama class had paid off. I could rival any of the Gossip Girls when it came to acting.

"Um, like, what are you talking about?" Brittany asked while flipping her stiff hair over her shoulder and glaring at me.

"Don't play dumb! We just broke up last week and now you're seeing him?! We're supposed to be best friends!" I shouted, throwing her expensive purse on the ground. Brittany's mouth flew open and she gasped loudly.

"That's my COACH bag!" she shrieked, stomping up to me in her Jimmy Choo heels. The bouncer was looking between us, not knowing what to do.

"And that's my boyfriend!" With that last line, I shoved Brittany with both hands and she stumbled backwards. Chaos broke out as everyone in line began to swarm us, chanting "FIGHT, FIGHT" and the bouncer instantly got lost in the crowd.

Just what I wanted.

"You can have him!" I yelled over the chanting, and then gave the bewildered girl another shove. She fell back into the crowd and I followed after her. Instead of going in for another shove (the poor girl had had enough) I expertly dodged around her and ran past the bouncer and into the club.

Well, at least what I thought was the club. It looked more like a fancy outdoor dining area. There was a long pool of water in the center of the courtyard and I was surprised to see a girl riding a swing that dangled above it. She waved at me and I tentatively waved back. The girl's attention was drawn to something behind me, and her expression turned confused. I followed her gaze and cursed when I saw George Foreman's twin and two equally buff security guards running toward me. Well, I guess my brilliant plan wasn't as brilliant as I thought it had been.

I quickly dashed around the water and into a door that led into the building. The inside was just as serene and beautiful as the outside, and just as empty. I needed a crowd to get lost in. I ran down the nearest hallway, my heels clicking loudly, hoping against hope that I would find the actual nightclub in Boulevard3. I heard the angry shouts of the guards behind me and I knew they were catching up.

Right as my feet began to tire out, my ears picked up on the sounds of deep, thumping bass, loud laughter and cheering. I was almost there.

Pushing myself to go faster, I burst out of the hallway and was met with a breathtaking sight.

I could see why Boulevard3 was so popular. It was huge. The expansive dance floor was packed to capacity with people dancing in outfits that ranged from dresses and suits to ripped jeans and tube tops. There was even a stage! Beautiful dancers, both male and female were dancing like video vixens onstage, making everyone on the dance floor seem like toddlers stumbling about. The entire place seemed so posh. Needless to say, I would definitely be visiting here again, with a proper ID and reservations, of course.

"Strawberry?" a female voice sounded from close by. I looked over and saw a woman standing next to a creamy chocolate fountain with a platter of bright-red strawberries.

"Are they for free?" I asked skeptically. The woman nodded and smiled brightly. Her smile disappeared as I snatched up a handful of strawberries by their leaves and dipped them into the gushing milk chocolate.

"Thanks," I called over my shoulder as I hurried away, leaving the stunned lady to the rest of her strawberries. I stuffed one of the decadent strawberries into my mouth and looked around the club, chewing. I almost choked when I looked back and saw the security guards talking to the strawberry lady. She was nodding vigorously and then she pointed at me. We all made eye contact.

I swallowed down my strawberry, dropped the rest, and bolted. I dove straight into the crowd on the dance floor and tried my hardest to wade through them and get into the very center. I almost bumped into a whirling man on stilts and a few angry people yelled at me as I pushed them aside. I ignored them and kept going until I got to the very center of the crowd.

I stood there for a while, trying to hunch over, wishing that I could somehow turn invisible. After a while of standing there, I realized that I looked like a complete idiot.

There I was, in the middle of the dance floor, hunched over like an old person, while everyone else danced. Oh yeah, I was definitely blending in.

I began to shift from foot to foot, trying to blend in with the other dancers who were gyrating to a Li'l Wayne song. Okay, so I had made it into Boulevard3. The Mystery Man had failed to mention what to do next. I glanced around, hoping to see the mysterious man from the hotel among the dancers. Seeing no one familiar, I let myself get lost in the music and began dancing along with everyone else. The beat was hypnotizing and I almost forgot about the whole reason I had come to Boulevard3 in the first place.

Suddenly, my phone, which was snuggled next to my pocket knife in my bra, vibrated and brought me back to the real world. I glanced around, and then dug it out.

There was another text message:

I SEE YOU. PLEASE TAKE A SEAT AND I SHALL MAKE MY APPEARANCE SHORTLY.

I glanced around before slowly putting the phone back in my dress. At least he hadn't stood me up after all I had done to get in this place. Deciding that the coast was clear, I battled my way back off of the dance floor, making sure to keep far away from the strawberry lady. I found an empty table near the dance floor and plopped down. Now all I had to do was wait and hope that I didn't get into any trouble for stealing someone's table.

I hoped that I was doing the right thing. This man could be a serial killer, for all I knew.

I watched all of the people dancing wildly to a remix of a Macklemore song out on the floor, and laughed under my breath when I saw some guy who looked like Napoleon Dynamite trying to do "The Worm" and completely butchering it. It looked more like "The Walrus".

"*Hola, bonita,*" a cool voice whispered right near my ear. I whirled around and nearly died. Next to me sat the most perfect-looking guy I had ever laid eyes on.

He looked as if he had come straight out of some magazine, one with guys that had dark hair, naturally tan skin, and were always posing with perfume or something girly like that. He had a sprinkling of stubble on his angular jaw, alerting me that he was not only out of my league, but out of my age range as well, if only by a couple of years. He was dressed in an unbuttoned white dress shirt and black slacks. It would have looked ridiculous on anyone else, but I immediately thought it was a good look on him. The only thing that seemed out of place about him had to be the stunning jagged tattoos that garnished his chest and arms.

I stared at him for a second, stunned. Guys like him had never approached me before. In high school, guys like him hadn't even existed.

I desperately searched for something to say, but for once, my mouth failed me. So I just sat there and stared stupidly for a couple of moments.

"What? I know I'm pretty good-looking, but you're acting as if you just saw an angel," the model teased, while stroking my chin like I was some dog. I hate to admit it, but if I was a dog, my tail would have been doing some serious wagging. I quickly pulled my chin away and found that my mouth was functioning again.

"The only thing hot in here is your breath. Now beat it, I'm waiting for someone," I hissed, turning away from him and looking back out at the dance-floor, chin in hand. Out of the corner of my eye, I noticed him check his breath a couple of times, looking as if he might have a heart attack. I held back a laugh. But no, not even the threat of having bad breath could stop this guy. He leaned in again, putting his mouth next to my ear.

"I know who you're waiting for, Lola Phillips," he murmured. I jerked away and looked at him. He quirked an eyebrow and held up his martini glass, waiting for my response.

What was up with strangers knowing everything about my life suddenly? "What else do you know, Inspector Gadget?" I asked, easing back into my seat and fixing him with an icy glare. He took a sip of his drink, the smile never leaving his face. Before he could say anything else, I was literally ripped out of my seat.

Appearing like ninjas out of thin air, the security guards were on me. "There you are!" George's look-a-like growled, jerking my arm so that I was pulled toward him.

"You've got the wrong girl!" I lied. "It was this other girl...she ran out the back! You'd better go catch her!"

"You think I'm stupid?" the bouncer nearly yelled. "I recognize that red Rihanna-wannabe hair!"

"At least I don't look like I should be selling grills..." I mumbled under my breath.

"What was that?"

"Hey, hey, let's calm down, everyone." My new "friend" had stood up and was giving the security guards a big "aw-geez-let's-have-a-beer-and-talk this over" grin. "What exactly did she do?"

George pulled me forward, like I was a prisoner. "This girl incited a fight outside of my club and then tried to sneak in here without paying!"

"Oh, really?" The model reached into his pocket and pulled out a crisp one hundred dollar bill. My mouth dropped open as he handed it over to the guards. The guards all exchanged a look before George pocketed the bill. He let go of my arm and gave me a disgusted look. I shot him back the same look.

"We'll overlook it this time, for you, sir," he mumbled with a nod before him and his herd of men in suits stalked off. I glared after them. If my wrist was bruised, I would be coming back here to sue him for every kitchen appliance he had ever created.

"You have some deadly looks, you know?" The model and my rescuer let out a loud laugh before he settled back into the table. He pulled out a pack of cigarettes and slid one out before popping the unlit stick in his mouth. He motioned for me to sit down and I did.

"Thanks, I guess, for helping me out with those guys," I said, rubbing my wrist. He shrugged it off and pulled out a lighter. He flicked it on under the bud of his cigarette. The bud sparked red before he put away the lighter. He inhaled deeply, removed the cigarette and blew out a long puff of smoke in my face. I coughed angrily and waved my hand in front of my face. I really hated smoking. The smell of it was enough to make me want to throw up.

"I always save a damsel in distress," he replied, giving me a smooth wink. The stranger chuckled and offered me the pack. I shook my head. He shrugged and puffed away at his own cigarette.

"So, Red, if you wanna know more about what we know, you'll come with me. I work for the man you shoved on the ground earlier today." He played with the umbrella in his drink while giving me a knowing smile.

Another thing my parents had taught me was to never go anywhere alone with strangers, not even ones that looked like models, and not even if they had saved you from being thrown out on your face. But, with a chance of finding them so close, I didn't know what to say.

"How do I know you're not just some sleaze trying to pick up a girl?" I said, half-joking. The guy's hazel eyes turned solemn. He reached into his pocket and pulled out a gold chain with a locket dangling from it. He flicked it open and my breath caught in my throat.

Inside of the locket was a familiar picture. I had been day-dreaming about it since the day my parents had went missing, so it was impossible not to recognize.

The photo was of baby me, being held by my smiling parents.

I reached out a shaky hand and grabbed the necklace, then looked up at the guy who had been holding onto it. A million questions blurred through my mind, mixed with the memory of my mom showing me the exact same necklace whenever she told me the story of how my parents first met.

"Why do you have this?" I asked finally, in a voice that was barely more than a whisper. His smile returned and he shrugged.

"You wanna know more, you'll have to come with me, hot breath and all," he teased while putting out his cigarette on the smooth table and dropping it in the ashtray. "Besides, can't you do this small request for me? I did just drop a hundred bucks on you." I felt a smile tugging on my lips and I fought it away.

I gingerly placed the necklace around my neck and clasped the ends together. I looked back up at him, my mind made up.

"Fine. Let's go."

Chapter Three

Next thing I knew, I was in the passenger seat of a red Ferrari, sitting next to the handsome stranger, and headed for who knows where at 80 miles per hour on a dark and lonely highway. I was seriously beginning to doubt my decision to come.

"Where exactly are we going?" I asked, for the tenth time. I was trying to sound brave, but I expected my face to be on the back of a milk carton by the next morning.

The guy just smiled knowingly at me. "You'll find out in a bit, Red. You'll find out in a bit."

Well, that didn't sound creepy at all.

Soon, we were out of the city limits and the skyscrapers were slowly being replaced with trees. My heart began to beat faster. There were no other cars on the road with us. I began to panic when we passed a sign asking everyone to report anything they knew about the disappearance of some girl named Georgina.

"I don't know what the heck you're trying to pull, but I'm telling you now…don't try anything stupid," I warned, keeping my voice steady despite the fact that I wanted to cry and jump out of the car. I should've known better than to ride off into the night with first cute guy who happened to have a picture of my parents.

The guy just laughed and snapped his seat belt into place, then grinned at me. "Calm down…and put on your seat belt." I looked at him as if he were crazy. There were certainly no cops down this road. But his eyes told me he was serious, so I snapped my seat belt on.

"As you wish, Daddy-dearest," I said in a sarcastic, high-pitched voice.

"Hey, I like that. Call me that more often, will you?"

I responded with a middle finger and then looked back out of the front window. The road we were on never seemed to end. We hadn't come across another person in about thirty minutes. Sure, it was 1 a.m. but in L.A., that was the time that everyone was up and about.

"Okay, hold on, Red," the guy piped up. I looked over and saw him gripping the steering wheel and looking strangely excited. I looked around for something to hold and grabbed onto to the sides of my seat.

Was he about to crash the car?

All of my questions were answered and about fifty million more were formed when suddenly the road before us suddenly opened up into a huge, square hole.

"Stop the car!" I yelled as we continued barreling toward it. He just laughed and pressed down on the gas. We were seconds away from falling.

I grabbed onto the stranger's arm and screamed as we drove right into the hole.

***

I always hated roller coasters. Being tossed and turned and flipped like hamburgers on a grill. Not fun at all. Fortunately, this was not the case for my current situation.

Instead of falling like I thought we would, I was shocked to see that the road hadn't simply disappeared into a giant hole where we would have fell to our end. Instead, the square section of the road in front of us sloped downwards into a deep, dark cavern, allowing the car to slip underground while its tires stayed on the dirt. I screamed like a madman as the driver drove right into the hole, as if he was used to the ground opening before him all the time. He flicked off his headlights, plunging us into darkness.

"What the heck is going on?!" I asked incredulously when my driver showed no signs of stopping. He smiled in the fading moonlight as we rolled deeper into the ground.

"Just relax, Red," he said in his soothing accent. "You'll be used to things liked this in no time."

"Used to things like this? Where are you taking me?" A sudden bump under the tires distracted me long enough to look back through the windshield. We were crawling through the darkness, surrounded by black on all sides. You literally couldn't see your hand in front of your face.

Enough was enough. "That's it. I've had enough of your games. So long and have fun pranking some other stupid girl," I said as I reached for my door handle.

"I wouldn't do that if I were you, Red," my driver said. I looked over at him but it was impossible to make out his expression in the dark.

"The name's Lola. Goodbye." I had no idea where I was going in the middle of the night in a pitch black driveway. Wherever I ended up, it had to be better than wherever he planned on taking me.

Just as soon as I pulled the handle, light returned in a bright flash. I froze like a deer in headlights. What were lights doing all the way down here?

"Shut the door, Red." My driver's voice was deep and authoritative. I hated when people told me what to do, but something told me I should listen. I slammed the door closed and squinted back out the windshield.

"It's Lola," I mumbled.

As my eyes adjusted to the light, I was surprised to see that we had drove to what seemed like a dead end. The wall in front of us was made completely from silver metal and was covered in bulbs that shone light at our faces.

"Now, stare straight ahead and don't move a muscle," my driver instructed. "That includes your mouth." I frowned at his insult but obliged. I didn't know what was going on, but I knew that I needed to listen to my new companion because there was no turning back now.

"SCANNING PASSENGERS," a loud, computerized voice blared out from the wall. I was speechless as the metal wall slowly opened like a garage door, revealing thick, black glass.

"What..." Another bright flash stopped me mid-sentence. After a few loud beeps, the computer spoke again.

"PASSENGERS CONFIRMED: AGENT RETRO REX AND RECRUIT LOLA PHILLIPS. ACCESS TO H CORPORATION GRANTED." A few more beeps sounded before the wall slowly shut again. There was some loud clanking beneath us. Suddenly, the platform we were on began to lower, taking us and the Ferrari with it. Metals walls rose on either side of the car to form a box of sorts. We were in a huge car-sized elevator, being lowered even further into the ground.

"This is insane...crazy...." I repeated in a murmur to myself as the elevator clanked and whirred with its descent. Amazingly, my comrade and his gelled-up hair seemed perfectly calm, as if riding in an underground car elevator was something he did on a daily basis.

"This is your new reality, Red," my driver said as he switched the car back into drive. "Welcome to H Corporation."

Right on cue, the wall in front of us lowered to reveal an expansive parking lot, surrounded by more metal walls and filled with all sorts of expensive vehicles: sports cars, trucks, RVs, and even a few school buses.

"Are you some sort of underground car dealership?" I asked as he maneuvered his car into an empty spot. "Because I don't have my license yet. I planned on getting it soon, though." I didn't really know what else to say, so I was reduced to nervous blabbering.

This got a good laugh out of my driver. "No, no," he assured me, "this is just our parking lot." He shifted the car into park before he turned it off and retrieved his keys from the ignition. He turned and looked at me, a serious expression on his face.

"You are Lola Phillips, daughter of Warren and Ruby Phillips, right?" he asked. I nodded slowly, still reeling from our elevator ride.

"Those are my parents. How do you know them?" I asked, while clutching the locket that dangled by my chest.

"I don't, at least, not personally," he admitted with a shrug. "But, that's not important right now. What's important is that you listen—"

"What's important," I cut in, "is that you tell me where I am and how you know my parents. I'm God knows where in some underground parking lot because you and that old guy told me you knew where my parents were. I think I'm the one who deserves to ask some questions and get some answers."

The driver sighed and ran a hand through his dark hair and exhaled. His hand fidgeted near his pocket, where I knew he still held his cigarettes and lighter. I guess dealing with me was more than he alone could manage. He looked back over at me and grinned.

"Yeah, I suppose you're right. But, first thing's first." He leaned towards me, making me shrink away, feeling nervous. First of all, I still wasn't entirely sure of this guy's intentions. Second of all, I wasn't used to guys, especially guys who looked like him, being close to me.

My driver gave me an amused smirk before he simply pulled the lock up on my side, unlocking my door.

"You have to hand-pull your door's lock," he explained, still smirking. I immediately felt embarrassed by my reaction and hurriedly climbed out of the door and slammed it behind me. The driver followed suit, then turned towards me.

"I'm not the one who can give you the answers you're looking for. I just work for the man who can," he informed me as he fixed his collar.

"And where is this man?" I asked as I placed my hand on my hip and stared at him.

"I'll bring you to him soon, scout's honor," he teased with a smile I didn't return. "But, like I said, first things first—we need to clean you up."

Clean me up? What was I—a Chihuahua? "Excuse me? I don't need to be cleaned up! I need someone to explain to me what the heck is going on!" Before I could go into full psycho mode, the driver pulled out a small, metal orb. I stared quizzically at the orb and then back up to its owner.

"What's that?" I asked. The driver didn't answer. Instead, he closed his hand around the orb and then opened his fist, revealing a white powder.

"Good night, Red. We'll talk again soon, *bonita.*" He raised his hand to his mouth and then blew the substance right into my face. I burst into a coughing fit as the white powder filled my nostrils and coated the inside of my throat.

"Wh-what is this?" I choked out in a raspy voice as I stumbled around. I grabbed the Ferrari to keep myself balanced as my vision began to fade in and out.

"It's better if you just go to sleep for now," the driver said while pulling out a cigarette. He lit it like an expert before taking a long drag on it. He blew out a string of swirly smoke that seemed to form shapes and letters. "Sweet dreams." His voice sounded so distant and far away. I suddenly felt so sleepy.

I slumped against the hood of the car, still coughing. Before long, my vision faded into complete darkness, mixed with a haze of cigarette smoke.

Chapter Four

"Lola, Lola, Coca-Cola, buy me a soda, little Lola.

Sweet and bubbly, just like you.

Buy me a soda, one or two.

Lola, Lola, Coca-Cola, buy me a soda, little Lola."

"Lola...Lola...Lola, wake up, dear." Someone was calling my name but I couldn't answer. I was surrounded by darkness. The darkness was like oozing tar, sticking to me. It seemed as if it was pressing down on me and I couldn't breathe.

"C'mon, open your eyes..." A soft, familiar voice broke through the dark mist. I decided to listen to it. I opened my eyes.

My vision was blurry and splotched with rainbow polka dots for a second, but the dots began to form into an intricate diamond patterned ceiling after I blinked my eyes a couple of times. I realized I was lying on my back, staring up at a ceiling. I sat up slowly, trying to ease the dizziness that sprang up and made me grab my head. After the dizziness had passed, I took a deep breath and looked around. Where was I? The room resembled a hospital room, with unused syringes littering the nearby desk and a small stand of magazines near the door. The door was on the opposite side of the room, with a sign on it that read "THE DOCTOR WILL BE BACK SHORTLY." I laid back on the bed I was on and sighed.

Had this all been some sort of crazy nightmare? Had I just dreamed of sneaking into the club and meeting the handsome stranger who led me to a world hidden underground? Maybe I had fell asleep somewhere and some kind stranger had taken me to the hospital.

I snuggled up in the warm covers of my bed and shut my eyes again.

Wait a second.

My eyes snapped back open and I scrambled to sit up in bed. I looked down at myself and nearly screamed when I saw that I was still in the dress I had stolen to wear to the nightclub. I reached up with a shaky hand and grabbed onto the locket on my chest.

That really had happened. I really had met that guy at the club, we really had drove underground, and he really had knocked me out with some type of sleeping dust.

A scary thought went through my mind.

Had I died without realizing it?! That would explain the pictures of angels decorating the walls. That had to be a sign that I had at least made it to heaven.

"Excuse me, ma'am! Are you awake?" I looked over and saw a pretty girl who looked as if she were around my age, yet she couldn't have been taller than four feet. She was dressed up in the silliest-looking pink, spandex, V-neck jumpsuit I had ever seen, paired with knee-high white boots and curly sandy brown hair that spilled around her shoulders. I pulled myself up into a sitting position and stared at her.

"...Am I in heaven?" I asked, and was surprised at how hoarse my voice sounded. I cleared my throat a couple of times, and tried to speak again, but my voice came out in a squeak. It must have been that stupid dust.

The girl laughed and flittered over to my side. "No, sorry! We're so far underground; we're probably closer to, y'know...the other place. "She whispered the last of her sentence and finished off with a big grin, waiting for me to reply. I was beginning to think maybe I had ended up in the other place, too.

"Right. Who are you and where am I?" I asked, my voice sounding almost normal now. The girl giggled again, her laugh sounding like skidding tires.

"I'm Lolli! And you're in one of the H Corporation hospital rooms. Are you feeling any better now?" the girl asked, smiling brightly at me. Too much enthusiasm this early could not be healthy for you. But she was also the only steady source of information in sight so I continued my investigating.

"What's the H Corporation?" I asked. Lolli tapped her chin, looking perplexed, and then sat on the edge of my bed.

"Retro didn't tell you anything about what was going to happen to you? Wow, you must be so scared! I remember when I was first recruited by the H Corporation! I was only thirteen and I was soooo nervous! I couldn't stop shaking and I was pretty tense and mean, kinda like you....w-well, not like you, but—," Lolli blabbered on and on before I finally cut her off.

"Okay, okay, I heard something about being hired. Who said I was trying to find a job?" I asked, giving her a hard glare. In fact, I was entirely tired of hearing people tell me that I needed to "get a job". How many companies do you know that would hire a hobo who hadn't taken a normal shower in months? Besides that, I hadn't missed that "mean" comment she had blabbed out.

Lolli smiled at me, her hazel eyes twinkling mischievously. She reached into her pocket and pulled out a long, silver object with a sharp point at the end. I backed away from her as her grin became bigger and bigger and she started to lean toward me.

"Stay back!" I warned, reaching for my own knife in my pocket, but I realized I was still wearing my mini-dress—which had no pockets. I grasped at my bra and then groaned inwardly. I remembered with a grimace that I had left it on the floor of the Ferrari.

Lolli laughed and poked the sharp object into an octagonal slot in the wall behind me and gave it a quick ninety degree turn. Suddenly, the wall behind me began to waver and shimmer and soon transformed into what seemed like a huge television screen with the all-too familiar face of the mysterious man from the Ritz-Carlton.

I scrambled backwards and almost fell off the side of the bed, but luckily Lolli caught me before I made an absolute idiot of myself. She laughed at me then turned her attention to the wall-TV.

"Sir, she's awakened! Should I bring her down to your office or clean her up first?" she asked. She glanced at me before leaning towards the wall and whispering loudly, "She's a little stinky." I snapped my head around to glare at her.

The man nodded once, never taking those silver eyes off of me. I stared back, unable to look away. So, he was the mastermind behind all of this.

"Just bring her here, Lolli," he said.

Before I could ask him anything, the screen flickered away and we were staring at a blank white wall again. Lolli hopped off of the bed, brushed off her jumpsuit and then grinned.

"Okay, let's get going, shall we?" she said, pleasantly. I nodded, suddenly feeling brave. I was excited to see the man who was in charge of an underground business and also excited to get a chance to punch him in the face for making me go through an obstacle course just to get to him.

I followed Lolli out of the hospital room and gasped. Somehow, it seemed as if I had just found myself warp into a new world.

Everything from the ceiling to the walls to the floor was made entirely out of shiny, white metal. The ceiling panels were striped with neon lights that ran down the ceiling's length and switched from blue to green every couple of seconds, as if they couldn't make up their minds as to which color they wanted to be.

I stared around at the decor in amazement before someone rudely bumped into me, almost knocking me to the hard floor.

"Excuse you!" I snapped, while turning around to face the culprit. I nearly had a heart attack when I saw that the person was a man dressed in a vibrant purple jumpsuit with spiral tattoos circling his eyes, giving them the illusion that they were bulging out.

"Never mind," I quickly sputtered out when he fixed me with an angry glare. I took a step back, only to bump into an even more frightening person with piercings jutting out from their large, protruding forehead.

"Your face!" I cried out in surprise. The two men continued to gaze at me angrily before Lolli quickly jumped to my rescue.

"Sorry about that," she apologized, "This is the new girl Harv wanted." Something about her statement made the men do a complete one-eighty.

"That so? My apologies," Bug-Eye said while backing away with his hands up. Piercings mumbled an apology as well before he and his scary companion scurried off. I stared after them and noticed for the first time that the hallway was crawling with other freaky-looking people in jumpsuits similar to Lolli's, except they were all in different colors. I noticed that while the men had jumpsuits with turtlenecks, the women's' jumpsuits had necklines that were cut into a deep V that ended in the middle of their chests. They observed me with suspicious eyes as we made our way through them, our heels clicking loudly on the metal floor.

This was insane. This was unreal. Where in the world was I? In any case, I made sure to stick close to Lolli.

"Sorry about that," Lolli said as we dodged the staring masses. "So, what's your name? You know I'm Lolli, and the guy you met earlier in that nightclub is named Retro," she explained. Those were weird names. But in a world where some people had the audacity to consider the naming someone Hashtag, I supposed that Lolli and Retro weren't that abnormal.

"I'm Lola. It's nice to meet you," I replied. Lolli nodded.

"That's a pretty name! I wish I could remember my original name! I'm sure I was a Delilah! That's what I like to think, at least!" she chirped. I stared at her vacantly, wondering who would have their name changed to Lolli.

"Here we are!" Lolli's high-pitched voice snapped me back to reality. We were standing in front of a set of stairs that spiraled so far down into darkness, I couldn't even see where they ended.

"Am I supposed to go alone?" I asked after a moment. Lolli nodded.

"Yep! His office is the first and only door at the bottom of these stairs. Good luck!" With those last well wishes, Lolli had skipped back down the hallway, leaving me to face the ominous stairwell. I took a deep breath before I took my first step.

Click.

I nearly jumped out of my dress at the sound of a nearby light bulb on the wall flicking on by itself. I took a second to let my heart settle down before I continued my descent, guided by the fluorescent blue bulbs that flicked on with every step I descended.

I circled down the stairs for what seemed like hours before they came to an abrupt halt in front of a door. The door was made from a black metal and bore the letter "H", carved in shiny gold, at the center of it. This guy was nothing short of dramatic, although I'll admit the lights were useful.

The door seemed to loom over me, causing me to hesitate. I took a deep breath before rapping against the door twice, then I let my hand fall to my side. A couple of seconds passed before a pudgy man in a tight, green jumpsuit opened the door. Some people were not meant to wear certain things, and this man and his jumpsuit were the perfect example.

He studied me for a second, his dull, sunken eyes unreadable, before he opened the door a bit wider and motioned me inside. I took a second to gather myself, and then stepped inside. It didn't take long to spot who I was looking for.

Seated behind a desk made entirely of gold, perched my newest "friend", the ever elusive Mystery Man. He was dressed in his designer white tuxedo with a yellow rose dangling from his breast pocket.

He leaned back in his black leather chair, smirking at me, with his cane resting on his desk. The green-clad man excused himself, and then exited the room, leaving me and the Mystery Man to ourselves.

We regarded each other in silence. Neither of us spoke for what seemed like an eternity. He decided to speak first. "Have a seat, dear. No need to look so hostile," he remarked in his deep voice, waving one of his hands towards the vacant seat in front of him.

"I'm not your dear," I corrected him, before plopping down in the chair. I made sure not to take my eyes off of his for a second, suspecting him to have a secret button that would cause a hole to appear beneath me. He chuckled, as if he had read my mind. He leaned forward, his elbows presiding on his desk and his chin resting on his fists.

"Miss Lola, is that what you would like for me to call you?" he asked, politely. I felt as if we had just stepped back into the 1940s.

"Just Lola. And another thing…"

BAM!

In one quick movement, I had punched the man right in his nose. A string of curse words poured out of his mouth while blood poured out of nose.

"That's for sending me on a wild goose chase just to find you! Ever heard of Skype?" I yelled, my anger getting the better of me. I slammed my fist on his desk for good measure. *Ouch, that hurt.* I shook my hand in pain and resisted the urge to cry.

I didn't feel the need to mention that I had no access whatsoever to Skype.

"It wush aw fer a goo caww," the man uttered as he gently pinched his nose and tilted his head up. I wanted to tell him to tilt his head down so he didn't swallow his blood, but the sound of him pulling out a drawer from behind his desk stopped me.

There it was—the button I knew he was hiding. He hit the button with his fist while sighing in frustration. I gasped and backed away. Before I could make a run for the door, two women in matching white jumpsuits raced in, carrying loads of medical equipment, as though he had just suffered from a major heart attack. I slowly sat back in my chair. What a baby. I hadn't even broken it, I'm sure.

After a few minutes of pampering and shameless flirting, the women were gone and he and I were left to scowl at one another.

"I'm glad to see you've recovered nicely, at least," he said, after a moment. I couldn't help but smile some. He returned the smile and then leaned forward.

"I'm sure you're curious as to why I've put you through so much. You see, I was testing you."

I cocked an eyebrow. "Testing me? For what?" I asked, sitting up in my chair a little straighter. The man's silver eyes gleamed as he reached into his gold desk and withdrew a sleek, black jumpsuit.

"Lola Phillips, what are you willing to do to get your parents back?"

Chapter Five

"Anything," I answered immediately. Harv nodded approvingly and went to hand me the jumpsuit. I shot the ugly jumpsuit a disdainful look. "But I'm not getting within a two foot radius of that jumpsuit," I added as an afterthought.

He laid down the jumpsuit on the desk and gestured with a twirl of his hand for me to sit back down. After a moment of hesitation, I did.

"We'll get to the jumpsuit in a moment. You see, all that you just went through was testing you," he stated. I stared blankly at him, waiting for him to make his point. He carried on.

"I wanted to see just what you were willing to go through to get to your parents. And you passed with flying colors...although your attitude could use an adjustment," he added, while tentatively touching his nose.

"So, I've been told," I said with a shrug.

"When I first approached you at the hotel, it was just to make sure you were the correct girl. I could tell right away from your similarity in…'temperament' to your mother, the lovely Ruby, you were her and Warren's daughter."

I smiled at the reference. From what I could remember about my mom and the stories my aunt told me about her, she could be pretty feisty.

"I'll take that as a compliment," I quipped. The silver-eyed man chuckled.

"Very well. I'm sure you found that, being a seventeen year old, homeless, young lady, it was quite the difficult task to get into such an upscale club."

"Understatement of the year."

He ignored me. "I must say, you impressed me when you were able to materialize a proper outfit and get inside. Your entrance was a bit sloppy, but we'll work on that." I opened my mouth to tell him to try and do better, but he was on a roll.

"Retro, the young man you met there, was just a distraction, to see if you'd be distracted easily by members of the opposite sex," he said, while sending me a wink. "Now, the elevator itself is the only way into my facility, so it was more of a necessity than a test. It took my engineers years to come up with such a brilliant device. They would also make sure that a lethal gas would be administered to all who were not in the personnel database. Thankfully, I put you in ahead of time, Lola." I listened carefully as he elucidated and felt my blood run cold at the thought of what could have happened to me in that elevator.

"...So, where are my parents?" I asked, getting straight to the point. They were the whole reason I was there. If he had lied about that, I was liable to break more than just a nose or two.

The man nodded and folded his hands on his desk. "Your parents worked for my corporation."

This came as a complete shock. I think that this would be something to share with the family at dinnertime. He continued on, oblivious to my insights.

"They were in the International Affairs department and dealt with communicating and trading with other secret organizations similar to my own, and big-name corporations throughout the world. One such corporation that used to partner with my own was called the E Corporation. They focused on globally uniting the world, you know, one mega-nation, led by one person. Except they went about it the wrong way, building nuclear weapons and other dangerous means that would force countries to join their mega-nation. I decided to cut them off as partners and work against them. They, of course, held it against me." He sighed and shook his head before continuing.

"I noticed my agents disappearing, one by one. Their decaying bodies were found soon thereafter. Of course it was the E Corporation's work. I'm afraid that your parents were also captured by them, which left you..." The man hesitated for a moment, obviously searching for the right words. "...well, alone. The only bizarre thing about their disappearance is that we were never able to find their bodies, which leads me to the conclusion that they may still be alive."

By this time, my heart was racing and my head felt sore. It felt as if time had slowly come to a halt in the world around me.

"I can see you have many questions on your mind," he said as he climbed to his feet. He extended his hand toward me with a slight smile. "Let me answer one. It's about time we got acquainted. My name is Harv Magnum III, President and CEO of the H Corporation. My establishment specializes in maintaining the balance of power throughout the world, researching technology, and stabilizing countries that get out of hand. And we do so by hand-picking people like you, Lola, to fulfill each goal we have set for ourselves. I need you to become an agent and help me find your parents."

I was dumbfounded for a second as I shook his hand without actually realizing that I was. "An agent? Like a spy" I sputtered stupidly. This was too unreal. I felt like I was delving into some hidden society, which I guess I was.

Harv laughed and drummed his fingers on the desk, a cheerful smile on his face. "You could say that. Are you interested, Lola? You are the only person I think would be capable of accomplishing this admittedly tough job," he said, his smile dropping into a serious line. I looked down at the floor. My head was starting to throb with all of these sudden realizations. I looked over at his face and could tell that he was. I couldn't doubt his seriousness, seeing that I was in a secret corporation miles underground.

Really, what was the worst that could happen? I had always told myself that it would be me who found my parents. Besides, this was the biggest and undoubtedly real lead I had ever came across. If I declined, my chances of ever finding my parents would be reduced to zero. Maybe it was because I was so excited at the chance of finding my parents that I didn't think to ask any more questions, important questions, until later.

"…Do I have to wear those ridiculous jumpsuits?" I asked instead, as an unexpected smile tugged at the corner of my mouth. Harv grinned and clapped his hands together.

"This is wonderful! I've had my eye on you for a long time, Miss Lola," he cheered, his bright grin almost blinding me. I was about to remind him to drop the "Miss" but the black jumpsuit had suddenly been flung on my lap, and out-of-date titles became the least of my worries.

"I said no jumpsuit!" I whined, holding the jumpsuit up and examining it with my lip curled. The V-neck was sure to show too much cleavage; disregarding the fact that I barely had any to begin with. "What's the point in wearing this ugly thing?"

"It is not ugly, my dear. I just like my employees to look like a team." Harv said, while dusting off his sleeves.

"A team of go-go girls?" I suggested dryly.

He ignored me and waved his hand toward the door. "Lolli is outside, waiting for you. She'll help you get situated here. I'll summon you later," he declared, like he was a grand king. I huffed and got up, slinging the ugly piece of black fabric over my shoulder. I had almost reached the door when Harv's voice stopped me.

"Before you go, Lola, I must have your agreement that you will do whatever it takes to get back your parents. This job won't be easy, I assure you."

I looked over my shoulder and was surprised at how serious his voice and expression had become. His silver eyes had misted over and now looked almost black. I almost gave my decision a second thought.

But all it took was the weight of my parents' locket dangling from around my neck to make me stay firm in my decision.

"Whatever it takes," I repeated as I exited his office. In the next second, I was tackled by a flying flash of magenta.

"Oh, Lola! You're one of us, now!" Lolli squealed, squeezing me tighter in her death hug. I could barely breathe with her short arms wrapped around my neck.

"I won't be for long if you hug me to death," I managed to squeak out. Lolli laughed and let go, practically radiating the dark stairwell with her cheerfulness. I was going to have to invest in a pair of sunglasses if I was going to hang around this girl.

"So, what color did you get?" Lolli asked. Figuring that she was talking about my jumpsuit, I pulled the wretched piece of stretchy fabric off of my shoulder and showed it to her. Lolli took one look at it before she put her finger down her mouth and gagged. My sentiments exactly.

"He stuck you with that? I thought you'd look cuter in yellow!" she protested, holding up her hands and framing my face. I put her hands down and laughed.

"With my hair, I'm not so sure that would work," I joked.

"So, Harv said you would get me situated." Lolli's hand flew to her mouth and she gasped.

"Oh, right! C'mon, we're gonna be roomies!" she said, grabbing my arm and nearly dragging me up the stairs.

My mind was still reeling at how fast all of this was going. Okay, so I was a spy now. A spy for a secret underground organization that was trying to save the world or something in that category. In all of the James Bond movies, being a spy looked pretty cool. Lots of explosions, guns, and a cute guy every now and then. The bonus part was that I was getting a room. Granted, I had to share it with Lolli, the living ray of sunshine, but a room was a room. Homeless people couldn't be picky.

Finally, we emerged from the dark stairwell and back into the lighted hallways. I blinked my eyes a few times as they readjusted themselves to the light.

"You'll get used to it!" Lolli promised, then began leading me down the long, winding hallway. I noticed the people in jumpsuits who had been watching me as if I were some lab monkey were now smiling and saying hi. Almost all of them looked as freaky as the two I had met earlier. Most had long, tribal tattoos that ranged from outrageous facial tattoos to hand tattoos and seemed as if they extended under their jumpsuits. I tried to ignore the agents and their creepy tattoos and kept close to Lolli.

Soon, we made it to a hallway that resembled a prison. The walls were made from the same chrome metal that lined the rest of the tunnels, and I realized just how cold it was down here. The fluorescent, neon lights that were built into the ceilings were all flickering and seemed as if they were on the verge of turning off completely. Shiny, black numbers labeled each of the metallic doors that lined the lengthy hallway.

I followed Lolli down the hallway until we made it to door number 101. She took out the long, pointed object from earlier and held it out for me to see.

"These are what we like to call our all-access keys. We'll go get yours soon," she explained. She gave the pointed end a couple of twists, causing the light on the tip to change from red to all spectrums of the rainbow. She settled on pink and then stuck the point into a slot on the door. She twisted the key a few more times before there was a low chime and the door slid over. Lolli sighed and stuck the key back in her pocket.

"I've been telling Mr. Harv that instead of a beep, our doors should play back our favorite ringtones! Wouldn't that be so cool?" she asked, looking excited. I coughed in my hand to hide a laugh, imagining what kind of ringtone Lolli's door would play.

We stepped into the room and I was pleasantly surprised to find that it looked more or less like a hotel room. I was half-expecting some weird alien lab, complete with a brain in a jar. There were two queen sized beds, a huge flat-screen TV, a beige sofa, and a small kitchen and dining area. The only difference between it and a regular hotel room was that most hotel rooms didn't usually have walls and floors that were made from glowing metal parts. Still, I was so relieved to find something slightly normal in all of this madness that the metal didn't bother me one bit.

"Nice," I murmured, as I walked around the room, my heels clicking loudly on the metal. I had almost forgotten was it was like to have a room. I peeked into a chrome door on the far end of the room and discovered a bathroom, complete with a huge bath and lighted vanity. My skin tingled in anticipation at the thought of taking my first hot bath in days. It had been such a long time since I had had a proper bath that I could barely remember what one felt like.

"I know! It's going to be so fun being roommates! We can stay up and watch TV and do each other's nails!" Lolli squealed. She fell onto her fluffy bed, the one furthest from the door as I exited the bathroom and leaned against the cold wall, still taking everything in. "But, before anything else, I'm sure you have lots of questions."

"Lots of questions" was an understatement. I had so many questions that it felt as if my head was liable to explode at any second.

"Did you know my parents?" It was the first thing that came to my mind.

Lolli rolled over to look at me, a sympathetic look on her round face. "No, sorry," she admitted. I sighed and sat heavily on what I assumed would be my bed. The soft, fluffy sheets were a stark contrast to the thin, holey blanket and hard cement I was used to sleeping on.

"You don't have to apologize," I reassured her, giving her a small smile. Lolli smiled back and sat up.

"Don't worry about them, Lola! Now that you're here, Harv said it will be easy to find them!" she sang in a happy voice.

I crooked an eyebrow. "Hey, I just started working here. What difference could I make in finding them?"

Lolli shrugged and jumped off of her bed. "I dunno, but Harv picked you for the job, so you can do it!" she replied, as if Harv knew everything. "So, anyway," Lolli's wide grin turned mischievous. "You're gonna find your way around here really easily! It's just like living above ground, plus you've got me here to help fill you in! So, if there's ever any guy you like, I'm your *chica*!"

I made a gagging sound and fell back onto the cushiony bed, my arms splayed above my head. I then sat up on my elbows and grinned at her. Lolli was one of those people who you couldn't help but like after a while.

"Are there even any guys our age who live down here?" I teased. "Besides, boys are the last thing on my mind right now." Seriously, I had enough on my plate already. Before Lolli could reply, someone knocked on our door. Lolli pranced over and looked through the peephole. She turned and looked at me, making a disgusted face.

"It's my brother," she groaned. I tried not to join in on the groaning. It was enough to handle one Lolli, but two might be enough to drive me insane.

Lolli swung open the door and I just about keeled over. Outside of our door stood none other than Retro, my crazy and annoyingly handsome driving companion.

Instead of last night's Victorian era outfit, Retro was now decked out in the standard jumpsuit, which was a gorgeous midnight blue. I couldn't help but notice (now that he had on his spandex jumpsuit and all) that he didn't have those gross, bulky, bodybuilder muscles, but more of a toned, lean physique, which made him seem like even more of a model. Could he get any more perfect?

He was leaning against the door frame, his hazel eyes focused on me, a small smile plastered across his handsome face. Now that I thought about it, Lolli and he did look a lot alike. They both had brown hair, although Retro's was darker, and had the same tan skin, hazel eyes, and easy smiles.

"What do you want? I'm trying to get Lola settled in," Lolli complained, straining her neck to look up at Retro while folding her arms.

"Sorry, sister dear, but Harv personally asked me to guide Red through Labeling," he informed us, while shooting me a sly grin from over his sister's head. I ignored him and walked over to where the siblings were standing by the door. I was still angry at him for blowing that sleeping dust in my face.

I expected Lolli, who seemed like the persistent type, to complain about her original plan to be the one to show me the ropes, but once Harv's name was brought up, she didn't mention it again.

"You sure you're not going to blow some more sleeping dust in my face?" I asked, eyeing the metal orb that was strapped into the belt he had around his waist. Retro's face turned a shade redder and he gave me an apologetic smile.

"Sorry about that. You were just getting a little crazy on me back there, so I thought it would be easier for the both of us if you just…y'know…went to sleep."

"A warning next time would nice," I said with a simpering smile. "So, what's Labeling?" I was growing curious. Before Retro could speak, Lolli jumped in, bouncing between me and her brother.

"It's this thing where you get your new name. It's how we lose our old identity and are able to start helping out down here, y'know, without government interference. Harv deals with making up excuses for our disappearances," she explained.

I wasn't so sure about losing my identity. But when I thought hard about it, I barely had an identity to begin with, so what did I honestly have to lose?

"Is that how you became Lolli and Retro?" I asked. Lolli nodded, and a look of sadness washed over her face for a second. Retro rustled her hair and the look was gone in a flash.

"Yup. So, let's roll already, *linda*. Oh, and you'll need to wear your jumpsuit. I'm sure you'll look good in it." I couldn't battle off the heat that rose to my cheeks as Retro turned and left the room.

"Who's Leenda?" I asked Lolli as soon as the door shut behind Retro. I had no idea where he had gotten the name Leenda from. Lolli looked at me for a moment before she tossed her head back and let out an ear-splitting screech of laughter. Ouch. I felt my fingers curling up as my ears rang with pain. Finally, Lolli composed herself.

"*Linda,*" she explained in a Spanish accent, "means beautiful." I stared at her.

"Oh." I knew I was blushing and hated myself for it, but who could resist a guy with an accent?

Especially one who called you beautiful.

Suddenly, without any warning, Lolli pounced on me, tearing away my already ripped clothes.

"Hey, what are you doing?" I yelped, trying to swat her away, but her four feet of height proved to be too much for me. I surrendered and stood there, feeling violated, as a complete stranger helped me pull off my stolen dress.

"I'm so excited! I wonder what name you'll get? I bet it will be something like Rain or Stormy, something pretty but moody!" Lolli cooed as she began helping me into my jumpsuit, starting by yanking my feet into them.

I tried not to be too offended by the fact that she obviously thought I was moody. I winced as her sharp pink nails carelessly dug into my ankles and pushed away the urge to kick my feet out and give her a punt to the head.

Lolli pulled the jumpsuit up around my midsection, and then motioned with her fingers for me to pull it up the rest of the way. I obeyed, and then stuck my hands into the sleeves, struggling to get my fingers into the gloves that were attached on the end. After I managed to do that, Lolli zipped me up in the back.

"There! Oh, wow! You look *bonita!*" Lolli sang, leading me by the shoulders over to the vanity in the bathroom. I stared at the sleek and mysterious girl in the mirror. I couldn't believe it, but I could actually make a jumpsuit work. My head snapped up when I realized that Lolli had said a familiar word.

"What's that *b* word mean?" was all I could say to my reflection, as I twisted from side to side to study myself. I looked pretty darn good, if I did say so myself. I resisted the urge to do a dance that involved brushing off my shoulders, mostly because I was afraid that if I moved an inch, my jumpsuit would rip.

"It means pretty, silly!" Lolli explained, seeming happy that she was getting a chance to play teacher. I felt my face burning up as I remembered Retro calling me the same thing earlier in the nightclub and again when he blew dust in my face.

That thought definitely calmed the butterflies.

"And now for the finishing touches..." Lolli's voice trailed off as she stood on her toes to spike my red hair up with her small fingers. I surprised myself when I didn't swat her hand away like I usually did when people touched me. It looked pretty, *bonita,* whatever you wanted to call it. I was beginning to feel like an agent now.

Lolli proceeded to grab a pair of her black stiletto boots and pushed them on my feet and up to my knees to complete my outfit. I took a second to wonder how Lolli could still be so short even though she was wearing heels. Her actual height had to be 1'2".

Lolli nodded, incapable of hearing my thoughts, and then slapped me on my back.

"Well, get a move on, Lola! Your new life is waiting for you!" she cried, dramatically throwing her hands into the air. "Full of mystery and wonder and cute guys!"

"Right. Thanks, Lolli," I said sincerely, although I had to fight the urge to laugh. She might be loud and overenthusiastic, but she was being a good friend to me. I had definitely not been the same to her, considering all of the unkind remarks that I was making about her in my head.

Note to self: be nicer to Lolli.

Lolli beamed and shook her head, her brown waves of hair going everywhere. "No problem! Now hurry, hurry, hurry!" Lolli cried excitedly, while pushing me toward the door, "I can't wait to hear what name you get!"

She shoved me out of the door and slammed it shut behind me, causing an echo to sound throughout the cold, empty hallway. I glanced around, searching for Retro. I didn't want to run into anymore of the tattooed freaks, especially not alone.

I stood there for a while, leaning back against the wall, playing with my gold locket. I flicked it open and smiled at the picture of my parents and me. I was closer to finding them than I had ever been before. I kissed the picture and shut it quietly.

After a few minutes of waiting for Retro, I gave up and began walking down the hallway. I could find the stupid place myself. I could've asked Lolli, but judging from the sounds of SpongeBob Squarepants and her laughter emanating from her room, I could tell she was busy.

I made it to a point where the hallway split off into four different directions without bumping into anyone. One hallway led to the dark stairwell that went down to Harv's office. The hallway to the right seemed like it was for business affairs. Everyone was rushing around on phones and typing away at extraordinarily expensive-looking computers. The last hallway was blocked by a thick, metal chain and a sign dangling from it that read "AUTHORIZED PERSONNEL ONLY".

Deciding on the business hallway, I made my way over to the nearest desk. A bespectacled blonde woman in a white jumpsuit sat there, typing away at a computer. She was typing so fast, I could almost see smoke flying from her fingers.

Clack clack clack clack...

"Hi. Could you tell me where I go to get a new name or whatever?" I asked. The woman continued typing rapidly, not bothering to look up at me.

Clack-clack clack clack clack....

I stood there, waiting patiently and feeling as if my head would explode with every key she pressed.

Finally, the robot spoke. "Continue down this hall, make a right and it's the second door on the left," she said in a monotonous voice, all while never missing a beat on her keyboard.

"Thanks," I said sarcastically before walking the way she had instructed. The hallway cut off to the right, like she said, and I followed it. I passed the first door on the left, which looked and sounded like it led to a dentist office, and then stopped at the second door.

The plaque on the door read "Labeling" in gold letters. There were brief instructions printed on a piece of copy paper taped directly below it. I squinted at the tiny words and read.

Directions – Please Follow These Carefully

- Say you're birth name into the microphone.
- When you hear the beep, reach in and grab two chips.
- Repeat your new name into the microphone.
- Receive your documents that will print out shortly.
- Step into the door that opens.
- Hold completely still until Labeling is finished.
- Step out of the door when the beep sounds.
- Take the documents to the Business Administrator.

Sounded simple enough. I had my hand on the handle, ready to pull open the door, when I heard the sounds.

Mostly, it was girlish giggling and low murmuring. A few tidbits of a Spanish accent were littered here and there.

"*Eres muy linda...Dar mi un beso.*" More giggling. Whoever was back there sounded as if they were having fun. Too bad; I couldn't wait all day.

I yanked open the door and almost screamed when Retro and some random brunette in green tumbled out. The office I had been expecting was no bigger than a broom closet, so I had no idea how they had both managed to squeeze in there.

The girl squeaked and quickly pulled herself together before racing off, mumbling sorry over and over again. Retro, on the other hand, looked anything but embarrassed. He smiled at me as he fixed up his jumpsuit and smoothed his hair back into place.

"Sorry. I lost track of time," he explained with a lopsided grin as he brushed past me. I turned around to face him with folded arms, feeling slightly amused.

"That was…Rebel, I believe." he continued when I didn't reply. "I'll introduce you two sometime."

"No, thank you," I said with a chuckle and a shake of my head. Luckily, I was used to getting things done myself, so I wasn't too offended by the fact that Retro had dumped his obligations to me so that he could seduce the first girl who had passed him in the hallway.

Retro frowned and now looked slightly remorseful. "Sorry, Red. I can help you now—"

"Once again, no, thank you. I'll be okay," I assured him as I stepped backwards into the small office. "But you might want to go check on Rebel. She seemed kind of flustered."

Retro studied my face intently before cracking a smile. "If you're sure, Red. I'll be around if you need me. I'm pretty good at helping you out of tough spots, if you haven't noticed."

"Thanks, I'll keep that in mind. Bye, Retro." I closed the door in his face and waited. After a couple of moments, I heard Retro's footsteps fade away.

At least I had gotten to see this side of Retro before I did something completely stupid, like develop a crush on him. I undoubtedly had gotten a big, fat reality check. He may have looked like a model but he wasn't an angel.

I turned around to face the machine on the wall. Retro and his high hair instantly vanished out of my mind. The machine jutting out of the wall was in the shape of a huge, black cube with a small microphone attached to the side. Recalling the instructions I had just read, I leaned into the microphone and said, "Lola Phillips."

The machine glowed and hummed for a few more moments before a loud "beep" sounded. A small compartment opened, kind of like those old tape cassette players do. I hesitantly peered inside. There was nothing but darkness. Shoot. I was so going to cheat and pick the name I wanted.

I thrust my hand into the dark opening and stretched my fingers around, grasping for whatever a chip was. I felt a small token, almost the same shape and size of a bingo chip. I closed my hand around it and then felt around for another. When I had secured two, I pulled them out. The compartment closed with a "click".

I silently prayed for a name like Rose or Rain or Music. I crossed my fingers, and bounced up and down, my excitement getting the better of me. I looked down at the chips and wanted to slam my head against the wall.

The blue chip read Rue while the other red chip read Harlot. "I want a do-over!" I shouted into the microphone.

"That name is invalid," the machine droned, "Please read the red chip and then the blue chip, in that order, so that we may process your information."

"No! I don't want this name! Give me a new one!" I wailed at the machine.

"That name is invalid," the machine repeated. I groaned and sank back against the door. "Please read the red chip and then the blue chip, in that order, so that we may process your information."

I stared down at the chips in my hand. Harlot Rue. I'm sure whoever was in charge of putting names into the machine did not know the definition of either of my words.

I stood up and weakly leaned over to the microphone.

"Harlot Rue."

The machine beeped and hummed for a few seconds before the compartment opened up again. A sheet of paper popped out. I grabbed it and looked it over a few times. Then I looked it over a few more times, just to be sure I had comprehended what I had just read.

H Corporation
Birth Name: Lola Phillips
Age: 17
Position: High Intel Gatherer/Double Agent/ Assassin
Given Name: Harlot Rue

Chapter Six

I didn't remember signing up for any of those things.

Before I could question my new occupation further, I heard another "beep". I looked up in time to see the wall slowly opening up. Behind the wall was a room with white walls and floor and it managed to somehow be smaller than the room I was standing in right then. According to the instructions, I was supposed to go into it. I took a deep breath and stepped inside, leaving my documentation on the ATM-like machine. I stood there for a minute, glancing around to see if there was a camera I needed to smile at. Instead, there was a bright flash. My eyes fluttered as my vision turned completely white.

"Confirmed human presence," the computer said. My eyes began to clear up just in time to see the wall behind me beginning to slide back closed.

"No, wait!" I cried, as I tried to step out of the room and back into the first room. The wall slammed closed right in front of my face, shrouding me in complete darkness. I pressed my forehead against the cool, metal wall, listening to the sound of my own breathing. I was trapped in a tiny room. A very tiny room. I backed away from the wall and decided to see what happened next.

"Commencing…Labelization…," the computer continued. There was a clicking sound and then the noise of metal scraping against metal. I felt my fingertips curling up at the aggravating sound and I gritted my teeth with anxiety. Out of nowhere, I felt something cold and hard latch onto both of my wrists.

"Hey!" I shouted as I tried in vain to rip away from my captor. I winced as the cold bracelets that held me cut into my jumpsuit and nicked at my skin. They had to be chained to the wall. I stopped struggling with my arms and moved on to my feet.

"Hey!" I screamed as I kicked at the wall in front of me, "Let me out of this crazy thing!" Of course, no one replied. Right when I was about to kick again, the metal scraping sounded and bracelets latched onto my legs as well. I swung my body around wildly and cursed as loud as my voice would let me.

"Please remain still. Labeling will begin in 5…4…"

I didn't know what "Labeling" was, but if being held against my will was a prelude to it, then I didn't want any part of it.

"3…2…" I stopped struggling and braced myself for whatever was going to happen next.

"1." In an instant, the room was flooded in a bright red light. I squeezed my eyes shut and ducked my head to my shoulder. I could feel the heat of the light on my skin. It felt as if I was standing in my underwear in the mouth of a volcano. The heat only got worse and more unbearable as the seconds ticked by. It burned the worse right where my heart was. Sweat began to build on my forehead and drip down my face. I didn't dare move, though. I didn't want to risk getting zapped by a laser and being reduced to a pile of dust. Although, at this point, that might be a relief.

Minutes later, the heat died away and I sensed the room grow dark again. The handcuffs on my wrists and ankles clanked open. I slowly opened my eyes and looked around. The wall was open again. Not wasting a second, I flew back into the first room and thanked God for light over and over again. What had that been about? I didn't feel any different, except maybe a bit sore all over. I shrugged it off and grabbed my papers.

I threw open the door and was a bit embarrassed to find some of the other agents had gathered around, obviously listening in on me rant and rave. They all suddenly scattered like roaches, chattering like they hadn't just been spying on me. This was going to be like high school all over again, just add spies and ultra-high-tech machinery.

Just as I was trying to figure out just where the Business Administrator could be, I noticed one person had yet to run away from the scene.

It was a small, shrimpy guy, dressed up in a doctor's lab coat. He couldn't be much taller than Lolli. He was wearing huge eyeglasses and had dirty-blonde hair. He was leaning against the wall, his eyes flickering from me to the floor. I crossed my arms and fixed him with a hard glare, figuring he was going to ridicule me.

"Yeah?" I asked, icily. The guy flinched and swallowed hard. He glanced around nervously, as if he were searching desperately for an escape route. I realized he was around my age, even though he was the size of a middle-schooler. His lab coat and clothes underneath were way too big on his small frame. In short, he looked like an adorable yet sloppy little boy.

"Err, um...." he stuttered, scratching at his arms like a heroin addict. "I-I'm the Business Administrator's intern. I-I can show you where the office is, i-if you want me to, that is." I breathed a sigh of relief, glad I wouldn't have to go on another blind trip through the facility.

"Sure, lead the way," I said, giving him a smile so he would stop acting like I was going to eat him alive. The tips of his ears turned red and he quickly turned away.

"This way…" he mumbled, walking quickly down the hall. I had to work to keep up with him, but I soon matched his pace. I made another shocking revelation as I looked at him.

"Why aren't you stuck in one of these dumb jumpsuits?" I asked incredulously. He looked up at me, surprised, and then quickly looked back down at the floor.

"I-I don't do any of the field work so I don't need to wear one. I'm mostly in the office and working on the tech stuff," he admitted. I nodded, still a little jealous. He was wearing a red shirt with a cartoon character on the front and a pair of dark jeans underneath his white lab coat. They actually looked comfortable. I, on the other hand, had a killer wedgie in my jumpsuit and felt like my ribs were about to crack.

"Here we are!" The intern's boyish voice tore me out of my thoughts about my uncomfortable attire. We were in a small room, similar to a waiting room. There were a row of chairs against the wall, and a TV set up near the ceiling. A gray-haired older woman with startling purple eyes was sitting behind a glass divider, glaring at me and my escort.

"Hack!" she hissed through the microphone, her voice crackling with static as her voice carried over to the speaker in the waiting room. "Where have you been?"

Hack, the blonde, blushing intern, turned redder and he hurried over to where the broad-shouldered woman sat behind the glass. She opened the window that separated her half of the room from ours (I wondered why she hadn't done that in the first place) and glared at him. Hack's face paled.

"S-Sorry, Miss Margie, I went out for a second to see what the ruckus was about. Y-You know, the new agent," he explained. The woman sniffed and let her gaze fall on me. I stared back at her, not letting her intimidate me. She smiled a bit.

"You look just like your mother, ya know that?" she noted. I felt a blanket of warmth fall over me at the compliment. My mom had been a beauty, but I had never thought of myself looking like her. I always thought I looked more like my dad, with his cocoa skin, sharp features and brown eyes. My dad often used to say I had an attitude more like my mom's, though.

Margie hacked up a big loogie and spit it behind her. The blanket of warmth was replaced with one of disgust.

"Thanks," I grunted. Margie's smile grew and she focused her gaze on the paper in my hand.

"Let's see those papers," she ordered. For some reason, Margie demanded instant respect, so I handed her over the paper without a second thought. She scanned the paper for a moment before her lips began to quiver. I realized she was looking at my new name and groaned.

"Please, just get it filed so I can go cry myself to sleep," I begged. Margie choked out a laugh, which was stopped short as she paused to chuck out another loogie.

"It's not that bad, honey! One young gal got stuck with To Jam. I think yours has a nice ring to it, kinda fitting for you," she said as she fed the paper into some kind of machine. I bit my tongue to keep from replying.

She thought that Harlot was a fitting name for me?

Margie turned her attention back to me. "So, do you have any idea what you're gettin' yourself into?" she asked, propping her chin in her hand and grinning up at me. I shrugged and sat in one of the chairs by the wall.

"Nah, not really. All I know is I want to find my parents. If I have to do some crazy stuff, I'll deal," I answered truthfully. Margie laughed and slapped her knee.

"I like you, little Miss Harlot! Hack, I want you to watch out for this one, ya hear?" she barked. Hack jumped, startled at his name being mentioned so suddenly.

"Uh, r-right! I will!" he replied, snapping to attention like a soldier. I held back a laugh. It was almost cute, especially with him being the size of a kid.

"I could use all the help I can get around here," I assured him, trying to put him at ease. Hack nodded and smiled at me, looking excited.

"I can show you around, whenever you have time...if you want," he offered, blushing a bit. That was a good offer. I couldn't even remember my way back to Lolli's and my room.

"Right now's good. Do I need to do anything else, Margie?" I asked, standing up and trying in vain to get rid of my wedgie discreetly. Margie took the paper out of the machine and scanned it.

"One more thing." She slapped the paper on the counter, along with a syringe. I stared at both of them, dumbfounded. Margie looked at me and slapped her forehead.

"Right, right, you're new," she reprimanded herself. She held out her hand. "Turn around so I can do it, then." I continued to stare at her. If there was one thing I hated (and yes, I hated a lot of things) it was needles. I stared at the foot long syringe and then looked up at her.

"I'm not putting that thing in me!" I protested. Margie looked annoyed.

"Oh, it's not all that bad," she assured me, "Every agent gets injected with this stuff all the time for health reasons. Besides, I thought you said you'd deal with whatever it took to find your parents?" I mentally punched myself for that comment. Whatever it took, yeah, but a needle was pushing it.

"C'mon, we don't have all day, little girl," Miss Margie urged before spinning me around to face away from her. She began to unzip my jumpsuit from the back but paused.

"Turn around, Hack," I heard her say.

"What? Oh! Right! I'll just—go here." I heard Hack's feet shuffle to the corner. Miss Margie went back to unzipping me, stopping the zipper near the middle of my back. She pushed the shoulder of my suit off and paused again.

"Oh, I've never seen a label like this. These are beautiful, darlin'," she sighed, while brushing my shoulder fondly. I had no idea what she could be talking about. I turned my head a bit and was about to question her when I saw what she was talking about.

I gasped and tore away from an annoyed-looking Miss Margie.

"What the…when…how…?" I stammered as I stared at my shoulder in disbelief. My normally unblemished brown skin was decorated in spirals of black ink. My breathing turned irregular as I pulled my other shoulder down and saw that it, too, had been tattooed. I looked down at my chest and felt faint when I saw that not even it had been spared. In fact, it seemed as if the whole tattoo had sprouted from my chest. More precisely, in seemed as if it had sprouted from my heart.

Directly over my heart was a swirly, black capital H. Long, thorny, ink vines crawled from it to twist up my shoulders and down my back.

"When did this happen?" I yelled as I rubbed at my shoulders, hoping that this was somebody's idea of a Magic Marker prank and praying that my face didn't look like Bulgy and Piercings from earlier. I quickly stopped rubbing when I felt a burning sensation where I touched. I winced and then shot an accusing glare at Margie.

"It happened during Labeling, of course. It's called labeling for a reason," she explained in a "duh" voice. I gave her an incredulous look. .

She sighed in exasperation. "Really, hon, it's no big deal. But if you really want to know, the tattoos are a way of being able to withstand the extra pressure that's on all of us from constantly being underground. This," Margie paused to flick the syringe that she still had in her hand, "helps keep the ink in the tattoos fresh." She popped the lid off of the syringe and held out her hand again, obviously waiting for my arm. I still hadn't recovered from the shock of suddenly finding out that part of my body had been tattooed without my knowing, but I didn't say a word as she took my arm.

What was done could not be undone now (except maybe through months of harsh removal procedures).

"There's a good girl," Margie said with a smile before plunging the needle into my upper arm. She slowly pushed the silvery-white fluid into my skin, taking her sweet time. The liquid seemed strangely familiar, but I couldn't stare at it for too long without feeling queasy. I quickly averted my gaze from the injection site and focused on Margie instead. She had pretty ringlets of silver hair, falling down her shoulders and beautiful ebony skin. Her fierce purple eyes were focused solely on the syringe. *Wait, don't look at the syringe.*

I looked back at Margie. "Please tell me my eyes aren't bulging out," I practically begged her. Margie looked up from the drawing site, looking confused.

"What in the world are you talking about?" she asked.

"Tattoos," I explained, "Do I have tattoos on my face?" Hack, who still had his back to me, decided to pipe up.

"Oh, no! Only the older agents ever get those," he clarified, helping ease my worries. "They're more of a fashion statement." I relaxed after Hack erased my fears. As long as I wouldn't end up looking like that, I was fine.

"Okay, we're all done," Margie informed me. I looked back down and found that the needle was gone and I had a cute little cartoon character Band-Aid slapped across the injection site. I breathed a sigh of relief and zipped my sleeve back up, releasing Hack's arm in the process. Except for a little nausea, I didn't feel much different. "Sorry," I mumbled to Hack, feeling myself blush as I realized how much like a baby I had acted. Hack shrugged, smiling through his obvious pain.

"It's alright. Here's your key." He reached behind Margie's desk and pulled out a metal object that was similar to Lolli's key. I took it and slid it into the pouch on my thigh, which seemed to have been made specifically for storing the key.

Margie casually flung the used syringe over her shoulder. It twirled mid-air before landing in a trashcan a few feet from her. *Wow.*

She wiped her hands off, not acknowledging her insane throwing capabilities.

"All done here, sugar. You're officially an agent of the H Corporation," she announced, giving me a big grin. I don't know why but I felt excited when I heard those words.

"Yes!" I cheered, returning her grin before turning to face Hack. "So, what now? Can we do the tour?"

Hack jumped at the sound of his name. "Oh! Yeah! Uh, follow me." We waved bye to Margie and then walked back into the hallway. The halls were unusually quiet. No one was milling about; in fact, there wasn't a soul in the hall.

"Did someone die?" I half-joked, looking around. Hack laughed brightly and shook his head. I could tell he was starting to lighten up a bit. He pointed at the Rolex that was secured to his wrist.

"It's eight in the morning. All of the agents are in the cafeteria for breakfast," he explained. I grabbed his wrist and stared at the watch. Eight? I had come into the place at almost 2 in the morning! I felt my stomach clench painfully and I realized I hadn't eaten in a long time. My last meal had been the strawberries and Mary-Anne's cookie, if those foods could even be counted as meals. Usually, I was used to this, but the smell of sizzling bacon and fresh bread intensified my hunger severely.

"Could we go get something to eat? I'm on the verge of becoming a cannibal over here," I moaned, dropping his wrist. Hack laughed nervously and I noticed him shift away from me.

"Yeah, sure! The cafeteria is right downstairs." We made our way down the hall until we came to a pair of white stairs with metal railings. One led down while the other led upwards.

"What's upstairs?" I asked as we descended the other set of stairs.

"Oh, just the classrooms," Hack replied, while adjusting his huge glasses.

"What?" I cried, "There's school down here, too?" I wanted to smack myself in the forehead. School was like an annoying sibling; there was no escaping it.

Hack gave me a reassuring smile, noting my dismay. "It's not like normal schools. It's actually my favorite part of headquarters," he admitted, his cheeks turning a shade pinker. I just shook my head. If school was his favorite part, I really didn't want to see the rest of "headquarters".

We continued down the stairs until we came to a plain white room with one set of double doors on a wall adjacent from us. I heard lots of laughter and talking coming from the other side of the doors and I felt myself growing nervous. Hack pushed open the door before I could stop him and the smell hit me like a semi-truck.

I thought I had woke up to heaven for the second time that day as I breathed in the smell of fresh food. Nervousness flew out of my system and was replaced with hunger. Drool was literally pooling inside of my mouth.

Hack waved his hand in front of my face, forcing me to snap back to attention. "Did you hear me? I said you're free to eat wherever you'd prefer," he said. His eyes looked distant. "I'll just go sit, um…somewhere…" I saw his eyes wondering to a far off table that was empty.

The rest of the cafeteria was just like a normal high school cafeteria, actually. There were blue tables set up from one end of the spacious room to the other, each filled to capacity with rowdy people.

I noticed almost immediately that the agents were separated into groups. A bunch of the older, adult agents sat at tables together, while the younger agents were all crowded together, dressed in casual clothing. I also noticed that the adult agents' jumpsuits had a silver octagon badge over their hearts, with an H inscribed in the middle of it. I was happy to see that Hack had told me the truth when he said only the older agents got facial tattoos. None of the younger agents had them.

But, all of the agents had one thing in common. They were all gaping at us. I felt the nervousness return somewhat, so I turned my attention back to Hack, who was still waiting for my response. I sent him a playful pout.

"What, are you trying to get rid of the new girl?" I teased.

Hack's face turned beet red, matching his shirt. "Of course not!" he said, "I-I just thought m-maybe you didn't want to sit by..." Hack's voice trailed off as I started walking toward the buffet that had been set up at the front of the cafeteria, before he could finish talking.

"You're not getting rid of me that easily," I called back over my shoulder. This wasn't what Hack was expecting, judging from the shocked expression on his face. I thought for a second that he hadn't followed me, but a moment later he was at my side, his face still red, but he was smiling a bit. I smiled back.

We grabbed our plates and silverware then began fixing our plates. I piled my plate with biscuits and gravy, five pieces of bacon, a huge helping of scrambled eggs, two pieces of toast, and, to top it off, three chocolate glazed doughnuts. Food was literally hanging off my plate. I noticed Hack watching me with big eyes. I hadn't had food like what was piled on my plate in a long, long time. Living on Skid Row had taught me one thing—eat as much as you can when you have the chance.

Thinking about Skid Row reminded me of Tara and even old Mr. Frederick D. I hoped they weren't too worried about me. Seeing as I had lost the crappy phone Blackeye had given me, I had no way of getting in contact with either of them. I prayed silently that they weren't too worried about me and that they were able to get a good meal this morning as well.

Hack and I sat off by ourselves at a table in the corner. I noticed everyone stealing glances at us and I tried to focus on eating. It wasn't that hard. In ten seconds flat, I had already polished off my bacon and one of my doughnuts. I was just about to dive into my biscuits and gravy when I noticed Hack staring at me, bewilderment etched on his face.

I returned the look, still chewing rapidly. "What?" I asked, accidentally spitting some eggs on his face. We stared at each other for a second and I couldn't help but start laughing at the shocked look on his face. He joined in with a weak laugh as well, although he took the time to wipe his cheek off with a napkin.

It felt weird to have already made some sort of acquaintance in such a short amount of time. Usually, I would stay away from others while I was in school and had earned the nickname of "freak" in a matter of minutes. I could already see Hack and me becoming friends and the weird thing was, I didn't mind it.

"Wow, that was beautiful!" a smooth voice called out. Moment ruined. It was a voice I was sure I was going to, unfortunately, become especially familiar with during my time as an agent.

Like a male lion followed by his pride, Retro was walking toward our table, his hands shoved in his designer jeans' pockets, while about five girls walked beside him, giggling at Retro's statement.

I had to admit: all of the girls were gorgeous. They were like the Victoria's Secret angels, minus the feathers and halos. They rolled their eyes simultaneously when Retro came to a stop in front of me and quickly dispersed to wherever bony girls go during lunch.

I turned around and glared at Retro, swallowing the rest of my eggs. "There's more where that came from," I sneered, gesturing toward my plate. Retro just laughed and plopped down next to me, snatching away one of my precious doughnuts and stuffing it into his mouth.

"Did you come over here to talk or steal my food?" I grumped, while scooting my plate away from him. Retro simply gave me an impish grin and then turned his attention to Hack, who was smiling admirably at him. I got the feeling that the two of them were already good friends.

Retro held out his manicured hand and flicked one of Hack's blonde curls out of his face. "Hack, are you trying to hook-up with our new girl? Word of advice: she's a tough nut to crack," he teased, causing Hack's face to light up like a fire engine.

"Actually, he's been giving me a tour and being helpful, unlike some people," I cut in, knowing he'd catch the hint. Retro at least had the nerve to look embarrassed, but it only lasted for a moment. His expression reverted back to its natural flirty smirk.

"You're cute when you're jealous," he cooed, while pinching my cheek like I was a child. "But, I think you're forgetting the fact that I already helped you, *mi querida*. Does the name Boulevard3 ring a bell?" I pulled away and frowned. That was definitely an event I wanted to forget, but I knew Retro wouldn't stop hanging that over my head.

"Lola Bunny!" Speaking of distracting, I heard Lolli's high-pitched voice calling out. I turned in my seat and saw Lolli waving at me as she balanced her plate and walked at the same time. Her current attire caused almost as big of a stir as her brother's had. It consisted of a leopard-print tube top paired with a shimmering pair of purple and yellow skinny jeans and a set of neon green hoop earrings the size of baseballs.

One question: had she gotten dressed in the dark? Or did she actually know that she was dressed like she was ready for Mardi Gras and a trek through the safari?

Admittedly, she pulled off the look better than anyone else I knew ever could. Seemingly unaware of the chatter her entrance was making, Lolli sat by me and dropped her heavy tray on the table with a thud before letting out a sigh of relief. It was no wonder. Her plate was more loaded than mine.

"Hi, Lolli," I replied while scooting over to make room for her. Lolli was a far cry from being overweight, but had a healthy pair of hips.

She nestled into her seat before picking up a potato tot and popping it into her mouth. "I'm glad I caught you! And it looks as if you're already making friends!" she squealed happily, sounding like a proud parent.

"We're not friends—I barely know these guys," I grunted while playing with my food. Lolli shook her head back at me in a playful manner.

"We're all friends down here!" she exclaimed. She paused to take a sip from her Styrofoam cup of orange juice. "But if it makes you feel better, we can all make introductions!"

"No!" we all groaned in unison but Lolli was determined. She waved us off and scarfed down another potato.

"I'll start." To each of our horror and humiliation, Lolli brushed her off her attire and stood up. Multiple heads turned our way. Almost in unison, Retro, Hack, and I used our hands to shield the side of our faces from the onlookers.

"Well, you all know me!" she began, "I'm Lolli Maraschino! I'm almost seventeen, my favorite color is pink, and I love romance novels! I'm an Aquarius, but I always thought I should be a Libra. I like guys who are handsome, dress nice, and are handsome. Did I say that already? Anyway, I enjoy long walks on the beach and-"

Thankfully, Retro decided to cut in here. "Okay, you're not auditioning for *The Bachelor*, Sis. Sit down before you pass out from talking so much." Lolli's face pinkened and she sat down with an angry grumble as Hack and I tried to hide our laughing, unsuccessfully.

"Fine," she mumbled, "then *you* go ahead and introduce yourself, Mr. Funny." Retro blew out a huff of air and seemed to go into deep-thinking mode. He scratched his stubbly chin and shut his eyes.

Finally, he turned and gave me a beguiling smile that made my heart flutter against its will. "My name's Retro Rex, but I'm pretty sure you haven't forgotten it," he teased, while reaching across the table to stroke the back of my hand with his thumb.

"I'm sure your little closet buddy hasn't forgotten it either," I retorted with a wink. Retro laughed out loud as he slowly withdrew his hand.

"Touché," he replied while quirking an eyebrow at me. He gave me appraising look, as if he had really noticed me for the first time since we met, then smiled. "I like you, new girl." I smiled back, despite myself.

"Wait," Lolli interrupted, causing me and Retro to startle, "Who is this 'closet buddy?'"

I was more than happy to fill her in. "Well--" I began with a wide grin before Retro rudely cut me off.

"None of your concern, baby sister," he assured her, while giving me annoyed glance, "Let's let Hack have a turn."

Lolli was all for this and soon Hack was in the spotlight. He fidgeted with his watch before he began to speak. "Hack Remand, at your service. I'm fifteen years of age, I made a score of 144 on my IQ test last week, and I enjoy studying in what little spare time I can find." He literally flung the words at us so fast, I felt like pulling out some paper to take notes.

After his speedy introduction, Hack dropped his head to resume toying with his watch, and mumbled, "That's all I can think of."

"Tell us what kind of things you like to study," Lolli urged with an encouraging smile. Hack looked up in surprise before returning the smile.

"I enjoy studying science, physics, and I also dabble in web design whenever I get the chance. Miss Margie certainly keeps me busy, though, so it's hard to find time," he finished, this time speaking much slower.

"So you're a real nerd, huh?" I teased, playfully. "I hope you'll help me out whenever school comes into the picture." Hack nodded enthusiastically.

"Of course, Lola! Just find me when you need help," he said. His expression suddenly turned panicked. "I mean, find me if you want to. You don't have to." I couldn't refrain myself from giggling at him. He was so nerdy that it was cute. As a matter of fact, I was realizing that I liked all three of the people seated at my table. Well, I was still on the fence with Retro. I needed to feel him out a bit more.

"See? That wasn't so bad," Lolli quipped, while shooting Retro a pointed look. She then focused back on me, her eyes glimmering with excitement.

"So, tell me! What did you get?" Lolli asked, grabbing my shoulders and bouncing up and down like an excited dog. It took me a moment to think of what she could possibly be talking about. Then it dawned on me—my new name.

"Oh, nothing special," I said, truthfully. I looked back at my plate and frowned when I noticed yet another doughnut was missing. Maybe I was onto something in high school by staying away from my thieving classmates.

"Tell me, Lola! Or should I say Tornado? Or maybe Kiwi? Kiwi is cute!" Lolli began to list out a whole dictionary of names from Apple to Zebra. Suddenly, Harlot didn't sound too bad.

"I got Harlot," I blurted out. "Harlot Rue." This successfully brought Lolli's rambling to an abrupt halt. Our entire table fell completely silent. I heard a couple of snorts and I realized that Retro was laughing at me. Lolli got to her brother before I could.

"Shut up, Retro! I think it sounds, um...cute," she said with a big, forced smile in my direction. She was a bad liar, but at least she was trying to make me feel better.

I bit into my toast and chewed it. "I guess there's worse," I said with a shrug. "So, what happens now that I'm a fancy, labeled agent?" I asked, eager to change the subject.

Hack, who had been busy playing with his fork, looked up, his face looking surprised. "Harv didn't tell you?" he asked.

"Tell me what?"

Everyone looked at each other, obviously knowing something I didn't know. Lolli began twirling one of her brown curls. Hack suddenly became entranced with an invisible speck on the table. I stabbed my fork into my biscuit and glared at them.

"This isn't charades! What happens now?" I asked again. Retro decided to speak up. He lazily made a slicing motion across his throat with his finger.

"You go through a DM," he said cryptically, looking at me with half-lidded eyes.

Chapter Seven

I stared blankly at him.

"What's a DM? Dangerous Mountain? Dark Movie? Demented Monkey?" I joked, hoping that none of those were what a DM actually was. No one laughed.

Lolli played absent-absentmindedly with her food and shot me a sympathetic look. "It stands for Death Mission. It's a must for beginning agents!" she explained, sounding like someone advertising a product.

"Death Mission….What's that?" I questioned. This was getting weird. But for some reason, I was getting a thrill thinking about doing something dangerous and exciting. It was just like when I had stolen my dress from the Hot Stylez store. Maybe I was an adrenaline junkie.

Hack spoke next, his voice taking on a professional tone. "The Death Mission is a mandatory training mission for all beginning agents. Agents are paired with an older agent as a mentor and then are sent out on a mission in order to test your prior knowledge and capabilities. This mission will determine just where you're ranked and decide what classes you'll be taking."

"Why's it called a Death Mission?" I asked slowly. Everyone cast worried looks at one another and I felt a shiver snake its way down my spine. Their faces spoke only bad things and I suddenly wasn't too sure if I wanted to know the answer.

"Well," Retro began, matter-of-factly, "Many agents don't make it back alive." He propped his chin up with his hand, waiting for my reaction with an expectant look on his face.

In a normal situation, I would've stood up, wiped off my mouth, and then walked the heck out and never looked back. The weight of my parents' necklace on my chest was the only thing stopping me from doing just that.

"Why? What do I have to do?" I said, my voice shaking involuntarily. Retro seemed to enjoy seeing me all shaken up. He looked around, before leaning toward me, a cryptic smile on his face.

"It's a surprise."

***

After my enlightening breakfast, Retro paraded off to his adoring masses, while Lolli, Hack, and I decided to keep looking around the premises.

"So, we call this place headquarters?" I asked for the third time as we ascended a flight of stairs leading to the residence hallway, as Hack had labeled it. Hack, patient as ever, nodded. He had been answering all of my questions with ease. He seemed as if he was enjoying this teacher-student experience.

"Yes, or some may call it base. It's just a simpler term for headquarters," he explained. I noticed Lolli giving Hack an admiring look.

"You know so much about...everything!" she exclaimed. "How'd you get so smart?" This made Hack blush, which I found adorable.

"I-I'm not that smart, really. Its basic knowledge," he rambled, keeping his eyes on the ground. I sighed. We had been walking around for an hour and we still hadn't finished looking at what Hack and Lolli called the west wing. The west wing was where all the agents' rooms were, along with the cafeteria and the school. The east wing was where the official business went on, and we hadn't barely touched that part of 'headquarters'.

"Headquarters, base....whatever it is, it's killing my feet," I whined, while pausing to lean against a wall and examine one of my feet. Lolli's high-heeled boots were a size too small, so the comfort level was already a zero. Walking for an hour wasn't helping. I could feel the blisters already forming on the side of my toes.

"Oh, stop whining, Bunny!" Lolli sang, upbeat as usual. "You need to know these things for later! It's totally easy to get lost in here."

"What's with calling me Bunny all of a sudden?" I had to know. Lolli laughed.

"You know, like Lola? Bunny? The cartoon?" she explained with an expectant grin on her face, like she expected me to go

"Ohmigosh! That's awesome!" I settled on a weak laugh, which was quickly drowned out by Lolli's squealing laughter as she joined in.

I heaved a dramatic sigh and we continued our tour, with me hobbling behind my two guides. Lolli, noticing my limping, slowed down so that she was at my pace. "Well...maybe we can put off the tour until later," she suggested, obviously noting my pained expression. I gave her a grateful nod and let her position me so that she was helping support my weight. I wasn't very used to people offering to help me, so I was very thankful when she did.

Hack seemed a little disappointed at Lolli's statement. "Alright then...if you're sure," he mumbled. "I'll just head back to Margie, then." Before I could protest, Hack had hurried away, leaving Lolli and I alone in the hallway, staring after him. Lolli blew out a puff of air.

"He's so shy!" she exclaimed. "He always complains about not being useful, and then he runs off when people need him!" I looked back at Lolli, who was crossing her arms and pouting. She reminded me of a little girl.

"Why did he become an agent, then?" I couldn't help but ask. It was being nosy, but hey, I was naturally curious. Maybe my parents' had passed down some of their secret agent genes to me.

Lolli took a second to think about her answer. "I'm not exactly sure, but I think it's because his dad works here, too," she replied after some time of hard thinking.

"Really?" I was caught off guard for a second. Hack and I had more in common than I had thought.

"Yeah, but he's not so good with the physical stuff, so his dad got him a Techie position."

"Techie?" I asked.

"It's short for technical staff. He deals with computers and all of that confusing stuff," she explained. "You see, we have Field Agents, like you and me, who are sent out on missions. Then, we have Operators, who specialize in driving the shuttles in the parking zone. Lastly, we have the Techies, who stay here and back us up." Lolli shrugged her shoulders. "We also have cooks and doctors but no one has ever really thought of nicknames for them."

"Miss Rue?" Lolli and I looked up to see a squat man in a gray jumpsuit approaching us. I noticed he was a senior agent, judging from the badge on his suit and the disgusting tattoo curling up his forehead. Lolli instantly snapped to attention. She drew an H over her heart before she went back to helping me keep my balance.

"Yeah, that's me," I replied, earning a sharp glare from Lolli. I ignored her and waited for the man's response.

"You are to come with me. Mr. Magnum has summoned you," he commanded, his voice firm.

Was he serious? These weren't the medieval days and I wasn't a peasant.

"He says to come immediately," the man pressed.

"Well, tell His Majesty that he will have to wait. I need to go change out of these heels before my toes fall off," I said, wincing as I went to take a step. The man and Lolli shared a shocked look. His mouth opened once, then closed, then opened again. He resembled a large fish, flailing about. I got the feeling he wasn't used to being talked to like a normal person. Lolli quickly jumped into action and attempted to smooth things over.

"Harlot, when Mr. Harv calls, we kinda have to go...like immediately!" she urged, giving me a wide grin. I noticed that she was giving me an almost imperceptible shake of her head. I took it as a sign that I needed to go now and ask questions later. I sighed.

"Fine, fine, let's go already," I urged. I reached down and pulled off my boots. I wasn't surprised to find blisters already forming on my pinky toes. The man stared down at my feet in horror before he quickly turned around and began walking away.

"Go, go, hurry!" Lolli urged me, while taking her boots from me. I laughed and imitated the gasping fish face the man had made earlier.

"Why, I never!" I huffed in a deep voice as I followed after the man. I heard Lolli squealing with laughter behind me. The metal felt like ice on my bare feet and I nearly sighed with relief as the burning sensation in my feet faded.

One trip down a spiraling set of stairs later, I was there. Harv sat at his golden desk, scribbling on a piece of paper. I waited by the door, unsure of what to do next. The squat man, who I decided to call Fish Face, rapped twice on the wall.

"Sir, Miss Rue is here," he announced. He shot me a snide glare. "And if I were you, sir, I would give her a stern talk about her attitude." My mouth dropped open as Fish Face brushed past me and left us alone in the room. I heard Harv clear his throat.

"Have a seat, my dear. Those heels couldn't have been too comfortable," he murmured with a hint of sarcasm in his voice, He didn't look up from his paper. I stubbornly took my time walking over to his chair and then plopped down in it. I threw my feet on his desk and folded my arms, wanting to tick him off. I still wasn't quite over the whole "almost-kill-Lola-to-make-her-aware-of-her-parents-whereabouts" plan.

"You called?" I asked, after I grew bored of watching him write on his little piece of paper. "Or should I say, summoned?" Harv ignored me and continued writing. Resisting the urge to keep bugging him, I huffed and leaned back to stare at the ceiling. I was surprised to see a replication of the famous Michelangelo artwork. There were baby angels peering down at me, smiling sweetly. They danced around on clouds, their feathery wings splayed out behind them, innocent expressions on their faces. It was beautiful, although it was something I hadn't expected to see in Harv Magnum III's office.

"So, what's with your little underground base?" I asked while still admiring the ceiling. "Why are we all cooped up down here? Are you afraid of someone?"

I was surprised when he actually answered. "Solitude," he replied, "Solitude and secrecy from others who are better off not knowing we exist."

"As for me being afraid..." Harv paused. I kept my eyes on the hypnotic ceiling. "I'm certainly not afraid of anything in this world," he finished with a soft laugh. I smiled with amusement and looked back down at him. He was still writing away on his paper.

"So, what, you're afraid of aliens?" I bantered. Harv chuckled loudly at this before finally dropping his pen.

"I see you clean up nicely, Miss Harlot Rue." His tone made my smile instantly dissipate. The way he was staring at me was the way the Big Bad Wolf probably stared at the 3 Little Pigs, waiting for his chance to snap one up.

"And I see you need to be reminded of the underage law, Mr. Child Predator," I cooed sweetly, batting my eyes at him and grinning widely. Harv laughed and leaned back in his chair, giving himself a better view of me. He was still wearing his stylish white tuxedo, giving him the air of a gentleman, or maybe an albino penguin.

"You should know that I don't follow the rules, Miss Rue," he replied, with a hint of mischief in his voice. I felt the heat rise to my face and I quickly looked away.

"Well, aren't you a cool kid…" I teased, trying to ease some of the tension from the room. I moved my feet back to the floor. "So, why'd you call me up here? Unless it was just to stare at me."

Harv grinned, causing the corners of those silvery eyes to crinkle. "No, but that was a bonus for me." *Ugh.* "Actually, I'm sure you've already heard of it."

I felt my heart begin to pick up its pace. "The DM," I breathed. Despite Lolli and the others' apprehension, I was still excited for my Death Mission, scary name aside. I was ready to get out there and do something that could lead to finding my parents, not wander around underground like a mole.

"Yes," Harv said, with a nod, "…I won't waste time by giving you the rundown then. I have high hopes for you so I'm not going to give you something easy." He met my eyes. "Your DM will most likely be an assassination."

"No!" The word had left my mouth before I even had a chance to think about it. It was like a reflex, like when your doctor does that annoying knee-jerk reaction test.

Harv gave me a surprised look. He slowly put his pencil down and then folded his hands together, fixing me with a level stare. "Harlot," he spoke in a clear voice. "That's not the answer I'm looking for."

"I don't care what you're looking for!" I shouted, standing up and meeting his intense gaze with one of my own. The very thought of having to kill someone was enough to make me feel nauseous. "I'm not killing some innocent person, not for this corporation, and not for you!"

I turned around and made my way over to the door, ready to go pack my bags. If this was what I would have to do in order for their assistance in saving my parents, I would just have to do the saving myself.

I stopped dead in my tracks when I heard Harv's next sentence.

"But would you do it for your parents?" Harv's smooth voice seemed to echo off the walls. I kept my hand on the doorknob.

Turn the knob. It's not that hard. Just push open the door and walk out of this crazy place while you still can. My hand shook as I grasped the doorknob tighter and tighter before I dropped my hand back to my side.

I couldn't open the door.

I slowly turned back around and faced Harv, feeling helpless. Harv nodded his head at my chair. With a scowl, I walked back over and sat down, making sure to look anywhere but his silver eyes. I tapped my foot like a jackhammer on the cold, hard floor.

"Harlot, don't forget we had an agreement. Besides, no one is asking you to kill an innocent person," he alluded. I looked up at him then, confused.

"But you just said I had to assassinate—"

"Yes, you may have to assassinate someone, but I never implied that they were innocent. In fact, they're far from it." Harv slid a packet of papers toward me. Warily, I picked it up and scanned over the front page.

A picture of a fat, fleshy-faced man stared back at me. He had curly black hair and a ratty-looking goatee that hung to his chest. Under the picture was a caption listing the man's personal information. His name was Eduardo Hernandez, 43 years old, and the owner of the popular chain of Mr. Taco restaurants. He was also a convicted serial killer who had somehow managed to get out on parole. He had murdered five young women who just happened to be around my age. But what really caught my eye was under all of that, there was a caption that read: "Agent of E. Corporation", the corporation who had possibly kidnapped my parents.

I noticed an unexpected flicker of anger in my chest as I stared at the man. I quickly slid the papers back toward Harv, who picked them up and put them back in his desk.

"Harlot, we're the good guys. I wouldn't send you after an innocent man," Harv said, reaching across the desk and patting my hand. I pulled my hand away. Harv smirked and folded his hand over his other.

"I chose this job especially for you," he continued, "so you'll know what you'll be up against in the future. I'm not saying this will be easy, but I also know that you need to be able to do this." I glanced back at the ceiling. The chubby little baby angels were still smiling at me, giving me the go-ahead.

I looked back down at Harv and shrugged. "What do I need to do?" I asked. Harv's smile returned and he sat back so he could dig through his desk.

He pulled out one of the all-access keys and gave it a few twists. "We know firsthand that this man has important information about his corporation, maybe even about the disappearances of our agents. I need you and your instructor to get this information, which should be somewhere in his house, and bring it back here. You may be able to do this without so much as seeing the man, if you're careful enough," he explained. I felt as if a sumo wrestler had just climbed off of my chest. I could get the job done without hurting anyone, even if he deserved a few good punches.

"Sure, alright. I can do that," I said, feeling my confidence coming back. I had broken into a few houses before, when things had been really bad. If there was a contest for breaking-and-entering, I would win first prize, and possibly jail time, but that's beside the point.

"Who's gonna be my instructor, anyway?" I asked, half-hoping that it would be Margie, the Business Administrator. I was pretty sure we would make a pretty deadly team. With my nose-breaking and her spit-hurling, Eduardo wouldn't stand a chance.

The look on Harv's face told me that he was proud of who he was about to introduce. He fixed his tie and looked behind me, towards the door. I turned around right as the door swung open.

"Harlot, I'm sure you've met Agent Retro Rex," Harv declared. Retro strolled into Harv's office, giving me a sly wink as he went and stood by Harv's side. I groaned. I didn't particularly dislike Retro, but I would've preferred someone who seemed as if they were actually serious about their duties as an agent.

"What's behind curtain number two?" I asked, making Harv's face scrunch up in confusion while Retro laughed under his breath.

"What's the matter? Most of my female agents love getting partnered with Retro," he said, looking between the two of us. Retro shrugged but couldn't keep the smile off of his face as he stared at me. I suppose he knew that I wasn't particularly fond of him and he was enjoying the show.

"Nothing, I guess. As long as we don't run into any closets or girls, I guess we'll be fine," I retorted, successfully wiping the smile off of Retro's face. He frowned and looked away while Harv tried to suppress his laughter. He was doing a bad job of it.

"Now, now…" Harv cooed after he managed to get his laughter under control, "Hack is waiting in the Business office to give you all you need before you go. Get going, you two." As an afterthought he added, "And try to play nice."

I left the office, not bothering to wait for Retro. *Why was the universe against me today?* I needed someone who was going with me to get the job done, not to play around.

I climbed up the winding stairs, pouting. The sound of heavy footsteps echoing behind me told me he wasn't far behind.

First of all, I should point out that I really didn't hate the guy. He was okay. I guess we had just gotten off on the wrong foot. Blowing sleeping dust into a girl's face isn't the best way to make a first impression, though.

"Red, wait up!" I looked over my shoulder and saw Retro climbing the stairs two at a time to catch up with me. Deciding to cut the guy some slack, I slowed my pace until he was able to step beside me. He took a moment to catch his breath before he began talking. "Look, Red. I'm really sorry about before…you know, leaving you hanging during Labeling." I could tell from the sincere expression on his face that he meant it. To tell the truth, I really wasn't that bothered by the fact that he had left me high and dry during Labeling. It was just fun teasing him about it.

"You don't have to be sorry. It's okay, really," I assured him. Retro shook his head, vehemently.

"No, listen." He stopped climbing the stairs and faced me, while putting an arm out to the side, forcing me to stop as well. I looked over at him, curiously. He raked his fingers through his hair before dropping his hand back to his side, where it twitched near his cigarette pocket. "I really am serious about helping you. Harv told me on the day that I was supposed to pick you up from the club that I needed to take care of you while you were down here. I already messed up."

"Wait, wait, wait…" I held up my hand to stop him. "Who said I needed anyone's help?"

Retro nodded towards Harv's door. "Mr. Harv. It's my duty to make sure that you remain in one piece while you live here with us, however long that may be." He exhaled before digging into his pocket and pulling out his pack of cigarettes. He looked at them before angrily shoving them back into his pocket.

"Let's start over, okay?" He reached out his hand to me. "I'm Retro Rex and I'll be your instructor for your DM." I laughed and shook my head, but still grabbed his hand and gave it a firm shake.

"I'm Lola…I mean, Harlot Rue. It's nice to meet you," I played along. Retro smiled, still holding onto my hand.

"Harlot? Nice name," he teased, making me laugh again. The corner of his mouth lifted up a bit as he stared into my eyes. I tried to look away, but found myself unable to.

"You have beautiful eyes, Harlot." I blinked rapidly as his words sunk in. I quickly pulled my hand away and looked down, my heart fluttering.

"Aren't there rules about interoffice relationships?" I joked dryly, while keeping my eyes downcast. No one had ever told me that there was anything about me that was beautiful. A warm, unfamiliar but welcome feeling seeped into my chest and I struggled against the smile battling to make its way on my face.

Retro shrugged, grinning at my joke. His attention was drawn to my feet and a confused look crossed his face.

"Lose your shoes?" he asked, while stifling a laugh. I looked down and remembered that I was indeed shoeless.

"Long story," I said while resuming our trek up the stairs. I kept my pace up this time, making Retro fall behind a bit. I needed time to shake the warm feeling that had enveloped me after his compliment.

It was just a stupid compliment! Why was I letting it affect me so much? I hesitantly looked back over my shoulder at Retro, who had succumbed to the call of his cigarettes and was puffing happily away. I coughed once and turned around, still smiling.

"So, Harv said you have to 'take care of me' while I'm down here?" I asked, not bothering to turn around. That would explain why he kept popping up everywhere I went.

"That was the plan. So far, I haven't been doing the best job of it," he replied.

"Well, that's okay. I've been taking care of myself for most of my life, anyway."

Retro didn't reply right away. After a few seconds, he asked, "What do you mean?" I didn't feel like going into my sad, sob story of a life, so I shrugged.

"Nothing really." We finally emerged from Harv's endless staircase.

"No, what were you—"

"Let's go find Hack," I cut him off abruptly, already starting off down one of the hallways. Whenever I brought up my story to someone, their view of me changed. I suddenly became a big charity case and that's not how I wanted to be viewed. I had gotten as far as three feet before Retro called after me.

"Hack's office is over this way, Red."

I wanted to slap myself. I turned around and brushed past him, muttering, "I knew that." Retro just laughed and followed me at a close distance. We found Hack in the Business office, sitting behind the desk where Margie had been, looking fidgety and anxious. He gave my bare feet a quizzical look but didn't bother asking.

"Yo, Hack. What's the DL on the DM?" I joked, flinging myself in one of the chairs that lined the side of the room.

"DL?" Hack asked with a confused face.

"Down low," I explained patiently. Hack's face brightened with understanding.

"Right, right. Check this out!" Hack was up in a flash, his hands gathering up papers and objects at lightning speed. He beckoned me up to the counter with a smile. I came up to the counter as he laid out all of the materials he had gathered.

"Well, this is what you'll need," Hack announced, sounding more like a college professor. He adjusted his huge glasses with one hand while picking up a pretty metal cuff bracelet with the other. "This is what we like to call a Brace. It's a high quality, versatile device. It can be used for communicating with other Brace-wearers and also for listening in on hard to hear conversations by switching into snoop mode by swiping down on the touchscreen. I've already programmed yours to communicate with me and Retro. It's quite handy, you know, if you two ever get separated."

I picked up the cuff bracelet and studied it. I flipped it over and over in my hand and squeezed with my nails until one of my nails broke. I held it up to the light, looking for any hidden buttons.

"It's just a bracelet," I concluded after my thorough examination. Hack and Retro looked at each other and shared a hearty laugh, as if I were a two-year old who couldn't figure out how to open a door. Hack reached out toward my Brace but stopped halfway. I looked at him questioningly.

"May I?" he asked politely, a shy smile gracing his childish features. I laughed and handed him my Brace. Hack turned it over and pressed a tiny, microscopic, you-couldn't-see-it-without-a-magnifying glass button on the inside of the bracelet. Suddenly, part of the bracelet opened up to reveal a small screen. On it were two cute little cartoon faces labeled "Hack" and "Retro". Hack's face was pale and freckled with oversized glasses and mad scientist blonde hair. Retro's had tan skin and hair that was crazily big. I laughed out loud.

"You've got Retro's face right!" I sputtered, while Hack's face turned redder and he laughed nervously. Retro laughed mischievously.

"Well, I see he's got you down to perfection as well," he taunted. I gasped when I saw that my face had also been programmed into his. I had my spiky red Kool-Aid hair and the biggest frown ever on my face. *It was so me!* I couldn't help but laugh again and this time Hack (who looked likely to faint if I hadn't liked it) and Retro joined in.

Hack was the first to settle down and get back to business while Retro and I continued to tease each other. "Here, try it out, Harlot. Just tap on Retro's face," he explained, gesturing towards my Brace. I slid it over my wrist and then gently tapped on "Retro's" icon. I heard a slight vibration coming from Retro. He held up his Brace with a grin. I saw that his screen had lighted up and my little face had appeared on the screen and was blinking.

"Oh, that's so cool, Hack!" I cried, feeling excited. It was just the thing to replace the phone I had got from Blackeye. And this one even had a touch screen!

"*Oh, that's so cool, Hack!*" My voice repeated itself from Hack's desk. I looked back at all the other objects that Hack had laid out. "Where'd that come from?" I asked. I noticed a little black ear bud and I picked it up.

"That's your earpiece. You'll be able to hear anything we have to tell you from that. Go ahead and put it in," Hack said, sounding like he was enjoying himself. I did as he said, noting to myself that Hack didn't seem to stutter when he was excited. Retro took the other ear bud and stuck it in his ear, then looked at me, a devious expression on his face. He whispered something into his Brace and then looked back up at me, expectantly.

"*I'll get that story out of you sooner or later,*" a soft voice murmured into my ear. My breath caught in my throat and I felt myself blush all over. So, he hadn't forgotten.

I looked up and noticed that both Retro and Hack were watching me. Hack looked a little peeved for some reason, while Retro was just giving me his infamous smirk. I smirked back and whispered into my Brace, "*It's not a big deal.*" Retro seemed disappointed as he lowered his hand from his mouth. I turned back to Hack.

"Anything else?" I asked. Hack, glad to be back in the circle, nodded with his face full of energy.

"Yes, well, Harv mentioned that this may be an assassination, so..." Hack's voice trailed off as he laid out two pocket knives, encased in metallic black. I picked up the knife carefully, twirling it around a few times. It reminded me of my old knife, but not quite. I tried to imagine plunging it into someone's chest, but I couldn't without cringing and cutting the image short.

"Is that it?" I asked quickly, trying to get my mind off the knife as I stuffed it in the same pocket where I kept my all-access key. "We don't get guns, or smoke bombs, or sleeping dust?" Hack shook his head, and then stood up, still smiling.

"That's what makes this mission a test," he explained. "Besides, I think that's all you'll need. Now you just need to head over to the parking zone, and they'll take you where you need to go," he explained. He extended his hand out to me, looking embarrassed. "I'm here if you need help while you're out on the field."

I smiled and shook his hand. "Thanks," I replied, causing his face to flood red. If I didn't know better, I would say this guy had a serious crush on me. Hack quickly let go of my hand and laughed nervously. "W-well, good luck you two!"

"We don't need luck with my skills, Hacky-Sack," Retro gloated, giving Hack a hard, but friendly slap on the back. He looked at me, his hazel eyes gleaming.

"Let's hit it."

Chapter Eight

Soon enough, we were herded into a bus-like vehicle parked in the first place I had set foot in down in H Corp—the parking zone. Lolli had conjured me up a new pair of boots that were actually my size, and still in my favorite color, black.

The driver of our bus, or Operator, looked too young to drive a Tonka truck. I had to admit though, he was stylish, even though I didn't really go for the skinny-jean, high hair, V-neck shirt type. His dark hair was even higher than Retro's and was striped with platinum blonde highlights.

He explained to us the rundown of the mission: he was to drop us off at Eduardo's house, we run in, grabbed the info, and came back. If anyone saw us, we would take them out. I gave the Operator a curt nod, still praying that things wouldn't get that far and I wouldn't be forced to hurt anyone.

I sat in the far back seat, which extended to both sides of the bus instead of splitting when it came to the aisle. Retro plopped next to me, headphones already popped into his ears. He leaned his head back against the seat and shut his eyes.

"This is gonna take a while. Feel free to get comfortable," he purred, smoothly slipping an arm around my shoulder. I laughed and shrugged his arm off, while scooting over a bit.

"Feel free to keep your hands to yourself," I teased back while kicking my feet up on the seat in front of us. Retro grinned and followed suit.

"You make that difficult, but I'll try." He leaned his head against the seat, while folding his hands behind his head to form a pillow. He looked over at me and smiled. "You ready for this?"

I bit my lip before nodding once. "As ready as I'll ever be, I guess." Retro nodded.

"My DM wasn't as dangerous as yours might be, but I'm here to help you, Red."

"I know. So, if any guys try to shoot me, you'll take the bullet, right?"

I laughed as Retro's eyes popped open and he looked at me with a startled expression.

"Whoa, let's hope it won't come down to that." After a few moments of silence, I figured that he had dozed off, so I kept myself busy by toying with my Brace.

"Remember how I said that Harv told me I was in charge of your safety while you were down here?" I looked over at Retro, surprised to find that he was staring at me.

"Yeah, what about it?" I asked, while pretending to study my Brace again.

"Well…it's only a promise I can keep if you promise to keep yourself alive out here."

I felt a trickle of nervousness find its way into my stomach. Everyone kept hinting at the possibility of death out here on my DM.

"Finding my parents might be a little hard if I were dead. I plan on sticking this thing out 'til the end."

Retro smiled at my reply before he shut his eyes and exhaled. "Good to know, Red." A few minutes later and he was snoring.

I laid my head back against the seat, ready to catch some Z's of my own when suddenly the bus jerked forward, and I knew we were on our way. I looked out the window and sure enough, we were in the familiar metallic walls of the car elevator. My arrival in H Corp wasn't exactly a fond memory, but I was starting to get used to all of the super technology around every corner.

"Okay, so let me lay down some rules, okay?" Our Operator suddenly piped up, turning around in his seat. He lifted his index finger and pointed it at me.

"No kissing, no hugging, and please don't try to get snappy with me. I heard all about your little attitude, and let me tell you, Marc Mojo will have none of that on his shuttle!" he announced, finishing his rant with a snap of his finger. I just stared at him and wondered whether to laugh or tell him where his finger would go if he pointed it at me again.

"I see you're speechless," Marc continued while smoothing some of his blonde-streaked hair upwards. "Just respect my rules, and we'll get along!" He turned back around in his seat with emphasis on rolling his neck.

I gave a dry laugh and said, "Sure thing, Beyonce."

This was going to be one long bus ride. I stared out of the window as the minutes flew by, my mind suddenly weighed down by a ton of thoughts.

This was by far the biggest lead I had ever found on my parents' whereabouts. Harv was basically training me to find my parents and I was lucky enough to meet him.

I still couldn't figure out why my parents wouldn't have mentioned something as monumental as working as secret agents for a hidden organization miles underground.

There had to have been signs. I let my eyes slide shut as a memory, as fragile as glass, materialized in my mind.

* * *

"Where are you going?" I was back in our old home, in front of the television that always used to intimidate me with its humongous widescreen. My parents, who were dressed in their lab coats and headed out of the front door, froze in place. They shared a brief look before my dad turned around and walked towards me, grinning.

"Didn't we tell you, Little Lola? We have a business trip we have to attend," he explained in the soothing voice he usually reserved for his patients. I pouted and crossed my arms over my chest.

"You guys always go on trips and leave me here. Why can't I come?" I whined, my lower lip protruding as far as I could make it. My parents shared another look before my mother decided to step in. She squatted down in front of me so that we were face to face. She smiled, making her brown eyes crinkle in the corners.

"Now, sweetie, we talked about this. You can't go with us because we can't bring children on our trips. We would if we could, darling, but we can't." I was not pacified so easily. I pulled away from her and scooted over to the far side of our couch.

"S'not fair. I'm bored when you guys leave," I whimpered while swiping at my nose. My parents chuckled before Dad swooped me up in his arms and kissed my nose.

"How about we make a deal?" he asked. I wiped my nose and smiled a bit.

"What kind of deal?"

"If we leave you for this one eensy-weensy, teeny-tiny trip, we'll bring back all kinds of souvenirs. Toys, candy, you name it. How's that sound?" Now, how could any kid resist the promise of toys? In my six-year old mind, I had just hit the jackpot.

"Hmmm…I guess that's okay, then. You can go now," I said with a big smile. "Shoo, shoo!" I waved my hands toward the door, making my parents laugh.

"The girl wants us out now, Warren," Mom said with a wink at my father. "We'd better leave." Our heads all turned at once as the sound of a car horn blared from outside. My stomach instantly dropped. Even at a young age, I despised my mother's younger sister.

"There's your Aunt Rochelle," Dad said as he put me back down on the couch. I groaned and curled my knees up to my chin. I watched as my parents hurriedly gathered their suitcases and other traveling essentials. After they were finished, they showered me with hugs and kisses and promises of tons of souvenirs.

"If you need anything, you know our number, babe!" Mom cried as she pulled her suitcase out of the door.

That's when I saw it. As my mom's suitcase bumped down our driveway, a small, glass vial tumbled out from an unzipped area. I rushed over and picked it up, ready to hand it over but the pretty liquid inside stopped me. It was glowing white and thick like cream. I studied the vial closely, watching as the bubbles pushed from side to side as I twirled it in my hand.

"Give that here, Lola!" I gasped in surprise as my mom snatched the vial from my hand, a terrified expression on her face. She shoved it back in her suitcase and made sure to zip it all the way closed. I stared at her in shock, not sure if I had did something wrong. She took a deep breath before turning around to face me. A forced smile took the place of her earlier expression.

"Thanks, sweetie. We'll be back in two days." Mom leaned down and hugged me before she and my dad climbed into their Honda Odyssey. They yelled a few orders to my aunt, who nodded and smiled almost as brightly as her bright attire. My parents waved and shouted their goodbyes at us as my dad backed out of the driveway. Soon, they were speeding out of the neighborhood.

My aunt, her sunglasses perched on her recently reconstructed nose, took me by the hand and waved after them, screaming, "You guys be safe! Lola and I are going to have so much fun!" As soon as their car was out of sight, she dropped my hand and groaned.

"Why am I always stuck babysitting you, you whiny little rat?" She glared at me, her green eyes full of disgust behind her sunglasses.

"You know, Daddy doesn't like it when you call me names," I said. My aunt blew a bubble with her chewing gum, which popped loudly before she smiled at me.

"Ask me if I care. You should already know the answer to that by now."

She continued talking, all the while smacking loudly on her mint gum. "You know the rules. Go up to your room and don't speak to me until your parents are back. If you get hungry or thirsty, you better call and order out for pizza." She paused and stooped down to my level. She lowered her designer sunglasses, revealing a pair of jade eyes. I always wondered how someone with such pretty eyes could be so evil.

"And what's the most important thing about me staying here?" She stared at me expectantly, waiting for my reply. I shrugged.

"You won't be here for long?" I replied innocently. My aunt smirked and grabbed my cheeks with her sharp, acrylic nails.

"Hahaha, you're a little snotty comedian, aren't you? The most important rule is..." she squeezed my cheeks tighter and smiled, "...I'm. In. Charge." She let go of my cheeks, still laughing before she made her way inside, already on her cell phone, ready to invite her college friends over to my parents' house.

* * *

I snapped out of the memory and returned to my ride on the car elevator, feeling enlightened, but also exhausted. My aunt could turn any memory sour.

More importantly, that vial that I had picked up so long ago had to be carrying the very same liquid that Margie had injected me with after my Labeling. So, my parents really had been agents. I always knew something was up with their frequent "business trips", but I would have never guessed that they were secret agents. I wondered briefly what they would think about me becoming one. Proud, I would like to think. It was all for them.

I was brought back to the present as the bus came to a jerky halt. *Why in the world had we stopped?* I stood up and walked to the front of the bus. We were outside of a large, circular door laced with metal. I looked at Marc, who was fiddling with some switches on the dashboard.

"Don't worry, I'll have it open in a jiffy!" he said, although he clearly had no idea what he was doing. His eyes finally landed on a bright red button labeled OPERATE GATE (oh, could that be it?) and he slammed his fist on it. With a huge groan and lots of flying dirt, the metal gate spiraled open.

I couldn't believe it. We were back above ground. Tall, green and leafy trees gently swayed in the wind around us and there was a shimmering stream a few yards away. I leaned up toward the front window to get a better view of the fluffy clouds playing peek-a-boo behind the leaves of the trees.

We had come up in the middle of a forest. I suddenly realized that being underground had been very bland. We were surrounded by cold, metal walls at all times and everything felt so artificial. The agents were very dedicated to their cause if they were willing to give up living above ground.

Marc gave me a satisfied smile before cranking up the bus and setting off through the woods. I looked behind me, out of the far back window, and found that we had literally driven out of the mouth of a cave. I watched in amazement as the circular door swirled shut again before it flickered and morphed to look like any other cave. I shook my head in amazement before plopping down in the seat behind Marc. H Corp was beginning to seem like another world to me.

"We have underground facilities like these around the globe. And many of them are linked by tunnels like these," Marc informed me as he expertly maneuvered the bus through the trees. "Europe, Africa, Asia, you name it. Cool, huh?"

"Very," I replied in amazement.

Soon, we were on the all-too familiar interstate that would take us to Los Angeles. I felt my stomach start to churn with nervousness. *What if Eduardo saw me? Would I actually be able to kill him, even if he had killed other people, and possibly stolen away my parents?* The knife in my pocket seemed to grow heavier and heavier by the minute.

"Here we are!" The Operator's high-pitched voice snapped me out of my thoughts and nearly caused me to have a heart attack.

"We're there? Already?" I panicked, my voice coming out like the squeaking of a mouse. Marc nodded and kept smiling. "Yep! This bus can really pick up speed! Have fun, you two!" he chirped. I felt the urge to slap him. *We weren't going for a picnic! And talk about un-stealthy. What kind of secret agent gets dropped off by a bus?*

Before I could decide on slapping him or kicking him out of the seat and driving back to headquarters, I felt a hand grab my wrist.

"Alright, see ya, Marc," Retro waved before practically dragging me out of the bus. As soon as we were off of the bus, I yanked my arm away.

"I can walk myself. I'm not a dog," I snapped before pausing to check out my surroundings. We were in one of the prettiest neighborhoods I had seen yet in Los Angeles, so I knew that we were either in Palos Verdes or Hidden Hills. All of the houses had at least two floors and an in-ground pool in each yard. They were the kinds of homes that people fantasized about.

"You think these houses are fancy?" Retro said, coming up behind me and startling me. I hadn't realized I had said anything aloud. I looked over my shoulder at him without turning around to fully face him.

"Well, yeah. They even have a pool," I noted, lamely. Retro laughed at me, making me feel as if I had just said something stupid.

"What? You don't think that these houses are fancy at all?" I asked, feeling angry and slightly embarrassed. Retro studied the huge houses looming around us before giving a dismissive shrug.

"I guess so. My summer villas in Puerto Rico are bigger than these, though." My mouth dropped open as Retro's words sunk in. *Was this guy for real? Who had summer villas at all at his age?*

I could tell he wanted me to be impressed, which I was, but I'd never admit that to him. "Yeah, right," I said instead.

"I'm serious, Red. If you want, I'll show you them one day," Retro offered as he took a step toward me.

"I'll pass," I replied as I stepped away, my face burning. I know what you're thinking: what kind of idiot would turn down a free trip to Puerto Rico with a guy like Retro? Retro's ego was already huge, there was no need to inflate it even more.

Retro smiled, unfazed by my answer. "Maybe you'll change your mind." His expression turned quizzical. "Why do you keep looking over your shoulder?"

I stopped myself in the midst of doing just as he said and bit my lip. I wasn't going to tell him that I was keeping an eye out for Blackeye, my supplier.

"No reason. I'm just ready to get this DM started," I lied.

I looked up at the house our Operator, Marc, had dropped us in front of before speeding off. It looked like any other normal house you'd come across. I was half-expecting Eduardo to live in a big castle, complete with bats, cobwebs, and maybe a few cute, glittery vampires. But no, the guy even had some lawn gnomes wearing bathing suits in his front yard.

"Are you sure this is his house?" I asked, looking over my shoulder to consult with my mentor, but Retro was nowhere in sight. I looked around worriedly. "Retro?!" I whispered loudly, suddenly feeling scared. My wrist vibrated, stopping me from going into hysteria. I looked down at my Brace and saw Little Retro's face on my screen.

"Okay, Red, it's time to start your DM." Retro's warm, velvety voice sounded in my ear. *"You ready?"*

"Could you warn me before you run off? Get over here!" I whispered angrily into my Brace.

"No can do, Red. I'm just here to make sure you don't get into trouble and to grade you on how well you do. The real mission is up to you."

I felt my heart drop at his words. I was going to have to go in there all alone, with a murderer who could chop me into bits and store me in his refrigerator.

"Retro, I'm not going' in there alone!" I whined, not caring how much like a baby I sounded.

"Red, I'll be close by, don't worry. Now go; and that's an order," he said in a playful but firm voice. I cursed and dropped my hand back to my side. I stared up at the house, which seemed to grow taller and taller by the second. I took a deep breath and shut my eyes. I pictured my parents inside, needing my help, only a few doors away. I could almost see my mom's curly brown hair and big brown eyes, wide and afraid, and my tenacious father, his cocoa hands clasping onto my mother's ebony ones.

I opened my eyes and brought the Brace back up to my mouth, giving Retro's face a quick tap. "Alright. What do I need to do?" I asked. I heard Retro make a satisfied sound and then he went into what I could only call "business mode."

"Okay, Red, I want you to make this break-in as clean as possible. No breaking windows or doors. We don't want to leave anything that would suggest it was a break-in."

"Leave it to me." Feeling completely self-conscious and suspicious in my stupid black jumpsuit, I made my way to the front door and stood in the shadows of the porch. I tried to peer into one of the windows but I couldn't see through it because of a set of yellow curtains. Praying that Eduardo wasn't in the house, I grabbed onto the door knob and slipped a bobby pin out of the back of my hair. I bent it into a semi-straight line and then quickly stabbed it into the keyhole. I twisted the pin and the jiggled the knob a bit. No luck. I kept twisting and jiggling until I heard a click. I gave a silent cheer and then pushed the door open. I stepped inside.

It was quiet. I carefully made my way to the side of a bookshelf in the fancy, green-oriented living room, cringing at my loud heels smashing against the tiled floor.

"*Nice, Red.*" Retro sounded in my ear, making me smile. "*Now all you have to do is grab the papers. They should be upstairs in his bedroom.*"

"Got it," I replied and then began walking toward the stairs. *Click. Click. Click.* I groaned out loud and ripped off my high-heeled boots. Harv obviously hadn't been thinking of stealth when he designed these outfits.

I took a step. No click. I sighed with relief and plodded my way upstairs, sticking close to the wall. I was on the last step when—

"ARF ARF ARF!" A huge dog rounded the corner and slammed right into me. It pinned me on my back with its heavy paws, its huge jaws inches above my face. I barely had time to scream before the dog licked me. *Yes, licked me. On my face!*

"Ew, back off! Get off of me!" I whispered loudly, trying to swat the mammoth dog away, but it just barked and kept licking away. I managed to wriggle away and stand up, but the dog was insistent. It pushed off of its hind legs and put its front paws on my shoulders, then continued licking my face, leaving it coated in a thick layer of gooey slobber.

Obviously, this dog wasn't a vicious attack dog, or if it was, it was a terrible one. I've never really been a dog person, or any other kind of animal for that matter. I gave its head a few cautious pats and it finally put its paws back on the ground. It looked up at me, its tail wagging like crazy.

"Hey, big guy. I'm going to need you to be quiet while I steal your owner's stuff, okay?" I cooed, giving it a good scratch behind its ear. It simply licked my nose in reply. I ran my sleeve over my face and tried not to gag. I noticed a colorful squeaky ball sitting on the stairs. I picked it up and the dog jerked its head upwards. Its gaze was intent on the little round toy, its mouth clamped shut. I moved my arm to the left; his eyes followed. I moved my arms to the right; his eyes did the same. I could tell he meant business.

"Thanks, Scooby Doo. Now, fetch!" I tossed the ball down the stairs, and in a flash, the dog was after it, barking wildly. I breathed a sigh of relief and climbed the last step to the second floor.

I brought my Brace up to my mouth. "Retro, which one is his bedroom?" I asked, looking around. The hallway had at least five doors on either side and each door looked exactly the same.

"*I could tell you, but then I'd probably have to dock points off of your score*," Retro replied pleasantly. Whatever. I decided to start with the left side of the hall, keeping close to the wall. Feeling like a ninja, I put back on my boots and kicked in the first door and jumped inside. I sighed happily when I realized the room was empty. I tried the next two rooms and they were the same.

"*You know, you could have just used your Brace to listen for anyone on the other side of the door instead of kicking them down*," Retro voiced.

"Now you tell me," I muttered.

I came to the fourth room and was about to take out the door when I heard something. It was like a quiet grumbling of a bear. I put my Brace into snoop mode, pressed it to the door and listened. Sure enough, I heard low snoring. I cursed and backed away from the door, praying my loud door-kicking hadn't been enough to stir him.

"Retro," I whispered, feeling panic rising into the pit of my stomach, "I think he's in his room."

It took longer than usual for Retro to reply. When he did, it was just a simple, "*Go get 'im, tiger*." I wanted to throw my Brace out of the window and then jump right out after it.

This wasn't right! Eduardo wasn't supposed to be in his house! I had played it all out in my head and in no scenario had I prepared myself for the actual case of him being in his room.

Okay, I had to get a hold of myself. I took a couple of deep breaths and then grabbed the door knob. If I could just sneak in quietly enough, I could grab the papers and leave. My grip on the doorknob tightened and I slowly pushed open the door.

The bedroom was innocent enough. The walls were painted a pastel yellow. A pair of green curtains cast an emerald tint to the furniture in the room. I lowered my hands back to my side as my eyes finally landed on the bed.

Whoa.

The photo Harv had shown me had not captured the size of the man sprawled across the bed. He wasn't even overweight. He was big, alright, but muscular, too. He looked like he could karate chop a tree trunk in half and break me over his knee, all at the same time.

I had wasted enough time. I crept up to the dresser beside his bed. Trying to be as silent as possible, I began to rummage through his drawers. I stopped each time he grunted or rolled around in bed.

I found a couple of family photos of him posing with who I suspected was his wife and his young son. In each photo, he was smiling and looked like a totally different person from the photo Harv had shown me. Feeling my heart tug, I put it back and moved on.

I spotted a small suitcase. Inside laid a row of binders. I shuffled through them until I came across a black binder with a huge white E stamped on the front. I silently thanked Eduardo for being unknowingly helpful and labeling his binder, before I swept up the binder and shut his dresser.

"Nice, Red, nice. Now come back outside and we're ready to go." I nodded, guessing that Retro was watching me, and made my way to the door.

I was in the doorway when a deep, rumbling voice stopped me dead in my tracks.

"Who are you?"

Oh, shoot. I quickly hid the binder behind me and then turned around slowly, praying that he was talking in his sleep. No luck. Eduardo was propped up on his elbow, glaring right at me. I swallowed hard. I tried to make my hands grab my knife, but they seemed to have frozen.

"I asked, who are you?" Eduardo asked again, louder this time. It was now or never. I took a deep breath.

"Hello!" I chirped in a French accent, "I'm your new maid, Evangeline!"

Chapter Nine

Eduardo and I stared at each other, none of us moving a muscle. I could feel the back of my neck growing sweaty.

Evangeline—really?! I wanted to slap myself. I couldn't have thought of another name? There was still time to end this. As the seconds ticked by, the knife seemed to be calling out my name. But I knew I couldn't kill him. He was someone's father, someone's husband. I couldn't take him away from them.

Finally, Eduardo spoke. "What kind of maid dresses like that?" he grumbled, standing up and stretching. Now that he was standing, I could see that he was easily six feet tall. I swallowed hard, trying to think of a good excuse for a maid to be wearing a black jumpsuit and heels. At least he couldn't see my tattoos with my jumpsuit on.

"Oh, you are so funny!" I said in a horrible French accent, and then threw in a high-pitched giggle. "They said you ordered the…um…the Red Hot Maid! So, ooh-la-la! Here I am!" I wanted to either laugh or cry at my poor acting, but Eduardo would probably think I was insane if I did either. Instead I forced a big smile and hoped he bought it. He stared at me, scratching at his greasy, black hair before he shrugged.

"Must've been George's bad idea of a joke….Well, go clean or whatever," he grumbled, waving me away. I did a lame curtsy and then backed out of the door, careful to keep the binder out of sight.

Now to get the heck out of here. I sprinted down the stairs as fast as my boots would carry me but stopped short at the front door. Our Operator's, Marc's, face flashed into my head and then his instructions repeated in my mind: he was to drop us off at Eduardo's house, we ran in, grabbed the info, and came back. If anyone saw us, we would take them out.

I couldn't leave now—he had seen me. I had to kill him. I turned back around and stared at the staircase. Maybe I could just leave. I was sure that Retro hadn't seen me or heard Eduardo talk. I could just lie and say he was fast asleep and—

"I think you're forgetting something, Red." There was Retro, right on cue. I crossed my fingers.

"What're you talking about? I have the info and I'm heading outside," I babbled, talking way too quickly. I heard Retro sigh.

"Red, he saw you. You've gotta take him out." he said quietly after a short pause.

"Why?" I practically begged. Remembering just exactly where I was, I lowered my voice. "He just thinks I'm a maid. I can just leave and he'll never think about me again." I could even hear the desperation in my voice.

"What happens when he figures out that no one hired him a maid? What happens when he finds that his important information has disappeared? The E. Corporation will find you and you'll end up just like your parents...or worse." That was harsh. But it was also true. I sighed and didn't bother to reply to him. I knew what I had to do, as much as I hated it. I reached a shaky hand to my pocket, ready to retrieve the knife.

Before I could even take out my knife, Eduardo had rushed downstairs and was charging right toward me. I noticed he was carrying the small suitcase.

Before I could utter out a scream, Eduardo stopped in front of me and spoke. "Listen, do you have any experience in waitressing?" he asked, sounding out of breath. I didn't know what to say.

"Uh..." Eduardo shook his head and grabbed my wrist. He carelessly swung open the front door and started dragging me toward a black Acura.

"Whatever, you'll learn. Get in," he ordered. I hesitated for a moment before I obeyed and cautiously climbed into the passenger's seat, wondering what in the world was going on. I managed to throw the binder under me before I sat down. Eduardo climbed into the driver's seat and hurriedly turned the car on. He threw his arm around my seat as he backed out of his yard, running over a couple of his lawn gnomes in the process. He then switched the gear into "Drive" and sped down the road.

"Sir, is something the matter?" I managed to say after a bit. Eduardo jumped a little, seeming as if he had forgotten I was in the car. He glanced over at me then quickly focused his attention back on the front window.

"I have an important meeting at one of my restaurants and it looks as if they're a tad low on waitresses." He glared at me. "You gotta problem?" Heck yes, I wanted to say, but I simply shook my head and gave him my most girlish smile. He just grunted and turned away. I was in no position to question the guy right now, seeing as he could drive off the road and kill us both if he wanted to. Another option would be to simply blow his horrendous breath in my face. That would be a one-hit K.O.

I looked out of the window as Eduardo turned on the radio. I heard the latest Taylor Swift song playing and I couldn't help but laugh inside when Eduardo started mumbling along.

"*Red, may I ask what the* infierno *you're doing?*" Retro's lazy voice reminded me that I was still on my DM. I couldn't very well reply at the moment so I hit the tiny red X next to Retro's face to mute him. I would figure out some way to get rid of Eduardo on my own and I didn't need him distracting me or reminding me.

Suddenly, Eduardo spoke.

"Those tattoos…where'd you get them?" he questioned, and I didn't miss the hint of suspicion in his rumbling voice. He was glaring at me from the corner of his eye while one of his hands gripped the steering wheel so tightly I thought it might snap.

Without knowing it, my jumpsuit's low V-neck had slipped down a bit to reveal the tiniest sliver of my tattoo. I felt the urge to confess everything but somehow managed to keep myself under control.

"A little parlor in France! This style is quite common, they told me." I lied between my teeth while batting my eyes up at the hulking man. Eduardo considered me a tad longer before he grunted and focused back on the road. I relaxed back in my seat, feeling as though I had just dodged a bullet.

After about ten minutes of driving, we pulled into the parking lot of a Mr. Taco restaurant. I snorted at the giant Mr. Taco sign that read, "Tacos + Beer = Right Here!" I don't think this place could have gotten any cornier.

"Get out." Eduardo's gravelly voice snapped me back to attention. He was already out of the car and had opened my door. He stood there, glaring at me and tapping his foot impatiently. I offered my hand and a shy smile, thinking he would help me out of the car, but he didn't even acknowledge it.

"Fine," I muttered, climbing out of the car myself. I kept the binder held behind my back and prayed he didn't find it suspicious. Eduardo slammed the door shut and then began walking to the back of the restaurant. I guess he expected me to follow, so I did. We came to a door labeled "Employees Only". Eduardo gave three quick knocks and then folded his arms. After a moment or two passed, a tiny blonde woman opened the door. She grinned brightly at Eduardo.

"Hey, Mr. Hernandez! What brings you here?" she said, giving him a big butt-kissing smile, and showing off her gap-teeth. Eduardo pulled me forward roughly by my arm.

"I brought help. Show her the ropes." he ordered gruffly before walking away. The girl kept staring after him until he had disappeared from sight. Her smile quickly dropped into a frown as her gaze flittered over to me.

"You'll do, I guess," she sniffed, before dragging me inside. I was instantly hit by the delicious scent of sizzling, seasoned beef and baking tortilla shells. Dozens of chefs milled about the white kitchen, giving my jumpsuit strange looks.

"Follow me," the girl ordered, yanking me toward a closet. She opened it up and began digging through a basket of clothes. She pulled out a red dress with a yellow apron and held it up to my chest.

"That'll do," she said with a nod. "Now hurry and get dressed. We're really busy at this hour." She tossed the clothes at me and walked away. I shot a middle finger and a big grin at her retreating back and then slammed the closet door behind her. I struggled to unzip and strip out of my jumpsuit.

I had went from being an agent to a maid to a waitress, all in under an hour! This whole DM was getting out of hand rather quickly. When I tried to form a plan on getting rid of Eduardo and escaping this place, nothing came to mind. There was no way I could kill him in front of crowd. Retro would probably demand that I killed all of the witnesses. Running wasn't an option, although that's what I felt like doing.

As I stood naked in the cold storage closet, I took the time to drink in my Labeling tattoos and made a startling discovery. The entire tattoo seemed to stem from the letter H inked directly above my left breast. I had found myself scratching incessantly ever since I gotten Labeled. It looked like a small tree that branched out across my chest and wrapped around my torso before it spread out and ended just past my knees and elbows. Seeing the tattoo reminded me of my mission and I hurriedly grabbed the waitress uniform.

I slid the binder under the empty shoe rack then hurriedly pulled on the short, flared dress and tied on my apron. I was sure I looked like a clown. I looked down at my feet. Of course, the Wicked Witch of Mr. Taco hadn't bothered to give me a pair of shoes. I sighed and threw back on my boots, making a mental note to burn them when I got back underground. I made sure to slide my pocket knife into my boot, just in case things turned sour.

"Come on, it doesn't take all day!" Miss Rude commanded from the other side of the door while knocking like that would make me go any faster. *Ooh, after all of this was over, I was coming for her.*

I threw open the door, plastering a fake "Evangeline" smile on my face.

"I'm so sorry! This dress, it's cute, no?" I said, making small talk as Miss Rude ushered me out front to the cash registers. She wasn't exaggerating when she said they were busy at this hour. Every table was filled to capacity with loud and rowdy people downing beer and tacos. I was staring at all of the people when one table caught my attention. Eduardo was sitting there, holding onto the black suitcase like it was his child. He looked nervous and kept fidgeting with the salt and pepper on the table. I wondered who he could be meeting that was making him as fidgety as a boy on his first date.

"Here you go!" Suddenly, two heavy plates were dropped into either of my hands and I almost fell over. Miss Rude grinned evilly at me and gestured out at the tables.

"They go to Table One. And I have five more orders for you when you get back," she said and then she sneered and headed back into the kitchen. I was tempted to stomp after her and slam both plates in her gap-teeth, but decided against it. Instead, I put on a big smile and headed out into the restaurant, wondering just what the heck I was doing.

How did you know which table was which? I passed by table after table and they all looked exactly the same to me. They were all covered with a checkered red and yellow tablecloth and was littered with napkins and dirty silverware. Finally, I spotted a table with the number "1" pasted on the wall next to it. I walked over to the table, where a happy couple were sitting, holding hands and whispering quietly to each other. I dropped their plates on the table, unceremoniously. The plates clanged loudly, causing the couple to jerk apart and look down at their plates then up at me, as if I were a crazy person.

"Enjoy," I grunted unenthusiastically, deciding to drop the "Evangeline" persona while I was away from people that were acquainted with Eduardo. The dopey smiles were hurting my face, and it wasn't like I was sticking around to receive a tip.

The next few orders were the same. I was beginning to think I was doomed to work as a waitress at Mr. Taco for the rest of my life when suddenly, Miss Rude pulled me back into the kitchen, the veins on her forehead looking ready to burst.

"We're getting complaints about a certain waitress being unfriendly and rude. You know something about this?" she nearly yelled. I smiled innocently and shrugged.

"Oh, really?" I quipped in a French accent. "Whoever could they be talking about?" Miss Rude's eyes went heavenward as she smacked her forehead with the palm of her greasy hand. I loved getting under her blotchy skin.

"YOU!" she shouted, throwing her hands in the air, "YOU!" Like I hadn't heard the first YOU. In fact, I had heard it and felt it, via the spittle flying from her purple painted lips.

She handed me two more platters, both containing huge burritos covered in melted cheese and a side of re-fried beans. "Now take this to Table 8. And I don't want any more complaints or I'll have you shipped back to France or wherever the heck you came from."

Hopefully, after I managed to get out of this situation, I would get a chance to ship my fist across her face, because that's what she seemed to be asking for. Since that was impossible at the time, I just gave her a forced smile and a curt nod.

"Of course!" I chirped before heading back into the restaurant. I glanced around for Table 8 and my eyes landed on Eduardo's table. I stopped dead in my tracks. He wasn't alone anymore.

Across from Eduardo sat a man clothed in a white collared dress shirt with a navy tie and a long, black trench coat over it. A black fedora graced the top of his slicked back raven hair and he had on leather gloves. The little skin he had showing was like porcelain: cold, white, and shiny. It was almost as if he would shatter into shards if you touched him.

I couldn't quite see his face because he was wearing an expensive pair of aviator sunglasses and his fedora was pulled ridiculously low. Everything about him seemed surreal and I got a sudden sense of déjà vu.

What the heck?

Deciding to play it cool, I calmly approached the table and put their plates down. I noticed that Shades (I decided to give him that nickname) was flipping casually through the black suitcase that Eduardo had brought. Eduardo didn't bother to acknowledge me; however, he kept a worried eye on the man.

"Here you go! Enjoy your meal, sirs," I said sweetly. Now I understood how waitresses and waiters who hated their jobs felt. You had to have been a cheerleader to have all of the enthusiasm required for this line of work.

Eduardo either didn't hear me or didn't care as he began to devour his food. Shades, at least, tipped his hat.

Just as I had turned my back to them to walk back to the kitchen, I heard Shades speak. "It's missing." Two little words made my blood run cold. I knew he could only be talking about one thing.

"What's missing?" Eduardo spoke, his voice filled with panic and fear. I started to pick my pace up a bit. I needed to get out of there. Even if I failed the mission by not killing Eduardo, Harv would most likely appreciate the fact that I arrived back underground with the information he wanted, instead of in a casket.

"The files on the H Corporation. They're missing." Shades spoke again, his voice still neutral, as if he weren't angry at all.

"B-B-But, I had just put them in there this morning! No one else has been in my room! Except…there was this girl."

It looked as if I would be clocking out a little earlier than expected. I sped-walked back into the kitchen and walked right past Miss Rude, who shot me an incredulous look. I went into the closet and grabbed the E binder then quickly walked back out. My mind had went into panic mode and all I knew was one thing: I needed to leave, and quickly.

I was almost to the exit door when Miss Rude grabbed my arm and spun me around.

"And where do you think you're going?" she mocked, while shoving another plate filled with salsa, shrimp and cheese nachos at me. "You're here all day, in case you didn't know."

I didn't even think about it. I took the plate and smashed it right into her face. Miss Rude screeched in horror as the plate clattered to the floor. The kitchen staff went into an uproar of gasps and laughter. Salsa and cheese dripped down her face and I do believe I saw a chunk of tomato in her gap.

"Did I do that? *Excusez-moi*!" I said, while flashing her an apologetic smile. She inhaled and then shrieked again before running off. I followed her with my eyes, feeling triumphant, until I saw who was standing directly in front of her.

Game over.

Eduardo was charging at me, his face red with anger.

"Come here, you thief!!" he bellowed, his huge hands outstretched to grab me. Luckily, Miss Rude was directly in his path. He crashed into her, sending both of them to the floor. I quickly jumped over both of them and raced out of the front entrance of the restaurant, followed by the bewildered cries of the customers.

I had never ran in high-heeled boots before but I was a quick learner, especially when it came to escaping serial killers. Putting all of my energy into my legs, I ran down the sidewalk, dodging some pedestrians and nearly crashing into some. My energy obviously was no match for Eduardo because I soon heard his heavy footfalls behind me. I tried to run faster but it was no use.

Suddenly, a hand grabbed onto my shoulder and I was slammed back onto the sidewalk. Pain shot up my spine and the back of my head. I arched my back and winced as I began to see spots. A shadow fell across me and my heart felt like it was going to burst. I looked up into the angry eyes of Eduardo and, for the first time, he looked like someone capable of murder.

He grabbed me by my neck with his strong hands and then yanked me up so that we were face to face. I could barely breathe because of how tightly he was squeezing. He dragged me over into a dark alleyway, cutting us off from the outside world.

"Before I kill you, tell me who you work for," he growled, squeezing my neck tighter. I gasped for air and clawed like an animal at his hands but didn't say a word. Even if he killed me, I wouldn't let him take down H. They were the only other ones trying to find my parents and I wouldn't ruin their only other option of rescue.

Eduardo squeezed even tighter and my vision began to get splotchy. I struggled to suck in air but none made it to my lungs. I couldn't focus on his face anymore...it became a swirl of neutral colors, that began to slowly fade away. My chest, which had been itching, began to burn intensely.

I couldn't believe I was about to die. Whenever I played out my death, it had never involved getting choked to death by an ex-serial killer. I had imagined me lying down, feeling at peace because my parents had been found.

My parents.

No, I couldn't die yet. I had to find them. I promised I would find them and it wouldn't happen if I was dead

"Get the heck...off of me!" I choked out before pulling back my leg and hitting him right in his groin with the heel of my boot, with as much strength as I could muster. Eduardo let out a low whistle of air and released me to hold onto his "precious commodity".

My chest was burning with such an intensity, I thought I was on fire. My vision was a cloud of red, as if someone had wrapped a sheer, red blindfold around my eyes. Suddenly, it felt as if my mind and body went into autopilot. Without realizing what I was doing, my hand reached into my boot and retrieved the knife.

"What you did to those girls, I'm going to do to you, but ten times worse," I said in a voice that I barely recognized as my own. Eduardo looked up at me, still in pain. I laughed weakly before I pressed the heel of my boot to his stomach and kicked with more strength than I thought I had left. Eduardo stumbled backwards with a muffled cry of pain before he fell onto his back. I stumbled over to him, still laughing. I climbed on him and pinned him on the ground, grinning, my knife still clutched in my hand.

He was going to pay for what he did to those girls, what he may or may not have done to my parents, what he tried to do to me. "Not so tough now, are you? Are you?!" I shouted. Eduardo cursed at me in Spanish before trying to swing at my face. I caught his fist without even trying and bent it backwards. He winced in pain before trying the other fist. I grabbed his hand like one would do with a lover before pinning it by his head. I halted bending his first fist so that I could grab my knife.

"Play nice, Eduardo," I whispered before plunging the knife into his hand. He cried out in pain and writhed around like a madman. I felt a smile pull at the corners of my mouth as I held the knife there. The burning in my chest was out of control at this point, but it felt so good.

"You're crazy! Get away from me!" Eduardo yelled. I giggled and twisted the knife, making him scream again.

"Lola! What are you doing?!" I looked up and saw Retro running toward me at full-speed. "Just kill him, don't torture him!" Just like that, the burning in my chest flared up, causing me to scream, and then abruptly stopped. The red, cloudiness evaporated from my vision, leaving me feeling drained.

"Retro…" I mumbled while slumping forward. What was wrong with me? I felt as if I had left my body and came back to find it completely zapped of energy. My thoughts were scattered and my head throbbed.

"Lola, look out!" Retro shouted. I looked up just in time to meet Eduardo's fist with my face. I rolled off of him, my nose gushing blood. I looked over and saw Eduardo pull himself off of the sidewalk. He pulled my knife out of his hand with a wince and tossed it angrily to the side. I curled up in a ball and screamed in terror as I prepared myself for the incoming onslaught. A loud noise rang out, sounding like a clap of thunder.

I waited.

And waited.

But nothing happened. I cautiously opened my eyes and screamed in terror when I saw Eduardo's blood-soaked face right next to mine. I hurriedly scooted away from him and bumped into someone's leg. I screamed and covered my face.

"Lola, it's over." I tentatively looked up and nearly cried with relief when I saw that it was Retro I had bumped into. A smoking gun dangled from his hand.

"You…I…"I couldn't even form a sentence. I scratched at my chest feverishly and sobbed at the same time. What was wrong with me? I was going psycho on Eduardo one second and then crying like a lunatic the next.

I was surprised when Retro bent down and wrapped his arms around me. "It's okay, Red. You're okay," he repeated. I stiffened at his touch at first, feeling uncomfortable. Slowly, I allowed myself to melt into his embrace without hugging him back.

"Red," Retro spoke, his voice sounding uneasy. He pulled away from me and grabbed my chin, tilting it from side to side. "I saw what you were doing to that guy earlier. What was that? You seemed like another person."

"I-I don't know," I admitted while looking down at the sidewalk, my chin still in his hand. "I just…felt different." Retro studied my face for a few more seconds. I noticed his gaze slowly crawl down to my lips. I felt my face grow hot as he began to lean closer. I had never been kissed before, not ever. Having Retro as my first didn't exactly appeal to me, but I wasn't repulsed by the idea of it. I quickly pulled my chin away and looked elsewhere, successfully stopping him in his tracks. Retro didn't speak for a few moments.

When I finally looked back at him, his smile had returned, although it looked a bit disappointed. He helped me up to my feet. "Well, in any case, you failed the DM," he announced in an upbeat tone. I probably would have made an uproar about this if I didn't feel as if I were about to throw up everywhere.

Instead I gave him a weak smile and said, "I thought we weren't allowed to have guns," before I collapsed on the ground.

Chapter Ten

"Spare me a quarter, spare me a dime

Even a nickel would do fine

Orange and lime, grape and cola

Buy me a soda, little Lola."

When I opened my eyes, I was staring up at a familiar diamond-patterned ceiling. I felt panic set in. Where was my parents' necklace? I desperately grasped at my neck until I felt something hard and cold. I sighed with relief, the panic vanishing.

I sat up on my elbows and looked around. I was back in the exact same hospital room I had awakened in the first time I arrived in H Corp. I felt a tingle in my chest and I couldn't help but scratch at it.

Just like that, the events of my DM came flooding back to me and I collapsed back on the bed, feeling like the room was spinning. I still couldn't process what exactly had taken place outside of Mr. Taco. Eduardo had been on the verge of killing me and I felt as if I had snapped. I remember taunting him and feeling as though I was the most powerful person in the world. The vision of myself twisting the knife stabbed into the palm of his hand made me feel nauseous.

Then Retro had appeared and I felt like someone had turned on a light switch in my brain. I was happy that he did. I really didn't know what I would've done if he hadn't shown up at that exact moment. Snapping like that had never happened to me and I planned on it never happening again. I would just keep that incident to myself and hope that Retro did the same.

After returning to normal, I promptly got my butt handed to me by Eduardo and I knew that I was going to be killed. Fortunately, Retro had come through on his promise to take care of me and had shot him.

"He saved my life," I mumbled aloud, the words sounding strange to my ears.

"I see you're awake." A deep voice interrupted me from my thoughts and nearly caused me to fall out of bed. I looked over and saw that a tall, blonde doctor had just entered the room. He was handsome...and strangely familiar. I couldn't quite put my finger on it, but there was something about him that made it seem like I had already met him.

"Did I break any bones, doctor?"

"Dr. Payne," he replied in a kind tone. I guess I wasn't the only one who had been stuck with a horrible name. "And no, you're in the clear, ma'am," he assured me, "Just a couple of bruises and a minor concussion that seems to have cleared up now. You'll be better in no time." He gave me a warm, reassuring smile. It was the type of smile you couldn't help but return. I breathed a sigh of relief and felt myself relax. I was afraid Eduardo had fractured my skull or something.

"Thanks, Doctor Payne."

"Oh, I almost forgot." The doctor gathered some papers from his desk and gave me another smile, although this one was more playful. "You have some visitors. My son was going to tag along, but Miss Margie needed him a little longer."

His son? Miss Margie? Could this doctor actually be Hack's dad?

Before I could question him, he had left the room and I was attacked by a mass of curly, brown waves.

"You're awake!" I nearly fell off the bed when Lolli popped into my vision from out of nowhere.

"How'd I get here?" I asked, motioning around the room with my hand. Lolli laughed and jerked a thumb over her shoulder. I looked where she pointed and felt myself blush when I saw Retro walking into the room, his arms folded. He gave me a small salute and smirked.

I owed him once again. This was the second time he had had to save me. I would end up being his servant before the day was through.

I quickly brought my attention back to Lolli, who was going on and on about the DM. "Everyone's talking about the DM! Did you actually take out that whopping guy with just your knife?" she asked, looking at me with widened, excited eyes and a big grin on her face.

Twisted

Took him out with my knife? More like had a nervous breakdown before I almost got myself taken out. I glanced over at Retro to get some idea of what she was talking about, but he was staring up at the ceiling now, like there was something oh so intriguing up there.

"I—" Before I could tell Lolli about her mistake, Retro came up to my bedside and threw his arm around his younger sister's shoulders.

"Yep, Red here was a natural. She not only took him out with her knife, but she got in a few blows to his face," he said smoothly, while giving me a meaningful look. "Now, go play with your Barbies or something, and let Red rest." He swiftly guided a complaining Lolli to the door and shoved her out, then closed the door behind her. He turned around and walked back over to me, a small grin on his face.

"Why are you lying for me? I could have handled explaining to Harv why I couldn't kill that guy. I really could care less if I passed the DM or not, at this point," I said, deciding to voice my thoughts. Retro shrugged and pulled out a cigarette. I noticed that he looked as tired as I felt, so I figured he would hit the nicotine.

"Look, if you hadn't passed that DM, you wouldn't have been able to become an official agent. Is that what you wanted?" he asked. I blinked at him. That was admirable of him.

"…So, what do you think happened to me back there?" I asked. Retro's face took on a distant look.

"I'm sure it was nothing," he said. "You were under a lot of stress. It happens." I nodded, feeling a bit better.

"Why do you care so much that I become an agent?" I asked bluntly. He was showing way too much interest in my life.

Retro looked embarrassed before he shrugged it off with a puff of his cigarette. "'Thank-you' is the standard response when someone does you a favor." I couldn't help but smile. No matter what his ulterior motives were, he did still save my life. He had also proved to me that, despite his aloof attitude, he was serious about keeping his promise to protect me.

"Thanks, Retro," I mumbled, allowing him a tiny smile. His smile brightened before he took a drag on his cigarette. He blew the smoke on my face, a habit he seemed to be forming, then sent me teasing smile. "A kiss is also standard, in some countries."

"Don't push it," I warned, still smiling. Thinking about kissing Retro brought me back to the DM. It seemed as if he were about to kiss me, but it could have just been a fluke. Staring at him now, and thinking about all he had done for me, made me hope that maybe he had been about to.

"Suit yourself. You don't know what you're missing," he joked. I shook my head and lay back on the bed, letting my eyes slide shut.

"Whatever, Retro. But seriously, I owe you one or two," I said, feeling myself getting sleepy again. I could have been imagining things but, before I heard the door slam, I thought I felt him brush my bangs away from my face and whisper "It's my job, Red."

I fell asleep with a smile lingering on my face. Maybe I should have kissed him after all.

***

My recovery time was not nearly enough. As soon as the bruises around my neck had cleared up and I was able to breathe without sounding like a gorilla, Harv sent for me and soon enough, I found myself back in his golden office. I sat at his desk, watching him thumb through the binder that had nearly cost me my life to get.

I felt a trickle of nervousness run down my spine. Hopefully, Retro had lied to Harv about the DM as well. He'd probably label me as useless and kick me to the curb.

I sat up straighter when Harv looked up at me, his face expressionless. Suddenly, he broke out into one of his charismatic grins, making me release a breath I had no idea I was holding in.

"You, darling, are a natural. The daughter of Warren and Ruby, that's for certain. Congratulations on passing your DM," Harv complimented me. I smiled. I hadn't actually killed Eduardo and had basically failed my DM, but I enjoyed having my feathers preened by Harv, just a little.

"I can't believe you doubted me. I've seen all of the James Bond movies," I joked, trying to sound as natural as possible. Harv laughed at my terrible attempt of a joke and nodded, while putting the binder in his desk. He pulled out a sheet of paper.

"Believe me, I won't ever doubt you again. Now," Harv pushed the paper toward me, "You have rightfully earned a place here as beginning agent and can start your classes."

I moaned. "Can't that wait? I want to know what's in the binder," I begged. My foot tapped anxiously at the thought of possible leads on my parents' whereabouts.

Harv shook his head, looking appalled by the very idea. "I'm afraid not, Miss Rue. The higher-level agents will go through all of the documents." I opened my mouth to complain, but Harv raised a hand to stop me.

"But…I promise you that I'll inform you if we find anything on your parents." I smiled gratefully and nodded in submission.

"Thanks, Harv," I replied. Harv smiled back.

"No, thank you, Miss Rue. Now, on to your classes…"

"I can't seem to get away from school," I muttered, picking up the paper he had laid on his desk and giving it a scan. It was my schedule. Classes started at 7a.m. and didn't end until 4p.m. A list of teachers were lined up beside insane subjects such as Deadly Arts, Stealth, Weapon Design, First Aid…and History. Couldn't forget that.

Despite that fact that I hated school, I still felt myself getting excited at the more interesting subjects listed on my schedule. "So, I get to learn stuff like walking on ceilings, and hitting pressure points and all of that cool stuff?" I asked, practically bouncing in my seat while I gripped the sides of my chair. This definitely beat public school.

Harv smiled and waved his hand toward his door. Clearly, he had better things to do. "I'm sure you'll get to that. Keep in mind that we are agents, not ninjas," he teased, with a wink. I blushed a little, realizing I was acting like an overexcited kid.

"I know that," I breezed, forcing myself to look disinterested. "Oh, yeah, I kind of…'lost' my jumpsuit during the DM. Hook me up with a new one?" I asked, while walking backwards toward the door to leave.

"One will be sent to your room. Although…I wonder how your clothes could disappear like that." My attention snapped back to Harv, expecting to see accusation written all over his face. Somehow, he must have figured out that my DM hadn't gone as smoothly as I played it off to be.

But instead of accusing, his expression was the opposite. He was leaning back in his chair, a suggestive smile on his face. I felt the heat rise to my face as I realized what he meant.

"Your hormones are worse than a teenage boy," I shot back, before storming out of his office. Seriously, right when I was beginning to think that he was a decent guy, he had to say something perverted.

The smile was back on my face as I climbed the staircase. I thought back to the beauty of above ground Los Angeles. I thought of its beautiful skyline, which I knew was lit up and shining at this time of night. Its buildings had always reminded me of stone trees jutting out of the earth and reaching for the moon. Being back above-ground had reminded me of the surreal beauty of the City of Angels.

But the fact was, it had never really been my home. No one had accepted me, had helped me, when I lived back there. No one except my friend Tara. Not Blackeye, that's for sure. At first, I thought he was just being helpful, getting me whatever I needed. I didn't know I would end up needing to pay him back. But here, I belonged and people were trying to help me find what I needed— my parents.

Did I miss L.A.? Not in the least.

***

Finally, I was back in the metallic hallways of H Corp. I looked around and was surprised to find them empty.

"I guess even here people need to sleep," I mumbled to myself as I walked down the halls. I tried to remember where the dorms were, but it took me five tries until I finally came to the right hallway. I silently cursed myself for not letting Hack finish giving me that tour the other day.

"97, 99, 101!" I proclaimed as I came up to me and Lolli's shared room. I went to knock but stopped short when I noticed one of those all-access keys taped to the door along with a little sticky note attached to it. Curious, I plucked the key from the wall and looked at the sticky note. It was written in big, loopy cursive, with hearts replacing the dots of the i's.

Here's your key, Bunny! Feel free to come on in! And don't forget: my color code is pink, blue, pink, pink!

-Lolli :)

I couldn't help but laugh a little at her naivety. Lolli was a bit too trusting, but at least we were in a safe community down here and hopefully no one would get the idea to try and break in. In fact, Lolli had known me for less than a week, and she was already acting as if we were best friends. I twisted the key so that the tip glowed pink and put it in the keyhole, then gave it a twist. I yanked open the door and walked in, ready to chastise Lolli but stopped short when I saw Lolli wrapped up in her covers, tears pouring out of her eyes.

"Lolli? You okay?" I asked, hesitantly. I walked over to her and sat carefully down on her bed beside her. She was practically sobbing. It was not pretty at all. I mean, blubbering and snot all over the place.

"Hey, it's gonna be okay," I said, trying to comfort her. I couldn't stand to see people crying. Usually I'd just tell them to suck it up, but Lolli looked as if someone had not only just ran over her puppy, but had backed up and did it a couple of more times.

"Lolli? What's—"

A sharp "shh" escaped Lolli's lips as she turned to me, holding a finger up to her mouth. My mouth slammed shut at the scary expression on her face.

Lolli slowly lifted her finger from her mouth and pointed at the TV, which I hadn't noticed, was on. I looked up and wanted to fall over. She was watching *Titanic*. And she was at the famous scene where Rose and Jack are holding onto each other in the water. This movie had to be the cheesiest movie of all time.

"Really, Lolli?" I teased, playfully pushing her shoulder. "I thought your idiot brother had got hit by a bus or something." Lolli laughed but it quickly changed into another sob.

"I love this part…!" she cried, while gasping for air.

"Breathe, Lolli," I reminded her. I looked up at the screen and felt myself smiling against my will.

"I'll never let go, Jack," Lolli and I cried out at the exact same time, mimicking Rose, although I made Rose sound like a hillbilly. By the end of the movie though, I hate to admit, Lolli and I were both sobbing and bawling on her bed like a bunch of big of babies.

"That…was so sad!" Lolli cried, blowing her nose into her blanket. I nodded, swiping at my own tears.

"I-I guess," I choked out, ending my sentence with a sob. "How did I end up crying?" Lolli shrugged and giggled a bit, causing me to do the same. I realized Lolli had unintentionally helped lift my mood a bit after the DM.

I couldn't help but laugh when I saw Lolli crawl up to the top of her bed and retrieve a big, oversized green teddy bear. Lolli's tan face flooded red and she clutched the teddy bear close to her.

"What? Frumplebuns helps me sleep better!" she said defensively, looking just like an oversized baby in her pink footsie pajamas. I just shrugged and hid my laughs while I made my way to my own bed and laid down. I shut my eyes to go to sleep, but Lolli's voice stopped me from reaching my goal since this morning—sleep!

"Harlot, if you can't go to sleep tonight, I can stay up with you."

I leaned up on my elbows and looked at her. Lolli was patting 'Frumplebuns', but looked as if her mind were elsewhere. "I mean, if you have nightmares or anything. I had them, y'know," she murmured in a quiet voice. I was taken aback by her statement. I hadn't given it much thought, but I realized that Lolli had to have taken the DM when she had first become an agent, too. She had probably killed someone. I looked at Lolli, with her angelic face and her bright, sunny attitude and couldn't imagine her hurting a fly. But, she killed someone. I felt a chill go down my spine and I looked away, back at the ceiling.

"Thanks, Lolli, but you can go to sleep. I'm fine," I promised. Lolli yawned and I could practically hear the smile coming back to her face. I turned back over to look at her. Her eyes were shut and she was wrapped up tight in her blankets, Frumplebuns snuggled close to her chest.

"Lolli…how did you wind up here?" I asked. The question had suddenly popped into my mind. She just seemed so out of place in an organization that dealt with assassinations and stuff like that. *Why would Harv choose someone as sweet as her?*

Lolli's eyes slowly opened back up and her hazel eyes met my brown ones. "It's kind of a long story…" she said, her voice trailing off. I yawned and propped myself up on my elbow, so I could get a better view of her.

"As long as it's interesting." Lolli cracked a small smile before shutting her eyes again. Her next words shocked me.

"Retro and I, we don't know who our parents are."

A thin silence hung in the air as I took a second to analyze this. Lolli continued on with her story, her voice quiet and soft.

"Well, at least our real parents. We were put into foster care when we were only little kids, like three or four. Retro said we were born in Puerto Rico, but I don't really remember. Our foster parents were always kind to us, but Retro always thought they just wanted government money, so he would be really bad until they gave us back up." I kept watching Lolli. She was staring into space, obviously reliving the memories she was telling me about.

"One day, they split me and Retro up. He went to live in New York and I stayed in California. I missed him…a lot. We didn't get to see each other for about five years, I think. I heard about him, though!" Lolli's eyes suddenly perked up and she gave me a big, sunny smile. "Did you know he's a professional model?"

"That explains a lot," I muttered, wanting to slap myself in the forehead. The slender physique, aloof attitude, and abnormally beautiful looks (not to mention having the hook-up in certain big-name nightclubs, but I was trying to forget that unfortunate incident of my life) all pointed in the direction of a fashion model, and a big-name one at that.

It seemed as though Retro had been able to maintain some of his ties to the above-ground world, judging from his summer villas and steady income as a model. Was I the only one who had to cut off all, if barely any, ties to the top world? Or was Retro the only one who was allowed such treatment?

Before I could question this, I noticed that Lolli was speaking. Lolli sat up now, her eyes looking excited. "One day, I decided to run away to find Retro. Except I only got to, like, the stoplight near my house. I was sitting there crying, when Harv showed up. He knew all about me and told me that Retro had sent him to find me. And that's when I came down here and Retro was here! I decided to become an agent, like Retro, and I've been living here since then!" Lolli finished, her eyes sparkling with excitement. I nodded, a bit deterred by how similar our stories were.

"Why did Retro become an agent?"

Lolli shrugged. "He never said. Maybe Harv asked him, too?" she guessed. She grabbed her ankles and rocked back and forth, smiling fondly. "Harv saved us and brought us here so we can find our parents together!" she said, admirably. I made an agreeing sound as I lay back down on my bed. I guess Harv had provided me with an opportunity to find my parents. I didn't worship the ground he walked on, like Lolli seemed to, but I was appreciative of him taking me under his wing.

"What about you, Bunny?" I looked over and saw that Lolli was staring at me, ready for story time. I rolled over with a grunt, so that my back was facing her.

"Basically like yours, minus the brother. I'm an only child, spoiled rotten." I admitted with a smile. I decided not to go into all of the details right then. "All I want to do is find my parents."

"Me too," Lolli whispered in a barely audible voice. "Maybe, we can all look for them together!"

I felt a smile tugging on my lips. "It's a deal."

I heard Lolli yawn behind me and the bed made a squeaky sound as she lay back down. "G'night, Bunny! We have class in the morning!"

I inwardly groaned and slapped my hands over my eyes.

Chapter Eleven

It turns out that Lolli is one of those girls who just adore school. As soon as her Tweety Bird clock went off at 6 a.m., Lolli shot out of bed like an arrow while I covered my head up with my covers and groaned. I was excited to learn, but five more minutes of sleep sounded even better. It was, after all, my first time in a long time waking up in an actual bed.

"No, not five more minutes! More like five more seconds!" Lolli said, ripping the covers off of me while brushing her teeth at the same time. Oops, had I said that out loud? I curled up in a fetal position and yawned.

"Lolli, give me my covers back!" I whined at her.

"Nope!" Lolli chirped. I watched her as she skipped over to the light switch by the door. I noticed she was wrapped up in a big, fluffy towel and had a shower cap on so I figured that she had already showered. She sent me a wicked little grin before flipping the light switch upwards.

The bright light almost blinded me. I cried out in pain and tumbled out of bed and onto the floor, feeling like a vampire who had just been exposed to sunlight.

"C'mon, Harlot! School's fun! Besides…" Lolli paused to blow on her newly painted fingernails, "…I don't want to tarnish my perfect attendance! And that includes tardies!"

I sighed and got up off of the floor. I went into the bathroom and grabbed an unused toothbrush and began to scrub at my teeth. "Fine," I said, submissively, "but I'm not going to class wearing this." I motioned with a sweep of my hand toward my greasy waitress uniform I had yet to take off.

Lolli laughed and went over to her closet and threw it open. "That's the cool thing about classes and free-time! We don't have to wear our uniforms! So, you can wear something of mine."

"No more butt-hugging jumpsuits? School's sounding better and better," I said with a grin.

Lolli giggled. "That's more like it. Ooh, how about this?" Lolli pulled out a mini-skirt and a green halter top and held it up to me. Her face fell and she frowned. I looked down at the clothes and immediately noticed the problem. Lolli's clothes were designed for people four feet and under. Being almost 5'6", her clothes were out of the question.

"…I guess my clothes aren't going to work," Lolli admitted. She rubbed her chin in thought. Suddenly, her brown eyes lit up. "Ooh, I know!"

Lolli rushed over to the opposite side of the wall, her brown curls bobbing wildly. I followed. She took out her all-access key and twisted it until it glowed silver and then tapped the wall. I watched in amazement as the metal wall wavered and shifted to resemble a big computer-like screen, just like when I had first arrived in H Corp, except this one was a bit different. There were a few icons labeled "Internet", "Call", and "Order".

Lolli sent me a grin over her shoulder. "World Wide Wall," she joked with a wink before turning back to the wall. She stood on her toes and used her key to tap on the "Order icon". The wall wavered again, and then changed to a new picture, showing a list of items that ranged from "Accessories" to "Toiletries". Lolli swiped her key on the wall in order to scroll down and then tapped on "Clothing", then "Juniors' Clothing".

My mouth dropped open when I saw pages and pages of cute clothes pop up. "Is this all for free?" I asked incredulously.

Lolli simply nodded as if it were nothing. "See anything you like?" Lolli asked, while eyeing a pink mini-skirt paired with black floral leggings. She quickly tapped the "Order" button under it, wrote her size, and then used her key to drag it to her cart.

"That would go great with my cheetah-print off-the-shoulder top and pink feather boa! Doesn't it scream—diva?" she beamed, while fanning her hands outwards. I shook my head at her over the top fashion sense and then turned my attention back to the screen. It was like walking into the mall with your parents' platinum credit card, minus the repercussions.

"This is okay," I said, pointing at a black sleeveless top with red lips plastered across the front. It included a pair of red, fingerless gloves that looked pretty cool.

Lolli sighed and made a choking motion in the air with her small hands, obviously not pleased with my selection. "I am gonna get you away from all of these dark colors, *chica*!" she promised, but she still ordered it for me. I picked out a pair of dark-blue, ripped jeans and black studded flats. Lolli completed our order while I took the time to take a much-needed shower.

I came back in the room just in time to see Lolli finishing our order. She twisted her key to black then tapped the wall again. It fizzled like a static for a second and then reverted back to its normal, metallic state.

"So, now what? We wait two weeks for it to be delivered?" I asked, plopping back down on my bed. I could do that. No clothes meant no school.

Lolli gave one of her squealing laughs and waved my comment off. "No, silly!" She threw open her closet and I was amazed to see that our ordered clothes had already appeared inside, hung and ready. I was more than a little amazed—I was creeped out.

"How'd they manage to get this in here so quickly?" I asked, while poking my head inside of the closet to search for little elves or some other phenomenon. I was starting to believe that anything could happen here.

"We have our office people keeping check on that!" Lolli explained with a wink. She gasped when she looked over at her clock. It was now 6:45. "Now come on, come on! We're gonna be late!" Lolli ripped off her towel and quickly pulled on her new leggings and pink skirt and then threw on her cheetah top. She did a little twirl and then grinned at me. I grimaced at the fact that she hadn't even bothered to cover up or go somewhere private before she decided to bare it all. We weren't at that level of friendship just yet.

"How do I look?" she chirped, giving me a Miss America wave. I gagged and decided to be honest.

"You look like one of the Cheetah Girls," I said bluntly. That's what friends are for.

Lolli pouted for a second, but her smile was back in half that time. "Joke's on you, Harlot, 'cause cheetahs don't have feathers!" she teased in a singsong voice, while throwing a purple feather boa around her neck. I sputtered out a laugh and Lolli soon joined in.

Her laugh turned into a gasp as she looked at the clock again. "6:57?! We've gotta go! Class starts in three minutes!" she panicked. I thought she might start hyperventilating so I gave her a comforting pat on the back.

"Hey, stop being so nervous. I'm the one who's the new girl, remember?" I reminded her. I was starting to feel nervous myself. It had been over a year since I had dropped out of high school and I wasn't too keen on going back to that type of environment. I didn't deal well with drama or gossip, but I was sure I would be the hot topic when it came to the gossip of H Corporation, thanks to Retro's white lie.

Lolli sent me a grin. "I keep forgetting that! You already seem like you fit right in, Bunny!" she said, giving me a big hug. "Now come on!" Lolli yanked me out of the door before I could do protest.

We practically ran down the hallways, dodging other late students and some older people too. We made it to the flight of stairs that led down to the cafeteria and the flight of stairs that led upwards. I smelled the lingering aromas of sweet oatmeal and bacon and I wanted to cry when Lolli took the stairs that led up, up, and away from my precious food. Clearly, breakfast was out of the question.

The stairs led us to a long and narrow hallway that was lined with surprisingly normal-looking lockers. The hallway was still shaped from metal but the lockers added a bit of normalcy to it.

Students dressed in everything from American Eagle to Gucci were scrambling about, slamming lockers shut, and racing to their designated classrooms. It was like I was warped right back to Dairywood High, where I had attended when I was living with my wicked aunt. I forgot for a second that I was miles underground, but Lolli's sharp pull brought me back to reality.

"Who do you have first period?" she asked in a hurried voice. I thought quickly.

"Deadly Arts with Haze?" I half-asked. I was still getting used to the weird names that were used down here, including my own. Lolli let out a low whistle and shook her head. I didn't take that as a good sign. She might as well have did that throat-slicing motion and said "You're dead!"

"His class meets in there," she informed me in a pitiful voice, while pointing to a door at the far end of the hall. She perked back up immediately and gave me a bright smile. "Good luck!" With those last well wishes, Lolli dashed off towards her own class. She turned around and gave me one last smile and a wave before she disappeared inside.

Just then, the bell rang and I was left alone in the hallway. I suddenly wanted Lolli, no matter how hyper she was, to be back with me.

I slowly made my way down the hallway, my palms sweaty and my stomach cramping. I was so not ready for this. I stood outside of the door Lolli had pointed out, staring down at the handle. It was my first day, I was late, and I was sweaty. This wasn't going good so far.

After saying a quick prayer, I pushed open the door and was about to step inside, but froze in the doorway.

I wasn't in a classroom. At least, not the normal type with desks and chairs. Instead, I found myself in a room that resembled a dance studio. There was some pretty hardcore training equipment pushed against the mirrored walls, and big blue mats were scattered around the wooden floor.

That's when I finally noticed the other students. I stared open-mouthed as people wrestled each other on the mats like they were feuding bears on Animal Planet. People were getting drop-kicked and karate chopped out there. One poor girl was getting her face smashed into the mat. This could not have been my class. It seemed as if Lolli had accidentally directed me to the H Corporation's zoo.

Just as I had turned around to leave, a sharp, deep voice called out. "Where do you think you're going?" I turned back around and saw that all of the sparring people had stopped mid-punch to stare at me.

"Is someone talking to me?" I asked, pointing at myself. A tall man lumbered over to me, his arms crossed, his golden eyes narrowed into slits. He looked like an extremely ticked-off Billy Blanks who was ready to try out some new Tae-Bo moves.

"Is someone talking to you? Are you the only one going somewhere?" he roared in my face. All of my usual smart-aleck comments flew out of the door and I wanted to go right with them. I stared up at his golden eyes and felt like I was going to wet myself.

"W-Well, I was—" I began but his sharp voice cut me off.

"You were what? Trying to skip my class?!" he roared again, keeping his arms folded as he leaned toward my face. I tried to back away but I bumped into the door. I was going to be murdered on my first day of school.

"No, I wasn't, I was just—"

"No, what?

"No, I wasn't going to skip—"

"No, *what*?"

"No…sir?" I asked, my voice coming out in a squeak. This seemed to pacify the beast, because he closed his eyes and took a calming breath. He opened his eyes and fixed me with his golden-eyed stare.

"What's your name?" he asked, tilting his head upwards and looking down at me.

"Lola—I mean Harlot Rue…sir," I quickly added. He nodded and then pointed to an empty mat.

"Go sit there while I get you into the system," he ordered. I did as he commanded and plopped down on the mat, my palms still sweaty from my encounter with who I knew had to have been Mr. Haze. I cut my eyes at all of the other students who were still staring at me, daring them to say a word. They all quickly went back to their death matches, talking in hushed whispers. Mr. Haze's heavy footsteps alerted me to his approaching. I quickly stood up and faced him.

"Okay, Harlot. Welcome to Intro to Deadly Arts. Here we learn the moves that could save your butt out there during a mission. Let's get you a partner so we can see where you're at." Mr. Haze motioned a finger and I was surprised when a beautiful girl strode over to us, looking bored senseless.

She could have passed as a foreign model. Her dark hair fell like waves over her narrow shoulders and ended at the small of her back. Her skin was flawless, as if she had never once had acne in her entire life. Her brown, narrow eyes were glazed over with boredom as she studied her nails.

"Harlot, this is Carma. Carma, Harlot. She's new, so go easy on her," Mr. Haze said. "And no hair-pulling or hitting anywhere near the face." He nodded at us, then stepped back, waiting for us to move.

Carma and I stared at each other for a few seconds before Carma put her hands on her bony hips and squinted her nut-brown eyes at me.

"Hey. Your hands better not come anywhere near my face or I'll have you and your bad dye job tossed right back out in the streets," she said, cutting her eyes at me and then turning away and walking over to her side of the mat. I stared after her in disbelief. Forget about her face: I was going straight for her throat.

I walked over to my side of the mat and faced her, ready to kick her scrawny butt. I had been in plenty of brawls on Skid Row and back in Dairywood and I had never lost one.

"This is just a practice match, Harlot, so don't feel bad when you lose," Mr. Haze explained. His confidence in me was unbelievable. "I just want to see where you're at so I can pair you with someone who's at your same level." He stepped off the mat.

His confidence in me was unbelievable. I would show him and Miss I-Wear-High-Heels-To-A-Fight. I definitely wasn't about to lose to some uppity—

BAM!

In one quick movement, Carma had sent me a sharp kick to my stomach with her heel. I gasped and doubled over in pain. Maybe Mr. Haze should have also mentioned to take off any sharp objects. I saw another flash of purple coming toward me and I quickly dodged to the left and automatically swung hard with a right hook. I felt my fist connect with her cheek, feeling pleased with myself. The pleasure quickly faded as I realized I had done just exactly what Mr. Haze had said not to—punched her in the face.

With a hysterical cry of complete rage, Carma had tackled me down on the ground and put me in a headlock. I struggled against her in vain. Although she looked to weigh less than a twig, she was able to keep me pinned to the floor.

After a few minutes of struggling, I sighed and gave up.

"Okay, get the heck off of me!" I choked out. Carma sniffed haughtily and stood, straightening out her purple peasant blouse, while I stayed on the ground, curled up in a ball. I looked up and noticed her cheek was a bit red. I couldn't help but smile with satisfaction.

"You're not as tough as everyone's been saying," she said, successfully wiping the smile off of my face. She gave me a disdainful look and then, with a flip of her lustrous hair, she walked away. I glared after her but didn't dare move. My neck felt as if it had been run over by a semi. I gingerly flipped over on my back and sighed. Mr. Haze walked over to me and towered above me. He shook his head.

"Pitiful, just pitiful," he remarked. "Take a break and then we'll try you with a few others." He shook his head at me one more time before stomping off to shatter some other innocent student's ego.

A pale hand with dark blue nails came into my vision. I followed the hand up to its owner and was surprised to see Marc, the Operator from my DM, grinning at me. I took his hand gratefully and he lifted me to my feet, causing me to wince a bit at the pain that surged through my neck.

"Wow, Carma did a number on you!" he said, dusting off my clothes like he was my mom. I looked away, embarrassed.

Marc patted my back and gave me a reassuring smile. "You shouldn't be embarrassed. Carma's the best fighter in class, and you managed to land a hit!" Marc gave a weak punch in the air that wouldn't have knocked down a gnat. He gave me a sheepish grin before continuing. "She's gone undefeated for a year, so she's basically a pro boxer in stilettos. Don't feel so bad," he joked. I cracked a smile at the visual image. Marc gasped, bringing his hand up to his chest in a dramatic manner.

"Did you just smile? And I heard that you were the Ice Queen on Earth!" he said. This time I laughed out loud, but it quickly died away.

"Seems like everyone's been hearing a lot about me," I said with a touch of bitterness to my voice. I had only been here for about two days and my name was already a hot topic underground.

Marc gave me a shocked look. "Seems like? You're the new girl who took out that giant on her DM with only a pocket knife. Everyone's talking about you!"

"Stop exaggerating," I said with a nonchalant shrug. On the inside, I was dying with laughter. Retro had certainly done a number on the masses.

"I'm not!" Marc huffed. "But really, don't worry about Carma." We both shot Carma a hateful look. She was now flirting with a couple of guys who looked like they were under a spell, judging from the way they all were leaning toward her as if she were a magnet. Sensing that we were looking at her, Carma looked our way and gave us a rueful grin and a little wave then went back to her flirting.

"She really gets under my skin." Marc eyed her purple stilettos. "Though she does have incredible taste in shoes." I laughed and pushed him playfully while he laughed too.

Even though I was laughing, I felt that familiar stubbornness churning inside me. I was going to beat Carma, even if it took me the entire year. But I'd say it would only take a week.

***

After a few more failed sparring matches, the bell for next period rang. Marc and I walked out of class, bruised and tired.

"You say we only spar once a week, right?" I asked Marc in a breathless voice.

Marc looked worse than I felt. He nodded and checked his nails, sighing once he saw they were all still intact. "Once is more than enough for an Operator. I'll take hearing Haze scream lectures at us over fighting those amazons any day," he harrumphed. We were both laughing at this until our laughter was drowned out by a bunch of loud shouting and talking coming from ahead.

A large group of students had surrounded two boys engaged in a heated argument by the lockers. Marc and I looked at each other and then edged closer to the crowd, our curiosity getting the better of us. I had just formally met Marc last period, and I was already taking a liking to him.

The two kids couldn't look any different, besides the fact that they were both male. One was gawky and tall, with glasses that rivaled Hack's in size and a crooked, green and yellow bowtie tied around his neck. The other was built like a sturdy house, wearing a sideways cap and an oversized ego.

"So, what you're saying is that we should stay cramped up in this hole and go out only once every two years to try and stop the E Corp?" the jock was saying, while jeering at the onlookers in the crowd. Some students made sounds of agreement and nodded at each other.

"Exactly! We're safer just staying here instead of trying to incite a full-blown war!" the geek shot back, earning a few shouts of agreement from the crowd.

"We could end this stupid rivalry with the E Corp in one blow instead of sending us off to die every now and then!"

"Yeah, we'd all die at once!"

"What a wimp. Why don't you just go back to the classroom, Techie? That's all you guys are good at." The jock gave the nerd a small, dismissive wave and turned his back on him, while the crowd "oohed" including Marc, of course. I was a bit offended by his dismissal of Techies. I knew that Hack was one and he was helping out in the best way he knew how.

The nerd's face went from pasty white to beet red in a second. "Techies do more than Field Agents like you, you testosterone-filled jerk!" he shrieked at the top of his lungs. The excited crowd "oohed" again and then gasped when the jock took a step toward the geek and shoved him back into the crowd. The geek, his glasses slightly askew now, scrambled forward, swinging his arms like windmills.

Before any real action could happen, Mr. Haze had stomped out into the hallway, his golden eyes blazing. "Get your ends to class before I drag you there myself!" he shouted. All of the students scattered quickly, even Marc, leaving me standing there alone. I glared after him. How was I supposed to know where my next class was supposed to be?

I heard heavy footsteps behind me.

"Rue, was it?" I heard Mr. Haze's baritone voice growl from behind me. I hesitantly turned around. Mr. Haze was towering over me, his bulging, muscular arms folded. He shook his head.

"I see you're gonna be a troublemaker," he muttered. "NOW GO!"

He didn't have to tell me twice. I scrambled toward the nearest door marked Class D—First Aid, and quickly went inside. I looked around and sighed with relief when I noticed it was just a normal classroom. I didn't think I could take one more spar, at least not without winding up in the emergency room.

Everyone was already in their seats, chatting excitedly about the action in the hallway. A wide majority seemed to mostly be leaning toward the "full-blown war" side of the argument. I didn't actually have a side. I just wanted to get the job done and get my parents back. They could participate in however many wars they wanted to when we were gone.

I noticed a young woman perched behind the front desk, a pretty blonde dressed in a white skirt-suit, who I guessed was the teacher. She smiled at me and waved me over, looking much too excited for someone who had to teach a class full of hormonal teenagers. I smiled back and walked over to her.

"Hi," I said, once I reached her desk, "I'm Harlot Rue, the new student. Am I in the right class?" She nodded and smiled wider, leaning forward, like she had a big secret to tell.

"Yes, you are and I know who you are!" she squealed in a flighty falsetto voice. "I've heard all about you! Please, take a seat wherever you like and we'll get started with class." I nodded, a little unnerved that even a teacher had been gossiping about me, then turned around and scanned the classroom for a seat. There was one empty seat, in the far back. It was smack in between two people I was in no mood to see at the moment—Retro and Carma.

I was a bit taken aback to see Retro in a classroom. He couldn't be younger than twenty and he was sitting at a desk with the rest of the teenagers. Then, I noticed that there were a few other older students scattered around the class, mingling with the other students. It reminded me a bit of how a college setting must be.

I walked over to the empty desk and sat down, trying not to look to my left, where I knew Retro's smirking face awaited, or to my right, where I knew I'd have to face Carma's inhuman beauty and scowl.

"Are you telling me that I'll be graced with Red's presence every day during this class?" Retro's silky voice reached my ears above the noise of the other students. I turned in my seat to face him and had to do a double take at his appearance.

I had yet to see him in his casual attire and he still looked just as aggravatingly handsome as ever in his long sleeved, turquoise shirt and dark jeans.

"You okay, Red?" I snapped out of my thoughts to find Retro giving me a curious smile. I flushed, embarrassed.

"Yeah," I mumbled, while trying to maintain a neutral expression, which was becoming harder and harder to do around Retro.

Retro glanced around before he rotated in his seat to face me. He gestured me over with a tilt of his head. I looked around curiously before I leaned over. Retro leaned over in his seat as well, putting his mouth near my ear.

"How are you liking the hero treatment?" he whispered with a hint of a smile. I smiled back. Although I still felt guilty about how things went down, including my unforeseen mental breakdown, I was starting to enjoy the perks of being a hero.

"It's okay, I guess. What exactly did you tell everyone?" I whispered back. Retro cocked his eyebrow and shrugged, innocently.

"The truth—that you are a very talented student-agent."

I guffawed at this. "Yeah, right. Everyone's looking at me like I just resurrected Lazarus," I joked. Retro's face became confused.

"Lazarus? What's that?" he asked, as if he had never heard the word before.

"It's not a what, it's a who. You know, from the Bible?" I hinted.

A look of recognition crossed his face. "I haven't looked at that book since I signed my first modeling contract. I used to read it a lot when I was a kid. *Mi abuelita* would read me the stories all the time." I smiled at the thought of a young Retro being read to by his grandmother.

"My parents read them to me when I was younger, too. What was your favorite story?" I asked, as I relaxed my strained position and rested my elbows on my thighs. Retro seemed to give my question some legitimate thought before he answered.

"The one about the boy and the giant," he announced with a frown. "I can't remember their names, though."

"David and Goliath, right? I like that one, too."

Retro nodded, a smile lighting up his sharp features. "Yeah, that's it. I liked hearing about someone doing the impossible. Y'know, being able to stand up to someone so much bigger than him." His face had a more serious tone to it now. I hadn't been able to read much of the Bible since I had run away from my aunt's house, but I always remembered the stories in it. Most days, those stories were the only things that were able to keep me going.

"You'll have to show me that one about Lazarus sometime," Retro said, breaking into my thoughts. I sat up and stretched.

"I didn't come down here toting the Holy Bible," I reminded him with a yawn.

Retro chuckled as he leaned back in his seat, our secretive conversation over. "There's a whole section of religious books in the library. I can show them to you whenever you'd like," he offered. I spun back in my seat to face the front. Our teacher was beginning to gather her papers and looked ready to start class.

"Sure," I replied. Someone nearby me had begun to loudly clear their throat, obviously trying to grab someone's attention. I looked over and saw Carma eyeing Retro and me out of the corner of her eyes while she applied a fresh shade of rosy pink lipstick. Her face had disgust written all over it.

As interested as I was in that little soap-opera waiting to happen, Mrs. Frankie began to talk and I didn't get a chance to think too much about it.

"Hello, hello class! How are we this morning?" she practically sang. We all murmured half-hearted, "fine's" and Mrs. Frankie beamed, her perfect white teeth practically blinding me. Lolli and she must get along great.

"That's great! Well, before we get started with class, I would like to introduce everyone to a very special young woman. You may have heard of her already." She caught my eye and gave me a big wink.

Oh no. I sank down in my seat, chewing my bottom lip. *Please, don't let her call me, please, don't let her call me, please don't let her—*

"Miss Harlot Rue!" *Shoot.* "Please stand up so we can all get to know your pretty, little face!" Feeling my pretty, little face burning up, I slowly rose from my seat and crossed my arms over my chest. I focused on Mrs. Frankie's face, although I felt all of my classmates' eyes drilling holes into me.

"Everyone, this is Harlot Rue! Harlot, why don't you tell us something about yourself?" Mrs. Frankie asked, completely oblivious to the embarrassment she was causing me.

I exhaled through my nose. "Um…well, my name's Harlot," I said lamely. A few laughs sounded around the classroom and I heard Carma mutter something that sounded like "duh". If I had the power to disappear at anytime and anyplace, I would be using that power right about now.

Mrs. Frankie gave a tiny laugh before she continued my torture. "Well, yes, Harlot! But, why don't you tell us about yourself! What type of things are you interested in? Besides beating up bad guys!" she added with a cheerful grin. I was surprised when some of my classmates clapped and whooped with delight. I felt a little of my confidence return as I began to answer her question.

"…I like food, too." Laughter erupted around the classroom and Mrs. Frankie tried unsuccessfully to get the room to quiet down. Mrs. Frankie shot me a grin that looked a little forced this time.

"Why, that's, uh, great! We should probably get on with class," she suggested quickly. I sat back in my seat, grateful that my torture was over.

"That was very eloquent, Red," Retro said while shaking his head at me and laughing. I shrugged again.

"It was the first thing that came to mind," I admitted. I heard Carma snort from beside me.

"I bet it was," she murmured while pretending to focus on the front of the classroom. I turned around in my seat, ready to ask her what her problem was, but Mrs. Frankie's voice stopped me as she began to teach class. I slowly turned back in my seat, feeling confused. Somehow, I had managed to make an enemy out of Carma.

***

After class, I quickly headed toward the lunchroom, my growling stomach demanding it be fed. I thought I had outrun Retro, but the pretty boy was quick, and soon I had acquired a walking companion. I don't know why, but I found myself beginning to enjoy Retro's presence, which was dangerous. I didn't want to become too close to Retro, who seemed to enjoy being around me as well. He was a good guy at heart, but I didn't want to get distracted while during my stay in H Corp.

"Hey, why didn't you wait for me?" Retro asked, sounding genuinely hurt. I was going to throw him an insult but decided against it. He had saved my neck a couple of times, so I guess I could be a little sweeter.

"I couldn't wait all day while you flirted with Mrs. Frankie," I voiced, but I slowed down my pace for him to catch up. Retro snickered as he threw an arm around my shoulders.

"First of all, it's Miss Frankie…" he said, stressing the word "miss", "…and second of all, jealous much?" he teased, tickling my chin with his other hand. I snapped at his fingers with my teeth and he quickly drew away, cursing. I cackled at his freaked out expression, but he didn't seem to find it as funny as I did.

"Were you a piranha in another life?" Retro muttered as we continued our pace. "Another life" brought something to mind that I had almost forgotten about.

"Lolli told me about how you were able to reunite with each other so that you can look for your parents together," I told him. Retro's expression suddenly darkened and he looked at me, his eyes uneasy.

"Really...," was all he said. I was a bit thrown off by his reaction but I decided to continue talking.

"It was sweet," I declared. Retro looked surprised by my words. He tried to turn his head away from me, but I could see that his complexion had turned red.

"Awww, you're blushing!" I cooed, while gesturing toward his face with my index fingers. Retro turned his head even more, trying to block his face. This just made me laugh harder.

Retro finally looked at me, and I could see that his blush had died down a bit. His smile looked a little shy and I couldn't help but notice how cute that was.

"So, what about you? What were you up to before you became Harlot?" Retro asked. "From what Harv told everyone, your parents were kidnapped and you've been living with your mother's sister?" I noticed he had changed the subject, but I decided against calling him on it.

I didn't feel like discussing the not-so-pleasant life I had led before I came here, but I knew hi story, so it was only fair. "I was homeless," I said, making sure that my voice was devoid of emotion. I heard Retro's footsteps come to an abrupt halt. I kept walking.

"Homeless?!" Retro nearly shouted, "You didn't have a house to live in?" His hand had shot out and grabbed my wrist, forcing me to stand where I was. I looked over my shoulder at him. His face was etched with concern and pity. I already knew where this was headed. I was so sick of everyone pitying me, acting like I was a lost puppy or a charity case.

"Harv never mentioned that you were alone out there," Retro speculated, talking more to himself than me. "Where did you live? Did you even live in a house?"

I yanked away from his grasp, surprising him. "I don't need you to feel sorry for me," I assured him in a harsh tone. I began to walk away but he grabbed my shoulder this time. I ripped away from him again, feeling tears building in my eyes. I hated when people treated me like I was less than them, just because I was homeless. I didn't like the feeling of being looked down on.

Retro was insistent. He grabbed onto my wrist again and pulled me so that I was facing him. I frowned up at him, knowing that I wouldn't be able to keep running from this conversation.

Retro fixed me with a hard look. "Why shouldn't I feel sorry for you?" he asked, sounding angry. "No one should have to be alone, not when we're so young!" We gazed at one another in silence. The only noise that I could hear was his angry breathing as his chest heaved up and down. He took a deep breath to calm himself before releasing my wrist. He looked away, fixing his hazel eyes on the wall behind my head.

I hadn't missed the "we" part of his speech. Obviously, there was something about his past that he wasn't telling me. I waited for him to say more.

Finally, he did.

"I had to live like that, too, at one point. So, I don't feel sorry for you. I just…I understand how it is." His eyes never left the wall and I felt as if he were reliving some time, long ago. "I just want to let you know that you don't have to live like that anymore. We have a home here." Without realizing what I was doing, my hand began to reach out for his own, but I stopped myself just in time. I let my hand drop to my side and instead gave him a weak smile.

"You're right. I'm sorry. I guess I shouldn't have assumed," I apologized. Retro looked up at me, and I was relieved to see that he was wearing his old smirk, although his eyes still looked a little distant.

"You know what they say about assuming."

"Ha," I jeered. "You know, whenever you're finished with modeling, you should become a comedian." This earned an honest laugh out of Retro, and I felt myself smiling as well. I felt as if I was starting to see the true Retro, past the veil of cockiness and aloofness he hid behind. I still couldn't help but want to know more about his past life. I wanted to know about his foster parents and how it felt to be separated from Lolli, the only family he had left to hang onto. I knew there was much more to his story than he was saying, but I wouldn't push it—for now.

Besides, he was right. We had a new home here. Sure, it was different, but we were all together here, pushed down below by the unforgiving hand of fate. We were all connected by the loss of loved ones, by the fact that we had nowhere left to go. I had a newfound respect of Harv, the man who had created all of this and brought so many of us together for a good cause.

I sped up my pace again as we entered the cafeteria, and Retro didn't bother to keep up. I figured he wanted some time to himself. The cafeteria line moved quickly, and soon I had piled a pepperoni and cheese calzone, crispy fries, and salad on my plate. I grabbed a can of lemon-lime soda and then looked around for a table to sit at. I was surprised to see Carma, the evil wench, waving at me from her table, which was smack dab in the middle of the cafeteria. I shot her a confused look.

What did she want with little, old me? Deciding to see for myself, I cautiously approached her table, which was full of jocks and preppy looking girls. *Why did I feel as if I had just walked onto the set of some corny teen flick?*

"What is it?" I asked flatly. There was no need for niceties; she had already made her distaste of me well known. Carma took a second to reapply her lip gloss in her compact before giving her reflection a smack. She closed the compact and smiled sweetly at me.

"Harlot, right?" she said, as if she had forgotten my name in the course of five minutes. "I just wanted to tell you that I'm sorry if I was too hard on you in Deadly Arts today," she said, giving me a sympathetic pout. I resisted the urge to punch her in the mouth and tried my best to smile.

"Don't worry, I'll get you back next time," I said, good-naturedly. Carma's friends all snickered and whispered "as if." "As if" I wasn't standing right there.

"Oh, I seriously doubt that. But feel free to try." She batted her lashes at me and then turned back to her friends. I was clearly dismissed. I stood there, staring at her. I couldn't believe such an abomination was walking the Earth. Seriously, what gave some girls the idea that they were better than someone?

Carma turned back to face me. "Um, you can run along now, *Harlot*," she jeered in a disgusted voice and then she flicked her hands dismissively in the opposite direction. I was at a loss for words, as her faux friends continued to giggle at me. I would never understand why girls felt the need to be catty towards one another. But, like the saying goes, two can play that game.

"Sure thing, Carma. And...you might want to hold off on that calzone." I leaned down and whispered the next part in her ear, but it was loud enough for her entire table to hear. "Your face is looking a little swollen." Carma gasped and clutched her cheek, still swollen from the solid right hook I had delivered earlier.

With wild laughter echoing behind me, I strolled away from Queen Carma and her Clones of the Lunch Table, with some serious swagger in my step.

I felt like laughing myself. Even miles underground, there was still the typical Queen Bee and all the drama that came with her. The only difference was that somehow I had worked my way onto her Most Hated List and for that last stunt, I'm sure I jumped up to number one on the list.

At my old school, I had stayed under the radar, away from the other students, always awaiting the day I turned sixteen and was officially allowed to drop out. I hadn't had to deal with peer pressure or any of the stuff that everyone says happens in high school. Luckily for me, it seemed that H Corp was not in short supply when it came to high school immaturity.

"Hey, Bunny, over here!" I looked around and saw Lolli, Hack, and Marc waving me over from the table in the far corner. I was happy to see that they were all already friends. Sighing with relief, I headed over to them and sat down heavily in front of Marc and next to Lolli. I couldn't help but notice that Retro was missing, but I didn't bring it up.

"I saw the claws come out over there with Carma!" Marc said, pawing at me like he was a big cat. I laughed and swatted his hands away.

"No claws came out, at least not that much. What's Carma's problem?" I pondered aloud, before taking a big, gooey bite out of my cheesy calzone. You would think that H Corp was trying to fatten us up like pigs, judging by all of the greasy yet delicious foods they fed us on a daily basis.

"What's not her problem?" Marc jested while stabbing at his salad. He looked up at me with a mischievous look. "I heard she was raised by trolls for parents in the Far East. She ended up eating them."

Lolli gave him a condescending look. "That's not true and you know it, Marc! She's just…," Lolli was obviously struggling to find the right words to describe Carma. She twirled her petite hands around, as if she were trying to grasp for the necessary word in the air.

Her face lit up and she snapped her fingers. "Confused!"

"Confused?" Hack asked questioningly. Lolli nodded, smiling as if she had just found the cure to cancer.

"Yes, confused! She doesn't mean to be so mean! I don't think that she knows she's hurting other people."

"Oh, she knows," I muttered, while rubbing my sore neck.

Marc snapped his fingers and I noticed a feverish look take over his face. "Oh, that reminds me!" he bubbled, his face glowing with the excitement of gossip. "Did you guys hear about how Carma totally went to town on Har—?"

"Marc, your food is getting cold," I said loudly, expertly cutting him off before he could drop the bomb on my friends. I didn't want the world to know that I had been beaten up by Carma during my first day of class.

Marc sent me a knowing grin and shrugged before returning to his chicken tenders. He dipped one of the fried strips into his honey mustard dip and bit into it. "Fine, fine. I won't say a word," he promised with a mouthful of chicken. Lolli began to immediately pester Marc with questions, so I was glad when Hack piped up.

"I-I'm glad you're back safe, Harlot," Hack said while repeatedly dropping his eyes from mine to his platter of fries.

"Me too," I responded truthfully, with a smile that Hack returned shyly.

Lolli wrapped her arms around my neck, thankfully forgetting about Marc's earlier comment, for the time being. "My new best friend was almost killed! But have we got something to lift your spirits!" she mused while giving the rest of the table a devilish smirk. I looked around at my newfound group of friends, a sense of happiness flooding my emotions. I wasn't sure of the exact definition of friend, but these three, along with Retro, seemed to fit the bill.

I noticed that Marc was giving Lolli the same devilish smile while Hack looked utterly confused. "What are you talking about?" Hack and I asked at the same time.

Marc leaned toward me and whispered, "One word: par-tay."

"That's two words," Lolli voiced. She giggled. "You're so dumb sometimes." Marc gave Lolli a mock concerned look and patted her hand sympathetically.

"Of course it's two words, dear."

"I didn't hear about any parties…." Hack mumbled, looking dejected and as out of the loop as always.

"What kind of party is it?" I asked. I didn't know whether to be excited or not. I had never been to a party before. I had never been invited to one either, so that's probably the reason why.

"Dorm party in Room 217 to celebrate your successful DM. Word is you brought Harv some pretty valuable info and everyone wants to celebrate!" Marc cheered, while pumping his fist skyward. Lolli joined in and they began to chant "Party, party!" I covered my face with embarrassment but laughed. I had never met anyone like the people I was seated by at that moment.

"Room 217?" Hack squawked. "B-But that's my room!"

"Are you sure?" Marc asked with a confused look.

"Well, it was my room the last time I checked!" Hack cried, seeming completely outraged. I'm sure I would be outraged as well, if someone had decided to throw a party in my room and hadn't had the decency to tell me about it.

"A party in my honor? I'm flattered," I said, lifting my hand to my chest. I couldn't battle away the feeling of guilt creeping up on me. I had done absolutely nothing to deserve a party. "Speaking of flattery," I said, "where's your brother at, Lolli?" Lolli finally removed her arms from my neck so that she could look around the cafeteria. Her face brightened and she pointed with her finger at a table just a few yards from our own.

"He's over there with his girlfriend!" she beamed.

Wait, girlfriend?

I looked in the direction she was pointing and felt as if someone had dumped a cooler filled with freezing water over my head.

Retro was sitting at a familiar table. In fact, it was a table that I had recently made a short pit stop at. He was seated by Carma, smiling in admiration as she ran her fingers through his hair.

I had to be hallucinating.

I continued to watch as Retro removed her hand from his hair and brought it to his mouth. He gave it an affectionate kiss, making Carma's face light up.

Why wasn't the hallucination going away?

"He's such a cutie. He could do so much better than that trashy thing," Marc interrupted my wishful thinking with a sigh. He sent jealous rays at Carma, who couldn't care less as she continued to paw at Retro's hair.

"Marc, for the last time, my brother does not play for your team," Lolli said, giving him a sympathetic pat on his hand this time. Marc snatched his hand away with a grunt and flung his eyes toward the ceiling.

The whole time I couldn't tear my eyes away from the nightmarish scene playing before my eyes.

Retro was dating Carma.

Carma was dating Retro.

It wasn't trigonometry, it wasn't even kindergarten math. Retro was with Carma. *But…but why was he always so nice to me?* I knew all of those times he had complimented me and made me laugh hadn't just been him playing nice. It had to have been, though. Guys liked to toy around with girls and their emotions, right? That's what Tara always used to tell me. I had already seen him doing the same thing with Rebel during my Labeling.

A bitter, putrid feeling bubbled in my chest, but I refused to call it jealousy. It had to just be gas. Nauseous, stomach-clenching, teeth-gritting gas. I tore my eyes from the couple, feeling disappointed.

"But, if he has a girlfriend, why does she put up with him flirting like he does?" I asked, trying to sound as disinterested as possible.

Hack cleared his throat, raring to go into Einstein mode. "Well, from what he tells me, they both have some type of agreement that it's okay to talk/flirt with members of the opposite sex as long as previously mentioned persons know that Retro and Carma are the ones who are actually in a dating relationship," he explained, giving me a headache in the process.

It was confirmed. Retro was a polygamist in the making. I couldn't help but steal another look at them, along with the rest of my friends. Carma was now cackling loudly at something Retro had said. She leaned towards him and began whispering something in his ear that he found just oh-so hilarious.

I sounded so jealous. But I wasn't. I was not jealous of stupid Retro or his lenient girlfriend, who seemed to be enjoying each and every second of touching his hair.

I needed a slap to the face. The only reason I was acting jealous was because he was dating Carma. Anyone else and I wouldn't have cared.

Nope, not at all.

I turned back to my friends. I could barely feel the pain that came with squeezing my plastic fork a little too hard.

"So, enough about them!" I said, sounding louder than intended. "Who decided to throw me this party?" It was a desperate attempt at a subject change, but I needed something else to focus on. Lolli smiled widely.

"Hack's roommate! My brother, of course!"

Of course.

Chapter Twelve

Finally, the school part of the day was over. Lolli and I were trying to find something suitable to wear to the party that night, by way of the World Wide Wall. I had already talked Lolli out of a puffy-sleeved pink monstrosity of a mini-dress and tiger-print pumps while she had shot down my dreams of wearing a cute black corset top and red skinny jeans with my black flats.

We were at a standstill.

"Lolli, I know that you're prejudiced against black, but you're going to just have to deal," I joked, struggling to reach around her and tap my dream outfit with my key. Lolli blocked me with her short arms like a middle school football player.

"I love you, Bunny, but I'm not going to allow you to become emo!" she bawled, as if she were the spokesperson for a tobacco-free campaign. Her melodramatics were enough to make me give in. I fell back on her bed laughing and eventually Lolli fell beside me, her cheeks rosy from laughter.

I smiled at her. "I'll wear something that doesn't have too much black in it if you wear something that doesn't have pink in it." I watched Lolli bounce this around in her head before she beamed and bobbed her head in agreement.

We sat up and began our search with renewed energy until we had found the perfect outfits and ordered them. Lolli hopped over to the closet and swung out our two new outfits, grinning from ear to ear.

Lolli had settled on a cute, strapless, purple top paired with a denim mini and a pair of matching purple and zebra-print pumps. She had tried to get the outfit in 'magenta' but I had countered that it was too close to pink, as was carnation.

My outfit consisted of a white romper with a chunky gray belt around the waist and a pair of dark heels with wood platforms. It was girly but somehow I still liked it. We got ready while Lolli rushed to fill me in on all of the boys to talk to at the party and which ones to avoid.

"Dip is this really cute guy, but he has this really bad habit of chewing tobacco, so you might want to stay away from him," Lolli informed me, giving me a disgusted face to make her point. She pulled her top down over her curls and pulled it around her chest. "Then there's Stag. He's okay, I guess. If you're into guys who burp a lot and talk about nothing but cars. I guess it comes with being an Operator. And then there's Trigger and Magnet." Lolli paused and gave me a low whistle when she saw that I was fully dressed. "Bunny, you look absolutely magnetic!"

"Magnetic?" I questioned, raising an eyebrow as I studied myself in her floor-length mirror. I hoped she meant beautiful. The romper fit me perfectly, successfully drawing attention away from my flat chest and more on my long legs. "You mean like…static…?"

"No," Lolli laughed, "I mean like attractive!" I smiled at her and did a pitiful excuse of a curtsy.

"Well, in that case, you look magnetic too, Lolli," I returned. Lolli curtsied in return (which looked a trillion times better than mine) before she shone her teeth at me.

"So, what're we waiting for? Let's go to your party!" Lolli hummed a melody as she began dancing her way to the door.

"You were about to tell me something about these guys named Trigger and Magnet," I reminded her as she opened the door. She waved their names off as if they were ghosts.

"Oh yeah. Forget about those two. Last year, they were part of this prank that got them suspended from missions for three months." I logged that little tidbit of info away as we made our way down the hall. I could already feel the bass from Room 217 throbbing through the hallway before we had even made it to the door. Once we made it inside, it was almost deafening.

Retro's room was double the size of me and Lolli's room, and every inch of it was covered with teens dancing and partying in the dark. In typical Lolli fashion, we had to arrive right on the hour the party was scheduled to begin. I was surprised that a horde of people had already shown up.

"Hey, look! It's our very own assassin!" a drunken voice called out. Immediately, all eyes fell on Lolli and me.

I inclined my head nervously at the onlookers while Lolli smiled and waved like we were the star float in a small town parade.

I was surprised when people began to chant my name, which embarrassed me even further. Eventually everyone went back to dancing and I sighed with relief. I hated being the center of attention, especially when I didn't rightfully deserve to be in the spotlight.

"Let's go stand somewhere so we can scope the room a little better," Lolli shouted in my ear, forcing me to bend down so I could hear her. I nodded. This was completely out of my element. I had no idea what I was supposed to be doing at a party, so I'd follow Lolli to the moon and back if she suggested it.

We made our way over to the corner of the room, making sure to dodge the corners that were laden with touchy couples wrapped together.

We stood there for a while, watching the party around us and bouncing slightly to the music. "Hey, I like this song!" Lolli cried as a loud dubstep song filled the room. A cheer from the masses proved that everyone else agreed. I had never heard of it. Before I could say as much to Lolli, she had grabbed my elbow and dragged me to the middle of the makeshift dance floor.

"What are you doing?" I laughed as Lolli began to jump from foot to foot and dance like a wild person.

"C'mon, don't tell you can't dance!" Lolli mouthed while grinning. I laughed in shock as Lolli grabbed my hands and we began dancing together. Usually I wouldn't dance in front of crowds, but no one seemed to be paying much attention to us, so I decided to just loosen up and have fun.

We were laughing and dancing back to back when I heard Lolli gasp. "Ooh, there's that cute kid from my computer class!" Lolli squealed, tugging my arm and pointing at a cute guy with tattoos and zigzags braiding all around his head. He looked over at us from across the room and flashed a smile. Lolli grinned back, instantly enraptured. I could see there was no changing her mind.

"He's cute. Why don't you go dance with him?" I offered, although I didn't really want to be left with no one to talk to.

"You don't mind me leaving you here, do you?" she asked, looking up at me with sympathetic eyes. It would probably make for a boring party, standing alone by myself, but I didn't want to ruin Lolli's night.

"Sure, go ahead," I said. Lolli squealed with delight. I couldn't help but laugh behind my hand as Lolli approached the guy, who looked entirely dazzled by Lolli's smile. Soon, hey were dancing together. Lolli sent me a thumbs up and I sent her one back, laughing even harder when she jerked the thumb into her mouth as she noticed her partner's gaze return to her.

I retreated back to the corner and watched them dance. Lolli looked happy, as did he. Although I was stuck by myself in a corner, I felt happy as well.

Who would believe that a girl like myself, a supposed orphan with no place to sleep besides the pavement, would be at a party, dressed in expensive clothes? Who would believe that that same girl would eventually find a home with a warm bed and food, friends, and a chance at a new life?

I couldn't be happier, even if I was stuck at a party by myself. I wondered briefly what Retro was doing. Maybe if he were here, I could at least have someone to banter with.

Just when the thought crossed my mind, I felt two arms entwine around my waist and pull me back into the corner. Suddenly, I was pressed against some guy I couldn't see and his mouth was right next to my ear. A pair of lips brushed against my ear.

"You didn't have to dress up just to impress me, Red." My breath caught in my throat at the sound of Retro's smooth voice in my ear as his arms tightened around my waist. My first instinct was to stay in that comfortable position for as long as possible, pretending that he wasn't spoken for. Of course, that was purely crazy talk.

I forced my body to pull out of his grip, then turned around to face him, my temper flaring. My face was as hot as the surface of the Sun, but I was able to hold myself together as I stared him down.

"My choice in clothing tonight was definitely not made with you in mind," I said with more venom than I had meant in my voice. I tried hard to fight the jealousy out of my voice, but I was losing the battle. I wasn't jealous, though. Really. I just couldn't get Carma's hands crawling through his hair out of my head.

Retro, oblivious to my new knowledge of his girlfriend, smiled and pulled me back over to him, this time with me facing him. I tried to pull away but Retro held me fast. I looked up to tell him that no meant no, but his expression looked dark and serious.

"What's wrong?" I asked cautiously, peering at his face. Retro shook his head and then nodded behind me. I twisted my neck somewhat to look over my shoulder and was surprised to find two guys staring at me, whispering quite obviously. They were leaned against the opposite walls, studying me with curious looks. It was too dark to make out their features, but it was as plain as day that they were watching us.

"What's their problem?" I asked, hoping it was loud enough for them to hear. It didn't seem like they did because they continued with their poorly hidden observation. I had a feeling they were gossiping about Retro's and my proximity or why he was even wasting his time talking to someone like me. The chasm between our lifestyles—a former homeless girl from Skid Row and a male model—seemed to grow even wider.

Retro shrugged as if he didn't know, but I could tell from the look in his eyes that he did, or at least knew a little. "They have nothing else to do, I guess," Retro ventured. His gaze slowly came back to me and the smirk returned to his face. "Now, can you explain why you are all alone tonight? This party is in your honor. You should be having fun."

"I was having fun, until I was suddenly groped by a certain someone," I hinted as I continued to struggle out of his hold. Knowing that his hands were the same that grabbed Carma's made me feel sick, but it was no use. For someone who was so lanky, he was pretty strong. I sighed and gave up. "And we both know that I don't deserve this party," I admitted in a quieter voice. Retro's smile drooped.

"Red, no one deserves this party more than you do. You may not have 'officially' passed the DM, but you showed more skill than almost any other agent I've seen."

I smirked at this. "Are you buttering me up for something?" I asked. Retro chuckled and pulled me closer. This was so wrong. I shouldn't be in a corner with someone else's boyfriend, but there was little I could do about it.

Besides, things were starting to get interesting.

"It's the truth. Buttering you up would be complimenting you on how beautiful you look tonight," he marveled as he raised a hand to brush some of my bangs that had fell on my forehead back into their upright position. "You're so beautiful, Red. Does anyone ever tell you that?"

Here it came again: the brain freeze. I was at a loss of words as Retro studied me like I was the most precious jewel known to mankind. "I knew you were special, Lola," Retro said, calling me by my original name, "I just wish..." His voice trailed off as he began to lean towards me. My heart began to pound against its ribcage as his face, full of emotion, got closer and closer to me.

I opened my mouth to come up with something witty to say but was cut short by Retro's lips suddenly covering my own. All thoughts and inhibitions poured out of my mind like a waterfall and vanished like vapor.

Retro was kissing me.

Retro was kissing me...and I was enjoying it.

It was almost like someone put me in autopilot, and soon, I was kissing him back. He pulled me closer to him as the kissing intensified, and I snaked my arms around his neck and upwards to play in the hair that he loved so much. *And Carma*, a voice whispered in my head.

I was surprised at how right yet how wrong it felt to kiss Retro. It felt natural, as if it were meant to be. As if it were meant for us to be the ones that were together.

Shoot, what was I doing?!

Retro.

Had.

A.

Girlfriend!

"Stop!"

I pushed Retro away from me, causing his back to slam against the wall behind him. He stared at me like I was an insane person. I glared back, breathing heavily and feeling like I was on fire.

"You have a girlfriend!" I shouted. "Why do you keep coming onto me?" The fact that he had a girlfriend seemed to dawn on him as well. He backed up a bit, looking hesitant.

"You know about Carma," he said, sounding more like he was stating a fact than asking a question. I bobbed my head up and down vigorously, my blood still pumping fast from our kiss.

Retro blew out a long huff of air and raked his fingers through his hair. "Carma and I have an agreement, Red. You're in the clear," he said. I noticed he didn't make another advance.

"That's not the point. I have a little more respect for myself than that!" I yelled. I didn't feel the need to point out that I had kissed him back. It was irrelevant.

"You did...kiss me back," Retro noted, voicing my thoughts exactly.

"Shut up!" I whisper-yelled, covering his mouth with my hand. I didn't know why I bothered, since everyone in the party had probably seen us in the act.

I removed my hand. "You kissed me first!"

Retro shrugged and smirked at me. "You kissed me back, Red."

I wanted to punch him, but I stopped myself. It was true—I had kissed him back. I hadn't been strong enough to listen to my brain and back away.

We stood in silence as I contemplated this. A slow song heavy on violin began to float through the claustrophobic room. We turned to watch the dancers. All of the couples were close and intimate now. I spotted Lolli, along with her dance partner, cozied together as they swayed across the dance floor.

"So..." Retro said after a bit, "...what does that mean?" I glanced over at him.

"What?"

"That you kissed me back."

I turned my head and saw that Retro was staring back at me, his liquid gold eyes twinkling playfully. I didn't know what to say. Since I kissed him back…that meant I liked him. Despite my promise to myself that I wasn't going to fall for him, it had happened.

"What do you think it means?" I said. I saw the corner of his mouth lift before he turned to face me. He reached out and grabbed the side of my face, stroking my cheek with his thumb.

"I hope it means that you'll do it again." I smiled at his words and found myself leaning toward him without thinking. As much as I tried to deny it, there was an undeniable chemistry between the two of us. Rather than think with my head like I always did, I loosened up and let my heart take the lead. I guess I could forget the fact that he had a girlfriend, and that he was a model while I had been sleeping on the sidewalk up until recently. I could forget all of that just for this moment. His lips were inches from mine, and that's all my mind could register. My heartbeat quickened as the distance between us grew smaller and smaller…

"Retro!" A sharp voice caused us both to jump apart right before our lips met. I looked over and saw that Carma, along with her Clones, had finally made their appearance. Dressed in the same outfit, but in an array of colors, they made their way over to us.

"Retro, what the heck are you doing here with her?" Carma hissed, looking at my hair as if a rat had crawled up there and died. "Get your inspiration from Elmo, Harlot?" I patted my hair insecurely and shot Carma a dirty look. I couldn't think of a reply quick enough; my guilt was getting the best of me.

Seemingly from nowhere, Lolli, Marc, and even Hack wandered over, looking defensive. "Is there a problem over here?" Marc asked, popping his gum at Carma and giving her a disgusted look.

Carma rolled her dark eyes. "No, not at all. I was just wondering why Harlot here was all over my boyfriend." I felt the smart remark I had planned die on my lips. I couldn't think of anything witty to say to that. I stood there, feeling embarrassed and disgusted with myself as Carma continued on, focusing her rage on Retro now. She shot him a furious glare, causing Retro to flinch a bit.

"Retro, why are you here with her? I told you to come pick me up so we could arrive here together."

Retro rolled his eyes but I couldn't help but notice he slid away from me. "I'm sorry, Carma. I completely forgot. Please forgive me," he droned, sounding as if he were reading from a script. He stepped away from me and walked over to Carma's side, his eyes downcast and his hands shoved into his pockets. Carma's face turned sympathetic.

"Aw, it's okay, sweetie. We all make mistakes," she said, while shooting me a glare. I just wanted to curl up in a ball and fade away. *How could I have been so stupid as to kiss Retro?*

"As for you," Carma returned to frowning at me. "Stay away from him. He's mine, okay? M-I-N-E. Got it?" I bit my tongue to keep from slinging a mouthful of curse words at her. If there was one thing I hated, it was being talked to as if I lived during the prehistoric days.

I glared at Retro as she prattled on, hoping he would say something to calm his beast of a girlfriend. All he had to say was that I wasn't coming onto him and that it was the other way around. *Say something…anything…*

"I'll stay away from her, okay? That way you won't have to worry about it.," Retro intoned. That wasn't exactly what I expected him to say. I stared at him, open-mouthed. Carma sent me a satisfied smirk before running her dainty hands through Retro's hair.

"That's even better. You're the best, Retro," she purred. Retro sent her a smile that others might think was handsome, but I found it to look fake, like plastic.

"Well, you've made your appearance," Marc said before sweeping his hands toward the door, "Now feel free to make your exit."

Carma sneered at him. "Sure, even if this technically is my boyfriend's room. I don't know why I even came to this party," she scoffed while grabbing onto Retro's hand. "Let's go hang out in my room." She, along with Retro and her Clones, turned to leave.

I wanted to vomit, cry, and attack Retro and Carma all at the same time. I was mortified. I was embarrassed. I felt stupid and used. Retro didn't like me; he didn't even like me a little bit. The fact was I had kissed another girl's boyfriend.

What was I expecting? For him to leave her and jump into my arms? Why would he? He was a model with someone just as beautiful and what was I? I was and would forever be a girl from Skid Row.

"Should we let them just walk away?" Marc asked while giving Carma a dirty look. She smirked in return.

I just forced a tight smile and nodded. "Yeah. I don't want anything to do with either of them," I said, staring vacantly at Retro. He met my eyes for a moment, a sad look plaguing his golden-hued eyes, before averting them back to the floor.

"Same here, Harlot," Carma hissed. She flipped her hair over her shoulder and dragged Retro out of the party with her Clones right on their heels. My friends instantly flocked around me.

"You okay, Bunny? Sorry about my brother," Lolli soothed, while rubbing my upper back. Hack and Marc joined in on the rubbing. I shook my head and forced myself to smile.

"I'm alright," I promised them. I really was alright. I was embarrassed and felt a little used, but still, I would be alright. Retro was just a guy. I wouldn't start bawling my eyes out over a boy who wasn't even mine (M-I-N-E) to begin with. I decided at that moment to not let myself fall for another guy while I was down here. I had to stay focused on my main priority—finding my parents. Guys could wait, especially if all they brought were confusion and embarrassment.

"Carma can be a witch," Hack whispered out of nowhere. We all turned around to stare at him. He blushed and started fidgeting with his glasses.

"Th-Th-That's how the saying goes, correct?" he stammered with an embarrassed shrug. We all giggled at our slightly awkward friend, easing some of the tension from our group. Even Hack joined in after a while.

Just when I decided that everything was going to be okay, the walls began to shake and quiver and I realized that, no, things might not be okay.

There was a loud *BOOM* and then the whole room began to fall apart.

Chapter Thirteen

Everyone in the party began to scream and run around in a panic as layers of rock and debris began to fall around them. The expensive stereo that had been pouring out the music was the first thing that was smashed. After that, it was the other students. I didn't know what was going on, but I knew we had to get somewhere safe.

I remembered reading somewhere that in the case of an earthquake hitting, people were supposed to get in a bathtub. *Or was that a tornado? You would think that someone who lived in California would know.*

Either way, we had to hide somewhere. Debris and rocks were falling from the ceiling, squishing kids from left to right, while others were choking from the ash that was sent flying in the air. Some were trying to make it to the door, but were stumbling and tripping over one another. Lolli was crying and screaming, right along with Marc and Hack.

I ducked my head and covered my nose and mouth with my hand. "Follow me!" I shouted in a muffled voice, trying to be heard over the chaos. They apparently didn't hear me because they continued to scream and cry. I maneuvered myself so that I was standing in front of them. They all instantly looked up, looking scared out of their minds. I grabbed them, shouting, "Stay low and try not to breath in the ash!" then led them into the walk-in closet close by. We huddled in the darkness, screaming each time the room shook abruptly.

Somewhere in the back of my mind, I felt as if this were different than an earthquake. The shaking only lasted a few short seconds and seemed to be happening periodically. It felt more like something hitting the walls with a gigantic fist every few seconds.

After one last quake, the room eased into silence. We sat there for some time, huddled together. The only sound heard was our rapid breathing.

"Is it over?" Hack whispered, while trying to use his Big Bang Theory shirt to rid his glasses of the dirt that had clouded them. I listened for a second. Outside had fallen deathly silent.

"I think so." I pulled myself up into a crouching position and then tried pushing the closet door. It wouldn't budge. I pushed harder, but there was something blocking us in from the other side of the door. "Come on!" I cried, while ramming the door with my shoulder. The door toppled over, along with me, and I ended up in a pile of dirt that I couldn't even recognize as a room. I pulled myself up and looked around. Huge chunks of rock had flattened the furniture and jagged rocks poked out from the metallic walls. The lights above our heads flickered on and off.

"This looks like something from a movie," Hack mumbled. We ventured out into the room. I couldn't help but notice a few limbs hanging out from under the rocks and held back the urge to throw up.

"This cannot be happening," Marc repeated as he gingerly stepped from one patch of clear floor to the other, with Lolli and Hack close behind him.

"Where's the door?" I asked out loud, as I looked around. I waved my hand in front of my face, trying to get rid of the lingering dust in the air. The ashes and debris were still airborne and we would surely choke to death if we couldn't get out of the room.

Lolli wandered over to the edges of the wall and began to move rocks out of the way, only to discover wallpaper. "No door over here," she announced. We quickly followed Lolli's example and began to dig around by the walls.

"None over here either!" Marc proclaimed. I was beginning to think that we were going to die a slow, painful death of suffocation when suddenly, Hack piped up.

"Wait! I think I found it!" Hack said, his voice excited. We all cheered and raced over as tiny Hack struggled to push a huge boulder out of the way to salvation. He heaved and grunted and coughed until finally, the boulder rolled to the side.

"Ah!"

We all cried out in surprise when a limp and bloody body of a teenager fell out from behind the rock and landed right on top of Hack.

Hack's face turned pale but he didn't scream. He gingerly moved the body to the side, letting it slide to the floor, where it landed in a slumped over sitting position. I had to hand it to him: he knew how to deal under stress. I had seen my fair share of dead people while I lived on Skid Row, but never one that was as mutilated as the one Hack had just put aside. The poor body was mangled and jutting out bones all over. I felt bile rising in my throat and quickly averted my eyes.

"Let's hurry!" Hack urged, and we did. We managed to push through the door and were surprised to see that the hallway was just as trashed as the room. A few bodies were scattered about and we made sure to avoid them as we slowly made our way down the hall, hands covering the lower-half of our faces.

"This wasn't an earthquake..." Lolli said quietly as she ran a hand against the charred remains of a metal wall. I nodded in agreement as I walked over to inspect the wall. It looked as if someone had blasted it with a crate filled with dynamite.

"I was just thinking the same thing," I murmured. Suddenly, we heard a static sound followed by three loud beeps that rang throughout the hallway. Lolli, Hack, and Marc snapped to attention like soldiers. They stayed completely still, staring up at the ceiling as if they were all possessed.

"Hey, what's wrong?" I asked hesitantly, while waving my hand in front of Lolli's face. No one replied; Lolli didn't even blink.

"Guys, now is not the time to—"

Marc cut me off with a quick "shh" before returning his focus to the ceiling. I glared at him but decided to not argue. I folded my arms and decided to stare up at the ceiling as well. I was surprised to see that the normally blue fluorescence of the ceiling had changed to a dark red, resembling blood. It flowed along the ceiling in waves, fading to black and then flashing back to a bright-red, before resuming its dark color. After a few moments of silence, a familiar voice filled the hallways.

"All agents, please report to the cafeteria at this time," Miss Margie's voice instructed. There was another static sound, three beeps, and then the room fell back into a hushed silence.

Hack, Lolli, and Marc relaxed and smiled at one another. "Let's go, guys!" Lolli said, enthusiasm back in her voice. "Mr. Harv will fix everything!" She began to skip away, followed closely by

Hack and Marc. I followed at a distance, forcing myself to look at the bodies of some of the agents who hadn't been as lucky as we had. Most of them I had never seen before, but a couple of them had been kids from my class. I realized with a wave of sadness that I would never be able to get a chance to know them. I couldn't help but keep my eye out for Retro. Don't ask me why. I was still angry with him but I didn't wish anything bad on him, or even Carma.

I didn't see either of them, so I sped up my pace to get back with my friends. Soon, we found ourselves in the cafeteria, along with what seemed a small country of people packed inside like sardines. I had no idea that there were this many people working in H Corp. The people already seated all looked up at our entrance, so we quickly shuffled over to our table and took a seat. Everyone was either crying or talking loudly, demanding to know what was going on.

"This cannot be happening. Nothing like this has ever happened here," Marc said. He paused to examine his nails. "But at least I didn't break a nail." I shook my head in disbelief, but couldn't resist the urge to check my own. Of course, my middle fingernail had been chipped.

I scanned the cafeteria, and felt a surge of relief course through my body at the sight of Retro, perched at a table with one leg tossed over the other. He looked quite calm, considering the current circumstances. I was just wondering where Carma could be when she appeared at Retro's side. She sat by him and wrapped her arms around him before she began to sob. Retro put one arm over her shoulder and attempted to console her, his face still neutral.

I turned back around to face my friends, forgetting about Retro and Carma for the time being. My quarrel with them seemed insignificant in light of the events that had just occurred. Suddenly, the atmosphere of the room changed. The chatter died away to the point that you could actually hear a pin drop. I looked at my friends and noticed that they were staring at something behind me, relieved looks on their faces. I glanced around and saw that their eyes were transfixed on Mr. Harv Magnum III as he strode into the cafeteria.

He was dressed in one of his usual white tuxedos, dashing as always. He walked with complete and utter confidence, his cane twirling effortlessly in his hand. He was followed by two women, who were dressed in matching black tuxedos and heels. I watched, amazed at the sense of order and calmness his presence brought to the room.

Harv strode to the center of the cafeteria and smiled around the room at the agents, while his women stood behind him, their faces blank. Harv's eyes fell on me for a second and he smiled a bit. My mouth twitched before I found myself smiling back. With Harv in the room, everything would be okay. Everything would be fine.

"My fellow agents, greetings. I trust none of you have been hurt too badly," he asked in that deep voice, looking around with a worried expression. We all answered in unison, "We're okay!" and Harv smiled again.

"Good, good…. Now, let me answer the question on everyone's minds." He gave his cane a light twirl to the side, so that he held it with both hands in front of his chest. "It seems as if the E Corporation found that it would be a good idea to bomb us with heat-seeking missiles that are able to move underground." Loud gasps sounded throughout the cafeteria and were followed by worried murmurs. The calmness that I had experienced a second before quickly died away as I registered his words.

"Bombed?" I asked aloud, echoing the many other voices rising in the room.

"Calm down, please," Harv ordered, and immediately everyone listened. His smile never faltering, he waved his hand around the room. "If there are any suggestions as to what we should do right now, please, feel free to speak." Almost immediately, everyone flew to their feet, shouting angrily.

"We go bomb them!"

"We can't let them get away with this!"

"My friend is dead!"

Harv listened to everyone carefully, moving from person to person, seeming as if he genuinely cared. I had to hand it to him—he was a great leader. The room was gradually calming down, but there was still plenty of shouting and turmoil going on. Lolli covered her ears and put her chin on the table.

"Why are they all so loud?" she complained, shooting daggers at Marc, who was waving his hands in the air and shouting along with everyone else. Hack was studying the people in silence.

"Hey, can I say something?" Someone spoke up from the table Retro and Carma were seated at. The shouting faded away as a handsome guy climbed to his feet, a jaunty grin on his face.

"Yes, Mr. Magnet, go ahead," Harv said, but I noticed he looked somewhat annoyed. The guy stood up so I was able to get a better view of him. He was tall and muscular, with smooth, honey-brown skin and eyes that seemed to shimmer from brown to gray, depending on where he looked. He seemed a tad over-confident, which might have been the reason Harv didn't seem to care for him.

"Well, Harv," Magnet began, casually calling Harv by his first name, "I think the first thing should be to repair the damages. I don't wanna sleep in rubble, if that's alright with you." This earned a few chuckles, giving everyone a much-needed gasp for air. With the newfound knowledge of the bombing, everyone needed something to chuckle at.

Harv cracked a tight smile. "Of course, Magnet. That will be taken care of right away. Perhaps you have plans for what we should do after that?" Harv asked, quirking an eyebrow.

Magnet shrugged, the grin still on his face. "After that? We get E back, of course." His response was met with loud cheers of agreement but I held my applause. Something of this magnitude needed to be dealt with, but I wasn't sure if that should mean more bloodshed.

"I'll take that into consideration," Harv stated before turning to face the rest of the cafeteria. "So for now, you can all return to your daily routines. Those who have lost your room, follow my assistants and we will provide you with a temporary resting place. I will provide further instructions by and by." With that last line, Harv left the room, his women and a few other now homeless people following behind him. As soon as he was out of the door, the chatter started up again. Others, looking depressed, got up and left, turning in for the night.

Marc yawned and stretched his arms skyward. "Well, tonight's been interesting!" he said in a voice muffled by his yawn. I nodded in agreement, although I wouldn't have used the word interesting to describe the night. It had been confusing, wrong, and tragic. A lot of agents that I hadn't had the chance to meet yet had been murdered.

"Interesting isn't the word I think you're looking for," Hack suggested, voicing my thoughts exactly. Lolli yawned and looked over at Retro, Carma, and Magnet's table. I noticed that her eyes were particularly glued to Magnet. *Could she have a crush on him?* He was a handsome guy, so I couldn't blame her.

The group of popular student-agents were chattering loudly and I couldn't help but overhear their entire conversation.

"Magnet, you idiot, we don't need to go out there like blind…idiots!' Carma was hissing. She was leaning across the table and seemed as if she were in an intense staring contest with Magnet.

"Just 'cause your scared doesn't mean we are," Magnet replied, giving her a flirty half-smile. The rest of the males at the table whooped and bumped fists with each other while the girls started hurling insults at them.

Carma sighed in exasperation and stood up, her Clones doing the same. "I'll leave you cavemen to your powwow," she huffed. She gave her thick, dark hair a toss and clicked out of the cafeteria, her Clones hot on her tail. I noticed that Retro didn't follow her. He and the rest of the boys were now talking in low whispers, making it impossible to hear them. I craned my neck and leaned forward, trying to figure out what they could be talking about.

"Hey, you can come sit over here if you want to listen in." I nearly fell off of my bench when I looked up and saw that Magnet was grinning at me. Of course the other guys at his table were now staring at me as well. I noticed Retro giving me a funny look, but when he saw me looking at him, he quickly turned away.

"It's okay," I managed to say before I spun back around in my seat, my face burning with embarrassment. Laughter floated behind me, making my face burn even more.

"That was pretty embarrassing," Marc announced while Hack and Lolli nodded in agreement.

"Who is that guy?" I asked.

"Magnet Fury," Marc informed me, looking as if he was ready to dive into some juicy gossip. I stayed quiet, awaiting the details, but Hack jumped in.

"He's not the most well behaved Field Agent. He's actually very intelligent, but he and his friend Trigger cause all sorts of problems," Hack said, casting an angry glance in Magnet's direction.

"So, this is the guy that you said played a prank?" I asked Lolli.

Lolli nodded vigorously. "Yep, that was him. Except it wasn't really a prank."

"They jacked a shuttle and loaded a bunch of agents on it so they could go party above ground," Marc cut in. He grinned mischievously. "I was on it and the trouble we all got in was worth it."

"How were they able to get a huge shuttle out of here without anyone knowing?" I asked dubiously.

Marc shrugged. "Don't ask me. I just went with it."

"Yeah, Lolli giggled, "You went with them all the way to suspension." Marc stuck out his tongue at her but didn't seem to have a comeback.

I was impressed. Anyone who was able to get something past people with such high technology was special. I risked another look at Magnet's table. He was laughing next to a shaggy-haired boy who made me do a double take.

Magnet's companion, who I suspected was Trigger, had an appearance that might scare others. His shaggy hair was a stark white and nearly blended in with the paleness of his skin. His eyes scared me the most. They were a pale, sickly pink, like scrubbed blood spilled on a white shirt. His off-putting eyes were cast downward as Magnet continued to talk to him. He would nod from time to time, but seemed as if he were in another world.

"What's wrong with him?" I asked in a low voice, afraid that Trigger might overhear.

Marc shook his head. "Trigger? No one knows," he said with a dismissive shrug.

"We just leave him to himself," Lolli added, looking a bit unnerved. "He never talks to anyone but Magnet, anyway."

"Why does he look like that?" I asked carefully, as I continued to stare at him. Hack cleared his throat.

"We don't know, really. He might be an albino," he explained. Something about the hurried tone in Hack's voice made me think that Trigger was a subject that no one liked to talk about. Right at the moment, Trigger's bloodshot eyes looked up to mine. I froze as our eyes locked. A familiar burning began to tingle my chest. I reached up and pressed my hand to my heart. Trigger stared at me a bit longer before he dropped his eyes back to the table. I lowered my hand back to my side, the burning still lingering.

That was the definition of weird. I hadn't felt that burning feeling in my chest since my DM. One look at this Trigger guy and it had flared up again. Something about him had brought the burning to the surface and I had a feeling he knew why.

"Harlot? Are you okay?" I looked back to my friends and saw them staring at me with weird expressions. I suddenly felt very sleepy, as if the weight of the day had come slamming back down on my shoulders. I put my hand to my head, which felt like it was swimming in thick, murky water.

"Yeah, I'm just…tired. I want everything to go back to before the party," I said. "You know, before things got crazy. Before, before." My tongue felt like cotton as I looked around at my friends. Their faces were blurry and began to mesh together into a swirling palette of colors. I moved my hand to cover my eyes.

"You guys look kind of funny," I tried to say, but I couldn't hear myself speak. Someone gently grabbed my wrist.

"Harlot, let's go get you to bed. You sound weird," I heard Lolli say. I uncovered my eyes and felt relieved to find that my friends' faces were back to normal. They were all staring at me with concerned expressions.

Lolli helped me to my feet, leaning my weight on her. I shook my head no, then nodded. Bed sounded good. "Okay. Good night," I whispered at Marc and Hack who scrunched their eyebrows together but nodded at me. Lolli and I passed Magnet and Trigger's table, moving at a slow pace. I felt someone's eyes on me as we exited the cafeteria. I turned my head and saw Trigger smiling directly at me, his sunken eyes gleaming. The door closed behind me, shutting off my view of him.

I began to feel better as soon as we were out of the lunchroom. I straightened myself out, relieving Lolli of her duties.

"Feeling better?" Lolli asked with a tired smile. I nodded. Even Lolli's enthusiasm was taking a hit with tonight's casualties.

It was strange seeing the agents so sullen. Older agents were already clearing out the debris in the hallways, while some of the younger agents stood around, eyes red from crying.

"Trishie! Trishie!!!" Lolli and I were knocked aside as a girl a bit older than we were barreled between us. She rushed up to a pair of senior agents, who were putting a young girl's body in a silver body bag. I realized with a sinking feeling that the dead girl had a striking resemblance to the one rushing towards her.

"Trishie," the girl wailed, "Noo!" The first girl tried to tear the body bag from the senior agents, who shielded the bag from her.

"Agent, control yourself!" the male senior agent commanded. He held her back by her shoulders while his female counterpart finished zipping the bag.

"You don't understand! That's my sister! She can't be dead. She can't be," the girl cried. She collapsed to the floor, sobbing loudly into her hands. The senior agents hoisted the bag between them and glanced remorsefully at the crying sister.

"We'll be showing the bodies of those killed at a later date," the female announced in a neutral voice before they walked off, taking the bag with them. The sister continued to cry on the ground, her shoulders wracked by sobs.

I watched her, my throat burning with tears. I had never known the bond between siblings, but I could only imagine the pain. I knew from the tears in Lolli's eyes that she was affected. She tugged on my arm gently. "We should go," she said. I hesitated but nodded. I felt bad leaving her alone, but I'm not sure she would want a stranger trying to console her.

I was grateful to see that Lolli and my room was still intact after the bombing, although there was some debris scattered about. Lolli fell asleep as soon as she touched her bed, but I was wide awake.

After rolling around restlessly for some time, I decided to take a shower, since sleep didn't seem to be an option. I quietly got out of bed, being careful not to wake Lolli. I went into the bathroom and shut the door behind me.

I loved the showers down here. There was a control pad on the outside of the glass door that let you choose the settings of your shower. I scanned my options. The lighted labels read "Cold", "Warm", "Hot", and "Sauna" temperature settings. The nozzle could be set to "Spray", "Mist" or "Jet" with one tap. I tapped on "Hot" and "Spray", then swiped the screen to start the shower. I heard the water spurt on from behind the glass door. I shed my clothes, which were coated in dirt, before slipping into the shower.

The spray of steaming hot water against my dirt-caked skin felt great. I sighed happily and pressed my palms against the wall of the shower. I watched as the water at my feet became brown with dirt and was sucked down the drain. I reached up and placed my hand over my heart, where the letter H was drawn in jet-black ink.

Tonight had been terrible. People were dead, people that I hadn't even had the chance to meet. Now was not the time for me to have a mental breakdown. The memory of my sluggishness in the lunchroom earlier was already beginning to fade away like a bad dream. I had felt tired and dizzy, right after I saw that Trigger guy, with pink eyes.

"No, that can't be right," I mumbled aloud to myself. I had to have been imagining things.

I cupped my hands together under the nozzle and let the water pool in the bowl they formed. I splashed the water on my face and breathed in deeply.

What had I been thinking about? I climbed out of the shower and dried off. Every time I tried to think back to the lunchroom, I kept drawing blanks.

It was probably no big deal. I went over to my dresser and pulled out a short pajama set Lolli had ordered for me and tugged it on. I climbed into the bed and laid on my back, staring up at the ceiling. I said a silent prayer for my parents, like I did almost every night and then turned my thoughts elsewhere.

E Corp's bombing didn't sit right with me. Something about the timing was too suspicious. I had just completed my DM the day before. *That couldn't have been the reason...*

I sat up in bed so fast, my head spun with dizziness. *They couldn't have bombed us because of me, could they?*

My chest began to heave as the facts started lining up. I had just completed my DM and stole their information. The next day, they bomb us. It was too coincidental.

I grabbed the sides of my head and gritted my teeth together, holding back the scream bubbling in my chest.

It couldn't have been my fault.

It was just a coincidence.

Pictures of the limp bodies being crushed by chunks of rock and metal flashed in my mind. I gritted my teeth harder, feeling as if they might shatter.

"It wasn't my fault," I whispered in the darkness. I grabbed my pillow and curled up in a ball, repeating the line in my head over and over until I was able to fall into a fitful sleep.

***

That night, I had the Dream. I was a little shocked because I hadn't had the Dream since I had come to the H Corp.

I wasn't eight this time. I was my current age, seventeen. Dad and I walked side by side on the clouds, barefoot. The clouds felt cool, soft and feathery beneath my warm feet. When I looked down, I couldn't see Earth like I usually could. Instead, all I could see were dark, angry storm clouds.

"Dad? What's going on?" I couldn't believe it, but I was able to speak this time.

Dad sent me a warm smile and patted my head. "Do you like Heaven, Lola?" he asked me in a voice that wasn't his own. It was deeper, yet strangely familiar. I stared back at him in disbelief. His face began to change before my eyes. It twisted and churned a grotesque mixture of pink and ebony.

"Dad?! Stop it! You're not dead!" I shouted at him, trying to stop him from the horrifying change he was undergoing, but there was no stopping it. His face continued to bubble and churn until I couldn't stand it anymore. I covered my face and screamed as a deafening, roaring wind began to whip up, sounding like the moans of lost ones.

A loud, shrill voice rose above the rest of the cries. "Trishie," it wailed, "you killed Trishie!"

"No!" I cried. The ground began to tremble and quake. I backed away from my dad and curled up in a ball on the ground, sobbing and screaming. I couldn't hear my screams over the wind. Suddenly, a hand clamped down on my shoulder. The wind and shaking stopped. The only sound I could hear was the sound of my shaky, rapid breathing. I squeezed my eyes shut as the hand squeezed tighter. Frederick D's voice floated into my ear.

"Beware."

***

"Ah!"

With a startled yell, I tumbled out of bed, entangled in my blankets and covers. I landed hard on the floor, directly on my elbow. I lay on the ground for a few moments, holding my elbow and gritting my teeth in pain. After I was done nursing my elbow, I peered over the side of my bed, making sure that I hadn't awakened Lolli. She was curled up with Mr. Frumplebuns, fast asleep. I sighed with relief and climbed back into bed, my elbow still smarting.

That was the strangest dream I had yet to have. I had never dreamed of anything like that, not even when I was a little kid. I knew it had stemmed from the guilt of the bombing.

"It wasn't your fault," I confirmed again. I rolled over on my side but found myself afraid to shut my eyes. The wind and wailing, quakes and crying…I wasn't in a hurry to meet any of them again. After a while, I drifted off to sleep. Fortunately, the Dream didn't come again.

Chapter Fourteen

The next day, you could practically feel the buzz running throughout the school hallway. Adult agents were busy at work repairing damages from the bombing while students gathered in clusters to talk about last night's events.

Of course, school wasn't cancelled. I walked into my Deadly Arts class and was pleasantly surprised to see that Mr. Haze was nowhere to be found. Everyone was sitting around on the training mats, talking animatedly. I noticed a few of the kids shooting me dirty looks. I was happy when I spotted Marc lying back on a mat, looking peeved.

"What's shakin'?" I said as I plopped down next to him, careful not to let my miniskirt slip any higher than it already was. I had let Lolli talk me into ordering a dark-blue jean miniskirt and a red off-the-shoulder top, and now I was regretting it.

Marc sat up, his usual giddy expression now replaced with an irritated one. "Not these idiots around here! Everyone's all ready to go fight E and I'm so tired of hearing about it," Marc said, giving his classmates an evil stare. I couldn't help but notice how his opinion now was a complete turnabout from what it had been last night in the cafeteria.

"But those guys did bomb us," I informed him, wishing that I could relax and lay back like the rest of the students in the classroom, but in a skirt, this wouldn't have been too smart of a thing to do.

"Yeah, and we should go get them instead of talking about it. And when I say "we", I don't mean me," he said. He looked at me, giving me an once-over. "Are you feeling better? You were starting to scare us last night." I dug around in my jumbled memory of last night and recalled having Lolli escort me to our room.

"Oh, sorry about that," I apologized, while scratching at my sweater. I still wanted to find Trigger and ask him what he knew about whatever was going on with me, but he had pulled a disappearing act. Actually, he and a lot of the other male students were missing in action today.

"Where is everyone, namely our teacher?" I asked as I glanced around at the students.

"Everyone is setting up for the memorial," Marc said. "It's supposed to be later this week." I nodded, the guilt making my skin itch. This memorial wasn't happening because of me. I tried to convince myself, but it was getting harder and harder.

"Have they figured out why E bombed us?" I blurted out.

"Yeah, at least they think so. It's supposedly because of that information you stole during your DM. Apparently, it was something they really didn't want us to have. They've never done anything like this before."

My breath caught in my throat as my nightmare proved to be true. So, it had been my fault. At least I knew now why my fellow classmates were looking at me as if they were ready to take me to the guillotine. They all blamed me for the bombing.

Marc gave me a stern look. "Harlot, it wasn't your fault, okay? You didn't ask for this." I felt his hand cover my own. I tried to look up and meet his eyes but I couldn't. His words comforted me, but I couldn't stop myself from feeling as if it were my fault.

"You're right," I agreed, trying to convince myself. Before I could ask for more information, a familiar series of beeps rang throughout the class. Everyone did that weird meerkat head turn and fell silent. I almost wanted to laugh but the sound died in my throat when I heard the announcement.

"Harlot Rue, please report to Mr. Magnum's office. I repeat, Harlot Rue please report to Mr. Magnum's office."

Silence fell over the entire room as the intercom went dead. All of the meerkat's attention had shifted to me as the announcement ended.

"What did you do this time, Harlot?" Carma's voice floated from across the room, followed by mutters of agreement.

Great, I had gone from a superstar to the most hated agent down here in less than a day. I gave Carma an ugly face, said later to a ruffled Marc, and quickly left the classroom, dreading whatever awaited me in Harv's office.

***

"What is it now?" I growled as I slammed into Harv's office. Harv was sitting behind his desk, looking like he was on vacation instead of planning on how to get back at his rival. His smile lit up the room.

"What? Can't I just call you in my office to get a chance to see your beautiful face?" he said, his voice like velvet. "And I must say, you should wear skirts more often." I looked at him annoyed, although I was secretly a little flattered. I always did like to think I had decent legs.

"And you should keep your perverted compliments to yourself. Now, what do you want?" I asked. I knew I was being rude (even for me) but I was still mad at being called out in front of my entire class. It was bad enough that they already hated me.

Harv's smile never faltered. "Your attitude still needs some adjustment, I see. But you're right, let's get down to business, shall we?" Harv snapped his fingers and soon, a line of senior agents filed into the room.

They were tough. Their jumpsuits did nothing to hide their huge muscles and well-toned bodies. All of their faces were wrought with jagged tattoos that mingled with scars. With expressions that ranged from stony and neutral to completely murderous, I found myself inching closer to Harv's desk. They nearly filled the entire room.

"Harlot, meet my Elite Agents. They will be going on a special mission today to strike the E. Corporation where they will feel it most – their technology." Harv explained. "Say hi."

"H-Hi..." I managed to squeak out. No one bothered to reply.

"So, why am I here?" I asked. "These people look as if they could take on all of the Avengers and not break a sweat." I noticed one guy, an incredibly muscular, stocky guy with short black hair and a jagged scar running from the corner of his right eye to his chin, crack a tiny smile. I decided I liked him. Harv laughed a bit and shrugged his shoulders.

"You certainly are an extremely promising agent, Harlot, so I thought perhaps you would like to tag along with them and see how it's done." He gave me a smile, one that seemed as if it held a million secrets. "Especially since you did so well on your DM." I swallowed hard and hoped he didn't notice the sweat that had formed on my forehead. *Could he have known that I cheated on my DM?*

Harv didn't give me time to worry for long. "So, do you think you can do this?" he asked. I felt every set of eyes on me and my stubbornness kicked in.

"Of course I can keep up with them. I might need some steroids, though." Harv smiled at my reply, and he waved his hands around at all of the agents. They turned around and left the room, all except for Scarface, who stood quietly at the door. Harv turned his attention back to me.

"Just be there with them during the mission, and don't get into any trouble. You leave first thing tomorrow morning."

"So…does that mean I'm excused from the rest of my classes for the day?" I asked, feeling a ray of hope in all of this madness.

"No, you may return to class." It was worth a shot.

With an angry sigh, I brushed past Scarface and left Harv's office. I didn't miss the mistrustful glare Scarface gave me as I passed by.

***

"Soooo, what was that all about?" Lolli was asking me as we got our lunch trays in the cafeteria lunch line. Today's entree was stir-fried vegetables and golden lo-mein noodles with a crispy-looking spring roll. I shrugged and took a bite out of the crunchy spring roll.

"Beats me," I said with a wave of my half-eaten roll. We made our way to our table, where Hack and Marc were sitting. They looked as if they were going over some class work.

I noticed Lolli giving me an evil look that seemed to read 'tell me now or so help me,' so I swallowed my food before giving her the rundown. "Harv wants me to shadow the Elite Agents tomorrow when they go to the E. Corp. Fun, fun, fun!"

Hack, Lolli, and Marc all gasped together and I almost laughed at how comedic they looked. Marc leaned forward, the first to talk as usual, it seemed.

"The Elite Agents? As in, the top of the top agents?" he panted, then began fanning himself. I picked up my napkin and gave him a couple of flaps as well. Marc snatched the napkin away from me and tossed it at my nose, making me grin.

"The one and only. What's the deal with them?" I asked. Marc, Lolli, and Hack shared looks of disbelief.

"You haven't heard of the Elite Agents?" Lolli asked, her tiny mouth forming a perfect "o."

"Lolli, I've only been here for about three days, not counting the time I was knocked out in the recovery room," I reminded her as I finished my spring roll and then stretched my arms and legs out in a very unladylike way. Lolli gave a discreet point at my skirt to which I smiled and lowered my arms.

"I-I keep forgetting you haven't been here that long," Hack said, giving me a tiny smile.

"I know right! You're practically part of the Cool Crew!" Marc chimed in.

"The Cool Crew?" I asked dumbfounded. Marc laughed.

"Just an impromptu name I came up with for the group we have going on here," he said, while wrapping his arms around us.

"Group hug!" Lolli squealed. Marc immediately let go, looking cross.

"You ruined it, Lolli!" he complained while folding his arms. I smiled at all of my friends. It did seem as if I was falling into place here in the H Corporation, no matter what was going on. No matter how many other agents hated me, I had a feeling that these guys would stand by me, no matter what. Just when I was starting to get that warm, fuzzy feeling in my stomach, the sharp scent of expensive cologne and hair gel came to chase it away.

"Room for one more?" Retro stood behind me, smiling innocently. With everything else going on, I had almost forgotten about the party last night and the large part Retro played in ruining it. I resisted the urge to knock the smile off of his face and simply ignored him. Marc took out his nail file and set to work. Hack began to focus on something on the lunch table that was invisible to everyone but him. Retro continued to stand there, looking uncomfortable. It was funny, seeing him squirm.

Unsurprisingly, Lolli was the one to break the uncomfortable silence that surrounded our table. "Sure, *hermano*, take a seat!" she chirped, giving him a big grin. Retro nodded and sat between me and Hack. Another lapse of silence followed.

"So…what do you guys think about this whole bombing thing?" Retro said, leaning forward so that I was bluntly out of the group and left hanging off of the bench. In less than a nano-second, everyone launched into a heated debate about the bombing. So, he was going to pretend as if nothing had happened. Unfortunately, I wasn't that forgiving.

I stood abruptly, clutching my tray tightly. Everyone looked up at me in bewilderment, except Retro, who kept his eyes trained on the table.

"What's wrong, Harlot?" Hack asked.

"I'm going to go pack and get what I need ready for the mission tomorrow," I informed them, then turned on my heel and strode quickly out of the cafeteria, dumping my tray on the way. I couldn't wait to go on my mission tomorrow and let out some of my anger on someone, anyone.

"Hey, if it isn't Bomb-Girl!"

Perfect timing. I turned around and saw a group of three boys around my age lingering by the cafeteria door. They were giving me dangerous looks that automatically put me in defense mode.

"Hey, if it isn't the Three Stooges!" I greeted them with fake enthusiasm. "Didn't you guys get canceled or something?" The boys all glanced at each other. I could tell me joking with them was making them even angrier.

"Ooh, funny girl, huh?" One stepped forward, the tallest of the three. He glared down at me. "Well, I don't think my friend who got crushed to death yesterday would find you so funny." A trickle of fear ran down my spine as the other boys closed in on me.

"Look, I'm sorry about your friend, but I didn't have anything to do with the bombing," I said, my voice now serious. The shortest of the group gave a dry laugh.

"Nothing to do with it? The E Corp has never directly attacked us. But when you show up, they invent a whole new weapon!" His voice had steadily risen to a shouting level.

"Yeah, so explain that, Bomb Girl," the tall one challenged. They had all backed me into the wall and formed a semi-circle around me. I stared them down, refusing to be intimidated, although I was starting to get a little nervous. No one else was in sight and the guys were getting more furious by the minute.

"I'm as clueless as you three, but I do know one thing—if you don't get the heck away from me, E Corp and their bombs will be the least of your worries," I threatened.

Obviously not taking my threat seriously, the shortest of the boys pushed me, causing me to slam against the wall. Everything seemed to speed up after that. Another one raised his fist to swing. Acting fast, I ducked, dodging his fist just in time. His fist went flying backwards into the wall. The impact echoed throughout the hall.

He cursed angrily as he nursed his bright-red fist. I took this moment to sweep his legs out from beneath him, causing him to tumble to the ground with a shout. I stood up and dodged to the right as the short one swung wildly at me. I lashed out with my fist and connected with his nose, producing a sickening crunching noise. He fell to the ground like a ragdoll, nose pouring blood while he cried out in pain.

I was just turning to face the last one when a fist slammed into my cheek. I slumped to the floor, clutching my face. I looked up just in time to see a sneaker coming right at my face. It connected with a sharp jab that left me dizzy. I fell to the ground, my vision turning white as blood built up in my mouth. I sat up and held onto my jaw, which felt loose and swollen. I spit a pink-tinted glob to the side and glared up at my attackers. My chest was beginning to tingle again.

The tallest one grinned down at me. "This is what they had to go through," he growled. The grin on his face turned menacingly wicked as he raised his foot, ready to send another blow to my face. I could see all of the pain and anger he had endured with the night's bombing in his charcoal eyes. I realized that he was being fueled by rage and was unlikely to stop the beating.

He sent his foot forward.

Before the kick could land, a flying blur rushed out of the corner of my vision and slammed into him. I pulled myself into a sitting position as the two people landed at my feet and began to wrestle each other on the ground.

"Retro?" I cried in disbelief. Believe it or not, Retro was the one who had tackled the tallest of my attackers. He was currently beating the mush out of my attacker's face, making me proud. Retro certainly didn't seem to be the fighting type, but he was proving me wrong. The other two boys cowered away, watching in horror.

"Dude, get off! She deserves to die for what she did!" The tallest was able to disentangle himself from Retro and quickly scrambled away. His lip was busted and his left eye was already beginning to swell shut. I smiled in approval. He had to look worse than I did.

Retro stood up as well and stared him down, looking as scary as I had ever seen him. "What happened was not her fault. Stop looking for someone to blame and realize who bombed us in the first place," Retro said in a cool voice, his chest heaving. The shortest attacker, nose still leaking, stepped closer to Retro but the tallest of the trio (and apparently, the smartest) put his arm in front of him.

He shook his head, never taking his eyes off of Retro. A wide smile spread across his face, causing the blood running down his chin to flow even more. "We'll let her go…for now. You won't be around her forever, though." With those last haunting words, the three boys staggered off towards the dorms. I stared after them, making sure they weren't going to turn around.

When they disappeared around the corner, I felt my breathing return to normal. I climbed to my feet and faced Retro, who was already staring expectantly at me. I wasn't sure of what to say. Every time I tried to stay mad at him, he did something heroic and made it that much harder.

He smiled, successfully breaking the ice between us. "Things are never boring with you around, Red," he joked. I grinned back but winced when my jaw began to throb. Retro's face became concerned. He reached out a hand and gingerly took hold of my chin, causing my heart to flutter against my will.

"They hit your face?" His voice was low and sort of scary. I pulled away from him. With him so close, it was too easy to remember the night before.

"No big deal. I'll get them back later," I said, blowing it off. Retro frowned and shook his head.

"No, don't even think about it," he reprimanded. "Those boys were serious. There are a lot of agents that are like them and out for revenge. Don't be stupid. Just stay away from them and don't fight."

"Stupid? No," I fumed, "What's stupid is everyone blaming me for this bombing! I didn't exactly ask E to bomb us. So, if anyone else wants to come and fight me, I'll be ready." I spun on my heel and began to walk away from him.

"Wait, Red!" Retro reached out and grabbed my wrist. I stopped walking and frowned at his hand. He should know by now that I wasn't fond of being grabbed. Retro looked from me to my wrist before he dropped my wrist and raised his hands in the air. "Sorry. Just listen, Red, please." I sighed and turned to face him with my arms folded across my chest.

"Fine, I'm listening."

"Good. I didn't mean to make it seem like it was your fault. I'm sorry," Retro apologized. I bit my lip and lowered my head, feeling guilty.

"I know you don't think that. I...I'm just trying to make myself feel better, I guess," I admitted. "I shouldn't have lashed out at you. You did just save me...again."

Retro chuckled and the tension between us gave away. "It's part of my job, you know. I should be getting paid overtime, though," he teased, while lighting flicking my necklace. I laughed.

"You're a real trooper," I agreed. Silence fell. There were so many words that needed to be exchanged between the two of us, I didn't know where to start. Retro shifted from foot to foot, scratched his head, and cleared his throat. Finally, he decided to speak.

"Red, about last night—"

"Don't." I held up a finger to stop him and put a strained smile on my face. "Let's just pretend that all of that didn't happen, okay?"

Retro opened his mouth to say more but after a few moments, he shut it back and nodded. "If…that's what you want," he replied quietly, while looking troubled.

"It really is." I reached into my pocket and pulled out my all-access key. "I should probably go pack for my mission now."

Retro nodded in agreement. "Ah, right. Lolli told me about your new mission. Be careful out there, Red." He cracked a small smile. "I won't be there to save you this time."

***

The next morning, I was up, packed, and dressed in my new black jumpsuit by 7:00 a.m. Even Lolli was still asleep. It was Saturday and thankfully, there were no classes on this day. I put on my Brace and made my way through the nearly empty hallways. I was almost to the bus tunnel when I bumped into someone, knocking them and a load of gadgets to the floor. I felt myself tense up, ready for a fight. If it were one of my attackers from yesterday, I wouldn't back down.

"Oh! S-Sorry!"

Wait, I knew that stutter. I looked down and saw Hack scrambling to pick up the gadgets he had dropped.

"Hack! What are you doing down here?" I asked, while I knelt down and began to help him pick up his things. I was amazed at the technology that went into developing the gadgets. There were a few orbs of the familiar sleeping dust, some long tubes, and a handful of small, black marbles. I was extremely careful as I picked each thing up and handed it over to Hack. Although they looked normal enough, I didn't want to trigger anything.

We finished picking his items up and Hack gathered them back into his arms. I could tell that the load was a little too much for him to carry. "Well," Hack began, "I just came to wish you good luck! I mean, you're going out with the Elite Agents, so I was a little worried! I-I just came to see you off," Hack babbled, his face growing redder by the second. I laughed and punched him playfully in the shoulder, almost knocking him off balance.

"You know I'll be okay, Hack! But thanks," I said with a smirk. Ever since my encounter with the Three Stooges the other day, I had been feeling a little on edge.

Hack returned the smile. Suddenly, his eyes widened. "Oh! I-I almost forgot!" Hack carefully reached into his stack of gadgets and pulled out a pocket knife. And not just any knife. It was the one I had lost during my descent into H Corp, on that fateful night in Retro's red Ferrari.

"Hack...where'd you find this?" I asked cautiously.

"Retro said you might want it," he said with an oblivious smile. "Oh, and this, too." Hack pulled out another item that I wasn't as happy to see. It was the cell phone that Blackeye had given me. It seemed like a lifetime ago that I had last held either of my belongings. I smiled gratefully and slid both into my jumpsuit's pocket. My knife felt right at home.

"Thanks, Hack. And..." I hesitated. "Tell Retro I said thanks, too." Hack waved me off as I walked towards the bus tunnel. With my old knife in tow, I felt a bit more confident about my mission.

As soon as I was out of Hack's view, I whipped out the phone and flipped through the messages. It was riddled with messages from Blackeye asking where I was. Each text was angrier and more threatening than the last. I laughed at them and shut the phone before tossing it carelessly back into my pocket.

Blackeye no longer had any power over me. With my newfound home and training, I wasn't afraid of him. Besides, he had no idea where I was and he would never know. I was free of him. There was nothing he could use to hold over my head any longer and no way he could harm me.

I laughed to myself all the way to the shuttle area. My laughter was cut short when I was met by the not so pleasant surprise waiting for me by the bus.

Scarface, the scarred Elite Agent, was waiting by the bus for me, dressed in a black jumpsuit with silver shoulder pads and an H patch on his chest. I carefully approached him, feeling nervous. I stopped a couple of feet away from him. He was blocking the bus entrance, so there was no way around him, unless I wanted to attempt climbing through a window.

"Excuse me, but I need to get on there," I said, trying to be polite. Scarface gave me a stony look and shook his head.

"Before you get on, I would like to have a word with you, Miss Rue," he said, his deep voice layered in a thick German accent. I shrugged my shoulders and tapped my foot impatiently. The bus looked so comfortable and I was ready to get a few more hours of sleep in.

"Okay, what is it?" I asked, my voice sounding more than a little peeved. This didn't seem to faze Scarface one bit. He folded his arms and stared down at me, his dark eyes calculating and cold. I felt my confidence slowly diminish as he continued to glare at me.

"Listen carefully to what I'm about to tell you, Miss Rue. While on this important mission, you are to obey any and every command given to you without hesitation, and certainly without that attitude of yours. This mission should be a very simple one, but it will also be a sensitive one. I don't want any unnecessary problems being caused. Understand?" He spoke in a quick manner, barely pausing for a breath. I swallowed hard and fought back the urge to cry. I always used to cry when I was younger and my parents got angry with me. Years later, the crying had evolved into pouting, which was exactly what I did now.

"I'm not a two-year old, Commander," I growled, folding my arms right back and standing up straighter, so that I could have chance of competing with his height. "I know how to stay out of trouble." I lied but it was necessary.

Scarface leaned away from me and frowned. "You'd better hope you do," he warned, with a threatening vibe to his voice. He stepped aside so that I would just be able to squeeze into the bus.

Before I took a step, his voice stopped me. "You may call me Lukas, Miss Rue." I gave him a slight nod and climbed onto the bus. I was disappointed to see that our Operator was not Marc, but another Elite Agent. The front seats were also filled with the silent Elites, so I passed them by and sat in the very back. No one bothered to hide their evident observation of me. They craned their necks towards the back of the bus to gape at me, then turned back around to whisper to one another.

Deciding to ignore them, I threw my feet up on the back of the seat in front of me and rested my head on the seat behind me. I had no idea how long our trip was going to take, so I figured I would catch up on my sleep.

As soon as I shut my eyes, Lukas's voice boomed through the bus. "*Achtung*, Elites!" All of our attention was drawn to the front of the bus, where Lukas was standing. Once he was certain of our undivided attention, he folded his arms behind his back and continued. "I've just been informed by headquarters that our drop-off point will be in Slovakia, near a town named Bojnice. Because of the far distance, we will be Jumping."

His words were immediately followed by sounds of shuffling and murmuring. I peered over my seat and noticed the Elites unloading masks from the luggage racks above their heads. Following their lead, I retrieved my own mask from my luggage rack and studied it. It was transparent and made from a material sturdier than plastic but felt lighter than glass. I tried to press it to my face but it slipped off. It was a full-face mask with no type of strap to hold it in place. I gazed up at the Elites. They held their masks to their faces for a few moments before they released them. I was surprised when the masks stayed in place. I continued in vain to make my mask stick.

"Preparing to enter Hypersonic Mode," the Operator voiced. I cursed and raised my hand, feeling like I was in a classroom. I didn't like admitting I needed help but I certainly didn't want to be mask-less when we entered whatever "Hypersonic Mode" was. Lukas's eyes fell on me and he raised an eyebrow. I waved him over. There was no way I was going to admit in front of the Elites that I couldn't figure out how to put on a mask.

Lukas made his way back to me and sat beside me. "What seems to be the problem, Miss Rue?" he asked. I pressed the mask to my face for a few seconds, released it, and it slid to the floor. I gave Lukas a hopeless look.

"I think my mask is broken," I said. Lukas chuckled and took the mask from me. He pressed it to my face and held it there.

"You hold it to your face and only let it go when you feel it mesh with your skin," he explained.

"Mesh with my skin?" I cried. As soon as I spoke, I felt my face begin to go numb, like it had fell asleep. The feeling began to crawl throughout my entire body. Before long, I couldn't feel a thing. I tried to open my mouth but the lip area of my mask had clamped down over it.

Lukas pressed his own mask to his face. "This will make sure you stay asleep and also protect your body while we are in Hypersonic Mode. We will be travelling at a speed that would most likely kill you otherwise." His mask's mouth shut and he shut his eyes.

"Countdown to Jump starting...now." The Operator pressed a button before pressing his own mask to his face. My heart began to beat against my chest as black, metal shutters shut over the windows of our shuttle, casting everyone in total darkness.

"Commencing Hypersonic Jump in 10...9...8...." The computerized voice had begun the countdown. I fell back in my seat, my eyes already feeling heavy. I looked over at Lukas for reassurance. He was already fast asleep. I felt the bus slowly spinning to face a new direction.

"5...4...3...2..." I closed my eyes and let sleep take me.

***

There was a lot of noise. People talking, feet shuffling, metal scraping against metal. I just wanted to go to sleep. It was so nice and warm and fuzzy. I felt like I was sleeping while bundled in layers of cashmere and silk. I hadn't slept this good for as long as I could remember.

"Miss Rue, it's time to wake up." The German accent reminded me of where I was. My eyes snapped open and immediately shut again when they drank in the bright light surrounding me. I groaned and sat up and stretched, keeping my eyes squeezed shut. I felt as if I had been asleep for years.

"Don't move too quickly. You will be experiencing something akin to jet lag for some time,"." I cracked my eyes open and saw Lukas watching me. I nodded and yawned loudly. I felt as if I had just awakened from hibernating all winter.

I carefully stretched each part of my body before I allowed myself to open my eyes all of the way. The shutters were still down, so there was no way of telling where we were. I reached up and touched my mask. When I went to take it off, I was surprised by how easy it was. It slid right off. I put it back in the luggage rack before falling back in my seat and stretching once more. I looked over at Lukas, who was rolling his neck from side to side, producing loud cracking sounds. I cringed. I hated when people did that.

"So, Lukas, right?" I asked, making small talk. He finished his disturbing neck-cracking before giving a curt nod. I ignored his silence and continued on. "What exactly are we doing on this mission? Harv said something about messing with their technology." Lukas gave me another nod and for a few seconds I thought he wasn't going to speak.

"We are going to infiltrate a celebration being hosted by the leader of the E Corporation in Bojnice Castle. Once inside, a few people will cause distractions at the party while I and a few others will head to their base and disturb a few of their contraptions," he explained finally.

"A party?" I asked, my insides lighting up a bit. Was that really how simple this mission was going to be? Harv could have recruited baby agents to do something as simple as attend a party.

Lukas gave me a knowing look and nodded. "Yes, like a ball, of sorts." Shoot. My eagerness quickly shifted to dismay. A ball meant itchy dresses and people stepping on other people's feet as they tried to do dance moves that were invented in the 1800s. Not my idea of a party.

"And whatever shall I be doing during all of this distracting and infiltrating?" I asked with a sarcastic edge to my voice.

Finally, Lukas turned around to face me. He cocked an eyebrow at me and a hint of a smile played across his lips.

"Smile and look pretty."

Chapter Fifteen

"Smile?" I blurted out. "Are you kidding me?"

I was now facing him fully and leaned forward, extremely ticked off. I know that I didn't Jump through God knows where to stand around and smile. Lukas didn't back down. His arms were crossed and he sat upright sitting upright, but I could see a hint of smile on his face.

"Mr. Magnum's orders. Don't worry, Miss Rue, you will be playing an important enough role. You will be the one entertaining the guests, disguised as a wealthy princess from a foreign country."

"Which country?"

"Err, we haven't quite decided yet. We will probably just make something up," he admitted with a small, indifferent shrug. Even the big Elite Agents didn't seem to have it all covered.

"How about the beautiful land of Haju-Malibu?" I offered.

"Haju-Malibu?"

"Hey," I warned. "Don't get in the way of my creative juices. I'm a princess from Haju-Malibu, a beautiful island off the coast of Africa, kind of near Madagascar," Lukas chuckled a bit and turned away.

"Fine. You can be from Juju-Millieboo," he relented.

"Haju-Malibu! I don't want you to blow my cover!" I said with a dramatic eye roll which made Lukas's chuckles grow even louder.

"Captain Lukas, we're awaiting orders." A woman with a short afro stepped by Lukas, completely interrupting our conversation. Lukas nodded and climbed to his feet, all business now. He made his way to front of the bus before spinning around to face us.

"We have arrived in Bojnice, Slovakia. Everyone, suit up." Immediately, everyone climbed to their feet and began to remove their clothes.

I was suddenly surrounded by naked people. All of the Elite Agents were changing out of their jumpsuits and into fancy tuxedos and sparkling gowns they retrieved from their luggage racks. They seemed perfectly comfortable with baring everything in front of company.

Not me. I wrapped my arms around myself, feeling exposed even with my clothes properly in place. I turned and looked at Lukas, who was about to change himself. He caught my eye and fortunately put his shirt back down before making his way back to me.

"I apologize, Miss Rue. I forgot to tell you that your dress is in the bathroom," he said after reaching my seat. "Make sure you put on the hoopskirt before you put on the dress."

"Hoopskirt? What's that?" I asked as I climbed to my feet. Lukas shook his head and ushered me to the very back of the bus. There was a door, which I assumed led to the bathroom. I shot Lukas a glare before I went into the bathroom and slammed the door behind me. I was pleasantly surprised by the size of the bathroom. Instead of a tight square area, like most bus bathrooms, this one actually had room to walk around. It was sparkling clean, from the floor to the toilet. Harv definitely kept his agents pampered.

I walked over to a coat rack, which held floor-length plastic bag, dangling from a hanger. I pulled the bag off, careful not to tear anything on the inside. The unfolding bag slowly revealed a long, golden dress that swept the floor. I pulled the dress from the hanger and held it up to myself. I turned to face the door, from which a floor-length mirror hung.

The dress looked like something a fairytale princess would wear. It was long and golden, with crystals adorning the strapless bodice. The skirt was laden with soft, plush ruffles and white, fabric flowers. I twirled in front of the mirror, enamored by the beauty of the dress. I had never in my life held something as beautiful and delicate as it.

"I almost feel bad putting it on," I murmured as I went to put it back on its hanger. I was surprised to see that I had forgotten about one article of clothing. A smooth, white, dome-like skirt was still dangling from the hanger. I pulled it off and held it up to better inspect it.

It had to be the hoopskirt. I noticed something else lying on the floor, near the toilet. I stood the hoopskirt to the side and picked up the two items on the floor.

Had someone had the audacity put an actual corset in here? I held up the stringy corset and studied it in disbelief. I tossed it over my shoulder. There was no way I was cutting myself in half trying to squeeze into that. I looked at the other item I had picked up from the floor. They looked like a pair of pajama pants with frills at the ends.

"Oh well," I mumbled as I unzipped my jumpsuit and pulled it off. I pulled on the frilly pants and then carefully stepped into the hoopskirt. I tied the strings at the waist as tight as they could go, while sucking in my stomach. As soon as I exhaled, I felt like my intestines were going to pop.

Finally, I slipped on the beautiful dress, which spilled over the hoopskirt and ended right at the floor. I spun around slowly to face the mirror and was met by someone unrecognizable. I stared at the beautiful girl in the mirror in awe. Her expression mirrored my own.

This couldn't be me. I didn't even look like myself in a dress. I looked like and felt like a princess. I reached up and brushed down my flared bangs so that they rested neatly on my forehead. My hand trailed down to rest on my locket. I cracked a small smile, feeling tears in my eyes.

"You guys would be so proud of me," I whispered, my voice heavy with tears. "I look like I'm going to prom." I laughed quietly as a single tear broke free and crawled down my cheek.

"You would probably be the one to do my hair for prom, Mom. And you would kill me, Dad, if you saw that I've cut most of it off and dyed it red. We would take pictures before I left to prom, like any other happy family. If you could see me now…you'd see that I'm not a little girl anymore. We missed that part of my life, getting to experience things together. But I promise…I promise that we'll spend every day together once I get you back. I promise…" Tears were streaming down my face at this point. I buried my face in my hands and sobbed.

"I miss you guys so much…I just want to find you…" I cried.

There was a knock on the door, followed by Lukas's voice. "Miss Rue, are you almost finished?"

My head shot up from my hands. "Uh… y-yeah!" I called back, "Give me a second!" I wiped frantically at my face with my arms before grabbing the roll of tissue near the toilet. I ripped off a bundle and dabbed at my face.

This was no time to cry. I was closer than ever to finding my parents. I couldn't break down now.

"Don't forget to cover your labels with a bit of makeup," Lukas called from the other side of the door. I nodded despite the fact that he couldn't see me through the door. I looked around the bathroom until my eyes landed on a small bag and a pair of gold heels in the corner. I stepped into the shoes, then picked up the bag. I unzipped it. Inside lay bundles of foundation, eyeliner pencils, mascara tubes, concealer sticks, and more. I had never been an expert in makeup. The different brushes and specific shades for specific skin tones had always confused me, so I usually went without.

With a shrug, I picked up a compact filled with brown powder. I picked up a thick brush and began to apply layers of the powder over my dark labels. I was surprised by how well the powder hid the tattoos, especially since it seemed as if they had been growing in length lately. They now extended just past my collarbone. I didn't know what that was about, but I figured it was normal. I was beginning to learn that it was better to just go with the weirdness of my new life rather than question it.

I dabbed a bit of the powder on my face, shakily applied some black eyeliner and mascara, and rubbed on some dark lipstick. I was amazed at the difference makeup made. Girls could hide their entire faces behind makeup if they wanted to.

After I was certain that my labels were completely covered, I put away the makeup bag and grabbed my jumpsuit. I transferred my pocket knife from my jumpsuit to the bodice of my dress. I left the phone and tucked my jumpsuit by the coat rack. "Alright, I'm done," I announced as I threw open the bathroom door and walked out.

Well, tried to. Unfortunately, my dress had other ideas. Lukas and the others, now fully dressed, were gathered by the exit while I struggled desperately to get out of the bathroom.

This is why I hated dresses.

"Miss Rue?" I looked up and saw Lukas maneuvering past the other Elites to make it to me. He stopped in front of me and crossed his arms. He cleaned up pretty nice in his sharp black tuxedo. "Did you not hear? We must leave now."

"Yes, I heard you! I just need one second." I groaned as I ran in place, trying to squeeze the wide, wiry skirt through the small door. I struggled for a few more seconds then sighed in defeat and gave up with an exasperated sigh. I looked up at him, feeling embarrassed.

"I'm stuck," I admitted. Lukas and I stared at each other before a smirk appeared on his face. He gave his head a slight shake before he squatted down a bit, like a football player. I looked down at him as if he were the insane one this time.

"What are you gonna do? Tackle me?" I asked incredulously. Instead of giving me a verbal answer, Lukas reached out and grabbed the sides of my dress and tugged me forward. I tumbled forward with a pop and stopped myself about an inch short of falling on him and probably suffocating him with my dress. I steadied myself by grabbing onto his arm for a moment and then stood up straight, trying to summon my last shreds of dignity.

"Thank you," I said. I fixed my dress and got in line with the rest of the agents. Lukas got in line behind me, trying to put his serious face back on.

"Agents, prepare for dismount." All of the agents, dressed in their fancy clothes, gathered the hems of the skirts and straightened their ties. The Operator, still dressed in street clothes, raised a fist.

"Alright…go!" He slammed his fist down on a button and the shuttle's door slid open. I was hit by a blast of cold air and snow.

"Go, go, go!" Lukas yelled from behind me, nearly bursting my eardrum. We hurriedly rushed down the steps and out of the warm shuttle. I was shocked when my heel crunched into snow. I hugged myself tightly and looked around in amazement at our surroundings.

We were in a winter wonderland. Snowflakes fell slowly down to the world below where they met our exposed skin before melting away into nothing. The night sky clashed with the stark white of the ground below it. The whole world looked as if it had been sprinkled with layers of sugar. I had never in my life seen snow. It was beautiful.

My amazement lasted only so long. The cold was horrifying. My heels sunk into the crunchy snow, which bit sharply at my exposed toes. The whipping snowflakes nipped at our bare flesh like sharpened knives. I wrapped my arms around myself and shivered violently. My love of snow had officially ended.

"We will be back in around three to four hours!" Lukas was shouting at our Operator. The Operator nodded quickly, before slamming the door in our faces. He pulled a speedy U-turn and parked. The black shutters fell over the windows.

"W-W-W-Whoa," I sputtered as the bus glowed and vanished in thin air. "It's gone!" Lukas looked at me and shook his head.

"No, it is still there. See?" He scooped up a handful of snow and packed it into a ball before hurling it like a football at the empty air in front of us. I was surprised when it shattered with a splat against seemingly thin air.

"Camouflage," Lukas explained. I nodded, shivering furiously.

"N-N-N-Nice," I complimented. Lukas gave me a concerned look before turning to face the other agents.

"*Achtung!*" Lukas called out. The Elite Agents snapped to attention and faced Lukas. I got the feeling that he kind of ran things with this group so I stopped what I was doing and faced him, too. He strode to the front of our group and then faced us all, his business face on. He folded his hands behind his back and stared us down.

"We all know what we are here to do today. Group A will come with me to the basement of the ballroom and do the rewiring and whatnot." There was shifting and a small group of about three Elites pulled off to the side, obviously Group A.

"Group B," Lukas continued, "will be in the ballroom with Future, keeping tabs on everyone at the party. You will inform me immediately via Brace if there is any suspicion of detection in the slightest."

The remaining agents, which were about four, moved to the right led by a tall, beautiful woman with a shockingly bald head. She had stunning blue eyes and ruby red lips that were frozen in a thin line. Her expression was neutral as she walked to the front of her group, then tucked her hands neatly behind her. This left me stranded in the middle, with all eyes falling on me. I refused to flinch and simply stared back at Lukas, awaiting orders. I was determined to do well on this mission, even if I didn't seem to be playing a huge role. Lukas fixed me with an icy glare.

"Miss Rue, enjoy the party." He spun on his foot and walked over to where the bus was hidden. He circled it for a moment, putting his hand out to keep an idea of where the bus was.

"I-I-I'm freezing butt over here, L-L-Lukas!" I called out, ignoring the glares from the Elites. Lukas shot me a condescending look before returning his attention to the bus. After a few more circles, he paused and rapped twice, producing two metallic clangs. He took a few steps back and waited.

Suddenly, the ground in front of him slid open with a grinding noise. We all stared as two white limos drove out of the hole and pulled to a stop in front of us. My mouth dropped. Lukas walked back over to us and smiled.

"Let's go enjoy the party, H Corp."

Chapter Sixteen

Group A, along with Lukas, climbed into the front limo. It sped off in a flurry of snow, leaving me with Group B.

"Haste, agents," Future said, immediately taking over as the leader. She didn't have to tell me twice. I was the first one in the limo, where I was met by luxurious warmth. I sighed in relief as I sunk into the soft, cushiony seats and rubbed my hands together, grateful for the heat. The Elites climbed in after me, with Future pulling up the rear. She snapped a few words to our chauffeur before climbing to the back of the limo and taking a seat next to me. She cocked her head and stared at me for some time. Finally, she cracked a smile.

"So, you are Miss Harlot Rue?" she clipped in a British accent. I nodded my head slightly.

"I am pleased to finally meet you, Harlot Rue. I have heard much about you."

"Good things, I hope," I replied with a grin. Future's smile fell.

"No," she replied in a flat tone. My face fell.

"Oh." She was honest, at least.

Future's smile returned and she laughed. "Great things. I have heard great things about you, Harlot Rue. I am pleased that we are working together tonight." I returned the smile. Another Elite, who was sitting across from us, spoke up.

"Agent Future, we are approaching our destination," she said in the same monotonous voice most of the other Elites used. Future nodded at the girl and adjusted the Brace on her own thin arm. I tugged at my own Brace before my attention was pulled to the extravagant sight outside of our windows.

It was like a fairytale come to life. A short distance from where our limo was racing uphill loomed a beautiful castle, surrounded by crystal-clear water on nearly all sides, like a paradise island. Its pale-blue towers climbed towards the moon in the sky while its walls were illuminated by the skylights surrounding the castle.

I leaned toward the window in awe as the chauffeur maneuvered the car around the curved road. I couldn't believe I was in a limo headed for a castle that seemed straight from a children's fairytale story.

"Bojnice Castle. Beautiful, isn't it?" Future was leaning next to me, a small smile on her red lips. "It's normally used as a museum but the leader of E Corporation was able to rent it for his ball tonight."

I noticed more limousines, with flags representing countries from across the globe, ahead of our own limo. There were so many; I couldn't begin to tell where the line started.

"E Corp seems like a very big organization," I stated as I sat back in my seat.

Future frowned. "Bigger than one would think," she said in an annoyed voice. "It's partners with most major companies around the world, which doesn't make things any easier for us. Thus, our underground mole tunnel." She shut her eyes and tilted her head up. "I dream of the day when that wretched leader of theirs drowns in his own blood." She snorted out a humorless laugh and turned away from me.

Okay then. Strange didn't even begin to cover Future. She seemed nice enough, but seemed like she was missing a screw or two. I looked back out of the window at the castle exterior. E Corp was definitely not a rival to take lightly. Judging from the numerous flags on the other limos, they had worldwide connections. Their goal of global unification seemed to already be in motion. The agents back home would probably think twice about their crazy idea to take on E Corp head-on if they saw how many allies they had.

Finally, our limo reached the front of the line. "Let's go," Future commanded. We all began to spill out of the limo, one by one. I noticed a few of the agents taking fur coats from a large container before they stepped out I followed suit and exited the limo, wrapped in an expensive brown fur jacket.

The castle was all the more pretty up close. I stared up in wonder at the humongous castle before me. I still couldn't believe that I, Lola Phillips AKA Harlot Rue, was standing in front of a castle in Slovakia, dressed like a princess. I beamed.

I gathered with the rest of the agents near the entrance of the castle as Future began to speak. "Everyone, split up. Once inside, do not stay together. Scatter and blend. We must not draw attention to ourselves while Group A carries out its assignment," she said firmly. We all nodded. I didn't know about the rest of the Elites, but I just wanted to get out of the cold. I would perform a series of cartwheels in a hoopskirt, if it got us inside quicker.

Our group got into the line formed at the entrance of the castle, waiting to get in. I noticed Lukas and his group slipping around the side of the castle, probably looking for a more exclusive entrance. I couldn't help but want to be in their group. They were going to be doing all of the exciting stuff while I was stuck dancing in itchy long johns.

Taking Future's advice, I pulled out of line, letting those behind me take my place. With nothing else to do while I waited for the others to find an appropriate time to enter, I decided to walk around the premises.

It was hard to believe that places as surreal and beautiful as Bojnice Castle still existed in the world. I walked along the stone path, frozen trees on all sides of me. A fond memory seeped into my brain as I drunk in the beauty of the castle grounds.

* * *

"Lola, what are you doing?" The five-year old version of me looked up in alarm as my mother charged into my room, her eyes furious. She gasped when she saw what I was holding onto.

"What are you doing with my wedding dress?" she yelled before snatching the white garment from my chubby hands. I squinted my eyes up and sniffled, ready to work up a tantrum.

Mom wasn't buying it. "Let one tear come out of that eye and that'll be one hour in time-out, young lady." That brought a halt to all waterworks. I sniffled one more time before I crossed my arms and pouted.

"S'not fair. I don't have any pretty clothes like that," I whined while jabbing a finger at her wedding dress. Mom sighed and patted the dress as if it were a purebred. A fond smile spread across her features.

"One day you will, sweetie. One day, when you're older and you get married, I'll help you pick out the prettiest dress you can find," she promised. My face fell.

"But I don't like dresses. They're itchy," I pointed out. Mom chuckled. She set the dress on my bed before scooping me into her arms.

"Then why were you trying to steal mine, Sticky Fingers?" she teased while smooching all over my face. I giggled and tried to swat her away.

"Well, 'cause...you always look happy when you look at it, that's why," I explained. Mom's smile grew as her eyes were drawn back to her lovely white gown.

"This dress does bring back good memories," she said quietly. She stroked the fabric with one hand. I reached out and mimicked the gesture.

"Did you know that your mom got married in a castle, just like a prince and a princess?" Mom said suddenly. My mouth fell open.

"No...way!" I cried. "Like the Cinder-princess?"

Mom laughed. "Just like that. I forget the name now, but it was a gorgeous castle." She sighed, memories dancing in the brown hues of her eyes. "Oh, Lola, it was so pretty. It was like a fairytale come straight to life. We said our vows under a big tree outside of the castle, before the wedding had even begun. It was one of the greatest nights of my life."

"What were the other greatest ones?" I asked curiously. Mom shot me a playful look.

"Well, another one was when this little chubby chipmunk was born," she said while tickling my belly. I laughed and threw my arms over her shoulders.

"I can't wait to have my own happy dress," I whispered. She squeezed me tighter.

"You will one day, sweetie. I'll make sure of it."

* * *

"Oof!"

I cried out in surprise as I bumped into something and nearly fell flat on the ground. I had been so absorbed in my memory that I had walked right into something.

"Are you alright?" a voice asked. Or rather, walked right into someone. I collected myself before I looked up and came face to face with someone I thought I would never lay eyes on again.

It was Shades, the man I had seen meeting with Eduardo during my DM. He was dressed in the same clothes I had seen him in before: a long black trench coat paired with a black fedora and, of course, his expensive aviators. I knew he was hiding something if he was wearing sunglasses in the middle of the night. Either that or he was trying to look cool.

The only difference in his appearance was that this time, he had exchanged his navy tie for one the color of blood. He was standing not even two feet from me, his fedora tilted so low, it was a wonder he could see where he walked. He stared at me, his hands shoved into his coat's pockets. The golden light from the castle lit up his porcelain skin, making him seem ethereal.

"Oh, I'm sorry," I apologized, feeling flustered. I was about to hightail it out of there, for fear of him recognizing me, but he began to talk again.

"Don't you think this is all a bit over-extravagant?" His voice was as cold and quiet as the scenery. It gave me goose bumps. I knew he was talking to me, but I didn't know how to reply. Luckily, he continued to talk.

"Seems as if the host is trying to compensate for something," he smiled at the castle, "would you not agree?" I had no idea what he was blabbing on about, and frankly, I don't think he knew, either. He was staring up at the castle with a dreamy expression, like he was in a world I wasn't part of.

I raised an eyebrow and shrugged. "Aren't you a part of this so-called...extravagant ball?"

Oops, didn't mean to spill that last part. The cold must have frozen all of my brain cells. I looked over at him, awaiting his response with fear churning inside of my stomach.

Shades's head slowly turned so that those sunglasses were focused on me now. The dreamy smile was gone now. "You could say that. Then again, you could say that I'm a part of everything, actually. My services aren't limited to just E Corp," he explained. I wasn't sure if that meant that he was an enemy or not. I decided to keep digging.

"Then what are you?" I asked curiously. Shades's lips twitched up into a smile and he turned around to face the castle again.

"You could call me a friend," he remarked with a tip of his hat. "And what would you like for me to call you?"

"...Lola," I replied after a bit of hesitation. Shades nodded and looked over his shoulder.

"Have you visited the cavern beneath the nearby courtyard, Lola?" he asked suddenly. When I shook my head, he pointed towards a courtyard in the distance. "It's right beneath there. Perfect place to hide something, don't you think?

With those last mysterious words, Shades bowed and excused himself. He strode off towards the castle, hands still shoved into his pockets. I stared after his retreating outline until he became mixed in with the rest of the party-goers.

"Weird," I mumbled to myself. I hadn't felt any threatening vibes from him, yet I had seen him trading with an E agent. He claimed to be a friend. Whatever he was, it seemed as if he didn't want to harm me. I decided I would take his word for the time being.

I looked around and realized that I had ended up in a garden, where a tall tree with a thick trunk stood, its branchy fingers stretching towards the sky. I stared at the tree for a few moments before I turned around and headed back to the party.

"Welcome to Bojnice Castle," the greeter welcomed me as I passed him by to enter the warmth of the castle. Another man helped me shrug out of my coat, but I barely noticed him. My attention had been stolen by the elegance and beauty of the interior of Bojnice Castle.

High arched white walls covered in portraits of royals surrounded the swirling mass of dancers as they swished around the floor. The ceiling was meters above my head and decorated with dazzling crystal chandeliers that twinkled and glistened like ice in the light.

I gazed around in astonishment, trying to drink in the sounds, smells, and enchanting beauty of the castle. It was like I had just opened a door into the sixteenth century. The little girl in me wanted to squeal and try to find wherever the prince was hiding, but I kept up a calm and cool facade as I stepped into the room.

Couples glided across the floor effortlessly in their ritzy clothes, looking like royalty. I noticed a few familiar faces and realized that they were the rest of the Elites. They looked as normal as anyone else in the room, and I could only hope that the same went for me.

"Excuse me, madam." A cold, clammy hand clamped down on my bare shoulder, startling me. I spun around, ready to fight or flee. It wasn't anyone threatening, though. The guy was practically the opposite of the word threatening. He was short and squat, with thinning black hair and little facial hair. He seemed nervous and was sweating profusely. I regarded him with a steady glare and waited to see what he wanted.

"Um…," the man began, while mopping his forehead with his handkerchief and looking down at the floor. "I am Duke Harold of Europe. I was hoping to ask you for this dance, Miss…?"

"Raevyn, Princess of Haju-Malibu," I finished for him, giving him a smile and as graceful a curtsy I could manage. I wasn't exactly sure of how to dance at a ball, but it was better than standing around and sticking out like a sore thumb. I noticed the other Elites had found dance partners and had joined in on the dancing.

Without much hesitation, I grabbed a startled Harold's arm and dragged him onto the dance floor. We faced each other and waited. I tapped my foot impatiently and crossed my arms. Were we supposed to bust a move or what?

"Milady, if I could just see your hands?" Harold asked politely. I flushed with embarrassment and unfolded my arms with a meek grin.

"Sorry, we don't have too many balls in Haju-Malibu," I admitted, feigning a shy, painful smile. Harold seemed thrilled by this.

"No matter, milady! I am an expert!" Harold declared with a wag of his finger. In no time at all, Harold had grabbed onto one of my hands and held it out a bit, at shoulder-length and then put his other grimy hand on my waist, before pulling me much too close. I was about to tell him to get his sweaty hands off of me but he was speaking again.

"Now, dear, you put your hand on my shoulder." I inwardly groaned but did as told. I was surprised to see that we looked to be in the same position as the other dancers.

"Very good!" Harold complimented. I grinned in spite of myself. "Now, follow my lead."

I learned quickly that I could not waltz. Harold and I stepped on each other's toes and bumped into so many other couples that Harold excused himself and left the party entirely, complaining of an ill cousin. He limped and groaned all the way out of the door.

With a grumpy sigh, I made my way over to one of the empty tables someone had set up around the dance floor. I sat heavily in one of the hard wood seats and sighed again.

"Miss Rue." A voice buzzed in my ear. I reached up and realized that I had forgotten all about my Brace and the handy ear bud it came paired with. I tapped my Brace. The screen slid open, revealing my contacts, along with a new face.

It was Lukas! He had a giant head and giant ears and even his standard frown. Whoever designed our faces sure did get them spot-on.

His face was blinking, so I knew it was him contacting me (that, and the fact that no one else called me Miss Rue). "Yup?" I whispered into my Brace, trying not to look too obvious that I was talking into my bracelet.

"Did you manage to make it into the party with no issues?"

"Yeah, no problem, Commander," I breezed. It hadn't exactly taken a rocket scientist to figure out how to walk into a building. I would love to see what he and the other agents were up to, but I wouldn't complain, at least, not to him. No need to make Lukas think that I couldn't handle this.

"Good to hear," Lukas's rumbling voice replied. "We'll be finished down here in a few minutes. Call me if there are any problems." I heard a click and Lukas's icon stopped blinking. I was tempted to tap on Hack's face and hold a conversation, but realized that I had no idea what time it was back in California. Deciding against it, I sighed again for the fiftieth time that night and dropped my wrist back to my side. My first mission with the Elites was shaping up to be a pretty boring one.

"You know, it's considered quite impolite to sigh so much at a party."

I frowned and looked up, ready to tell whoever my intruder was to get away from me if he didn't like my sighing, but the remark died on my lips.

It looked as if I had ran into that prince after all. The man staring down at me had windswept jet black hair that looked like raven feathers and pale, porcelain skin that was a sharp contrast to his hair and his dark eyes. He was dressed in a handsome black tuxedo that held a single red rose in its breast-pocket.

"You might offend the host," he clipped in a sunny British accent, smiling at me, as if he knew something I didn't.

"The host offended me when he decided that this," I waved around at the dancers, "would be fun." I knew I was acting like a sourpuss, but I shouldn't have had to been there in the first place. This mission could have been completed without me wearing itchy long johns in the middle of Slovakia.

I stared out at the dancers again, hoping he would take the hint and walk away. *No luck.* Instead, he walked in front of me, blocking my view of the dancers and forcing me to look at him. He was still smiling, and I couldn't help but think that his smile seemed familiar.

"I'll make sure to tell him that so he'll keep it in mind for the next ball. What did you say your name was?" he asked. I narrowed my eyes at him suspiciously.

"I never said," I reminded him in a sharp voice. I realized that I was coming off as overly-suspicious so I tried to smooth things over a little. "But my name's Har—I mean, Raevyn."

The stranger's smile quirked up to the side a bit and he nodded, while chuckling a bit. "Raevyn, hm? That's a pretty name but I'm not sure if it suits you." I gasped at his words, making him laugh.

I felt my face grow hot. "So, what, I need to have an ugly name? Like Gertrude?" I asked heatedly, getting ready to find some punch somewhere and throw it at him.

He laughed again and waved his hands around in front of him, as if trying to wave away any negative vibes. "No, no," he said, while still laughing. "I was saying that you look more like a Scarlet, or perhaps a Lola."

I tried to make my face stay emotionless at the sound of my former name, but I flinched and found myself chewing at the inside of my bottom lip, a habit I have had since I was a kid. It happened whenever I was nervous. I knew the stranger had caught my reaction, but he didn't say anything.

"It's the name I'm stuck with," I replied, returning my eyes to meet his gaze after regaining my composure. The stranger nodded understandingly, but looked distracted by something. I followed his gaze and noticed he was staring at Future, whose bald head stood out in the ballroom. She was standing against the wall in her gorgeous, fitted black dress and was scanning over the guests.

"Raevyn, would you mind if I asked for your hand?" the stranger asked suddenly.

"My hand?" I asked, feeling confused. The stranger laughed again, and without another word (or my permission), he whisked me out to the middle of the dance floor and we stood in a waltzing position.

"I didn't say yes!" I cried. The stranger simply smiled that infuriatingly attractive half-smile and began to whirl me about.

This time, I have to admit, I actually enjoyed dancing the waltz. The band was playing a melody that consisted of mostly violins and a piano. We glided gracefully across the floor, while he twirled me around every now and then, helping me stay on track with the dancing. After a bit of spinning, and dancing I felt myself relax and smile some. Unlike my last attempt at dancing, I let my partner take the lead this time, and it worked out much better.

"You dance beautifully," the stranger complimented in my ear as we swept across the marble floor. I smiled and shrugged, keeping my eyes glued to our feet.

"Thanks. Sorry I keep stepping on your expensive shoes, though." His black dress shoes were a bit scuffed now, but he simply shook his head, although I noticed he was looking at his shoes a bit wistfully.

The song slowly came to an end and I found myself feeling a little sad that we had to stop dancing so soon. I had actually enjoyed it. We separated and face one another, smiles on both of our faces. I noticed the other women curtsying to their partners so I did a clumsy imitation.

"Thank you, stranger, for the lovely dance," I joked, when I had stood back up. The stranger bowed low and without warning, grabbed my hand and brought it up to his lips for swift kiss. I stared down at him, speechless.

The stranger kept his head down, but lifted his dark eyes up to meet mine. "A pleasure."

My heart was beating so loud, I was certain that he could hear it thudding inside of my chest. "S-So, you never told me your name," I blurted out, changing the subject, although I wasn't quite sure if I wanted to.

The stranger straightened up and tilted his head to the side, a perplexed look dancing across his face.

"You don't know who I am...?" he asked quietly.

"How would I know you? We just met a few minutes ago."

The stranger studied me for a second, before his handsome features contorted into a simpering grin. "Ah, so you don't. Well, Miss Raevyn, you may call me Kane E. Abel. I'm the host of tonight's party."

"The host...?" I asked. The music seemed to fade away as my head began to feel dizzy. If he was the host of the ball, then that meant that he...

"Yes. Perhaps you might recognize me as the leader of E Corporation."

This was going to be an interesting night after all.

Chapter Seventeen

We stared at each other for a while in silence. It was like the entire ball had faded out around us. The music had died away to a quiet hum.

A million thoughts raced across my mind at once. This was the almighty leader of the E Corporation? He couldn't have been more than eighteen! And I had been waltzing around with him like a star-struck dope.

I had the sudden urge to run. *He kidnapped your parents*, a tiny voice whispered in my head. My urge to run came to an abrupt halt as reality hit me.

I had been dancing with the man who had orchestrated the kidnapping of my parents.

I looked down and my trembling hands and curled them into fists. "Do you know who I am?" I asked quietly. Kane smiled politely.

"Of course I know who you are, Lola. I knew who you were as soon as I laid eyes on you."

"Don't smile at me like you haven't done anything wrong!" I yelled, taking a step toward him. My head was swimming with hate and my heart was thundering against my ribcage. "You're the reason my life has been a living nightmare! You're the one who took everything I had from me!"

By this time, most of the dancers had stopped to watch our scene play out. Kane shook his head at me. "You sad, confused girl," he said with a sad frown. "Your terrible life has nothing to do with me."

I was seeing red now. My hands clenched into shaking fists and I lunged. "You stole my parents from me!" I shouted, drawing my fist back and swinging it right at his face. He was faster than I was, though, and he quickly ducked under it. He looked up at me and laughed. *Laughed!*

I growled like an inhuman beast and shoved him with all of my might. He fell down on the ground, but grabbed my arm and pulled me with him. We began to roll and tumble on the floor, causing people to shriek and run out of the way.

"Where are they?!" I yelled, as we wrestled against one another. I reached into the front of my dress and pulled out my knife, rubbing off some of the powder that was caked on my chest. I flicked out the blade and pressed it against his throat, letting him see that I was dead serious.

"Tell me where they are or you won't be able to bid your lovely guests goodbye tonight," I warned. Kane's eyes flickered from my eyes to the labels that were now evident on my chest. His eyes darkened.

He shook his head at me, a sadness plaguing his dark eyes. "I cannot help you, Lola," he said in a serious voice. I pressed the knife closer, my chest burning up. I inhaled sharply as the pain in my chest doubled.

Oh no, it was happening again. My head began to feel dizzy. I groaned and dropped the knife, feeling like I was about to throw up. Kane took the moment to throw me to the side. He stood up, brushed off his suit and then pulled out a walkie-talkie from his pocket.

"Attention, men," he spoke into it, "We have H agents here. Kill on sight." He shot me a look that almost looked remorseful.

"If I could help you, I would. But it's too late." He reached up and took the red rose from his breast pocket. He tossed it at me. It landed by my feet, scattering a few petals on the floor.

"Goodbye, Lola." He turned and walked away, getting lost in the crowd.

Soon, men dressed in military garb burst into the room, shouting and yelling out commands, turning over tables, and causing mass hysteria. The guests were in full panic mode now. They were running for the exits, a few of them stopping to pick up a pastry from the dessert table on their way out.

I picked myself off of the ground, still woozy, and looked around for Kane. What had he meant by "it was too late"? It couldn't mean…he wasn't saying that my parents were…

"No," I whispered. "No!" A few of the panicked guests bumped me on their way to the exit, and I nearly fell a couple of times, but I barely noticed. My knife was knocked from my hand and went sliding across the floor, getting lost in the stampede of panicked guests.

"Kane! What did you do to my parents?!" I screamed over the chaos. My chest was heaving up and down and I felt something wet leaking down my face. Droplets of red splashed at my feet. Everything was red, like an artist had dumped a bucket of red paint over the entire scenery. The burning in my chest flared up like fire. I screeched in pain and grabbed the sides of my head.

When I looked up, I felt like I was in auto-pilot. "Kane!" I roared again. I didn't even recognize my own voice. I tore off my heels and hoopskirt and threw them to the side, then took off in the direction I had saw Kane running.

"Harlot! We must leave!" I heard Future calling from behind me, but I ignored her and kept running, as if pushed forward by some unseen force. Their mission could wait. Kane had answers about my parents that he was going to tell me whether he wanted to or not.

I weaved through the crowd, shoving people aside like they were ragdolls. Suddenly, I was tackled to the ground by a heavy body.

"We have an H agent!" A muscular E agent hollered into my ear as he struggled to wrestle me on the ground. I looked over his shoulder and saw more of the E agents heading our way.

With strength I didn't know I had, I struggled back against the bulky man. I pinned him beneath me before I began to swing wildly at his face.

"Get off! Get off!" I shrieked repeatedly as I pounded his face again and again and again. He managed to flip me off of him. He grabbed the side of my head with one hand and slammed it against the ground, while pinning my arms behind my back with his other.

The pain shot like a bullet through my head. The burning in my chest faded and I was left feeling like a zombie. My vision was still red but the anger had dissipated.

"Get…off," I mumbled, but I knew it was no use. My voice sounded strange and foreign to my ears. I felt tears welling up in my eyes as the sound of the approaching agents got louder and louder. I was going to either be killed or trapped in a cell for the rest of my life.

"Harlot!" A voice tore through the fogginess that was beginning to settle in my head. Suddenly, the huge E agent was knocked off of me and sent flying. He landed a few feet away from me, unconscious. I stared over at him, too tired to even move.

"Miss Rue, you must run!" I looked up and saw Lukas and Future standing over me. Future was clutching a, black, metallic rod while Lukas was holding onto a pistol and a black box. He held both out to me.

"Take these and run back to where our shuttle is!" He was talking again, but he seemed to be talking in slow motion. I reached slowly out for the gun but my head began to spin along with the room and I lost focus of the gun. My hand clutched at empty air before I let it drop to the floor.

"Can't," I muttered, my voice sounding thick and heavy. My tongue felt huge and fat in my mouth. I noticed Lukas and Future exchange worried looks before Lukas shoved the gun at Future and wrapped her fingers around it.

"Take her and go, Future! Remember what Harv said: we must keep her alive!" Lukas shouted. I couldn't make out Future's expression, but I could feel her hands wrap around my wrist. She placed her other hand on Lukas's cheek and stroked it gently, before taking the box. She made the H sign over her heart, while Lukas returned the gesture. With a sharp tug, she yanked me to my feet and we began running blindly through the ballroom.

"What about Lukas?" I mumbled. My head was starting to clear up now, but my vision was still coated in red. I could just make out the blurs and shapes of people running around.

"Lukas can handle himself," Future murmured in a calm voice, but I noticed it trembled a bit.

"Lukas may be G.I. Joe, but even he can't handle all of those guys!" I said, my voice a little louder now. It was starting to dawn on me—we were leaving Lukas behind so he could buy us time to escape.

"He will be fine," Future reassured me in a harsh voice. We had made it outside now. We raced through the garden and out into the harsh cold of the surrounding forests. I spared a glance over my shoulder and gasped.

Helicopters were hovering all around the castle now, lowering men down into the battlefield, while the ones already on the ground were fighting with some of the other Elite Agents that hadn't been able to escape.

"Keep running!" Future's sharp voice snapped me out of my trance and I continued running.

"Take her and go, Future! Remember what Harv said: we must *keep her alive!"* Lukas's words were echoing in my ears as we ran through the wintry forest. Why? Why was it so important to save me?

Finally, we stopped running. We stood there, in the darkness of the night, trying to catch our breath. Well, at least I was. Future was standing there, looking back in the direction from which we had ran.

"Future, we have to go back!" I protested, holding my throbbing head with one hand. Future simply shook her head, not tearing her eyes away from our path.

"The other agents knew this was a risk. We did what we came to do." She held up the small, black box and held it close to her.

"So, we're just going to let all of the other agents die?!" I whispered, tears forming in my eyes. They stung. "Lukas saved our lives and we just left him there, defenseless!"

Future fixed me with a steady look, her crystal blue eyes gleaming menacingly. I forced myself to glare back, despite the fact that Future was seriously intimidating when she was angry.

"Lukas made a choice. If you went back there, you would be of no help, anyway. You..." She looked me over, a disgusted sneer on her face, "...are weak."

I flinched at her words and looked away. She was right, I guess. I was weak. I hadn't been able to do something right ever since the moment I had stepped foot in H Corp. I kept messing everything up.

Future frowned at my silence and raised her Brace-clad wrist to her mouth. "Agent Future reporting in. Agent Harlot and I were able to flee the scene of the ball. We are awaiting pickup." She lowered the Brace and sucked in a deep breath then let it out slowly. I turned away from Future, refusing to let her see the liquid dripping down my face. The tears stung like fire as they trailed down my cheeks. I was surprised when I saw my tears land on the white snow and change it to a pale red.

Suddenly, the shuttle pulled up next to us. The doors opened and I was surprised to see Marc driving the bus. Lolli and Hack were sitting behind him, staring at me with worried looks. Future got on before me and sat in the back, clutching the box to her chest as if it were a baby. I shakily climbed on the bus slowly and stood in the aisle. Lolli took one look at me before she screamed.

"Your eyes!" she shrieked. I looked at Hack and Marc, who looked equally horrified. I reached up and gingerly patted near my eyes. I pulled my hands back and was shocked to find them covered in thick, dark blood.

"Oh my…what's happening to me?!" I yelled as I swiped like a madman at my eyes. My hands were shaking violently and I began to cry harder, making the blood come that much quicker.

Hack quickly jumped up to aid me. "Don't wipe at them, Harlot! It'll make it worse," he informed me in a stern voice. He guided me over to a seat and sat me down. He pulled out a handkerchief.

"Squeeze your eyes shut," he ordered me gently. I did as told. I felt him press the handkerchief over my eyes. Slowly, the burning began to fade away.

"Thanks, Hack. I've got it," I said while putting my hand over the handkerchief to hold it in place.

"What the heck happened?" Marc asked incredulously. I shook my head.

"I don't really want to talk about it," I said quietly. No one said anything else for a moment. I heard Marc crank up the bus and warm air slowly filtered in.

"You don't have to talk about it," Lolli whispered by my ear. I felt her stroke my hair. I nodded gratefully. I didn't think I could manage to talk about how much of a disaster tonight had been without breaking down.

My parents…were they dead? Was Kane telling the truth when he said that it was too late? I prayed that it wasn't true. I prayed that he was simply bluffing.

Hack patted my back. "My dad will check out what's going on with your eyes," he reassured me. I nodded again as I pressed the handkerchief harder against my eyes. I knew there was something wrong with me now. The burning in my chest, memory lapses, personality change…something was out of whack in my body.

"This was a tough mission. You'll feel better in the morning. Preparing for Hypersonic Mode, by the way," Marc added. He directed the bus towards a hole that was forming in front of bus—our ticket home. I removed the handkerchief from my eyes and got my mask ready.

Somehow, I highly doubted that things were going to look better in the morning. Lukas and the rest of the Elites had been captured because of me. And my parents, whether I wanted to believe it or not, might have been dead.

Chapter Eighteen

When I woke up, I was in the hospital ward…again. This place was going to be my new home pretty soon. My eyes were still sensitive, so I kept them squinted as I peered around the room. My eyes landed on Hack's dad, Doctor Payne.

"Good morning," he greeted me with a cheerful wave as he placed his clipboard on his desk. I waved back, feeling shy.

"Hi, Doctor Payne," I replied. Doctor Payne stood from his desk and walked over to me, smiling.

"Seems you had quite the scare last night, Harlot. Your eyes were leaking blood." He paused and gave me a serious look. "At first I thought you had diabetic retinopathy, but it seems the problem was much less severe." I smiled with relief. I was beginning to feel as if I were on the verge of dying.

He walked over to his desk and picked up his clipboard. He flipped a couple of pages before he looked up and gave me a reassuring smile. "This kind of thing usually happens with new agents. Some of the agents have a hard time adjusting to living underground or their bodies reject the vaccination you received." I nodded, remembering the shot I received from Miss Margie after I had been labeled.

Doctor Payne continued. "Fortunately, this usually only lasts for the first week or so. After a while, your body adjusts and the panic spells will go away."

"That's a relief. I thought I was going to die," I breathed as I patted my sore eyes. Doctor Payne laughed and laid down his clipboard.

"Well, that would be no good. You're a very promising agent, from what I've been hearing," he complimented me. "Now, get some rest and come see me if you have any more problems." I watched as he walked out of the room, dimming the lights behind him. I exhaled and sunk back into the warm covers. It was warm and cozy, like a hug from your loved ones. I just wanted to forget about what had happened last night. The night had went from a fairytale to a nightmare. The Elites were gone because of me.

I heard my door creak back open. I poked my head out from beneath the cover, figuring that Doctor Payne had forgotten something.

"Red." Much to my surprise, Retro was the one standing at my door. I pulled myself up on my elbows and smiled.

"Hi," I greeted him. Retro returned the smile before walking over and sitting on the foot of the bed.

"I can't let you out of my sight, can I?" he teased. "Every time I do, you end up in the hospital."

I laughed despite myself. "No one said taking care of me was easy."

"That's for sure." Retro's smile faded and he fixed me with a steady stare. "What happened out there, Lola? Lolli said you looked as if you were dead on the inside."

"That's a bit dramatic, don't you think?" I cracked, while falling back on the bed. Retro frowned at me, obviously not pleased with my evasion of his question. He scooted closer to me.

"Red, tell me what happened," he said. I placed my hands over my eyes and took a deep breath. I couldn't push this event to the back of my mind like I did with every other unpleasant memory.

"My parents are dead," I announced. I was surprised at how normal my voice sounded. "My parents are dead. I was too late to rescue them."

My words were met by silence. "…Why do you think that?" Retro asked after a moment.

"The leader of E Corporation, Kane E. Abel, told me himself." I squeezed my eyes closed even tighter. "He told me that it was too late. I couldn't find them in time, Retro." By this time, tears were flowing freely down the sides of my face. I felt Retro's smooth hands cover my own. He removed my hands from my face, forcing me to stare up at him.

"Do you really think that they are dead?" he asked in a serious voice.

I shrugged. "Kane said it. He kidnapped them. He would know."

"So, what are you going to do?"

I shrugged again. "I don't know. Go back above ground. Go back to how life was before I became an agent."

Retro frowned at me and dropped my hands like they were on fire. "So, you're just going to give up? I thought that you were better than that, Lola," Retro growled in a bitter voice. He climbed off of the bed and turned his back to me. I sat up on my elbows so that I had a better view of him.

"What else is there to do, Retro?" I yelled. "My parents are dead! D-E-A-D! I can't do anything for them now, can I?"

Retro spun around and glared at me. "You don't know that for sure! They could still be alive!" he roared back. I opened my mouth to say something, but Retro was on a roll.

"No, you just want to give up and return to…to what? Living on the streets? Starving half to death? Having no one?"

My mouth slowly closed as my mind registered his words. Life had never been as good as when I became an agent. Here, I had a home, friends, food, and the best thing of all—a chance to find my parents.

"But…" I mumbled, the fight slowly draining from my body.

"But nothing!" Retro yelled. "If there was even a chance that my parents were still alive, I would search for them until I found out the truth!" We regarded each other in silence. Retro's words hung in the air like smog.

"Your parents are dead?" I asked quietly. Retro's breathing slowly returned to normal. He dropped to the bed and put his face in his hands.

"I found out last year," he said in a numb voice.

"But, Lolli—"

"I haven't told Lolli," Retro admitted. "I can't do it to her. That's been her one wish, to meet our parents again. I found out last year that they were both killed in a plane crash while on their way to California. They had found out that Lolli and I lived here. They were coming to see us, but…" Retro's voice trailed off. He sat up and looked at me with glassy eyes and a coy smirk.

"Don't give up yet, Red. Please." I felt the urge to cry all over again. I wanted to cry for Retro, who looked like a lost little boy, and Lolli, who still didn't know that her parents were dead.

I sat up and put my hand on Retro's shoulder. "I won't give up," I decided. Retro smiled at me and grabbed my hand. He removed it from his shoulder and pulled me into a hug.

"I knew you wouldn't. You're stronger than that," he murmured. I couldn't fight off the butterflies that sprang into my stomach. Being in his arms again was enough to make me firm in my choice to keep looking for my parents.

I pulled away from him quickly. As much as I was starting to appreciate Retro, I wouldn't go down that road again. Retro studied my face with calculating eyes. When he began to lean towards me, I was already half-expecting it. What I wasn't expecting was my reaction.

My body moved on its own. I crashed my lips into his. Retro, shocked at first, took a moment before he began to kiss me back. Just like last time, my mind was completely blown with the feel of his warm mouth against my own. It was like feeling the warm ocean lap against your bare feet in the summer. Retro's fingers entwined with mine as the kiss deepened and I felt myself getting swept away.

I felt like someone had snatched away my oxygen when Retro suddenly pulled away from me like I was a disease. He quickly scooted off of the bed as if he were on fire. I swung my legs over the side of the bed and stared up at him, feeling confused. "What's up?" I asked. Retro was tapping his foot and rubbing at his hair like a drug addict. He blew out a long breath of air before speaking.

"I shouldn't have done that." Well, that was a shocker. Retro was being the responsible one this time.

"It was a mistake, a huge mistake," he continued in a strange voice.

Ouch. True, kissing Retro was definitely a mistake, but I wasn't expecting to hear the words coming from his mouth.

"Look." Retro finally turned around to face me, but he didn't meet my eyes. "I'm sorry, Red, but this," he gestured between me and him, "can't happen again. I'm with…Carma. It's not fair to her if I continue this fling with you."

Double ouch. He had labeled me as what I knew he saw me since the first time we met—a fling. A temporary fun time. I had knew it all along but sometimes, when he stared at me, I thought that maybe I meant a bit more than that to him.

"Fling? That's what I am to you?" I asked, careful to keep the emotion from my voice.

Retro's eyes climbed up to meet mine, but he lost the nerve and looked away.

"Red, you mean much more to me than a fling—"

"No, no, I get it," I said as I stood up and faced him with crossed arms. "You go be with Carma, the girl you want people to see on your arm, and come back to the shadows and play hero with me when you feel like it."

"No, Red, it's not like—"

"It's exactly like that, isn't it, Retro?" I yelled. "Stop playing with me. I'm not a charity case that you can come to and boost your ego when you feel like it!"

"Red, listen to me!"

"No!" I shouted. "I know how you see me, Retro. I'm just a charity case to you. Carma's the trophy girlfriend. Go claim her." I sat back on the bed and grasped angrily at the sheets. Retro didn't speak.

"I'm sorry, Red," he said finally. The sound of the door opening and then closing was my signal that he had left. I was surprised when I felt tears running down my face.

I sat there, replaying what had just occurred between us over and over. I had knew it all along. No matter how many times he saved me or held me or even kissed me, he would be saving, holding, and kissing Lola Phillips, the charity case. Lola Phillips, the girl who had lost her parents and needed help. I would never be seen as an equal in his eyes.

I forced myself out of the hospital bed and stretched. My body felt tired, but my mind was whirring with thoughts. As my eyes fell on the black jumpsuit hanging from the foot of my bed, I felt an ominous feeling wash over me. I hadn't forgotten about Lukas and the other Elites that had been left behind. I needed to push my hurt feelings aside and focus on what was really important. I knew where I needed to go for help.

As soon as I had changed into my jumpsuit, I dodged through the other curious agents out in the hallways until I found the staircase. I took the stairs two at a time, getting closer and closer to Harv's door.

* * *

"Harv, I need your help!" I announced as I burst into his office, not bothering to knock. Harv looked up from his paperwork, looking tired.

"Harlot, dear, I'm afraid I'm particularly busy right now. You can imagine all of the paperwork I'm going to have to do to cover the events of last night," he said before immediately getting back to his paperwork. I noticed that the small black box that Lukas had risked his life for was resting on Harv's desk.

"That's just it!" I cried, feeling myself growing impatient, "Some of the Elite Agents were left behind last night during the fight. We need to go get them!"

Harv didn't look up. He kept writing. "They did what they were supposed to do. There's no need to after them." I stood there, shocked. The only sound in the room was Harv scribbling on his papers.

"What the heck do you mean, there's no need?" I yelled, slamming my hands down on his gold desk. My hands stung a bit but I ignored them and glared at Harv. He kept writing.

Why wasn't he listening to me?

"They stayed behind trying to let me escape! I can't just leave them there and forget about them!" I continued, my voice rising with each word I said.

"But you did leave them." Harv's pen had stopped moving and his silver eyes were now finally focused on me. "It was a necessary action they took and we won't risk anymore agents' lives to bring back those who made a noble choice to save others." I bit my lip and looked down.

"But—"

"Miss Harlot!" Harv's voice was as sharp as broken glass. His silver eyes had turned the same color as storm clouds. "No one is going after them. They are gone—dead. We can't change what happened to them so we might as well move forward."

I stared at him, horrified. "These aren't animals! They're people! People you selected for H Corp! You can't just give up on them!" I screamed, tears threatening to spill over.

Harv sighed and rubbed his temples, looking his age for the first time since I had met him. "Harlot, we are through here. Do not discuss this conversation or last night's occurrences with anyone else, understand?" he asked in a much calmer voice. We glowered at each other in silence. I refused to answer. Harv cocked an eyebrow at my silence.

"I said, do you understand, Miss Harlot?"

I turned away from him and walked to the door. "No, I don't understand," I whispered under my breath before I pushed open the door and walked out.

I slammed the door behind me and stared angrily at the darkness. I didn't understand. But I did understand what I had to do now. I reached up and grabbed onto the locket that Retro had returned to me on the day that we first met. I popped it open and found my parents' faces smiling up at me. They were all I needed to assure myself that I was about to do the right thing.

I would find a way to find Lukas and the others and bring them back home. And I knew two guys who just might be willing to help.

Chapter Nineteen

"Magnet and Trigger?" Lolli was staring at me as if I had sprouted two heads after I asked her a simple question. We were in our room, getting ready for the memorial in honor of the bombing's victims. Everyone was required to wear their jumpsuits, so tardies were to be expected due to the difficulty in putting the things on.

"Yes, what are their room numbers?" I asked again, growing impatient. If my plan was going to work, time was going to have to be on my side.

Lolli continued to stare at me strangely but she asked no other questions. She dropped the brush she was using to detangle her curls and reached over to her nightstand. She grabbed a pink book labeled "Diary" and begin to flip through its patterned pages. She had only been flipping for less than five seconds before she had my answer.

"Magnet Fury is in Room 113. I'm not sure about Trigger's room number, though," she replied before snapping her diary closed. I stared at her.

"What?" Lolli asked, once she noticed I was still staring at her. "Don't you keep certain people's room numbers in your diary?" she asked innocently, as if I were the one with the creepy habit.

"I'd have to say no," I said. We both shared a laugh before Lolli resumed brushing her hair. I watched her, a wave of sadness washing over me. "I'm going to go ahead and leave for the memorial," I said, forcing a grin.

Lolli didn't bother to take her eyes off of her reflection in the bathroom mirror. She waved at me over her shoulder. "Alrighty! I just need to do my makeup and I'll meet you there."

I slipped out of the door, hoping that my performance was enough to convince her that nothing was going on. Instead of heading towards the memorial, I continued along the dorm hallway, searching for Room 113. The hallways, usually crowded with conversing agents, were empty due to the memorial.

"113," I said aloud as I spotted the door with the number printed across it. I crept up to it and stood there. I held up my fist to knock but froze.

What was I doing?

I didn't even know what I was planning on doing. When I had sat at Harv's door, feeling like I could tear up his entire office, I had already made up my mind. I was going to go and get Lukas and the rest of the Elites. It was going to be hard, mostly because I had no idea where they were, but I was determined. I just needed help.

There was no way I was going to involve Lolli, Hack, or Marc. What I was contemplating was completely against Harv's orders and I didn't know what the repercussions would be, which is exactly why I wanted to keep my friends out of it.

Unfortunately, this left me with absolutely no help in my rescue plan. I faintly recalled Lolli or Marc mentioning that Magnet and his friend, Trigger, had been able to slip out of H Corp, unnoticed, last year. If they had been able to do it, I figured they wouldn't mind telling me how it was done. I was desperate and they were my only shot. I went to knock on the door again but still couldn't bring myself to do it.

I heard someone clear their throats, making me nearly jump out my skin. I spun around to find Magnet and Trigger watching me like I was a crazy person. They were dressed in their jumpsuits for the memorial. Magnet's jumpsuit was a mustard yellow while Trigger's was a misty gray.

"We would like to get into our room, if that's alright with you," Magnet said with a crooked smile. Trigger didn't bother to speak.

I jumped away from the door, flushed with embarrassment. "Oh! Um, yeah, go ahead," I sputtered.

Wait, that wasn't what I wanted to say. "Wait!" Both boys paused and turned back to stare at me.

"What's up?" Magnet asked as he unlocked his door with his all-access key. The door slid open. Trigger slipped inside, leaving Magnet and I alone in the hallway.

"I need your help," I said, deciding to just be straightforward.

Magnet raised an eyebrow before his eyes locked onto my hair. He blinked rapidly, recognition dawning on his face. "You're that Harlot chick, right?" he asked, a broad grin spreading across his face. I nodded, not sure if his recognition was a good or bad thing. A lot of agents seemed to only know me as "The Bomb Girl.".

Magnet didn't seem to be one of them. "Hey, I've heard a lot of good things about you. Why would someone like you need help from guys like us?" he asked in a friendly tone.

I nodded behind him. "Can I come in?" I asked. Magnet smiled and stepped aside, allowing me enough space to walk into the room. Trigger was sitting on one of the beds, staring at the metal wall like a zombie.

"So," Magnet stepped around me, the door sliding shut behind him. "You want in on the Bomb Squad, right?"

I blinked. "What?"

"The Bomb Squad is what everyone's calling it now. You want in on the demonstration we're putting on during the memorial, right?" Magnet continued. He picked up a red spray paint can and tossed it to me. I caught it with one hand, still confused.

"What are you talking about? I'm not trying to bomb anyone and I'm not trying to paint graffiti," I said, tossing the can back to him. His confused expression mirrored my own.

"Then why are you here?" he asked, setting the can back on his nightstand. I looked behind me, making sure that the door had closed all of the way. I looked back at Magnet.

"I need help to get back the Elites."

This got Trigger's attention. He slowly turned around to look at me, his pink irises glazed over. As soon as we locked eyes, my chest started burning. Something about him always seemed to make my chest flare up. I figured it had to be nervousness. I scratched at it nervously before my attention was once again snagged by Magnet.

"Whoa, whoa, whoa. What are you talking about? What happened to the Elites?" he asked. I gave him the rundown of my night at Bojnice Castle, despite Harv's orders not to. By the time I was through, Magnet's mouth was hanging open.

"The Elites were captured?" he asked, incredulously.

"Maybe killed, according to Harv," I chipped in.

"Then why are you trying to go find them?"

I frowned at the floor. "Because I don't want to give up on them until I know the truth," I answered, recounting Retro's words.

Magnet studied my face for a long time before he smiled. "I can tell that you're serious about this," he said. He shrugged. "But, we can't help you."

Wrong answer, buddy. "Can't help me?" I echoed. "It's for the good of the corporation!"

Magnet jabbed a thumb over his shoulder at Trigger, who was still observing me in silence. "Trigger and I are expected at the memorial today. We're helping out the Bomb Squad to put on a little demonstration for the rest of H Corp," he explained.

"What's the Bomb Squad?"

Magnet's eyes lit up as he began to explain. "A bunch of the younger agents want to get back E Corp for the bombing. We tried to take it to the senior agents but they didn't want to listen. They said that they were gonna do it their way. According to how your mission went, I'd say their way didn't go as planned. So today, we're gonna show them that we can't be ignored." He picked up the spray can and grinned. "It's gonna be great. You in?"

I pushed the spray can away. "I told you, I have my own thing that I need to do." That and I wasn't quite for the "Bomb Squad's" cause. Like the old saying goes, don't fight fire with fire.

Magnet nodded, looking sad. Suddenly, his brown eyes lit back up. "Alright, how about a deal, Harlot?"

I raised an eyebrow. "What kind of deal?"

"You help us and we help you." When I didn't speak, he went on to explain. "You see, we could always use more people on the Bomb Squad."

I could see where this was going and I didn't like it. "I already said I can't do whatever kind of demonstration you plan on doing today. I've got to get a shuttle and get out of here."

"And how do you plan on commanding a shuttle? You know any Operators?" I frowned as his words sunk in. Marc was the only Operator I knew but I had already promised myself that I wasn't going to involve my friends.

Magnet's grin grew. "That's what I thought. Trigger here isn't an Operator, but he knows how to operate the shuttle like a pro. If you could find it in your heart to join the cause, maybe Trigger and I could show you how it's done."

I was between a rock and a hard place. There was no way I was going to attempt a Jump or whatever it was without proper guidance. I didn't want to end up as a pile of jelly or worse after attempting to Jump. If there's anything worse than being a pile of jelly.

"C'mon, Harlot." Magnet's grin was gone and was now replaced with a determined look. "Don't you think that what we're doing is the right thing? If we just stay here and shrug off the bombing like it was nothing, they're just going to keep doing it until our whole base is gone. We all need to band together and show them that we're not afraid to fight back."

"I don't know…" I was starting to cave, but I still wasn't sure I wanted to be involved in something that had nothing to do with me. The only reason I had become an agent was to find my parents. I hadn't signed up to fight wars and lead demonstrations like some kind of politician.

A new voice cut into our conversation. "Don't you want to get back at them for taking away your parents?"

I looked over and saw that it was Trigger who had spoken. He was staring up at me from his spot on the bed, eyes no longer glazed over. He climbed off of the bed and took four slow strides towards me. He stopped in front of me and fixed me with his glossy-eyed stare.

"Don't you think E Corp deserves whatever we can do to hurt them?" His voice was scratchy and soft, like he had been smoking his entire life. "Or do you not care that they ruined your life?"

"You know nothing about my life," I said sharply, feeling myself grow angry. I wasn't sure who my anger was directed at. The very mention of E Corp was enough to send my mind right back to Bojnice Castle. Just thinking of Kane Abel's smug face made me want to punch a wall.

"I know more than you think," Trigger said, his abnormal eyes flashing. "Now or you going to help us or not? If you aren't, good luck trying to get the Elites back on your own."

I could punch him in the face, but that wouldn't change the fact that he had made a valid point. My chances of getting the Elites back without their help were slim to none. Without their help, I wouldn't be able to rescue a soul.

"Fine," I said, throwing my hands up in surrender, "I'll join the Bomb Squad."

Magnet grinned at Trigger before slapping a hand on my back. "That's what we wanted to hear! Everyone's going to be hyped that you joined. Believe it or not, a lot of people look up to you."

I rolled my eyes at the ceiling. "That's hard to believe."

Magnet was insistent. "No, really! Yeah, maybe some people are a little angry about the bombing so they're not thinking straight. But the other kids think that you're something else."

"Because of my DM?"

"Not just because of that. Everyone knows what you're trying to do for your parents and they admire that." It had never crossed my mind that I wouldn't leap at any chance to save my parents. Children were naturally protective of their parents, in my opinion.

"Wouldn't anyone in my shoes do the same thing?" I asked, surprised.

"You'd be surprised," Magnet said. "Now let's hear the details. What exactly are your plans for getting the Elites back here?"

I faced them and lowered my voice. "I'll be honest with you guys. I'm not supposed to be doing this. Harv told me specifically not to go after them. If you don't want to help me, feel free to say no. This is probably going to get me into a lot of trouble."

"A lot? Try a ton," Magnet chuckled. "But, that's no problem. Where are we taking the shuttle to?"

I blinked, shocked. "We? I just need you guys to show me how to operate it."

"What's the fun in that? If someone's doing something that's against the rules, you know we've gotta be part of it," Magnet said while holding his hand up for five.

I eyed his hand until he dropped it. This wasn't a celebration. "So you're just in it for a thrill ride?" I asked dryly.

Magnet shrugged and shot me a bright grin. "We like to have fun. It's a plus that we get to help out someone. What's the plan?"

I wouldn't complain about their reasons for wanting to go. Agreeing to help was good enough for me. "I don't actually have a plan," I admitted after a short pause. I hadn't made plans for the next steps following getting their help. Trigger grunted and sat back on the bed, resuming his game of "Stare at the Wall". He had officially checked out of the conversation.

"What?" I cried. "I didn't think I would make it this far!"

Magnet blew out a huff of air. "Look, we don't want to go on a wild goose chase looking for the Elites. We need some solid facts and plans about where we're going and what we need to do once we get there."

I thought I was the serious one.

Magnet eyed my wrist. "Have you tried checking in with one of the Elites?" I followed his gaze and locked in on my Brace.

How could I have forgotten about my Brace? "That's it!" I cried as I quickly opened my Brace's screen and popped in my ear bud. I tapped on Lukas's icon and waited.

"Lukas?" I whispered. We waited with bated breath for a reply. After the ten longest seconds of my life, I heard a familiar German-tinged voice.

"Agent Rue?"

I nearly fainted with relief at the sound of Lukas's voice flowing from my ear bud. "Lukas! Lukas, where are you?"

It took a while for him to reply. "I'm not sure. They took me and the rest of the Elites to a cave, I believe. Harlot, did you manage to make it back to base?"

"Yes, all thanks to you, Commander," I said, smiling with eyes filled with tears.

"Harlot, listen to me," Lukas said suddenly.

"What's up?"

"I'm not sure how long they plan on keeping us alive down here, so I have a favor to ask." He paused. "If you see Eliza…Agent

Future, please tell her that I am okay. I don't want her to worry about me."

I thought of Future. I hadn't seen or heard a sign of her since we had made it back to base. Something told me that she wasn't going to be too happy seeing my face, judging from her harsh words she had for me the other night.

"You can tell her yourself, Lukas. Some other agents and I are coming to rescue you."

"No, Agent Rue!" Lukas's voice was so loud, I nearly had to pull out my bud. "You are to do no such thing. Stay at base. We will be fine."

"Yeah, right, Lukas! That's why you want me to send your goodbyes to Future! Tell me where you and the others are, exactly."

"Agent Rue—"

"You're not talking me out of this Lukas! Just tell me where you are!"

A long pause of silence followed. When Lukas spoke again, his voice was barely a whisper.

"We are still in Bojnice, Slovakia, in a cave." I turned my head and repeated the information to Magnet, who jotted it down. "Agent Rue, please…be careful." My ear bud fell silent. I looked at my Brace and saw that Lukas's icon had stopped flashing.

"They're still in Bojnice! We've got to go!" I cried.

"Whoa, wait, Harlot!" Magnet said, holding up a hand. "Trigger and I still have to do that demonstration, remember?"

I sighed, impatiently. "How long will that take?"

Magnet laughed. "You are something else. I guess we can find someone else to fill in for us, if I tell them now."

"Thank you, Magnet. And you too, Trigger. This means a lot," I said truthfully.

Three loud beeps sounded. Magnet's head snapped up while Trigger continued to stare blankly into space. "Agents," Miss Margie's voice sounded, "please report to the Ceremony Hall at this time for the memorial."

"There's our cue," Magnet announced with a smile. He turned to me, business face on. "If we're doing this, this is our shot to get out of here unnoticed and a chance to get some gear." Magnet nodded at Trigger and they both began to move around the room, gathering different items.

"We've got to move fast, before they notice that we're not at the memorial," Trigger noted as he started up the World Wide Wall. He typed "Winter" in the search bar and began to scroll through rows of coats, gloves, scarfs and earmuffs. He shot me a look over his shoulder. "What size are you?"

"Size 'none-of-your-business'," I replied while walking over to the wall. I snatched away his key and wrote my size under a black coat with matching gloves and scarf. Remembering how cold it was the last time I went to Bojnice, I also ordered a fluffy hat and earmuffs. I hit the order button and then handed Trigger back his key. He shook his head and then went on to order his and Magnet's outfits.

"How much time do we have to get out of here before they notice?" I asked as I went over to their closet. I threw it open and pulled out my ordered outfits, along with the clothes Trigger had ordered. I tossed their things on the bed before starting to pull on my new clothes.

"Fifteen minutes, approximately. They usually do a head count, so that'll give us some time," Magnet said, while zipping up his dark coat. "We still need to go get some gear, though."

"Gear? Aren't we wearing it?" I questioned.

Magnet laughed. "No, these are clothes. We need more gear like your Brace. We'll probably need a couple of Sandmans, maybe the L.E.N.S. too."

"Aren't things like that in Miss Margie's office? How are we going to get past her?"

"She's at the memorial," Trigger announced. "She's always in charge of events. We just have to walk in and take the stuff. Nothing too difficult about that."

"Wait, we're going to steal from her?" I gasped, stopping halfway into zipping up my coat.

Magnet nodded. He swung his bag over his shoulder and tossed me one. "Yeah. If we're going to do this, you have to be prepared to get your hands dirty."

I caught the bag and slung it over my shoulder. "I am prepared," I shot back. "Miss Margie is a nice person. It just doesn't feel right stealing from her."

"Get over it, Robin Hood," Trigger scoffed. "Given your background, it shouldn't be that much of a leap for you."

"Don't go there with me," I dared him, while stepping toward him, my gloved hands balled into fists.

Trigger laughed and stepped up to meet me. "What? I'm telling the truth, aren't I?"

"I…" I didn't have a response for that. I had resorted to stealing for a short time while I was homeless. I regretted doing it, so I didn't need him bringing up my past.

"You guys, calm down!" Magnet stepped between us, successfully defusing the brewing tension. He put an arm around both of our shoulders and pulled us closer. "We're a team now, so let's act like it, huh?" He shot us a big grin before letting us go. Trigger and I continued to glare at each other, but I was forced to look away from him when my chest flared up.

"Fine," I said. "Let's go get the gear and then get out of here."

"That's what I wanna hear!" Magnet cheered. He opened his door but didn't walk through it. Instead, he turned back to look at me. "You sure you want to do this? You know, this could ruin your chances of finding your parents."

My chest tightened. Would Harv really cut off his help in finding my parents? Could I really risk the chance of finding my parents for the Elites?

I had to make a decision. "Yeah," I said after a long pause. "Yeah, I want to do this."

Magnet smiled and nodded approvingly at me. "Then, let's get going, baby."

* * *

"Keep the lights off."

Magnet, Trigger and I walked into the Administration Office, being as silent as possible. This was a bit difficult for me, thanks to the loud heels on my pair of black boots.

The office was dark and silent. The only sound (besides my clicking heels) was the sound of static coming from the television mounted on the wall.

"All of the gear is behind her desk," Magnet said. We hurried to the door leading to the back of the office and went inside.

Miss Margie really needed to clean up her office. It looked as if a tornado had touched down right in the center of it. Empty chip bags, soda cans, candy wrappers, and crumbs were strewn all over the floor and desk. I was surprised there weren't rats slithering around.

"She needs a maid," I mumbled as we gingerly stepped through the ruins.

"We've been telling her that forever," Magnet sympathized. He glanced around. "She keeps the gear in the file cabinets. Grab anything you can, but Sandmans and a pair of L.E.N.S are what we are really aiming for."

We all went to work, digging through the messy file cabinets as best as we could in the dark. I gathered as many first aid kits and bandages as my bag could fit.

What did a L.E.N.S. look like? Or better yet—a Sandman? I dug around the bottom drawer, flipping through piles of papers and objects. There were glass vials, nail polish, and even a box of doughnuts, but I didn't see anything that reminded me of sand.

I grabbed onto something hard. I pulled it out and studied it in the light of my Brace. It was another glass vial, filled to the brink with black liquid. I studied it carefully, twisting it from side to side, before I tossed it back inside. I heard it clang against something hard.

I shone my Brace's light into the cabinet and was shocked to find bottles upon bottles of the black liquid. I popped the cap off the top of one vial and sniffed. I recoiled instantly in disgust. It smelled like really strong alcohol mixed with something that smelled old, like dust.

I dropped the vial back into the cabinet and shut it. Something that smelled like a uncleaned toilet could not be useful.

"You find anything yet?" Magnet whispered from across the room.

"Not yet," I whispered back. I moved onto the next drawer. This one was filled with familiar metal orbs. I grabbed a handful and turned to face the boys.

"These would probably come in handy," I announced, recalling the time Retro had used one on me. I felt the corner of my mouth lift a bit at the memory. There was a sharp pang in my chest, pulling me back to the present. I couldn't afford to think about Retro right then.

I held a few out to Magnet, who took them with a pleased smile. "You found the Sandmans, Rue! Let's stock up on these." He and Trigger began to empty loads of the Sandmans into their bags. I grabbed a handful and slipped them into the pockets of my jumpsuit.

"Now, we just need to find the L.E.N.S," Magnet said, as he returned to searching through the cabinets.

"What are those?" I asked.

"They stand for Legit Eyesight and Night Sensors. They look just like a normal pair of sunglasses but they can sense body heat, give you night vision, and even 20/20 vision."

Cool!

"I've got to have a pair of those," I said excitedly. I resumed my search, digging through cabinets with newfound speed. It wasn't long before I found a cabinet filled to the brink with rectangle, shield-style sunglasses.

"Are these Oakleys?" I cooed as I slid a pair onto my face.

It was like someone had pulled a film from over my eyes. I looked around the office. Everything was sharp and crisp, like everything in the room had been outlined with charcoal.

"Whoa."

"Pretty cool, huh?" I turned around to find Magnet grinning at me. With the sunglasses on, I could see every detail of his face, down to the nearly invisible mole on his cheek.

"Yeah," I breathed.

"You can switch into night vision and heat sensor mode by pressing the little buttons on the right arm."

I reached up and felt along the temple until I felt a small, round button. I pressed down on it.

"Oh!" My head snapped up as my vision turned green. The room, which was once almost completely black, had lighted up in a sea of bright, fluorescent green.

That had to be the night vision. I reached up and pressed the next button. I had to blink my eyes a few times to adjust to the rainbow colors that flooded my eyes. I swung my head around, trying to make sense of the wide array of colors.

My eyes finally landed on Magnet, who was lit up like a sunset. Cross hairs focused on him before the text "human" flashed in my eyes. In the bottom right of my vision, there was even a thermometer that read his body temperature.

"If you're through playing around, we need to go," Trigger's voice sounded, breaking into my world.

I looked up at the ceiling, annoyed, before turning to face Trigger. "Aye-aye, Cap…" My sentence died away when my eyes landed on him. Unlike Magnet in heat sensor mode, Trigger's body was on fire. There wasn't a speck of yellow or even orange in his outline. The thermometer was off the scale.

I pulled off the L.E.N.S. and stared at Trigger. His face turned uncomfortable under my scrutiny.

"Trigger…"

"Let's grab the stuff and go," Trigger said quickly, while striding behind me and grabbing his own pair of L.E.N.S. He shot me a glare while he pushed his sunglasses on top of his head, then sped out of the room.

I stood up from my crouching position and faced Magnet. "Tell me what's wrong with Trigger."

Magnet studied my face, the grin slowly dissipating from his face. He dropped his eyes to the floor.

"Trigger is really sick."

"Sick?"

Magnet nodded. "I mean, really sick. He's got a rare disease that made him look the way he does. He doesn't like to talk about the details of it, but the doctors say that he doesn't have too long to live."

"Is there a cure?" I asked. I was surprised that I was feeling sympathetic towards a guy that I had deemed an annoying jerk a bit earlier. But, he was risking his neck to help with the rescue mission, so I couldn't really be that angry with him.

Magnet shrugged, but I could see his eyes. They looked tired and sad. "No one's found one yet. They're working on it, but they haven't had much progress. All they can give him are meds for the pain."

"That's horrible…."

"Yeah, but don't let him see you feeling bad for him. He hates when people do that."

I could relate to that

Beep.

Beep.

Beep.

"Attention, all agents." Magnet and I froze as the intercom turned on and Miss Margie's voice rang out. "Field Agent Harlot Rue, Field Agent Magnet Fury, and Field Agent Trigger Reverse, please report to the Ceremony Hall at this time. I repeat, please report to the Ceremony Hall at this time. Senior agents are on their way to retrieve you from your rooms."

The intercom shut off.

"We've got to move," Magnet said. I was already on my way out of the door. I raced into the hallway, almost bumping into Trigger, who was on his way inside.

"We need to get on a shuttle before they close all of the gates," he said in a breathless voice.

"Let's hurry, then," Magnet said. We ran down the hallways as fast as we could, burdened down by our gear and winter clothing. We swerved around corners and ducked through hallways until we saw the parking zone a few yards ahead of us.

"Halt!"

Shoot. We looked over our shoulders to find five senior agents rushing towards us.

"This isn't good," Magnet murmured as we stood in place and faced down the agents.

"Wait for it," Trigger said suddenly. "It should be happening soon."

"What are you three doing out here?" one of the senior agents yelled as they approached us.

"What do we do?" I whispered.

"Wait," Trigger repeated. In the next second, the lights flickered and then died. The senior agents cried out in surprise, but I couldn't see them.

"Put on your L.E.N.S. and head for the nearest shuttle!" Trigger ordered. I hurriedly slid on my L.E.N.S and switched into night vision mode. The green, glowing outlines of the senior agents were fumbling around, using the walls for support.

"Harlot, come on!"

I spun around and saw Trigger and Magnet already rushing towards the parking zone. I glanced back at the agents before I took off after them.

We climbed into a black shuttle, the nearest one to us. Trigger sat in the Operator's seat and began to push buttons and pull levers.

"Hurry it up dude, hurry it up!" Magnet urged as he leaned over the seat and looked nervously out of the windows.

"I can't do anything until the Bomb Squad turns back on the power!" Trigger yelled back. I noticed his breathing was short and rapid, while his eyes looked wild and disoriented. He slammed his hands down on the control panel and cursed.

I grabbed his shoulder and forced him to look at me. "Now is not the time to throw a temper tantrum, Trigger!" I whispered loudly. The voices of the senior agents were getting closer by the second. It was only a matter of time before they managed to find us in the darkness.

"I know that!" Trigger yelled back. He pulled away from me and went back to pulling switches and spewing out curse words.

I turned to Magnet. "The Bomb Squad turned off the power?" I asked.

He nodded. "Yeah, for the demonstration. It's lucky timing for us, but they're going to be turning the power back on pretty soon."

There was no time to waste. "Trigger, go lay down in the back," I ordered. Trigger looked at me, face etched with confusion.

I pointed at the back and gave my best impression of my mom. "Go! You need to rest!"

Trigger eyed me for a few more seconds before he stood up and went to do as told. I took the Operator's seat and looked down at the rows of lights and switches.

"I thought you didn't know how to do this?" Magnet asked worriedly. I nodded absent-mindedly, while brushing my hands over different buttons but not activating them.

"How hard can it be?" I reached out and flicked on a switch.

"Whoa!" I grabbed onto the sides of my seat as the shuttle began to vibrate. Magnet fell on ground as the shuttle continued to vibrate like a cell phone.

"Why do they even have this switch?" I groaned as I flipped it back off. The vibrating stopped, allowing Magnet to climb to his feet.

"Maybe I should get Trigger back up here," Magnet pondered.

"No, I can do this." I scanned the control panel, searching for something that resembled a Jump button. Whatever those were supposed to look like.

Suddenly, the lights outside of the shuttle turned on. The shuttle beeped and whirred, the power returning to it. A small screen on the panel lit up, revealing a GPS system. I typed in Bojnice, Slovakia then searched frantically for the activation button.

"We're almost out of time! Just hit something!" Magnet yelled. He was already putting on his mask and instructing Trigger to do the same.

"Stop yelling at me!" I yelled back.

"Then hit a button!"

"Fine!" I slammed a button with my fist, then jumped up and grabbed my own mask.

The bus whirred again and I was relieved to hear the computerized voice announcing, "Commencing Hypersonic Jump in 10…9…8…."

The black shutters began to lower. I snuck one last look out of the shutters. The senior agents were running from shuttle to shuttle, yelling and ordering each other around.

My heart nearly quit when one of the agents looked up and caught my eye.

"There they are! They're in the A shuttle!" he yelled, while pointing right at me. I ducked in my seat and fixed the mask on my face. I felt the slight pinch as it meshed with my skin.

"5...4...," the computer droned. *Hurry, hurry!* I glanced behind my seat and saw Magnet and Trigger, already fast asleep in their seats.

"3...2..." There was a loud banging on the shuttle's door.

"Agents! Open up immediately!" Their voices were already beginning to sound far away and distant. My eyes slid shut, the faint sound of sirens ringing in my ear.

Chapter Twenty

When I awoke, I was on the floor of the shuttle, right next to a drooling Magnet. Trigger had somehow managed to stay in the same position. He was still sleeping peacefully at the back of the bus.

I sat up and stretched before popping off my mask. I yawned and then nudged Magnet.

"Magnet, wake up. We did it," I mumbled, still feeling groggy. Magnet grunted and slowly opened his eyes. He sat up carefully and stretched like a cat before taking his own mask off.

"Well done, Rue! I guess you deserve your Operator license after all," Magnet said with a dopey smile as he climbed to his feet. I laughed and shrugged.

"I just hit buttons. You guys did everything else. You gave me the plan, and the clothes, and the gear," I smiled. "Thank you."

Magnet smiled back and held up his hand for five. This time, I didn't leave him hanging.

"If you two are finished with Sappy Time on A-Shuttle, I think we'd better get moving."

Magnet and I looked over to see Trigger smirking at us.

"Ha-ha, you should make jokes more often. It's better than you frowning up like a little toad," I joked as I tightened my coat and pulled down my hat.

Trigger frowned at my comment and pushed past me to claim the Operator's seat. *Geez, someone couldn't take a joke.* "We need to get to the Elites as quickly as possible. They'll be after us soon," he said.

"Lukas said that they were in a cave," I said as I leaned over Trigger's seat to watch him work. Trigger tapped the control screen like an expert, scrolling around the map with his fingers. Magnet soon joined us.

"Are there any caves around here?" he asked. Trigger continued tapping a moment before he nodded.

"There's one that's famous. It's an underground cave near Bojnice Castle," he said.

That had to be it! "That has to be the one Lukas and the others are being held at!" I exclaimed. "Can you set the coordinates for there?"

Trigger nodded and with a few taps, he had programmed Bojnice Castle into the system. He shifted the shuttle into drive and we began to move forward.

I sat down behind the Operator's seat, nervousness churning in the pit of my stomach. The shutters over the windows were still down, so I knew that we were invisible to outsiders.

I felt my seat shift. I looked over and saw that Magnet had taken a seat beside me.

"You aren't getting nervous now, are you?" he asked.

"Am I not supposed to be nervous? We just stole a shuttle and snuck out of H Corp. Now the entire base is going to be looking for us," I exclaimed.

"Hey, it was your idea."

I looked away. "Yep. Stupid idea, right?"

Magnet shrugged. "It was the best you could come up with on short notice. Besides, we're doing the right thing by going to rescue the Elites."

I turned my head to look at him. "You think so?"

"I know so. You haven't been an agent as long as me, but I personally knew half of the Elites. Everyone in H looked up to them. They were role models for all of us. Especially Lukas." Magnet grinned and leaned his head back against the seat. "Lukas was the only Elite who would actually speak to you and when he did, he always said something that made you respect him that much more."

I smiled, thinking about Lukas. He was definitely a serious person, but he was also the only Elite who had been genuinely kind to me.

"I know what you mean. I hope Harv will understand that we had to do this."

My Brace suddenly vibrated, causing both me and Magnet to startle. I looked down at my Brace and was surprised to see the words "VIDEO CHAT" flashing on its screen with the words "accept" and "decline" below them I glanced at Magnet, who shrugged in reply.

"It could be Harv," he warned.

"If it is, maybe I can explain to him why we had to do this. Might save us some trouble when we make it back," I replied. I hovered my finger above the "decline" before I quickly tapped "accept". My screen crackled and fizzled with static. Magnet and I watched, not uttering a sound.

"Harlot! Oh my gosh!"

"Lolli?" I cried in disbelief. Lolli's round face finally appeared on the screen, looking worried and distraught. Agents of all levels were racing like horses in the background, shouting in different languages, bumping past one another, and making a mess. It was pure chaos.

"Harlot, where are you? Did you really run away from H Corp?" Lolli cried, tears streaming down her face.

"No, Lolli, I'm not running away," I said, trying to console her.

"But, that's what Harv said!" Lolli sobbed. "He said that you and two boys stole a shuttle and drove it out of here! Did you not like it here with us, Bunny? I promise, I'll let you use the bathroom first in the morning if you come back! And I'll try not to snore as much! I'll even let you wear black! Every hour, every day! Please, Bunny, please don't leave!" Lolli was sobbing her poor eyes out by this time.

"Lolli, get a hold of yourself!" I yelled. Lolli sniffled a couple of times but then began sobbing all over again. I sighed and tried again.

"Lolli, I'm not running away. I'll be back before you know it," I assured her. Lolli rubbed at her eyes, mascara dripping down her rosy cheeks.

"You…you are? Where'd you go?" she asked. She squinted her eyes at the screen before continuing. "And is that Magnet sitting next to you?"

"Yep. What's up?" Magnet greeted her with a nod of her head. Lolli's eyes nearly bugged out of her head as she locked onto Magnet.

"Oh! Oh, hi!" she giggled while attempting to wipe the snot and makeup from her face with the back of her sleeve. "How long have you been there?"

"Long enough to see that we're in trouble," Magnet replied, pointing to the crowd of panicking agents behind Lolli. Lolli glance behind her shoulder before leaning in closer to the screen.

"Oh, you guys aren't the only ones in trouble. Today, at the memorial, some boys thought that it would be a good idea to turn the power off. They spray painted this message on the wall that got everyone really upset. Harv's trying to find out who they were *and* where you guys rushed off to." Lolli pouted. "Harlot, what's going on? Where'd you go?"

"I can't tell you yet, Lolli," I admitted. "But, I'll be back soon. Just promise me that you won't tell Harv or anyone else that you talked to me."

"Bunny—"

"I've got to go, Lolli." I saw the twinkling lights of Bojnice Castle ahead and knew that I needed to cut our conversation short. "Hold things down for me while I'm gone."

"But, Bunny, I need to tell you—"

I ended the video chat and closed the screen of my Brace. I would have to finish my conversation with her later. We were fast approaching the familiar outline of the Slovokian castle and we weren't the only ones here.

"Looks like this is going to be harder than we thought," Magnet noted as he leaned over the seat and stared out of the front window.

Bojnice Castle was surrounded by military jeeps and men in uniform, patrolling the area. Helicopters circled the castle, their spotlights roaming the snowfields and trees beneath them.

Trigger slowly brought the shuttle to a halt and then looked over his seat at us.

"This is as close as we're getting to the castle," he announced. He shot me a challenging glare. "Where's the cave, Rue?"

"Excuse me? I wasn't the one who discovered that there was a cave around here. That was you, Sherlock," I retorted.

"I said that there was a cave. I didn't say that I knew where it was."

"Well, I don't know where it is either."

"Of course you don't."

"What's that supposed to mean?"

"Down, you two!" Magnet cut in. He glanced between the two of us. "Didn't I say that we were a team?"

"Yes," Trigger and I muttered in unison.

"So why are you two arguing like tween girls at the mall?"

"Don't ask me. He's the one who's had a problem with me from the beginning," I defended myself. I looked back over at Trigger, who met my glare with one of his own. "What's your problem? I've tried to be nice to you over and over again but you treat me like I ruined your birthday party."

"Do you really want to know?" Trigger asked. "Do you really want to know what my problem is, Harlot Rue?"

"I've got your soap box right here," I taunted, while gesturing at the ground. "And if you need a few tissues, I have plenty."

"You guys—" Magnet tried to intervene again but a sharp glare from Trigger was enough to shut him up. Trigger's eyes flicked back over to me, pink and narrowed.

Suddenly, his eyes fluttered, rolled to the back of his head and he fell like a rock to the floor.

Wasn't expecting that.

"Trig!" Magnet was at his friend's side in a flash. He helped him into one of the seats and laid him down so that his head was resting on one of the bags filled with extra clothing and gear.

I crept over and watched as Magnet pulled out a vial filled with a familiar black liquid. He pulled out a syringe and slowly drew the liquid into it. He flicked the syringe like a pro before injecting the fluid into Trigger's jagged shoulder tattoo.

Trigger twitched a bit but other than that, he barely flinched as the large needle pierced his flesh. I noticed his breathing slow back down to normal and soon, he looked as if he were sleeping peacefully.

"What was that?" I asked.

Magnet slid the syringe back into his pocket and climbed back to his feet. "He passes out a lot, y'know, because of the disease. I just give him a shot of this stuff," he waved the now empty vial around, "and he's back up in a few minutes, maybe an hour." I had to bite my tongue to stop myself from blurting out something as inconsiderate as "An hour? He's going to be asleep for the entire mission."

"What is that black stuff?" I asked instead as I took a blanket down from the luggage rack and draped it over Trigger's dozing body. He looked peaceful, for once.

Magnet frowned at my question. "This stuff? Haven't you seen it before?" I shook my head.

Magnet's face turned even more confused. "They didn't inject you with this after you were labeled?"

I dug around my memory, searching for any remembrances of a black vial. I remembered being injected with a liquid, but I remembered it being white.

I said as much to Magnet. His frown grew as I finished recounting the details of my Labeling and the injection that followed.

"That's weird. Most agents get this injection when they're first Labeled," he said, while studying the tattoos near the dip in the front of my jumpsuit.

"Maybe they changed it," I guessed, although I wasn't too sure. "Back to the matter at hand—I think it's safe to say that Trigger needs to sit out on the rest of the mission."

"Yeah, I wouldn't count on him getting up until much later. So, boss lady, what's the plan?"

I chewed on the inside of my lip while gazing out of the front window at the battalion of armed soldiers parading around the castle's perimeters. I had never been given the leadership role before but Magnet had certainly just passed me the title. I took a deep breath and tried to focus.

I spun around to face Magnet. "Okay, here's the plan," I said finally. "We're going to stand out like sore thumbs in our jumpsuits and giant coats, so those will have to be the first things to go."

"You want us to go out in that snowstorm with no clothes on?" Magnet said in disbelief as he pointed a finger toward the window, where sheets of snow flurried by.

"Um, no. I meant that we're going to have to find a way to blend in with the rest of the soldiers out there or at least blend in with the snow."

I began to tear through the luggage racks, searching for something that matched my description. "Look around the shuttle for something white or with camouflage." After a moment's hesitation, Magnet joined in on the search, tossing everything from swimsuits to wedding gowns to the floor.

"These things are usually only loaded with clothes needed for that day's mission, Harlot," Magnet said after only a few seconds of searching. "I don't think we're going to find anything that we need."

"Keep looking!" I ordered. "There has to be something up here!"

After a few minutes of completely trashing the shuttle, we had rounded up a few pairs of white socks, a wedding dress, and white sunglasses.

"I told you," Magnet huffed.

"Do you have a better plan, Mr. Negative? Please, share!" I urged in a sarcastic voice. When Magnet was silent, I muttered, "That's what I thought."

"We'll just have to brave it then," I announced as I pulled back on my coat and fluffy cap. "We'll head straight for the castle, dodge the helicopters' searchlights, find the cave and then get the heck out of here."

"It's not going to be that easy, Harlot!" Magnet warned. "We need to know where the cave is before we rush in there!"

I tightened my coat around me and cut my eyes at Magnet. "It's a cave beneath a castle. It can't be that hard to find." I pulled the lever to open the shuttle. The sharp, biting cold air met me with a blast, blowing my cap right off of my head. I looked back at Magnet, who was holding his own cap down so that it wouldn't do the same. "Are you coming? You said you wanted a thrill ride." I gestured toward the armed men and helicopters. "This will probably be the biggest one you've had yet."

Magnet stared at me before his old grin spread across his face. "You got me. Let's go, Rue, and hopefully we'll make it back to tell Trigger all about it." He dug around in his bag before tossing me something black and shiny. I caught it but was surprised by how heavy it was. I looked down and was even more surprised to find myself holding a pistol.

"When did you get this?" I asked as I studied the shiny object. I had never held a gun before. It was heavy and a little bit scary.

"Grabbed it while we were searching Margie's office," Magnet explained while sliding his own gun into the case on his hip. "We're going to need them."

Despite the fact that I had never fired a firearm before, I was positive I would learn fast enough if it came down to it. I slipped the gun into the case on my hip. I sent him a thumbs up before grabbing my cap and rushing out into the snow.

"Ah!" I cried out in shock as cold wind slapped me in the face, once again sending my hat flying. I watched it as fluttered away into the distance, disappearing into the thick, white air.

Magnet tumbled out of the shuttle after me and immediately began cursing and shaking up and down like a jackhammer.

"F-F-Forget the soldiers! The c-c-c-cold is gonna get us first!" he whimpered. I could feel his pain. Being from L.A., snow was something that I had rarely seen, especially not in sheets.

"Just start running!" I yelled, trying to be heard over the roaring wind. Magnet and I started to push our way through the wind, but it was like trying to run forward while a football player held his hand to your forehead. The wind was blowing right toward us, sending sheets of freezing, cold snow at our faces and slowing our movement.

We finally stopped to catch our breath behind a tree. I poked my head from behind the tree, squinting towards the castle. We were only on one side of the castle's moat while the castle loomed above us on the other side.

I turned back to Magnet, who was still jumping in place, trying to stay warm. "W-We're almost there," I yelled. "We just have to go around the moat to get to the entrance."

I couldn't tell if Magnet nodded or not, since he was still bouncing away. I took his head jiggle as a yes. I began battling my way from tree to tree, trying to keep my head down and hands in front of me. I trusted that Magnet was following, since there was no way I was turning around and risking the chance of getting blown away.

It wasn't until I saw a familiar tree in the distance that it hit me. It was the same tree that Shades and I had talked under the same night that the Elites were captured. The memory of my talk with Shades in the courtyard of Bojnice Castle flooded back into my mind.

"Have you visited the cavern beneath the nearby courtyard?"

"It's right beneath there. Perfect place to hide something, don't you think?"

That was it! I spun around to face Magnet, eager to tell him of my epiphany. I was surprised to see that he was nowhere around.

I decided against calling for him. I didn't want my voice to carry over to the soldiers. Instead, I squatted down and tried to see if I could make out his footprints in the snow.

There was a set of tracks that led towards mine but abruptly cut off. I looked around, my heart beginning to pick up its pace.

He couldn't have just disappeared, could he? He had been right behind me the entire time!

Unless someone had taken him.

I scanned the ground a few more times until I found what I was looking for. There was another set of tracks coming from the right of Magnet's that met his exactly where they ended. I followed the new set of tracks with my eyes. After meeting up with Magnet's, they veered back towards the way they came—in the direction we were headed.

I turned around just in time to dodge a fist that was coming right for my head. The soldier, bundled in a white fur jacket (at least he planned smartly), was fast. He sent another jab towards my face. I ducked to the right and then shoved him back with both of my hands. The wind made my shove less effective, so he barely budged. He shoved me back and, thanks to the wind, I went tumbling backwards like a ragdoll.

I rolled along the field of snow for a while until I finally came to a slow halt, facedown. My whole body was tingling with numbness from the snow caked over my entire body. I pushed myself up on my elbows, feeling like my whole body was numb from the packed snow. I was just climbing to my feet when I noticed a blur of movement from the corner of my eye.

I dodged to the side, barely missing another one of his shoves. I tried to run but my foot slipped and I ended up falling. I rolled over on my back to push myself up but instead found myself face to face with a gun.

"Move and I'll shoot!" the soldier shouted. I didn't move a muscle. The soldier held one hand up to protect his face from the cold wind while keeping the pistol aimed at my head. "Put your hands up slowly and then state your name and affiliation."

Think, Harlot, think! I looked around, frantically searching for options.

"Hands up now!" The soldier was fighting to stand still but the wind was blowing directly at him, making it difficult.

That was it—the Sandmans! I brought my hands up as slowly as I could manage, making sure to spill a few Sandmans into my hands in the process.

"They're up!" I shouted back.

"Name and affiliation!" I didn't speak. I squeezed my hands into fists and felt the satisfying crunch of the Sandman turning into powder.

"I said name and affiliation, girl!"

I cracked a tight, frozen grin and mouthed, "Sweet dreams," before I opened my hand, letting the sand flow from my hand…and off to the side.

Crap.

Using the brief moment of confusion to my advantage, I sat up and quickly knocked the gun from the soldier's hand. It slid to the right and I was right behind it. There was no way I was letting him get his hands on a gun again.

I dove for the gun, followed by the muffled shouts of the soldier. I landed on the ground, a few inches from the gun, but managed to slide forward and finally snag it.

I spun around and pointed the gun at the soldier who froze and put his hands in the air. I stepped toward him, never moving my aim from the center of his forehead.

"Where'd you take my teammate?" I yelled.

He didn't speak. I took a step towards him; he stepped back, nearly falling in the process.

"Don't play games with me!" I shouted, placing my finger on the trigger. "Where is the guy I was walking with? Where did you take him?"

The guy still had the guts not to say a word. I shifted my aim just a bit and pulled the trigger, sending a bullet flying just past his ear. The kick was enough to almost send me flying but I was able to keep my footing.

The solider, on the other hand, had crumpled to the ground, a hand clamped over his left ear. I noticed with a sinking feeling that there was a stream of blood leaking down his arm and dripping onto the white snow. He screamed out in pain and writhed around like a dying snake on the ground.

Oh, crap, I hadn't meant to actually shoot him! I tried to keep my composure, but my hands were trembling. "I told you that I'm not playing games! Tell me where my teammate is or off goes your other ear!"

After panting for a long time, the man finally spoke. "My teammate took him to the cavern with the rest of the H agents."

At least he was still alive. "Now, was that so hard?" I asked. I stuffed the pistol into my bag and then pulled out a few medical bandages. I walked over to him and held them out. He looked up at me, eyes filled with fear and confusion.

"Take them. Sorry about your ear," I said as I squatted down to his level. He slowly reached out his hand before snatching them from me. He regarded me with a dubious look before doing the same to the bandages.

"They're not poisoned or anything," I assured him before turning on my heel and heading back to the castle, leaving the man staring after me. I hoped that he would use the bandages.

I was alone for the first time on a mission. On my mission with the Elites, I had Lukas and the rest of the Elites there to watch over me. On my DM, Retro was the one guiding me through it. Now that it was just me, I felt like I was eight years old again and waking up to find my parents gone.

Breathe, Harlot. You can do this. I inhaled through my nose, counted to five, then exhaled through my mouth before continuing towards the castle. I circled the moat, keeping out of sight in the shadows of the evergreen trees, until I finally made it to the front side of the castle.

I was disappointed to find the parking area filled to capacity with military vehicles of all shapes and sizes. Men in heavy jackets paraded about, yelling into their walkie-talkies, while others searched through the snow with long devices that resembled metal detectors. They seemed pretty bent on finding something, and I knew it was clues about H Corp and whatever was in that precious black box Lukas had stolen.

Their white coats against the snow made it difficult to make out the soldiers. I slid on my L.E.N.S and switched them into heat sensor mode. Instantly, each soldier lit up like fireworks.

I sucked in a sharp breath as I took in the literally hundreds of soldiers roaming the grounds. They were all over the place, milling around like excited fire ants.

I was in over my head. I glanced down at my Brace, tempted to call for someone, anyone to come and take me away. My finger lingered over Retro's face for a moment before I dropped my wrist back to my side. No, I could do this. Magnet, Lukas, and the rest of the Elites were all counting on me. I was their only hope and I wasn't going to let them down.

I just needed a plan and I think I had one.

I pulled the hood of my coat over my ice-coated hair, drew my gun from its case and aimed it towards the line of vehicles. I focused on one car, a Hummer, and tried to aim for the fuel tank. I needed a distraction to draw them all to one area and a fiery explosion was just the thing to do it.

I placed a shaky finger on the trigger and pulled. The bullet collided right where I wanted it to go. I covered my ears and turned away, anticipating the fireworks.

Nothing happened.

I looked back at the car and saw that it was leaking fuel and nothing more. I sighed in frustration. The movies and every video game in the history of video games had lied to me!

"Did you hear that?"

"Yeah, sounded like gunfire!"

Shoot. My failed attempt at exploding cars had successfully drawn attention, but not to the parking lot. I ducked back behind my tree as the red forms of soldiers began to head in my direction.

I took off toward the parking area, where the lines of vacant military vehicles sat. I slid under one of the lower cars and hid there. I watched as numerous feet padded by me, all headed in the direction I had just come from. After searching for a few minutes, about four soldiers congregated together and began talking. It was too windy to hear them, so I switched my Brace into snoop mode and filled myself in.

"Did you guys see anything?" one of the soldiers asked. He spoke with authority, so I figured he was their captain.

"No, nothing, sir," the others replied.

"Well, keep looking! I know I heard something!" The rest of the soldiers hurried off, leaving the captain to himself.

"H scum, I know you're out there," he mumbled before he walked off as well.

I switched off my Brace and slid myself out from under the car. With some of the soldiers now M.I.A., thanks to my "brilliant" distraction, I had a straight shot towards one of the courtyards. I only hoped it was the right one.

Staying low, I took off towards the courtyard, struggling to stay upright against the wind. I slipped a few times but managed to make it without anyone spotting me.

As soon as I stepped foot on the stone ground of the courtyard, I looked for a new place to hide. There were a few trees, but they were right out in the open and much too narrow. I glanced up and groaned when I saw that the soldiers were returning to their original posts, which was near me.

I had to find something, anything…. Finally, my eyes landed on a hole in the ground not too far from me. I glanced around. When I saw that the coast was clear, I darted over to it.

Peering inside, I was surprised to find a small pool of water below, surrounded by a rocky edge. It had to be the underground cavern. I was pretty sure that the hole wasn't the actual entrance to the cave, but it would have to work.

I sat on the cold ground and draped my legs inside of the hole. I removed my L.E.N.S and put them back into my bag, then took a deep breath and pushed myself forward.

It was a long way down. I hit the cold water feet first and plunged beneath its surface. The water actually felt warmer than the freezing temperatures outside but I still didn't want to keep myself submerged for too long. I began to swim back up until I broke through the surface. I grabbed onto the rocky ledge surrounding the pool of water and pulled myself out. I nearly cried with relief when I saw that I had fell right into what seemed to be the underground cavern of Bojnice Castle.

The brown earthy walls of the cave were dimly lit by a few scattered lights placed along the ground. It must have been included as part of the museum that Future mentioned because there were guard rails along the rocky steps that would prevent tourists from falling into one of the nearby lakes.

I was happy to find that the cave was slightly warmer than outside. I threw off my wet jacket and thanked God that my jumpsuit was water-resistant.

The only thing was that cavern itself wasn't that spacious. There wasn't a sign of the Elites or even the soldiers to be found.

The L.E.N.S.! I pulled them out from my now soaking bag of gear and slid them back onto my face.

There they were! A row of orange figures were on the other side of the wall, sitting side by side. They were guarded by two soldiers who looked to be carrying heavy firearms.

Twisted

I took off my L.E.N.S. then drew my own pistol and pressed my back against the wall. I slowly edged along the wall until I came to the corner. I peered around it and sure enough, there they were—the Elites! They were all still dressed in their formal attire from the ball and were tied together by lengths of heavy chains.

I scanned each of the tired faces of the Elites until I came across two familiar ones—Lukas and Magnet. They were seated by one another, tied back to back. Magnet was hurling strings of threats at the guards while Lukas had his head hung forward, looking defeated.

I felt my heart wrench at the hopeless looks on each of their faces. They really thought that H Corp had forgotten about them. They might have, but I hadn't.

I raised my gun and aimed at the nearest guard, who looked half-asleep posted up against the wall. My hand was shaking from cold and fear as I placed my finger on the trigger. It would be my first time actually killing someone.

No, no, don't think like that. It had to be done. I slowly pulled the trigger. The shot echoed off of the cave's walls. The guard, with a bullet hole right between his eyes, dropped to the ground, dead. I had the urge to throw up but I pushed it away and aimed at the other guard, who was looking around in alarm, his gun aiming at every shadow that moved.

"Show yourself!" he shouted. *Yeah, right.* I pulled the trigger again, this time aiming for the heart. My hands were shaking insanely and I needed a larger area to aim for.

The man went down. By this time, the Elites were in a state of shock as they gazed at the dead bodies of their captors. I tried to take a step toward them, but my stomach lurched. I held a fist over my mouth, trying hold back the vomit climbing up from my stomach like thick tar.

I was able to fight it back down. I took a deep breath and rushed toward the Elites.

"Harlot!" Magnet cried as soon as he saw my face. I aimed my gun around, making sure that were no other guards before putting my gun away.

I shot Magnet a grin. "I would definitely not count this mission as a thrill ride." I walked over to him and Lukas and stooped down so that we were on the same level. Lukas was staring at me like I had just sprouted angel feathers.

"You came, Agent Rue," he said with wide eyes.

I smiled and winked at him. "Hey, Commander." I grabbed the chains that bound them and noticed that there was a lock on them.

"The guard over there has the key," one of the Elites said, nodding toward the man who I had shot in the head. I dropped the heavy chains and slowly walked over to the man, who had slid against the wall into a sitting position, a dark blood trail following his descent.

I swallowed hard before jamming my hands into his pocket and retrieving a silver key. I hurried back over to Lukas and Magnet and quickly unlocked their chains. The boys stood up, their chains tumbling around their feet. Magnet let out a whoop while the other Elites cheered.

"I'll get the rest. Guard the entrance," Magnet ordered, before getting to work on freeing the rest of the Elites.

I turned to face Lukas, who was still staring at me in amazement. "What?" I asked with a pout. "You thought I was going to get killed out there, didn't you?"

"Quite frankly, yes," Lukas said honestly.

"I'm touched by your confidence in my talents," I said sarcastically. Lukas laughed and I was shocked when he swooped me up in his arms and swung me around like I was a little girl.

He stopped swinging me and put me back on my feet. He held me at an arm's distance, regarding me with a warm smile. "It was a joke, Agent Rue. I believed that you would come from the moment you told me you would. You are a brave agent. Your parents would be proud."

I smiled at his kind words, feeling tears building in the corners of my eyes.

"Alright, you two." Magnet had wandered over, followed by the now unbound Elites. He threw an arm over my shoulder and mussed my hair. "You did good, Rue."

"Alright, already!" I laughed while pushing him off of me. "Let's get out of here while we can."

Lukas was back in business mode. "She's right. Where did you park the shuttle?" he asked.

"Near the back of the castle, on the other side of the moat," I said.

"That's not too far away. Let's split into groups and meet back there."

"You guys are all unarmed!" I criticized. "How do you expect to make it all the way back there?"

Before we could make any further plans, the entire ground began shaking.

"What's going on?" I yelled above the noise of the quaking ground. Rocks began to tumble from the top of the cavern, threatening to splatter us.

"Move it! Out of the cave!" Magnet began to direct us up a set of stairs but we were met halfway by armed soldiers. I pulled out my gun but the quake had grown worse and I was sent tumbling back down the stairs, along with the Elites, Magnet, and the soldiers.

The cave was collapsing. Rocks fell from above, splashing into the lake and crushing around the ground. I struggled to regain my footing and managed to climb to my feet.

"Oof!" A sharp kick to the back of my leg sent me tumbling towards the water. I grabbed onto the guard rail, successfully stopping myself from taking another cold plunge into the lake. I looked up and saw one of the soldiers standing over me, a gun pointed at my head.

"Stay down!" he ordered. Just then, a large rock the size of a bowling ball hit him on his head. His eyes rolled to the back of his head before he fell forward into the lake.

I pulled myself back up onto the ground and saw that the Elites and Magnet had already incapacitated the other soldiers, stolen their weapons, and were heading up the stairs.

Lukas turned and saw me running towards them. "Hurry!" he yelled while stretching a hand out towards me. The cave's floor was beginning to crack apart like dry skin, revealing dark canyons below it. I jumped from ledge to ledge, trying to dodge being crushed by the falling debris or dropping into the dark canyons opening at my feet.

"Hurry, Agent Rue!" Lukas shouted, his hand still outstretched. Magnet was by his side, glancing back and forth between me and the stairs leading to out the cavern. The rest of the Elites had already fled up the stairs to safety.

I was almost there when a fissure opened right in front of me. I teetered on the edge.

"Harlot!" Magnet and Lukas screamed as I was teetering back and forth. I fell back on my bottom, avoiding a plummet to the bottom of wherever the fissure might lead.

The fissure continued to grow in size. I scooted away from it. I looked up at Magnet and Lukas. "Run!" I yelled with a wave of my arm. "Just get to the shuttle!"

"We're not leaving you, Agent Rue!" Lukas shouted back.

"I'll be okay! Just go!"

Magnet and Lukas shared a look before Lukas turned back to me, a pained expression on his face. He was about to speak when a geyser of water shot up from the fissure, blocking him from my view.

Suddenly, the sound of whirring wheels caught my attention. I was shocked when a huge metal vehicle rolled out of the ground, followed by another, and another. They all began crashing up the stairs the Elites had raced up. I watched in amazement as the metal vehicles, now out in the open began to open fire from the pole shaped nozzles jutting out from every direction of their vehicles.

Had H come to rescue us?

I looked around for a way to escape. The only way seemed to be the stairs, which were on the other side of the giant crack in the ground that the vehicles had just drove out of. The only way across the gap would be to jump.

I backed up a few steps and eyed the gap. It was pretty wide—much wider than I wished. I backed up a few more steps then shot off like a rocket.

Right on the edge of the gap, I dug my foot into the ground and leapt. I felt like I was in slow motion for the few seconds I was airborne. The other side was just a few feet away.

Oh no. I was already starting to come back down. I reached out my hands and leaned forward but it wasn't enough. I screamed as my hands brushed the side of the ledge, just missing it, and I began to fall.

"I got you!" Suddenly, a hand shot out and grabbed mine, stopping me from plummeting to my death. I looked up and saw that it was Trigger who had saved me from certain death.

"Trigger! You're okay!"

He smirked at me. "Yeah, thanks for leaving me out of the action. You see what good it did you." He grabbed onto my other hand with his and then pulled me up.

Once I composed myself, we took off up the collapsing stairs. "What's going on?" I asked as we ran through the snowstorm and flying bullets. The vehicles were blowing up soldiers left and right as they tore through the beautiful gardens.

Trigger led me around to the side of the castle, in a part thick with trees, obscuring us from the view of the destructive vehicles. "That's H Corp. I guess they got wind of what we were doing and now they're here to take us back," Trigger said. "Magnet and the Elites are already headed towards the shuttle we brought here."

"Why are we running away from them, then?" I questioned, while glancing at H Corp's destructive machines. We did our mission. Let's go back and face whatever punishment they throw at us."

"It's not that simple, Harlot!" Trigger yelled. He grabbed my shoulders, forcing me to stare into his tinted eyes. "It's a bloodbath out there! They're shooting to kill and if we just waltz out there, they'll probably shoot us!"

"A-Alright, calm down!" I said. "Let's head back to our shuttle then."

"Now you're talking like someone with intelligence." He let go of my shoulders and began leading the way again. I followed after him, shivering. I had left my coat back in the underground cavern and the snowstorm hadn't eased up yet.

"Th-thanks for saving me," I said after some time of trudging through the snow.

Trigger glanced back at me, looking embarrassed. He turned back around, shoving his hands into the pockets of his warm, furry jacket. "What happened to your coat?"

"L-Left it," I managed to say. My hair was still wet from my dive into the water and now it felt as if someone had placed a hat on my head, filled with ice cubes.

Trigger heaved a sigh. He shrugged off his coat and held it out to me.

"B-B-But you—"

"Just take it already."

He didn't have to tell me twice. I snatched the coat away like I was a starving animal and it was a piece of meat. I pulled it on and pulled the hood over my head. It wasn't much better but it was an improvement.

"Thanks," I said again. Trigger shrugged off my thanks with a grunt and then continued on, with me close behind.

Finally, we made it to the back of the castle. We stepped gingerly down the hill until we came to the moat.

"How did you plan on us making it through that?" I said, eyeing the icy water with apprehension. Trigger didn't answer. I looked over and saw that he was no longer by my side. I turned back to the water and gasped when I saw Trigger already swimming across the moat like an Olympic champion.

"Trigger!" I hissed. "You're going to freeze to death in that water!"

He continued swimming until he made it to the other side. He climbed out of the water and then faced me, waiting for me to the do the same thing.

"I'm not getting in that water!" I yelled.

"You'll be fine, I promise!" Trigger replied casually. I was amazed to see that he wasn't even shivering.

I groaned in frustration but there was no way around it. I ran towards the water and jumped in. I shrieked in pain as the cold water touched the bare skin of my face and chest, feeling like thousands of needles going into me at once.

"Swim, Harlot!" Trigger was screaming at me. I tried to listen to him but I couldn't. I was gasping wildly at the searing pain and flailing about like a fish out of water. My heart had sped up to the point that I could hear its rapid beating in my ears.

I heard Trigger curse and soon there was another splash of water as he dove back in. I tried to remain calm but I literally felt as if I were dying.

Suddenly, Trigger was at my side. He grabbed me with one arm and began to swim back to the edge of the water. "Just stay calm, Harlot," he repeated over and over. "Just stay calm!"

Finally, we were back on land. I fell on my back, shivering uncontrollably. The wind stung at my face, feeling like hot oil. I screamed.

Trigger quickly clamped his hand over my mouth. "Shut up before you draw them!" he hissed. I nodded but I felt as if I were convulsing. He studied me with worried eyes. "I thought you would be able to handle it," he said quietly. I was too cold to even be angry.

He uncovered my mouth and then turned his gaze into my eyes. He stared intently at me, his brows furrowed in concentration.

"Ah!" All of a sudden, my chest flared up, burning like never before. I clawed at my chest, trying to pull out whatever was aflame inside of me.

"Stop it!" Trigger yelled while grabbing onto my hands to stop me from tearing at my flesh. I grunted and writhed around as my chest continued to burn away.

"What did you do to me?!" I growled. Another sharp pain hit me, making me scream and arch my back.

"I'm trying to help you!"

I huffed and panted until slowly the pain died away. I breathed slowly and heavily, feeling as though I had just ran a mile. I slowly sat up and held a hand to my chest.

"I'm warm."

And not just warm. I felt like there was a small furnace inside of me, making me feel hot and cozy.

"You're welcome," Trigger said before climbing back to his feet and starting toward the woods.

I scrambled to my feet and chased after him, yelling, "Wait, Trigger!"

He continued walking. I finally caught up to him and caught his wrist. I spun him around to face me. "What did you just do to me?" I asked breathlessly.

Trigger snatched his wrist away. "I saved your life…again," he said between gritted teeth. I noticed that his eyes had turned a darker shade of pink and that he looked tired. He turned around to keep walking.

"Trigger, I know about your disease," I stated. Trigger gradually came to a stop. He spun around to face me.

"Disease?" he scoffed. "Is that what Magnet told you it was?"

"Yes."

"Well, if you're wondering if my 'disease' is what just saved you, then your answer is yes."

"But, how?"

Trigger shrugged. "I don't know. That's why I don't call it a disease. It's more of a curse, a curse that lets me do things I don't even fully understand. But the fact is that you're okay now. Now let's move."

I had so many questions to ask about his so-called "curse" but he was right. I was okay and we were wasting time standing around and talking. I would ask him all about it once we made it back. We took off towards the trees again, my mind still riddled with questions.

"Harlot! Trigger!" In the distance, we could just make out the forms of Magnet and the rest of the Elites.

"Over here!" I yelled. Trigger and I ran over to them where we were immediately bombarded with questions.

"Are you hurt?"

"How'd you make it out?"

I held up my hands to stop the questions. "We're okay! We just need to leave—now." The sounds of gunfire and explosions had yet to cease and were only growing louder.

"Where's the shuttle, Trig?" Magnet asked. Trigger pulled out a keychain laden with keys and button pads. He pressed a button on one.

I looked around and saw the faint blue shimmering outline of the shuttle not even five meters from us.

"Over there!" Trigger ordered. He pressed another button and the metal shuttle glimmered into view. The door slid open, revealing the inside of the shuttle. We piled into it without a moment's hesitation.

The Elites took seats wherever they could find them and began searching for their Jump masks. Trigger hopped into the Operator's seat while Magnet and I stood behind him.

He tapped a few buttons on the control panel and then cursed. That didn't sound good. "What's wrong?" I asked frantically.

"H Corp disabled all Jump routes that lead back to base," Trigger announced. Everyone began murmuring at once, sounding worried.

"What can we do, then?" Magnet asked.

Trigger swiped the screen a few times. "We'll have to Jump as close as we can to base and then drive into one of the other entrances. Masks ready."

We all did as told, grabbing our masks but not putting them on yet, waiting for Trigger to maneuver the shuttle into the Jump Route. Trigger pressed a switch. A square section of the snowy field before us lowered, revealing the lighted path of the Jump Route.

BOOM!

We all screamed as the shuttle was rocked by a close by explosion. I glanced out of the window and saw that a few of the military tanks had strayed from the castle and were rolling towards us. One fired another missile, causing our shuttle to rock back and forth violently.

"Hold steady!" Lukas barked. Trigger cursed again and pressed a switch, closing the hole to the Jump Route. He shifted the shuttle into drive and pulled a quick U-turn before speeding away from the oncoming tanks.

"Where are we going?" I asked, holding tightly to my seat as Trigger pushed the shuttle faster and faster.

"To another Jump Route entrance," Trigger explained.

We all screamed as the bus flew off the ground with the impact of another missile exploding right behind us. The shuttle landed back on the ground and slid around wildly until Trigger managed to get it back under control.

"There's one up ahead!" Trigger exclaimed. "We're going to have to drive right into it!" I peered over his shoulder and, sure enough, another patch of land had lowered into the ground, revealing a glowing tunnel.

"We're going too fast!" Magnet yelled. Trigger either didn't hear him or didn't care. I sat back in my seat and put on my seatbelt. This wasn't looking too good.

We barreled into the slanted tunnel like a racing champion crossing the finish line. There was a loud, screeching sound as the roof of our shuttle and the roof of the metallic tunnel scraped against one another, reminding me of nails on a chalkboard. Sparks flew on every side of the shuttle until Trigger slammed on the brakes, causing us all to jerk around in our seats.

He put the shuttle into park and exhaled. "We made it," Trigger announced casually. I unbuckled my seatbelt, which had dug into my lower stomach like claws and stood up on shaky feet. I turned back to face the rest of the Elites. They looked up at me, faces dirty and tired, but happy.

"We made it!" I cheered. The Elites cheered with me, breaking the tough façade they always wore. There were tears all around as they hugged each other and let out whoops of delight. Lukas looked up at me and our eyes locked. He inclined his head to me. I did the same and we both broke out into smiles.

I turned back to Trigger and Magnet, who were watching me with intrigued faces.

"You did good, Rue! You can consider us your teammates any day of the week," Magnet said, while bumping my fist with his.

"Yeah, I guess," Trigger said with a shrug but I noticed he was wearing a lopsided smirk. I smiled back at them and felt the urge to cry. They had went through a lot to help a girl they hardly knew on her poorly planned rescue. I had barely spoke to them before this, but I hoped that we could continue to be friends once we were back in base.

I laughed. "I owe you guys. But let's take it easy on the thrill rides from now on," I joked. Magnet laughed and hopped back into his seat, Jump mask in hand.

"We just have this last one and we're done, baby," Magnet said with a wink before pressing his mask to his face.

"Preparing for Hypersonic Jump," Trigger announced before hitting the Jump button. The countdown began. We all fixed our masks to our faces, ready for the much-needed sleep. I would worry about the consequences of my actions later. At that moment, nothing could erase the smile on my face. We had successfully rescued the Elites and all was well. I clutched my locket and fell into the deepest sleep I had yet to have.

* * *

I dreamed I was walking through a field of sparkling red flowers, dressed in a shimmering white gown similar to the one I wore to Kane's ball. I waded through the tall forest of flowers that reached far above my head. The red rose petals cast a red glow to everything beneath them, including me. I was careful not to touch the giant thorns jutting off of their stems.

Finally, I made my way out of it and found myself in a grassy meadow. The sun was high in the beautiful, blue sky. I stared up at it, using my hand to shield my eyes. A few colorful birds flittered by, singing a high-pitched melody. I laughed and followed them with my eyes. They danced and darted around the sky before they swooped right over my head. I spun around to continue watching them but my attention was stolen by a small figure in the distance. It was a little girl sitting by herself, humming a song. She had black, curly hair and was dressed in a pair of overalls.

I walked over to the little girl and knelt beside her. She was staring at the ground, her mass of curly hair hiding her face from me.

"What are you doing out here?" I asked quietly. The girl ignored me and continued humming her song. I listened carefully and could just make out her words.

> *"Give me soda. Give me soda.*
> *Can't you spare a dime or two?*

*Your parents are dead, off went their heads
Little Lola goes boo-hoo."*

I slowly backed away from the girl as her singing grew louder. She repeated the song over and over until she was shrieking the words at me:

*"GIVE ME SODA! GIVE ME SODA!
CAN'T YOU SPARE A DIME OR TWO?
YOUR PARENTS ARE DEAD, OFF WENT THEIR HEADS
LITTLE LOLA GOES BOO-HOO!"*

The sky began to turn dark as storm clouds gathered above us. "Stop it!" I screamed, trying to block my ears with my hands. The little girl giggled and slowly looked up at me. Her curls fell out of her face, revealing the smiling face of my mother. The face twisted and morphed and became my father, and then back to my mother. It morphed back and forth, back and forth until I thought I was going to scream.

The little monster climbed to its feet and began to toddle towards me, its face still changing.

"Stay away from me!" I yelled. I took a step back and screamed when I began to tumble backwards, into a hole that hadn't been there seconds ago.

I fell and fell, the words of the girls chilling lullaby echoing around me.

* * *

I sat up with a start. My chest was heaving and my mask was foggy with sweat. The other agents were still fast asleep. I ripped off my mask and raced back to the bathroom. I slammed the door behind me and then raced over to the toilet, where I threw up everything in my stomach.

After I was done, I flushed the toilet and then scooted back to lean my head against the wall. I glanced down at my hands and found them shaking uncontrollably. I took a deep breath to calm myself.

"Just a dream, Lola, just a dream..." I told myself over and over again, while rubbing my upper arms. The chant wasn't working this time.

The lullaby the little girl had been singing had struck a nerve in me. I knew the melody. My dad used to sing it to me all of the time when I was afraid of going to sleep at night. He hadn't used the words the little girl had sang, though, that's for sure.

I knew the dream meant nothing. It had just stemmed from the brewing anxiety that was eating away at me. Now that we were closer to getting back to base, reality was starting to sink in. I had deliberately went against Harv's orders and I had to be prepared for whatever the punishment would be. I just prayed he would let me continue to be an agent.

There was a soft knock on the door.

"Agent Rue, we have arrived in Los Angeles. Are you alright?" It was Lukas's voice on the other side of the door.

"Yeah, just felt a little sick," I replied in a soft voice. "I'll be out in a minute."

I stood up and walked over to the sink. I ran cold water and splashed it on my face, then let the water fall off of my face and back into the sink. I looked up at my reflection and froze at what I saw.

My labels had grown once again. This time, the growth was more obvious. The labels shot up like black veins, crawling up my collarbone and ending right at the nape of my neck. Doctor Payne had told me that it was normal, but I was afraid they would continue growing until the claimed my face. I rubbed at them but quickly pulled away when I felt a burning sensation.

I decided to leave them alone. "It's going to be alright, Lola," I told myself. I squeezed the locket dangling from my necklace. I gave my reflection a smile and then walked out of the bathroom, ready to face reality.

The rest of the agents were up now. I travelled to the front of the bus, where Magnet and Trigger were plotting our next destination.

"Found an entrance yet?" I asked as I joined them.

Trigger nodded. "There's one nearby. We can reach it by joining traffic and heading to the interstate."

I couldn't help but wonder if that was the same entrance Retro and I had used. It seemed like a lifetime ago that I had first drove into H Corporation with him. So much had happened since then. I felt like a different girl than the one who had been struggling to survive on Skid Row.

"Everyone, sit down and try to look normal," Trigger directed as he pressed a series of buttons. "I'm shifting the shuttle into its bus guise." Everyone took their seats and buckled up as the black shutters over the windows rolled up, revealing the sides of cement buildings on either side of us.

We were parked in an alleyway. Trigger drove the shuttle forward, out onto the road. My eyes stung as the sparkling sunlight of Los Angeles poured through the windows.

I had forgotten how beautiful my hometown was. To the towering skyscrapers that reached for the bright sun, to the shiny cars speeding along the crowded streets—L.A. was beautiful. I gazed out at the people walking along the street, oblivious to the fact that they were walking above a hidden society.

One girl slumped against the side of the building caught my attention. She had long brown dreads, tied back into a low-hanging ponytail. She looked strangely familiar.

"Tara?" I whispered. I placed my hand on the window as we zoomed past the dozing girl.

No, it couldn't be. The girl I saw looked too thin and sickly, like a strung-out drughead. I craned my neck to try to catch another glimpse of the girl, but we were moving too quickly. I dropped my hand and fell back in my seat, feeling guilty. Although I had never stopped thinking about her or the rest of the people I had become friends with in Skid Row, I still felt guilty for not telling Tara about what I was planning on doing. She was probably worried sick about me.

"Harlot, come here."

I broke out of my thoughts and looked up to find Trigger's eyeing me from the rearview mirror. I got up from my seat and waltzed up to him, positioning myself so that my elbows were resting on the top of his low seat.

"What's up?" I asked. Trigger glanced around nervously before glaring at me.

"You better not say a word about what I did for you back there when you were about to freeze to death," he threatened in a low voice.

I chuckled. "Why? Are you afraid that people might think you're actually a decent human being?"

Trigger whipped his bangs to the side, revealing an embarrassed face. "I-I don't care what the other agents think of me." He looked away. "They're all afraid of me, anyway."

"Maybe it's because you've never actually talked to them," I suggested. "If you opened up some more to others, people might find that deep down…deep, deep, deep, deep—"

"I get it," Trigger muttered.

I continued on. "—very deep down," I smiled, "you're not half-bad."

Trigger gave me another embarrassed look before frowning and turning away. "Like I said, their opinions don't matter. The reason I'm telling you not to mention that is because I don't want anyone to know about what I can do," he explained.

I thought back to the times when Trigger and I had locked eyes and the burning in my chest had started up. "What exactly can you do?" I asked.

Trigger turned to face me, eyes gleaming. "Lots of things. Do you want to see?"

"No, thanks," I replied quickly. There was no way I was going through another round of the pain he had caused me again.

Trigger laughed quietly. "I don't know why I'm like this. I don't even remember if I was born with this disease or if it's something I contracted. All I know is that people are afraid of it." He shot me a meaningful look. "It's better if they don't find any more reasons to be afraid of me."

I nodded. I understood what he was getting at, even if he hadn't come outright and say it. He was afraid of what might happen if people realized that he was capable of doing things they couldn't understand. I didn't want to admit it, but Trigger's disease and the strange powers it gave him scared me, too.

The buildings soon were left in the distance and we found ourselves on the familiar interstate. The shuttle had fell into a comfortable silence. Everyone was gazing out of their windows, probably contemplating the future or remembering the past. I was thinking of both.

"We're coming up to the entrance," Trigger announced in his bored voice. I sat up in my seat, along with everyone else. It was the moment everyone had been waiting for. Would we be met with open arms or treated as traitors?

Trigger maneuvered the shuttle into the slot that opened before us and we rolled down, down into the ground, leaving the sunlight behind us.

"Getting nervous, Harlot?" Trigger teased from in front of me.

I blew air between my lips. "Psh, heck no," I lied. "I just faced down soldiers in the middle of a snowstorm in Slovakia. Why would I be afraid of...?" My voice trailed off as the wall in front of us opened, revealing rows upon rows of H agents, all aiming guns at our shuttle. We all slowly raised our hands above our heads.

The thrill ride was definitely over.

* * *

We were herded off of the shuttle and led down flights of stairs until we came to a large room that resembled a theatre, where we were told to sit in the hard, uncomfortable chairs lining the floor. I was seated between Magnet and an Elite woman with dark hair.

"Leader Harv Magnum III will arrive shortly!" one of the agents announced. The rest of the armed agents lined in front of us, where they kept trained eyes on our group.

"They're treating us worse than the last time we snuck out," Magnet noted with a frown.

I looked around the huge, dimly lit room to pass the time. We were seated in front of a stage, complete with red curtains. The curtains were drawn shut, hiding the back of the stage from viewers. The rest of the room was filled to the brink with rows upon rows of chairs.

"Is this the Ceremony Hall?" I whispered to Magnet, who nodded his head in response. I glanced around for the graffiti but found none. Maybe their demonstration hadn't gone as planned.

Suddenly, the double doors to the room slammed open and agents of all levels flooded in. I looked over my shoulder and watched as they filled in the seats behind us. I felt relief and happiness wash over me when I saw Lolli, Hack, and Marc walk into the room, looking scared and confused. Lolli's eyes met mine and her face lit up.

"Bunny!" she squealed.

Marc and Hack glanced around before they spotted me. "Harlot!" they cried. My three friends tried to head towards me but I quickly shook my head. I nodded towards the armed agents, who were eyeing them carefully. I didn't want the armed agents to think that my friends had been involved in any way.

Loll, Hack, and Marc exchanged glances before shuffling over to their seats. They never took their eyes off of mine.

"What happened?" Marc mouthed.

"Long story," I mouthed back. Marc raised his eyebrows, waiting for the details. I opened my mouth to try and give him the short version, but my attention was stolen when Retro and Carma sat down right in front of him.

Unable to look away in time, I locked eyes with Retro. I was instantly drawn back to our last time together, when Retro had labeled me as a fling and I had told him to stay away from me. Looking at Retro's face, I could tell he was remembering the same.

Carma leaned over and kissed Retro's cheek, successfully breaking Retro's concentration. He tore his eyes away from me and began to whisper with his girlfriend. I turned back around in my seat, my heart aching.

I glanced around and noticed that the talking had died away and the room had fell silent. The only sound was the sound of someone's feet walking down the corridor and the tapping of a cane. Everyone was looking to the right. I followed their gaze and saw that Harv Magnum III had entered the room.

He strode down the center of the chairs, cane in hand. He climbed the set of stairs leading up to the stage and then took a few, slow steps to center stage. He slowly turned to face us. The grin on his face seemed strangely out of place, considering the circumstances.

"Hello, hello, agents. How are you all this evening?" he asked pleasantly. There was a quiet pause before everyone mumbled out half-hearted replies.

Harv nodded, still smiling. "That's good to know, especially since it has been such a taxing day for us all. A lot of us have been busy, busy!" His eyes dropped to me. "It's good to see you back, my Elites." The Elites all drew H's over their hearts and bowed their heads.

Harv smiled and continued. "Do you all know why I tell you not to do certain things?" he asked, still staring at me. No one replied this time.

Harv's frown grew. "I repeat: Do you all *know* why I tell you not to do certain things?"

After a brief pause, some girl called out, "Because you don't want us to get hurt!"

"Exactly!" Harv yelled, pointing his cane at the girl. The smile was back on his face again. "I tell you not to do certain things because I don't want you to get hurt. You are my family and I care about each and every one of you deeply." He really seemed hurt by our disobedience.

"That's why I look out for you and try to protect you. Who brought you here when you had nowhere else to go?"

"You!" a few kids shouted.

"Who took you in when the world turned against you?"

"You!"

Harv's eyes met mine. "Who gave you the chance to do something you believed in?"

"You!" Every agent in the building was yelling now, all except me. I felt the guilt eating at my insides as his words sunk in.

Harv took a deep breath. "That's right, agents. And I do it because I want to help. I know how it feels to have nowhere else to turn, to have no one who cares about my well-being. That's why I do what I do" His smile faded. "But it seems some of you don't care about that. Some of you would rather turn a blind eye to that and do things that could hurt not only yourselves, but the entire corporation."

He snapped his fingers. Two senior agents came onstage and drew back the red curtains. I gasped when I saw what was painted on the wall behind Harv, in big, bright-red letters:

IT'S TIME TO STOP HIDING

The sentence was accompanied by pictures of bombs and body parts flying everywhere. So this is what the Bomb Squad had done. I could only imagine everyone seeing this same scene during the memorial. The rest of the agents gasped along with me, while others even began to cry.

"Is this what you want?" Harv yelled. "You want us to stop hiding and fight?" No one replied.

"Violence is the only way to get something done, is it?" Harv continued. "Going against orders is what gets things rolling, is it?"

Harv seemed like a different person when he was angry. But he had only just got started. He snapped his fingers again and the two soldiers disappeared backstage. When they came back out, they were leading a woman dressed in camouflage military garb.

"E agent!" The H agents all hissed and recoiled at the sight of the captives. The E agent's mouth had been gagged and her wrists were tied behind their backs. The senior agents led her to the front of the stage.

Harv walked over to the captive E agent and then faced us. "Here they are!" he announced with a sweep of his hand. "The ones that many of you are so desperate to chase and hunt down, picked up in the popular spot of the day—Slovakia!" He nodded at the senior agents. They nodded back before one pulled out a handgun.

I was starting to get a bad feeling about this.

My fear was confirmed by Harv's next sentence. "So, let's see you do it, hm?"

Everyone glanced around in confusion. Magnet and I shared a confused look.

"What is he talking about?" Magnet whispered.

"Don't be shy now!" Harv was unrelenting. "How about a volunteer? Someone who really just enjoys taking risks?" His eyes crawled over to mine and he grinned. "Miss Rue! Thank you for volunteering, my dear!"

Everyone's eyes fell on me. I opened my mouth to protest, but quickly shut it again. I was in no position to let my usual smart-aleck remarks fly. I slowly rose to my feet.

"Yes, come on up, Miss Rue!" Harv was the only one who clapped as I made my way through the rows of silent, staring agents. I heard Lolli whimpering from the back of the room.

I finally made it onstage, where I held my head up higher, trying to seem brave. Harv began to circle me, resembling a hungry vulture.

"Miss Rue had quite the exciting adventure today. Didn't you, Miss Rue?" I didn't reply, knowing that it was a rhetorical question.

"Miss Rue, along with Agents Magnet Fury and Trigger Reverse stole away from base today to bring back our precious Elites. Thankfully, she succeeded." There was slow, uncomfortable applause from the agents.

Harv went on. "But, as you know, Miss Rue has only been an agent for less than a month. She hasn't had the proper training to take on a mission in which such skill is required. I told her this and yet she found it to be a good idea to not only run off, but goad two other agents into doing the same thing!"

"We weren't 'goaded' into anything!" Trigger's voice yelled from the crowd. I looked out and saw Trigger standing up in the crowd, his chest heaving. "We went of our own free will!"

"That's right!" Magnet had jumped up as well. "We helped her because we wanted to!"

"Then you're just as bad as her," Harv declared, "if not worse for not trying to change her mind!" He turned back to me and pointed at one of the E agents. "Go ahead, Harlot. Since you don't see fit to listen to me anymore, you must want to do like the others and fight. Go ahead. Shoot her."

I watched in horror as one of the agents walked over to me and pushed the gun in my hand. The other agent yanked the woman a few feet in front of me. I looked down at the gun and then back up at Harv, wondering if he was serious.

"Don't make her do this, Harv!" I looked out at the ground and was surprised to find that it was Retro who had stood up this time. Carma stared up at him, jaw dropped.

Harv looked just as surprised. "Agent Rex, do you have something you would like to say?" he asked carefully.

"Harlot just became an agent! You can't expect her to behave like a perfect agent in such a short time!" Retro yelled.

Harv laughed. "Well, this lesson will certainly speed up the process." He turned back to me, the charming grin back on his face. "Proceed, Miss Rue."

"I'm not shooting her," I said automatically. I placed the gun on the ground. A collective gasp resonated around the room. Harv's smile never faded. He reached down and picked up the gun, then held it out to me again.

"I think that you will, Miss Rue. Or you can consider your brief stint as an H agent officially over."

The scenario I had dreaded since I had decided to sneak off had just came true. He was threatening to fire me. I would have to go back to living on the streets of Skid Row, struggling to survive, with no way of finding my parents. I would never be able to find them, I realized.

Not without the help of H Corp.

I reached out with a shaky hand and grabbed the gun.

"No!" Retro roared.

I slowly turned to the woman and aimed the gun at her head. The woman stared back at me, her eyes wide with fear. Blonde curls of sweaty hair spilled out of her hat and tumbled around her narrow, pointed face which was painted with fear.

I blinked. There was something familiar about the woman. I knew that I had seen her before, maybe even talked to her.

"What are you waiting for, Miss Rue? This is what war is all about!" Harv said with a deep laugh. "This is what the agents want!"

I placed a shaky finger on the trigger. The woman whimpered and I nearly dropped the gun.

"Don't talk to strangers, Mary-Anne, especially not to dirty ones. She doesn't look very becoming."

It was the voice that did it. The woman that I was staring at was Mary-Anne, the cookie girl's, mother.

I began to lower the gun, my throat burning with tears. I couldn't shoot her. Even if she wasn't kind to me the day that we first met, I still wouldn't take the life of another child's mother. I wouldn't put Mary-Anne through the kind of life I had had to live.

I'm sorry, Mom and Dad. I can't do it.

Right at that moment, a loud explosion went off above our heads. I jumped and a shot rang out.

No. Please, no.

I slowly opened my eyes and let out a strangled sob when I saw Mary-Anne's mother on the ground, blood leaking from her chest.

The rest of the room was in chaos as small chunks of debris rained down from the explosion, but I barely noticed the pebbles that fell on me. I dropped the gun I was holding and dropped to my knees, tears pouring down my face.

I killed Mary-Anne's mother.

It was at that moment that I noticed there was more than just pebbles falling from the ceiling. Small, white slips of paper floated down, coating the ground like snow. I picked one up, blinking to get rid of the tears blurring my vision. The white paper had three words stamped across it and a swirly signature written at the bottom in red.

PREPARE FOR WAR – From your dear friend, Kane E. Abel

I crushed the paper in my hand and sobbed over Mary-Anne's mother as the rest of the agents fled the room. It looked as if we were headed to war, rather we wanted to or not. And I had just fired the first shot.

About the Author

Brittany fell in love with writing at a young age, when she first discovered that she could make people laugh with words. She became interested in secret agents after years of playing James Bond video games with her siblings as children. When she's not writing, she enjoys spending time with her family and friends, dancing with music videos, and singing.

Her future plans include finding a career in writing, traveling the world (starting with Los Angeles), and getting her own dog. She currently resides with her family in Chipley, Florida where she spends her days attending college.

Upcoming Books and Information

Twisted is the first novel written by 19 year old author Brittany Hawes. Go to www.deepseapublishing.com for more information on Brittany and her upcoming book events.

If you like this story, you'll also enjoy:

- *Let Sleeping Dragons Lie*, by Tryone Burson
- *Hardt's Tale*, by Gwendolyn Druyor
- *The Good Fight*, by Ophelia Hu
- *The Gallivan Legacy*, by Sable Lewis
- *The Bryant Family Chronicles*, by Eddie Hughes
- *Capria Rodalia*, by Sidney McPhail
- *Miss Alice* by Sarah Gastright

Like *Twisted*, these award winning works are available in paperback and eBook form at Deep Sea Publishing's Online Store, BarnesAndNoble.com, Amazon, and Apple's iBookstore. The website also lists the shops and bookstores that carry the books. These books can be ordered from any bookstore as well using the ISBN.

Deep Sea Publishing (DSP) is a Florida-based company publishing fictional novels, young adult/teen fiction, children's books, photography books, and reference guides.

Made in the USA
Charleston, SC
07 March 2014